Marc didn't 
her.

Natalia made it from her hospital ... t
the nurses noticing. She tiptoed over to his bed and softly said, "Hello." If he *was* asleep, it shouldn't wake him.

He rolled over—and stared at her. It felt as if a tsunami had crashed over her. Her legs were shaking so badly, she didn't think they would hold her up. Stumbling backwards, she leaned against the wall so she wouldn't fall down.

"Are you okay?" he asked. "Do you want me to call the nurse?"

"No," she squeaked out. "I'm sorry. I should go."

"No. Wait, please come here."

She couldn't put one foot in front of the other, so she just stood there.

"You took the trouble to come to my room, why won't you come in? Who are you?"

"My name is Natalia."

He continued to stare. "You know, out of all the people who've come in here, you're the only one who seems familiar to me. Do I know you?"

"We were in the cab together when it had the accident."

"Oh. I'm sorry. Are you okay?"

She tried to pull herself together. The last thing she wanted was for him to see her like this. "I think I'm a little better than you."

"So, you know me. How about my wife?"

"I know your Aunt Mariella. I've never met you wife." She wasn't up to spending any more time with him and wanted to leave before she burst into tears. "Well, good night. I just wanted to see how you were."

"Will you come back and visit me again? I would like you to tell me how we know each other."

"I don't know. I'll try." She wasn't even out the door before the tears ran down her cheeks. The real sobbing didn't start until she was in back in her bed, alone in the dark.

She'd never met him before...or had she?

The last thing forty-year old Natalia Santagario expected was to be sitting on a Manhattan barstool ogling a man she's never met, but swears she knows.

He didn't know her at all...or did he?

The mysterious dark-haired woman at the end of the bar stops twenty-eight year old Marc Tremonti in his tracks. His head assures him she's a stranger, but his heart tells him otherwise.

Together they embark on an adventure that will change their lives forever.

Their attraction instant and enigmatic, they undergo past life regression and discover that, not only have they spent hundreds of lives together as lovers, Natalia holds the secret to Marc's puzzling birthmark.

But what should have been a joyful reunion is complicated by a kind, albeit confused, *almost* ex-wife, an unfortunate accident in a taxicab, and a bout of temporary amnesia that threatens to ruin everything. On top of all that, they must contend with a mischievious ghost from their past.

What else could possibly go wrong?

KUDOS FOR TWIN FLAMES

There is so much to enjoy in *Twin Flames,* by first-time author Debbie Christiana. This book is not a straight out romance. Sure, romance plays a part in the story, but the interesting thing is the way Christiana has fleshed out her story with the notion of past lives and their impact upon the central characters. *Twin Flames* grabbed my interest from page one with its tight storyline, and it held me in its thrall until the end...For those wanting some steam with their romance, you won't be disappointed. The sex is hot, and fits snugly into the plot. *Twin Flames* made me laugh, cry, and a few times growl in frustration—a stubborn woman suffering from the effects of insomnia will not always make the best of decisions. Special mention should be made of the level of research Christiana has obviously undertaken in regards to sleep therapy and past-life-regression. Both topics are handled with great skill, and the reader experiences each session with a sense of realism that is a the credit to the author. – *Taylor, Reviewer*

Twin Flames by Debbie Christiana is an interesting book. Although, women's fiction is not a genre I normally read or care for, I thoroughly enjoyed *Twin Flames.* The book is fun to read and contains some very interesting and enlightening concepts. It made me laugh, made me scream at the characters in frustration, and it also made me think. Christiana did her homework, too. The techniques she describes in both the sleep clinic and the past-life regression sessions are accurately portrayed. I checked, of course, but more importantly, the story has a ring of truth that only comes from extensive research. *Twin Flames* is a keeper that will make you want to come back and read it again and again. – *Regan, Reviewer*

TWIN FLAMES

By

DEBBIE CHRISTIANA

A BLACK OPAL BOOKS PUBLICATION

GENRE: Paranormal/Women's Fiction

TWIN FLAMES

Print ISBN: 978-1-937329-03-7

Published by Black Opal Books **http://www.blackopalbooks.com**

ACKNOWLEDGMENTS

My journey to publication would have never happened if it weren't for so many wonderful people helping me along the way.

My eternal thanks to Black Opal Books who decided to take a chance on a brand new author, who was naïve and green. They have been an absolute pleasure to work with and have made my first publishing experience a wonderful one.

Thank you to Lauri, Faith and Susan, the editors who worked so hard on my book. Marc and Natalia thank you as well for making their story come alive.

I want to thank Cindy, Candee, Annie and Kerri for muddling through the very long first draft for me. To Janet and Susan for reading the second, shorter but not quite finished draft for me.

Great thanks to Cindy Hammock, a dear friend, for her wonderful artwork and beautiful cover for my book. It's very special for me to have her be a part of this.

Many thanks to Nancy Connally and Kathy Olivieri for their help and priceless advice. I wouldn't be writing this acknowledgement page without them.

To Gloria Chadwick, author of *Discovering Your Past Lives.* I appreciate the time you took to email me and for all the valuable information on Twin Flame Soul Mates.

To Mary Lee LaBay. A consultant for past life hypnotherapy and author of *Past Life Regression-A Guide for*

Practitioners and *Exploring Past Lives: Your Soul's Quest for Consciousness.* She was so very gracious with her time and granted me permission to use her method of opening a door to our past lives. I was able to consult with her over breakfast on her deck. She is so cool and interesting!

Of course, I have to thank my family. My husband Bill, my two sons, Matt and AJ and my daughter Ellie, who have been patient and supportive while I sat at my computer for many hours every day. Even though I tried not to, I'm sure I neglected them a bit. I love you all very much.

DEDICATION

To my husband Bill, my kids, Matt, AJ, Ellie and my dad.

and

To my mother, who is no longer here, for handing me my first book on reincarnation when I was twelve years old.

CHAPTER 1

"What is a soul? It's like electricity – we don't really know what it is, but it's a force that can light up a room." – *Ray Charles, 1930-2004 Pianist and Soul Musician*

I thought you two came to cheer me up." Natalia took a long sip of her eggnog, the warmth of the rum soothing her mood.

The three women were huddled in Natalia's family room surrounded by boxes of Christmas decorations. Her two friends were visiting to help her decorate for the holidays or so she thought, but then, some sort of holiday "intervention" had begun. She loved them to death, but sometimes well-meaning friends were a pain in the ass.

"We did." Christine gave her friend a moderately sympathetic look. "Listen, I know you've had a rough couple of months—with Jacob leaving you at the altar."

"It was the Justice of the Peace," Natalia said, upset Christine had even mentioned the bastard's name. "I was a little late, and he overreacted."

"That may be so, but it doesn't change the fact that your fiancé was convicted of a felony a few days later."

"Ex-fiancé." Exasperated, Natalia began to rub her temples. "Can we change the subject? *Please.*"

"Sure, let's talk about our annual trip to New York City."

"I know your hearts are in the right place, but I'm not up going to New York this year."

They had dragged her up to the attic, gathered all the Christmas things together and made her lug the boxes down all by herself. After at least twenty trips up and down the attic steps, everything labeled 'Xmas' was stacked on the family room floor. As a reward for all her hard work, Ellie handed her a glass of eggnog complete with rum. Then they plopped her on the couch.

"Nat, there's only a few days until Christmas. You have to snap out of this funk and get some holiday spirit," Christine said. "I think coming with us is just what you need."

Ellie poked around in one of the boxes until she found what she was looking for. "Remember this?" she asked Natalia. It was a picture of them in New York last year.

"Yes." She sat the frame on her fireplace mantel and smiled at the memory it brought to mind. "I remember. We had a lot of fun that day, but I don't think I'll be much fun this year."

As Natalia spoke, a familiar cool breeze swept past her. She looked over at her friends who didn't seem to feel the gentle gust go by. Just like always. Why did she think this time would be any different? A string of lights lying on the coffee table crashed to the floor.

"Stop it, right now," she growled under her breath.

"Be careful Nat, you don't want those lights to break," Ellie warned. "Anyway, I know once you get to the city and start shopping, you'll have fun. If you're not having a good time, you can hop on the train and come home."

Natalia was about to refuse the offer one last time when her glass of eggnog tipped over and spilled onto the table.

"I said stop it and I mean it," she hissed, louder than she should have. She quickly turned to make sure her friends hadn't heard her. They had their backs to her, busily attaching gold garland and red ribbons to her staircase. Natalia watched them and groaned. These two were not going to leave one spot undecorated. Hadn't they ever heard "less is more"?

"I spilled my eggnog," she called to them. "I'll be right back." As she walked into the kitchen, a chill tingled at her neck. "Why do you want me to go to New York so badly?" she asked, standing completely alone in the middle of the kitchen.

The hanging light over the table rattled.

"How could I possibly meet someone while shopping with Christine and Ellie? Anyway, I'm not ready for that yet. Please, just leave me alone about it."

The kitchen drawers opened and slammed shut.

"Be quiet!" she hissed. "They'll hear you." Her irritation grew as the refrigerator door flew open. "I know you don't care if they hear you or not. You're not the one who has to come up with an explanation of what's going on in here. I do."

Water spit out of the faucet into the sink.

"Fine. Have your temper tantrum." She leaned back against the counter and crossed her arms over her chest. "Let me know when you're through." Natalia had lived with Giovanna, a mischievous apparition, long enough to know when she couldn't win.

When Giovanna's outburst was over, Natalia began closing the open drawers. A picture of her and her brother Robbie, which she kept on the counter, inched toward her.

"Yes, I know. I have to get him a present." Natalia shook her head in defeat. Between her friends and Giovanna, she hadn't stood a ghost of a chance. "You always get your way, don't you?" Grabbing a towel, she headed back to the family room. "It seems I'm always cleaning up your mess."

Christine and Ellie were spraying fake snow over snowman stencils on the windows around her front door. Natalia rolled her eyes. This is what happens when your friends have kids and you do not. She wasn't sure how much more of their decorating she could take.

"I think you both have done more than enough for me. I appreciate it. I really do. I'm at least an eight on the holiday spirit meter." Leading them back to the family room, she said, "Let's have some more eggnog."

"Oh my God, look at the time!" Christine hurried to the closet, grabbed her coat, and handed Ellie hers. "Nat, I'm sorry but we can't."

"I wish you'd reconsider and come with us on Saturday," Ellie said, trying to persuade her one last time.

She smiled. "Okay, you two. I'll come. I have to get Robbie a present. He's coming home for Christmas."

"Good." Christine hugged her. "You won't regret it, we promise. We found a good restaurant. Bring your famous appetite."

Ellie took a turn hugging her goodbye, and they rushed out the door.

Once Natalia saw their car back down her driveway, she got out the window cleaner and sprayed her front door windows. Within a few minutes, all the snowmen had melted away.

♨♨

With a hot cup of coffee and a donut in hand, Natalia and her two friends boarded a train for the hour ride to New York City. Grand Central Terminal was jammed with people, most of whom were watching a holiday light show flashing onto the ceiling. Having seen it plenty of times, the three women worked their way through the massive crowd on to Forty-Second Street. After taking in the obligatory holiday sights, the Christmas tree at Rockefeller Center, and a quick stroll down Fifth Avenue, they were ready to move on. They hopped on the subway to Christopher Street in the Village to their favorite out of the way stores for a day of shopping.

"Nat, are you almost ready?" Ellie asked.

"Yeah, and I'm hungry."

"Should we take Nat to that Italian restaurant we found last time?" Christine asked.

"Sure," Ellie said. "Want to try it, Nat?"

"Do you both think with a name like Natalia Santagario I don't get enough Italian food? I was hoping for a big juicy steak and bottle of red wine."

"I guess we could have steak, but this place is really good. Plus all the waiters are cute."

"You're both married," said Natalia.

"But you're not," Christine said, pointing a finger at her.

"Whatever. I don't care. I'm starving. Let's go."

A crowded subway ride later, they arrived at Tremonti's restaurant on West Fifty-Fourth Street.

Before they went inside, Natalia stopped her two friends. "Thank you," she said. "I really needed this. I'm glad you kept harassing me about coming with you."

"We told you so," said Ellie with a smile.

As they entered the restaurant, they were swallowed by a crowd of shoppers, tourists, and people reveling in the holiday season. Sandwiched between her friends and the other hungry inhabitants of the restaurant, Natalia couldn't help but notice the wonderful aromas swirling around the room. For a moment, she was a little girl in her grandmother's Brooklyn apartment, having Sunday dinner.

As she inhaled once more, a strange sensation took hold of her. Her body temperature seemed to shoot to a hundred degrees. Sweat formed on her brow. Light headed, she could feel the color drain from her face.

"Nat, what's wrong?" Christine asked, resting her hand on Natalia's shoulder. "You look like you saw a ghost."

No, I'm used to seeing ghosts. "I'm fine. It's hot in here, that's all. Let's try to work our way to the bar so I can get some water."

They started to push their way through the crowd when Natalia felt Ellie take her hand. "Hurry, those people are getting up," she said, dragging Natalia behind her.

No sooner had they hopped up on their barstools than a young waiter appeared.

"What can I get you ladies this evening?"

"Hi," said Natalia. "I would love a glass of wa—" She sat completely still, staring past the waiter.

"We'll have three glasses of Merlot, please," Christine chimed in. "Could you bring my friend some water? She isn't feeling well."

"Sure," the young man said and left.

"Nat, what are you looking at?" Christine asked.

"The man over there making drinks," she said, pointing to the side of the bar.

"Looking? Ogling is more like it," scoffed Ellie. "She's practically drooling."

"I know him from somewhere," Natalia said.

"His back is to us. You can't see his face."

"I don't need to see his face."

Having no logical answers to give them, Natalia ignored the rest of her friend's questions and continued to watch the fascinating man behind the bar. He was tall with broad shoulders and dark curly hair. His sleeves were rolled up, his strong arms and hands visible. He was good at his job. Quickly dipping his hand in the ice and dropping the cubes into the glasses, he had three drinks made in a just few moments.

Then something changed.

♨♨

"Hey, Marc. I need two Absolute Martinis and two Cosmos," the older waiter said patting him on the back.

"Okay, give me a minute."

Marc reached for Martini glasses on the shelf. The regular bartender couldn't have picked a worse night to call in sick, although Marc didn't mind helping out. It beat sitting home alone on a Saturday night, which had become customary as of late. He put the three drinks aside and started on the next order.

Getting four new glasses down, he suddenly felt warm and woozy. Leaning over, he reached into the ice with his right hand, relishing its coolness. He straightened abruptly and stopped what he was doing, as the same odd affliction he'd felt a month ago hit him once more. Within seconds, first his left, then his right shoulder burned as if hot coals were blistering his skin. He took a few deep breathes and the throbbing subsided a bit. Feeling startled, but not knowing why, his whole body twisted to the left knocking over the glasses.

Clutching a fistful of ice, he turned and gazed into the considerable crowd at the bar. What was he looking for? He didn't have clue, but when he saw it, he would know. Of that, he was sure.

He moved in a near-full circle. Then he saw her. She had a bewildered expression on her face but an intense gleam in her eyes. He cocked his head and gave her a curious look, knowing she had been watching him.

As he walked toward her, the pain in his shoulders all but disappeared. Feeling his whole body relax, the ice fell out of his hand onto the floor, but he kept moving.

"Marc! What are you doing?" asked one of the servers. "Someone is going to slip on the ice."

"Oh, sorry, I'll get it in a minute," Marc responded, never taking his eyes off the woman he was approaching.

When he reached his destination, he was at a loss at what to say. "Hi," he said, unsure of himself. "Don't take this the wrong way, but have we met before?"

When she hesitated, the woman beside her spoke. "You'll have to excuse her. She's not feeling well tonight. Nat, tell him you thought he looked familiar to you too."

"I thought you reminded me of someone I knew. That's all. My friend is overreacting. It was warm in here, and I was light-headed. I feel fine now." She gave him a kind smile.

"Yes, it can get warm in here. Do I know you from school? I went here in the city."

She looked amused. "Listen, hon. I'm a little older than you, don't you think? I grew up in Connecticut."

"I went to summer camp in Connecticut for two years." Her words and smile put him at ease, and he felt confident and even a bit flirtatious. "You could have been my camp counselor. Maybe I didn't appreciate you in your bikini when I was ten and you were..."

"I don't know. How many years ago were you ten?"

"Eighteen years ago."

"Oh."

"Like I said maybe I didn't appreciate you in your bikini when I was ten and you were..."

"I was twenty-two when you were ten. And I did look good in a bikini back then," she said with a smirk. "Sorry, I never worked as a camp counselor. Try again."

"I will. You have me intrigued. Anyway, they say forty is the new thirty."

"Does your wife know you flirt with all the women?"

He looked down at his wedding ring. "If it brings in good tips, she doesn't mind," he said, not knowing how his wife felt about much of anything lately.

"Good for her."

"I'm Marcos, but please call me Marc," he said, offering his hand. "It's nice to meet you."

"I'm Natalia. Same here."

The minute their hands met, a powerful shock traveled from his hand up his arm. He forced himself not to jump.

"Ouch!" she exclaimed.

"Sorry. It's that time of the year I guess," he said, concluding she received the same jolt.

"These are my friends, Christine and Ellie."

"It's nice to meet you." Marc shook their hands. "Can I get you something to eat?"

"Sure," Christine said. "We're starving. We had a busy day of shopping. We already ordered drinks."

They chose a few appetizers to share. Marc took their orders, gave Natalia another long look, and walked away. A safe distance from her in the kitchen, with his heart pounding, he rubbed his arm, still tingling from the shock. Amber, the cute, blond waitress walked by and winked at him. She had made it clear more than once she was available to help him through the present impasse with his wife. He'd rejected her advances and tried to convince her—as well as himself—he and his wife were on their way to working it out. With his wife off to find herself, it had been difficult for Marc, living alone these past eight months. Through bouts of loneliness and sadness, he had always remained faithful. However, the mysterious, dark-haired woman at the bar stirred something in him he had never felt before.

♨♨

"Nat, we have to go to the ladies room," Ellie said.

"Go ahead, I'll stay here. Put your coats on the seats to save them."

Glad to have a few minutes by herself, Natalia shook the arm that received the shock. It was prickly, as if asleep. She took a gulp of water and tried to relax. This was totally out of character for her, letting someone have this effect on her. He was just a man, albeit an extremely good-looking man. She sighed. An extremely good-looking *younger* man she swore she knew, who turned her insides to jelly, and was married. *Shit.*

To pass the time, Natalia picked up a pen and doodled on a napkin. As she watched her strange drawing come to life, she began to see things clearly. In an hour or so, they would leave, and she'd never see Marc again. It was harmless flirting. She enjoyed having some innocent attention from a man. It had been awhile. There was no need to read anything else into it. She would be herself and enjoy the food and wine.

Looking up, she saw him walking toward her, his hands laden with plates. She moved the napkin and pen aside to make room for their food.

"What's that you're drawing?" he asked.

"Nothing. I'm doodling until my friends get back from the bathroom."

"Can I see it?"

"Sure, I guess." She slid it across the bar toward him.

He studied the napkin for a minute and gave her a hard look.

"What's the matter?" she asked.

"What made you draw *that*?"

Natalia was surprised at the harshness in his voice. "I don't know. Why?"

"Are you trying to tell me you don't know what this is?" It sounded to her more like an accusation than a question.

"No, I really don't. What's the problem?"

"Nothing." He dropped their plates down harder than he should have and walked away.

Natalia sat there, stunned.

I guess I can add uptight to the list.

♨♨

"Angelo, can you cover for me for a few minutes? I need a break."

"Sure, Marc."

"Thanks."

Marc couldn't fathom how in one short hour his evening had turned so...*weird*. Nor could he explain the strange effect she had on him. It was no ordinary shock she had given him. And now the drawing! How could she have possibly known?

For the sake of his sanity, she needed to leave. He'd give them time to finish their meal and take them the check. Then she'd be gone, and things would be back to normal.

After a little while, he peeked out the kitchen door and saw her staring at him. He made his way over to her and started to say something when she interrupted him.

"I'll have a whiskey on the rocks."

"What?" he asked.

"You heard me."

"You drink whiskey straight up?"

"Yes."

He turned his back to them and reached for the first bottle of whiskey he saw.

"Excuse me. Is there something wrong with the Johnnie Walker Gold?"

He didn't turn around to acknowledge he'd heard her but grabbed the whiskey she wanted and poured her a drink. As he handed her the glass, their fingertips briefly touched. Shocks ignited between them. Their eyes locked.

"Who the hell are you, lady?"

He heard her mutter "*Faccia di stronzo*" under her breath.

"Natalia." Ellie nudged her. "Stop it. That isn't going to help, and you'll only regret it. You always do."

Marc was impressed as Natalia took a good size gulp of her whiskey and, without flinching, swallowed it. Setting the glass down, she said, "How about we stop with the silent treatment, and you tell me why my sketch made you so angry?"

He snatched the napkin off the bar and walked to the register, tabulated their bill, and handed her the check. "Someone will take this for you when you're ready."

"We aren't going anywhere until you explain to me what the problem is," she said.

"No."

She sipped her whiskey. "Fine. We're staying. Please send someone else over to wait on us. Your attitude has pretty much sucked tonight. I hope you're not expecting a tip."

He glared at her. She retaliated with a defiant stare. Now what the hell was he supposed to do? If showing her would get her to leave, that's what he would do.

"All right, ladies, follow me. What you want to see is in the back." When they hesitated he asked, "Change of heart?"

"No," said Natalia.

They were following him through the kitchen when Giuseppe approached them. "Marcos, what's going on?"

Marc ushered the three women into a small office and told them he'd be right back. Reaching in his pocket, he handed the older man the napkin. "This is the drawing I told you about, and the woman who drew it is in the office. I was upset when I saw it and didn't handle it well. Now she won't leave until she gets an explanation. But *I'm* the one who needs an explanation."

"Marcos, you've always been too sensitive about it, even as a child. Let me see that." He gazed down at the napkin then back up to Marc. "It's perfect," he said carefully. "It's exact."

"I'll show her, and maybe she'll tell me how she knew. Then can you please ask them to leave?"

"Of course, Marcos." The two men walked into the office.

"This is Giuseppe," said Marc.

"It's nice to meet you." Giuseppe extended his hand to the women.

Marc stood self-conscious and unsure. He gave Giuseppe a look, asking for some reassurance. When he nodded, Marc started to unbutton his shirt and take it off.

Natalia whistled at him.

Marc spun around angrily. "Jesus Christ, can't you control you forty-year old mid-life hormones?"

"What? Don't you dare, you—"

"Natalia!" yelled Christine.

She lowered her head, apologetically. "I'm sorry. I was only joking."

"Ladies," Giuseppe said, leading the women toward the door. "This way out. This is not a joke to him. Please leave him alone now. We'll have your check ready by the bar. Good night."

CHAPTER 2

"A soul mate encounter brings about a stirring of soul memory and one recognizes a soul mate intuitively from the very recesses of the soul." – *Jaime T. Licauco, 1940- Parapsychologist and Author*

The women walked up Fifty-Ninth Street to Columbus Circle. The temperature had plummeted and the wind was howling. Attempting to hail a cab proved fruitless. Every cab whizzed by, full of warm and content passengers.

Natalia played the evening over in her head. Knowing she'd contributed to the last part of the night's debacle, she felt a twinge of remorse. Still feeling, she knew him—and worse—was perplexingly attracted to him, she didn't want to leave things the way they were.

"Hey, will you guys come back to Tremonti's with me? I feel terrible about what happened and I think I should apologize. Then I can put the whole thing behind me."

"Nat, it's freezing! I don't want to walk all the way back there," whined Ellie. "It's over and done with. Can't we just go home? Look, there's a subway station."

"I don't know if that Giuseppe guy is going to let us back in, much less see Marc," said Christine.

"I need to try. Please," Natalia pleaded with them. They grudgingly agreed and began their trek back to the restaurant.

Natalia pushed her way through the large bar crowd. Christine and Ellie let her go and stopped to order a drink. She marched up to the kitchen door and looked in. When Marc saw her, he reluctantly walked over and cracked open the door.

"Hi. Can you come out here for a minute, please?" she asked.

"You're not shy, are you?"

"No. I would like to talk to you." She waited. "Do I have to beg?"

"Let me guess. You aren't leaving unless I come out and talk to you, right?"

"Right."

He walked out, grabbed her hand, and pulled her to the corner of the restaurant. Natalia felt the shock the second he touched her. "Sorry," they both half mumbled, and Natalia assumed he'd been stung again as well.

"So?" he asked.

"Look. What I did was inappropriate, and I'm sorry. I didn't realize it was such a sensitive subject. I was trying to lighten up a tense situation, but it came out wrong. I'd still like to see whatever you were going to show us. If you agree, I'll be considerate. I promise."

While he stood staring at her, she nearly melted into a puddle. His deep brown eyes moved slowly, up and down her body. She didn't mind and followed his lead. Beginning at his shoes, she let her eyes gradually wander up to meet his. He looked good in his white shirt that showed off his wonderful Mediterranean coloring. His open collar button revealed a long, sexy neck. When an amused look crossed his face, she knew he liked playing this little game with her.

But as much as she enjoyed gawking at handsome men, she didn't have all night. "Can I still see it? I'll come by myself, not with my friends or Georgio."

"His name is Giuseppe," said Marc. "Are you sober now? No whistling?"

"I wasn't drunk. It wasn't the whiskey. I probably would have whistled at you, anyway." She shrugged her shoulders and smiled at him. He raised his eyebrows. "Oh, come on!" she grumped. "Are you always this serious?"

He didn't answer but didn't stop her when she waved Christine and Ellie over.

"Can you wait here for me? I promised to behave, so Marc is going to show me whatever this thing is. It might be better without a crowd."

"I don't know if that's a good idea," Christine said, looking at Marc. "You two back there all by yourselves."

"I'm not going to hurt her. I'm not *that* upset with her."

"Oh, we aren't worried about her. We're worried about you."

The two women laughed and walked away.

♨♨

Marc and Natalia went back through the kitchen. A few men were still working and eyed her as she walked past.

"Hi, guys," she said.

The men whistled, obviously teasing him about going into the office with Natalia.

"Sorry," he said. "Just ignore them."

She followed him to the office door. Instead of going in, she looked back at the men, gave them the thumbs up, winked, smiled, and then went inside. They laughed and clapped at her as Marc shut the door behind them.

"Are you always like this?" he asked her.

"Like what?"

He chuckled to himself. Most women he knew would be offended or embarrassed by the men's catcalls. She seemed to enjoy it. At the very least, it didn't bother her. He wanted to be angry with her, but he wasn't. In fact, since she came back to the restaurant, he found himself even more captivated with her than before.

"Whose office is this?" she asked.

"Mine. Why?"

"I didn't think bartenders got private offices at restaurants."

"What if the bartender's last name is Tremonti?"

"So, you own the restaurant?"

"It's a family owned restaurant."

He leaned against the wall as she strolled curiously around his office. As far as he was concerned, she could walk around all night in fitted jeans that revealed her long legs and other *assets*. She was exceptionally pretty, with shoulder length, jet-black hair. She had big brown eyes with long lashes, a smooth olive complexion, and curves in all the right places. She did not look her age. His mind started to drift to a place it shouldn't, and he was somewhat annoyed when her voice took him from his daydream of her.

"I know this is awkward, but I want to help. Why don't you tell me about it before you show me? Maybe it'll be easier."

"I have a birthmark with a tattoo around it."

"And it looks a little something like what I drew?"

He didn't answer her.

"Where is your birthmark?"

"On my left shoulder."

"What if I turn my back while you take your left arm out of your shirt then show me." She faced the back of the office.

He sighed loudly, and removed his shirt. "Okay."

Marc felt her behind him and his stomach quivered. He looked down and was stunned to see he was holding the napkin in his hands. He didn't remember taking it out of his pocket.

He froze as she touched each of the six odd shaped marks on his shoulder. Her finger followed the ragged edge of the large port-wine birthmark that enclosed the six marks. A procession of shocks followed her moving finger.

Staring at the napkin, he went along on her journey as if he were reading a map. She began at the top of his tattoo, with one finger. First, she outlined the small yellow flame on the left and then the larger red flame on the right. She added a second finger and used both hands to trace the two colorful ropes that extended from each flame and met at the bottom.

Oddly, he didn't mind her touching him. In fact, it was the opposite. He found it quite soothing. He was no longer surprised at the shocks only she seemed to give him, but he didn't think it was appropriate. He was married, and even though he felt he knew her, she was a complete stranger.

"Wow," she said. "Can I see the napkin?"

He handed it to her.

"It's exactly what I drew. I can't believe it," she said touching his shoulder again.

"What are you doing? Please stop it."

"I'm trying to take it all in." Then out of nowhere, she got on her toes and kissed his shoulder.

Marc whipped his shirt on and turned to face her.

"You said, this time would be different," he snapped, raising his voice to her.

"No wait, I'm sorry. I don't know why I did that. It just happened. Please. I'm as surprised as you are. Don't be upset. It was almost like...I couldn't help myself."

"How were you able to draw it so well?"

"I don't know. It's so beautiful, especially the tattoo. I love it."

"You *do*?"

"Of course, I drew it, didn't I?" She smirked. He sat on the chair behind the desk. Without another chair available, Natalia jumped up on the edge of the desk. "Why did you get that particular tattoo around it?"

"I don't know. I had a burning sensation in my shoulder the day I got it. You really like it?"

He couldn't believe she wasn't put off by it. He knew it was unattractive. Some people tried to be nice about it. Others did not. He wished he had a dime for every time someone asked him why he didn't get it removed.

"I think it's pretty cool. Why does it bother you so much?"

"When I was kid, I got teased a lot. I'm still self-conscious whenever I have to take my shirt off. "

"A lot of people have birthmarks. It's a part of who you are."

"Yes, they have birthmarks, but not strange women drawing them on napkins."

"Yeah. I don't know what to tell you about that. I thought I could help you, but I guess I can't." Neither of them spoke for a few minutes.

"Now what?" he asked.

"I guess we have to put it down as one of life's mysteries. Sometimes there are things you can't explain. You just have to live with them."

"I don't willingly show too many people. I meant what I said before. I feel like I know you."

"I know. Me, too. You're easy to talk to, except when you get angry at people who sit at the bar and doodle a little."

"I get angry? *Faccia di stronzo?*" he said, repeating Natalia's Italian insult.

She looked surprised. "You speak Italian? I didn't mean to call you a—"

"SOB? I think you did."

"The literal translation is—"

"I know very well what the literal translation is."

"Well, at the time I meant it, but I take it back now."

"You're a strange woman."

"And you're being ridiculous. If having a birthmark is your biggest problem, you shouldn't complain. There are people in the world with real problems they have to deal with."

"You get right to the point, don't you?"

"Life is short. Why waste it pretending to be something you're not?"

"I guess you're right."

"Of course, I'm right. I'm old and with age comes wisdom."

He cracked a small smile.

"And you finally smiled again," she said. "You haven't done that since you thought I was your camp counselor. I'm glad. You have a nice smile."

She hopped off the desk and picked up the napkin. "It's a pretty good piece of artwork if you ask me." Reaching for a pen on his desk, she signed it.

Natalia, December nineteen, two-thousand-nine.

"A keepsake from a very unusual evening." She handed it back to him.

"Thanks."

"I should be going," she said. "I don't want to miss the last train out."

From the moment she touched his birthmark, Marc had an incredibly peaceful feeling wash over him. Earlier, he wanted her to leave, but now he was afraid this calmness would leave with her.

"They run more trains during the holiday." He didn't know what else to say.

"I know. I think we'll be okay." She didn't move.

If she had to go, he at least wanted to touch her again, to feel the electricity between them. As if she was reading his mind, she extended her hand to him.

"So," she asked. "Friends?"

"Friends," he said and slowly put his hand in hers, holding it longer and tighter than he should have.

"Ouch!" She jerked her hand from his. "Get a damn humidifier in here, will you?"

"Sure," he told her but knew it wouldn't help. He'd touched plenty of people tonight, and she was the only one who gave him a shock.

"Have a Merry Christmas."

"You, too," he said. "Will you come back and visit sometime?"

"I don't think that's a good idea," she said. "Good night."

He agreed. In fact, it was a dangerous idea, but Marc promised himself he would see Natalia again, one way or another. He wasn't a believer in life's mysteries. There had to be a reasonable explanation.

CHAPTER 3

"When my grandmother was alive, she used to tell me that every time God creates a soul in heaven, he creates another to be its special soul mate. And that once we're born we begin to search for our soul mate, the one person who's the perfect fit for our mind and body. The lucky ones find each other." – *Lurlene McDaniel, 1944 – Author*

Natalia was coming in the door when she heard the phone ring. 'Hello."

"Natalia?"

"Yes." A shiver of excitement and apprehension traveled down her spine at the sound of his voice.

"Hi. This is Marc. You know, the guy who acted ridiculous over his birthmark."

"Sorry, doesn't ring a bell," she joked, hoping to cover any trepidation in her tone.

"Excuse me?"

"Yes, Marc. How are you?" She laughed a little. "How did you get my number?"

"I got your name off the debit receipt and called information for Connecticut."

"Are you like, a stalker?"

"No. I didn't know any other way to find out your last name. Do you own Santagario Vineyards?"

"Like yours, it's a family business."

"Oh. First, I'd like to apologize for my *intense* behavior the last time you were here. It was an unusual evening, and I didn't handle it well. I would like you to come to the restaurant and have lunch. My treat."

"That's not necessary. I understand. It was strange for both of us."

"I would like you to meet my aunt. She owns Tremonti Dream and Sleep Center here in Manhattan. Have you heard of it?

"No, I'm sorry I haven't."

"She'd like to put a complimentary bottle of wine in each guest room, and I thought your vineyard might be interested."

"We're a very small operation. I could never supply a large business in New York, but thanks for thinking of us."

"I would still like you to come for lunch. When you came back to the restaurant that night, I let you apologize. You owe me the same courtesy."

Natalia hesitated but in the end relented. "I guess I could do a little shopping and pop my head in for lunch. I'll call you in a few weeks and arrange it."

"No! The weeks immediately following the holidays are slow for restaurants. It would be better for me sooner rather than later."

"Oh—well, I don't know."

"I bought a humidifier."

"How can I say no, then?"

"Good. Can you come on Thursday?"

"Sure. What time?"

"Be at the restaurant at 11:30 when we open for lunch. I'll be waiting for you."

♨♨

When Natalia arrived at the restaurant, Marc was outside pacing anxiously. "There you are. I thought you weren't coming."

Extending his arm out to her, she put her hand in his. They looked at each other briefly then down at their clasped hands. There was no shock, but she wore leather gloves.

"The train was a little late. I decided to walk instead of taking a cab."

"Come on in. I want you to meet my aunt."

She walked into the empty restaurant. The atmosphere was quiet and tranquil, unlike her last visit.

Marc led her to a table near the window. Sitting there was an attractive woman in what Natalia assumed was her early sixties. Her dark hair, sprinkled with grey, was swept up in a loose bun. Her skin was smooth, and her eyes were so deep brown they were almost black. She reminded Natalia of an older Audrey Hepburn.

"Natalia Santagario, this is my Zia Mariella Tremonti."

"It's very nice to meet you," said Natalia, offering her hand.

"The pleasure is mine, dear. Please have a seat."

"Thank you. Your family owns a wonderful restaurant."

"My brother opened it originally. Marcos' father. Now, a lot of the family has their hands in it."

"You two get to know each other," said Marc. "I'll be right back."

"I told Marc this wasn't necessary," Natalia protested. "But he insisted."

"I understand you two had a very interesting evening."

"He told you?"

"Marcos mentioned a little of what happened. We're very close."

Marc came back with a bottle of wine. "Is this okay, or do you want a whiskey?"

"Am I going to need a whiskey?" she asked.

"No, I don't think so."

"Good because I brought two bottles of our wine. I thought it was the least I could do since you're providing lunch." She pulled a bottle of Cabernet and a bottle Chianti out of her bag.

"That was very thoughtful of you. I would love to taste your wine," Mariella said.

"Natalia, what would you like for lunch?" asked Marc. "Please, anything you want."

"I don't want anyone to go to any trouble. I'll eat anything."

"Okay."

"Can you leave the corkscrew?"

"Sure, let me open the bottle."

"No. I have it, thanks. I do own a vineyard you know." She laughed a little, watched Marc walk away, and turned her attention to Mariella. "So, Marc tells me you own a sleep and dream center here in Manhattan."

"Yes, I do."

"Maybe you're just the person I should talk to. I haven't been sleeping well the last few months." Natalia pulled the cork out of the bottle.

"I'm sorry to hear that. Sleep deprivation is a huge problem in this country. With all the technology, everyone is always on the go. No one gives their brain or body time to relax."

"I don't think that's my problem. Shall we?" she asked Mariella as she poured the wine.

"Minor sleep issues usually last a week or two, not months."

"I'm sure it's nothing, and I'll be back to sleeping like my old self in no time." The two women put their glasses together and in unison chimed, "Salute."

"Natalia, your wine is very good. I wish you would reconsider. Marcos mentioned you believe your vineyard is too small to handle supplying my center. I don't think it would be as much of a strain as you think."

"I don't know. I've never ventured out of our local area."

Marc returned to the table carrying three plates of food, placing one in front of Natalia and one in front of his aunt. The table had an empty seat next to each woman. Instead of sitting next to his aunt, Marc put his plate down next to Natalia's and sat beside her. She felt the heat of his closeness and inconspicuously shifted away from him toward the window. Taking a whiff of the wonderful food in front of her, she relaxed. "This is *not* Risotto Smeralda!"

"It is. Do you like it?" asked Marc.

"It's my favorite," Natalia groaned, taking a bite. "Oh, this is delicious. Can I meet the chef? I would like to marry him and have his children."

"I'm sorry. I'm already married, but maybe we could work something out." Marc winked at her.

His comment and the sparkle in his eyes when he said it had her heart racing. She managed to ask, "You made this?"

"Yes. I'm glad you're enjoying it."

"I love it, but I'm a little embarrassed. I thought you were the bartender."

"I don't get the impression you ever get embarrassed about anything, but no, I graduated from the Culinary Institute in Hyde Park, New York." He picked up his wine glass and raised it toward her. "Let me return the compliment, Natalia. Your wine is excellent. We could be good together."

With a curious look, she mused over the handsome man next to her and their peculiar circumstances.

Her gaze turned to his wedding ring, and she said, "No, I don't think so."

♨♨

Marc rammed the swinging kitchen door with his right shoulder and walked in. For him, being a chef and having someone enjoy his meal was the highest form of flattery. And Natalia enjoyed her meal. His experience was, the female sex usually picked at their food when in the company of a man they didn't know well. Not her. In fact, she took the last piece of bread and wiped her dish clean. He smiled as he put her plate in the sink. Yes, she was unlike any woman he'd met before. She said and did what she wanted, not conforming to any rules of conduct—especially those expected of her gender.

Marc's problem was how he could touch her without being obvious. He refused to let her leave without knowing if her touch still resulted in a shock. He also had unanswered questions about his birthmark. That was the key to their strange puzzle, but he didn't know how to approach the subject.

While pacing around the kitchen, he realized he was playing with his wedding ring. Were his feelings for Natalia a result of being alone for so long? No, he didn't think so. There were too many coincidences to ignore. Either way, he should leave well enough alone. He told himself after Natalia left today, there was no logical reason to see her again. However, he wasn't sure he'd be able to heed his own advice.

He fixed two cups of espresso and went back to the dining room. He placed a cup in front of Natalia.

"Thank you. I think the coffee and a nice brisk walk back to the train station is just what I need. Otherwise, I may fall asleep."

Mariella pushed her chair back and excused herself from the table. "Natalia, please don't leave yet. I'll be right back."

Marc turned to Natalia, trying to make small talk. Her phone went off. As she bent down to reach into her purse, he knocked a spoon off the table onto the floor. Leaning over to pick it up, he deliberately brushed his hand against hers, aware of the spark between them. Together, they slowly straightened in their seats, staring at each other.

She glanced at her phone. "Oh, I have two messages. I never heard the phone ring." She gave him a half-smile as they sat in an awkward silence.

"Natalia, I'm sorry, but I have to ask. Have you given any thought as to how you drew my birthmark?"

"No. I think we should forget about it. I'm not going to magically wake up one morning and know how I drew it."

She looked away from him, this time out the window. With her back slightly turned to him, he leaned in closer. Her scent was intoxicating. He was content to sit there, savoring her nearness. Finally, he spoke into her ear.

"Well, I *have* thought about it. Drawing a complicated design you've never seen before is not an everyday occurrence. It's not something I can forget about. I think we should—"

"Natalia," Mariella said, suddenly appearing at the table. "Before you leave, I would like to introduce you to the rest of the family."

Marc, irritated by the interruption, reluctantly stood, let Natalia out, and followed them into the kitchen.

Mariella made the introductions. Giuseppe still looked at Natalia with some annoyance. Since Giuseppe was his uncle, and he'd always been a little overprotective, Marc forgave him.

His cousins, Angelo and Tony, recognized her as well. "Hey, Natalia, are you going behind closed doors with Marc again?"

"That was the original plan," she said, smiling. "But then I found out he could cook. Now I only want him for his culinary skills."

"Are you saying he cooks better than he—"

"Tony!" Mariella glared at him. "Mind your manners."

"I'm not saying anything," said Natalia. "You guys do the math."

"If you were to ask me," joked Marc. "I'd say I do both very well."

"That's enough," said Mariella. "You're all behaving like children." She led Natalia out the kitchen door. "I'm sorry about that, dear. Don't mind them."

When the women were gone, Tony walked up to Marc. "Hey, we really like her. She's a good sport. Who is she?"

"Her family owns a vineyard in Connecticut. Mariella would like to put a bottle of her wine in each of her guest rooms at the center."

"She'll be back, then?"

"I don't know. We'll see. I hope so."

♨♨

Mark caught up with Natalia and Mariella at the door as they were saying, "Goodbye."

"It was nice to meet you," Natalia said to Mariella. "But I want to make the three-thirty train."

"Please take my card. Go online and look at my center's website. I enjoyed your wine and it could be a good business opportunity for you. Maybe it's time you branched out a little. Just think about it."

"Okay, I will." Natalia hugged Mariella then turned to him. "Thank you for a delicious lunch."

"You're welcome." He offered his hand and closed it firmly around hers. She jerked—ever so slightly. He'd gotten his answer. The shocks were not a coincidence. When he felt her pull away, he let go.

"I thought you bought a humidifier," she said.

His lips curved in a playful grin. "I lied."

"Very funny." She checked her watch. "I'm sorry, but I have to go if I'm going to make my train. Good-bye."

And she was gone.

"Marcos, she was lovely," said Mariella. "I liked her very much."

"I know," he said softly. "I really like her, too."

"Marcos, what are you saying?"

"I don't know what I'm saying, much less what I'm feeling." He sighed and flopped down in a chair. "Every time I touch her, I get a shock. It doesn't happen with anyone else. Did you get a shock when you kissed her good-bye?"

"No." She sat next to her nephew. "Is there anything else you didn't tell me about the night you met?

"We thought we knew each other and had met before."

"Do you have her drawing? I would like to see it."

He reached into his pocket and handed her the folded napkin.

"Marcos, it's a perfect match. You gave me the impression it was *somewhat* similar. Why didn't you tell me?"

"Please. I need you to get her back down here," he pleaded, knowing his aunt would do anything for him.

"Her wine was exceptional. It's a small, relatively unknown vineyard, and I may be able to get her wine at a more reasonable price than a larger name. I'll call her in a few days and see if she has thought about my offer."

♨♨

Natalia unlocked the door, walked in, and threw her purse on the couch. Although she was relieved to be off the crowded train and in the coziness of her family room, there was no solace from the chaos spinning in her head. Since that cold December evening, Marc and his birthmark haunted her thoughts day and night. As handsome as he was, it wasn't reason she was attracted to him. There was something else, something deeper—something she didn't understand.

He was an exciting, but dangerous enigma, and she was tired of behaving like a teenager with a forbidden crush. Enough was enough. It was time to act her age and be sensible. She didn't need any more strange occurrences in her life. Living with Giovanna was plenty. There was no need for further contact with Marc. Fumbling through her purse, she found Mariella's business card and threw it in the garbage.

Later that evening, sitting at her computer, she spotted Mariella's card on the keyboard. "I know you're here, Giovanna." She felt a cool breeze blow past. "Why do you want me to go online and look at her Center?"

Natalia often wondered how and why she was able to have these conversations with Giovanna. It was telepathic, one-sided, but telepathic, nevertheless. She understood Giovanna's communication but heard it *in* her head, not with her ears. *She*, on the other hand, always had to speak aloud. Another unsolved mystery with no resolution in sight.

"Do you really have no one else to bother?"

The small garbage can next to her desk tipped over.

"I know I haven't been sleeping, but I don't think I need to check myself into a facility."

The computer booted up all by itself.

"You're a pushy ghost, aren't you?"

Typing the website into her browser, Natalia checked out the site. Mariella, as well as the other doctors on staff, were licensed sleep therapists, all accredited by the American Academy of Sleep Medicine. She clicked on *therapies* and thoroughly read about the services the center offered their clients.

"Okay, I read the whole thing."

She felt a slight nudge on her arm.

"No, I don't want to read that. It has nothing to do with me."

Giovanna prodded her harder. Giving in as usual to her unseen houseguest, she clicked on *hypnotic regressions*. Mariella had hired two new doctors specializing in hypnotic regression. Usually, the regressions only went as far back as childhood, using the procedure to uncover some trauma that had occurred during a person's younger days. Occasionally, though, it was used to go back farther—to look into past lives of clients.

This was a not a new phenomenon. People had believed in reincarnation for thousands of years. However, the therapy *was* new to Tremonti's Sleep and Dream Center, and they were asking anyone interested to contact them.

When she was through reading, Natalia heard Giovanna in her head and spun her chair around.

"What did you say? How do you know about Marc?"

The door to the library slammed shut.

Natalia got up, darted to the door, and opened it. "Come back here, right now!" She ran into her family room but didn't feel Giovanna anywhere. "I asked you a question and I want an answer."

Silence.

Walking over to the steps, she shouted up the empty staircase.

"You want to screw with me? Fine, you know there are certain individuals that can make unruly ghosts leave a person's home. We'll see how quiet you are when you're being shoved out the damn door."

She stood there, fuming, with her fists clutched at her sides. The threat was meaningless, she would never make Giovanna leave.

They needed each other too much and they both knew it.

CHAPTER 4

"One never consciously seeks out one's soul mate...The soul mate finds you. He or she merely appears in one's life when the right time and circumstances come." – *Jaime T. Licauco, 1940- Parapsychologist and Author*

It was a cold, miserable January day with the precipitation changing back and forth from sleet to snow. Due to the weather, Natalia couldn't go for her daily walk through the vineyard—which these days provided her the only respite from her embarrassing fixation with the young chef in New York. A week had passed since their lunch, and she hadn't had much success banishing Marc from her thoughts. She wanted to see him and his birthmark again, and that scared her.

Thankfully, Giovanna hadn't mentioned Marc again. Natalia still had no idea how she knew about him. "Great, I live with a ghost who reads mind," she mumbled.

What she needed was a vacation. What she *didn't* need was both Giovanna and Marc in her head. She went to her library and found a book about the ten places you should visit before you die. Curled up next to the fire, she looked for an exotic location that would make her forget Marc.

The phone rang.

"Hello, dear," said Mariella. "How are you?"

"I'm good," she replied slowly.

"Wonderful, but let me get to the point. Did you look at my website?"

"Yes. It looks like a very professional, state-of-the-art facility. I was impressed."

"Do you think we could help you with your insomnia?"

"I don't know, Mariella. I've never done anything like this before." The book she was reading fell off the chair, and she knew the cool breeze was eminent. "I'm not in the mood for you today," she muttered.

"Did you say something, dear?"

"No. Sorry."

"Why don't you come for a visit?" Mariella suggested. "We could kill two birds with one stone. Maybe I could convince you having your wine here would be good for your business *and* mine. Then you could look around and decide if our facility can help you. No pressure, I promise."

"Can I have another day to think about it?" A vase filled with flowers fell over with a crash and water spilled out onto the table. "Okay, now I'm pissed. Was that necessary?" Natalia growled through gritted teeth.

"Was what necessary? Are you angry with me?"

"No, not at all. Um...my cat knocked over a vase of flowers."

"So, what do you say?"

Creating a commotion, Giovanna swirled wildly around the room. Natalia knew her disruptive friend wouldn't stop until she agreed to Mariella's invitation. Against her better judgment, she heard herself telling Mariella she would meet her at the restaurant, and they could walk from there.

♨♨

Natalia arrived at Tremonti's a little before eleven a.m. The restaurant looked dark so she knocked, looked in the window, and saw Giuseppe walking toward the door.

"Good Morning, Giuseppe."

"*Buongiorno*, Natalia. How can I help you?"

"I'm supposed to meet Mariella here this morning. Is she here yet?"

"No. Please come inside and wait. It's cold outside."

She followed him into the kitchen. Tony and Angelo were sitting at a table with cards strewn across the top. She didn't notice Marc anywhere and was both relieved and disappointed by his absence.

"Hey, Natalia," said Tony. "How about a cup of coffee?"

"Sure. What are you guys doing?"

"We're playing cards. For some reason Marc insists we get here at ten a.m. We don't open until four, so we play for a little while. You won't tell on us, will you?"

She winked at them. "Not if you let me play while I'm waiting for Mariella."

"Sure." They pulled a chair over for her.

"I know a fun game my brother taught me. What to try?" she asked. "We just need some quarters."

"Why not?"

The men dug into their pockets and threw the coins on the table. Natalia looked in her purse and put her share in as well.

"Okay, everyone put in a quarter," she explained. "I'm going to deal everyone a card. Put the card on your forehead facing out so everyone can see it but you. Then we all bet. Highest card wins, ace high." The men looked at her with blank stares. "No, really, it's fun. Of course it's more fun if you've been drinking, but you'll see."

The three of them did what she asked while complaining about feeling silly having a card plastered to their forehead.

"Well, I must have a better card than you guys," she said, throwing in two quarters.

She watched the men gaze at her forehead, smile, and toss money into the pile. Tony ultimately won the two dollars and twenty-five cents with his high-ranking five of spades. After a few more hands, they heard someone in the doorway

"So, this is what goes on when I'm not here?"

The four of them slowly turned toward the voice, each holding a card on their head, and saw Marc standing there. Natalia gave him a small shrug and smiled.

"Good thing I'm the responsible one," Marc complained. "Natalia, I thought you were meeting my aunt, did you forget about that?"

"Marc, are you always this uptight?" she asked.

He gave her a foolish grin and opened his fist to show a handful of quarters. "Nah, I'm upset you didn't wait for me to play. Although, it looks like the silliest game I've ever seen."

"It is, but it's still fun."

They played a little longer until Marc's phone went off. "Hi, Mariella. Yes, she's here. Okay, I will. Bye." He put his phone down. "Sorry to break up the party but I have to take Natalia to Mariella's. Something came up, and she had forgotten to get your cell number. Apparently, someone never took the phone off night mode," he said, looking at Tony, who shrugged.

"Sorry."

"Come on, Natalia. We better get going."

"Thanks for humoring me and playing my one card poker game," Natalia said. "It was nice to see you all again."

They stepped out onto a congested Fifty-Fourth Street. Even though it was cloudy and cold, Natalia was happy to be outside and stretch her legs.

"It's this way," said Marc. "So, what are you meeting my aunt for?"

"I haven't been sleeping well, but I don't think I have the time to come to the city for treatment."

"They have great doctors there. I'm sure they'll be able to get to the root of your problem."

"We'll see."

"Maybe you could ask them how you knew about my birthmark," Marc murmured under his breath.

"I'm sorry. What did you say?"

"Natalia, I need you to ask them how you knew about my birthmark."

She stopped walking and glared at him. "No, I will not. If I talk to anyone, it will be about my sleep problems, not your obsession with a mark on your back. Anyway, how would a sleep therapist know anything about that?"

"They have doctors who can hypnotize you. Natalia, please," he said with a pleading look on his face. "We must have met before. It's the only explanation. Maybe we were drunk at a party and don't remember."

"You're serious, aren't you? I'm twelve years older than you are. You're grasping at straws. If it's that important to you, why don't you get hypnotized?"

He looked down at the concrete sidewalk. "I've always been skeptical about the work Mariella does there. She believes that dreams have meaning, and she's into the whole past life regression thing." He raised his eyes to her. "I like everyone, and they're great doctors, but they know how I feel. I can't act like all of a sudden, I'm a believer and ask for their help."

"So you want me to be the guinea pig? You're out of your mind."

"It's important to me. It should be important to you, too."

"Listen to me," she said, pointing her finger in the direction they'd come from. "You need to go back to the restaurant and leave me alone. I'll find Mariella's place on my own."

"It doesn't bother you that you drew something as obscure as the birthmark of someone you never met?"

"No. I haven't given it another thought."

"I don't believe you. You came back to the restaurant that night because you were curious. Now you say you haven't given it another thought. You're a terrible liar."

"Marc, I'm trying not to get pissed off, but I'm warning you, you need to drop this right now and leave me alone." She marched away down the street.

"Walk away if you want, but I'm not going to drop it," he yelled after her.

♨♨

Natalia arrived at the center, furious with Mark for putting pressure on her. His birthmark wasn't her problem. If he was so obsessed about it, let him be hypnotized. All that nonsense about why he didn't want to do it himself was probably just bullshit.

Mariella walked through the lobby to meet her. "There you are, dear," she said. "Where's Marcos?"

"I don't know where he is, and I don't care. This isn't going to work if he keeps bothering me about his birthmark. I want to forget everything that happened that night."

"I'm sorry, dear. It's been a problem for him since he was a child. Although, he's been more preoccupied than usual since he met you. You have to admit it's strange."

"Yes, it's strange. But so are a lot of other things. He needs to figure this out on his own. It has nothing to do with me."

"Natalia, it has everything to do with you."

"Not you, too?" she whined.

"You're right," Mariella admitted. "We're here to talk about wine and sleep, not Marcos. Let's go upstairs and I'll show you around."

To Natalia's surprise, the facility was beautiful. Each room was light and airy, not dark and dreary as she'd assumed.

"What were you expecting, dear? Dracula's castle?"

Natalia laughed. "Maybe a little. I didn't know what to expect."

"Just because we delve into non-traditional methods of treating people doesn't mean we've moved to the dark side." Mariella led her to the elevator. "Let me show you the rooms I would like to put the wine in."

Natalia didn't consider them rooms, but suites, and they were impressive. The kitchen was small, but the living room was large with a two-sided fireplace that faced into the bedroom.

"I would like to place a basket filled with wine, cheese, and crackers on the hearth. We could include a card showing your vineyard nestled in the beautiful hills of Litchfield County, Connecticut, as well as directions. Who knows? It may get you more visitors on the weekends. Can you picture your wine here?"

Natalia could easily envision her wine here and that worried her. Mariella was a savvy businesswoman and had done her homework. She was sure Mariella hadn't heard of Litchfield County before last week.

"Yes, I can picture it. I'm not sure we're a large enough vineyard. I promise to figure it out in the next couple of days and let you know."

"I have an apartment here in the building. Let's go up there where we can talk." As the woman pushed the button for the twelfth floor, Natalia felt herself moving toward a disaster of monumental proportions. She was heading to the apartment of a woman she had just met, who was the aunt of a man she thought about constantly. She was royally screwed.

Where was her earlier resolve to be through with this family? She was well aware she needed to stay away from Marc, but something deep in the recess of her soul told her she wouldn't be able too.

As they walked into the apartment, Natalia was struck by the view of Columbus Circle through a large picture window. She gazed down at the statue of Columbus standing tall, as if he were directing the traffic as it looped around him.

Mariella showed her around the small but stylish, two-bedroom apartment. The décor was a little more modern than Natalia usually liked, but she found it warm and inviting. She sat down and gently rubbed her eyes.

"Are you all right, dear?

"Yes, I'm just tired. It happens this time every day."

"Would you like to talk about your sleep problems?" Mariella asked as they sat on the sofa. "I am a licensed therapist. I do more in the administrative side these days but I think I remember a thing or two."

"I saw online that you have quite a few degrees."

"Yes, I was very career-oriented in my younger days. That's why Marcos is so important to me. I never had any children of my own."

"You never married?"

"No. I never had the time. Between taking care of Marcos, going to school, and opening this center, I had a lot on my plate."

"You took care of Marc? Why, did his parents work?"

"No, dear. He didn't tell you?"

Natalia shook her head.

"Marcos' parents died in a train derailment accident in Italy when he was four years old. His father, Salvatore, was my brother. To celebrate their anniversary, they went to Sicily then on to the mainland. They boarded a train headed for Rome, but never made it."

Mariella turned her head away. Natalia rested her hand on the woman's back. "Mariella, I'm so sorry. I would have never asked if I thought—"

Mariella put her hand up. "It's fine, dear. We still miss them, of course. Anyway, they named me as Marcos' guardian, and I was happy to raise him as my own. It was hard at first. He didn't understand where his parents were. But we are a big, extended family, and time does heal wounds, to a certain extent."

"Does Marc remember them?"

"He has pictures and home videos of them together. We told him anything he wanted to know about them. He has a few memories, but he was only four."

"You did a wonderful job raising him. He seems like a great guy." Natalia put her head down and whispered, "I really like him."

"I thought we weren't going to talk about Marcos anymore today."

"Yes." Natalia took a deep breath and straightened her shoulders. "Please no more about Marc."

"So, tell me about yourself. I seem to have done all the talking."

Natalia didn't like talking about herself. She walked back to the picture window and gazed down at the hustle and bustle surrounding Columbus.

"I grew up in Connecticut. My family has owned the vineyard for many years. I have a brother Robbie and some extended family. I went to UCONN and got my business degree then went to work at the vineyard. My brother and my parents had a falling out, and I took Robbie's side. They weren't happy with me, but they were more upset with him. They retired and moved to Florida and before I knew it, I was in charge. My relationship with my parents is civil, but strained."

"What about the men in your life?"

Natalia let out a small grown. The one thing she hated more than talking about herself was discussing her terrible track record with men. She sat back down on the couch with Mariella. "I've had a few serious relationships. The last one didn't end well."

"Do you think all this is impacting your sleep?"

"I don't know."

"Is that when your sleep problems started, after the break-up?"

"No, it was a few weeks, even a month or so afterward. It was around Thanksgiving."

"That's when Marcos got his tattoo."

"Mariella, you promised."

"Yes, dear, I know. Then after you met Marcos, did you sleep better or worse?

"Mariella! What the hell does that have to do with anything?"

"Answer the question, dear."

"It's been worse, but that doesn't mean anything. My sleep problems have nothing to do with Marc. They started before I even met him."

"You do know you're the only one who gives him a shock. I assume you only get a shock from him as well."

"What? How did you know?"

"Marcos told me."

"You don't really want to help me, do you? This is all for his benefit. How could I've been so stupid?" Natalia stood, angrily grabbed her coat, and walked to the door.

"Of course, I want to help you, but I think it's all connected. I've been doing this for a long time. There's more going on here then you think."

"I don't want to hear it. I'm going."

"Wait." Mariella took hold of Natalia's arm. "I promise to run all the proper tests with no mention of Marcos."

"I don't know, Mariella. I'm so exhausted right now I can't even think straight."

"Come sit down, and I'll make you a cup of tea."

♨♨

When Natalia woke up, it took her a few minutes to get her bearings.

Mariella sat, patiently waiting, in a chair.

"I'm sorry," Natalia said. "I didn't mean to fall asleep."

"Remember where you are dear. I have people falling asleep on me all the time." Mariella smiled. "Here I made you a sandwich. You must by hungry."

"Thanks."

"If we are going to move forward with this, there are a few questions I have to ask you." When Natalia gave her a warning glance, Mariella added, "Don't worry, these are strictly professional questions."

They went over Natalia's diet, sleep patterns, and exercise routines. Mariella faxed Natalia's doctor to get the results of a physical she had in December. She left the room and when she returned, handed Natalia a bottle filled with pills. "Here, take these for ten days. If you don't see any improvement by then, even a little one, we can talk about the next step. It will be entirely up to you. I won't call you. You get in touch with me if you want to continue."

"What are they?"

"It's a mixture of different herbs that will help you relax and soothe any anxiety you may have. It's chamomile and a small amount of synthetic melatonin. Melatonin is what your body produces to help you sleep." She handed her a piece of paper. "Follow these directions and hopefully you'll get some sleep."

"Thank you, Mariella."

"I want you to use these ten days to think about my business proposition as well."

"I will." The two women hugged and Natalia left.

♨♨

When she was gone, Mariella picked up her plate and walked into the kitchen. This may be a little harder than she'd initially thought, but she wasn't too worried. Her new friend had a strong and stubborn personality, but strong and stubborn had nothing on human nature. Human nature always won.

Natalia would be back. She wouldn't be able to help herself. They would go through the motions of therapy, but Mariella knew what she really needed and would do whatever was necessary to get her to that point. Unfortunately, that included giving her placebos instead of herbal supplements. Mariella had a small pang of guilt but it was short-lived. She was becoming quite fond of Natalia. It was too bad she was already exhausted and wouldn't be getting much sleep in the next ten days, either. In this particular case, the end would justify the means.

CHAPTER 5

"When soul mates meet, there is from the very beginning instant recognition of each other stemming from the very core of their being, and this recognition has an aura of certainty that defies logic. This is commonly called 'love at first sight.'" – *Jaime T. Licauco, 1940- Parapsychologist and Author*

Sam, what do you think? I have to call Mariella and tell her what we've decided. I promised." Natalia looked affectionately at the man she had come to love as a father. Sam Belfry had been at Santagario Vineyards for twenty-five years, and she couldn't have kept the vineyard running without him. He was an expert on grapes, from the vine to the bottle.

They sat in front of her computer, looking at Mariella's website. Natalia explained to him everything she and Mariella discussed.

"I think we could do it," he replied. "We may have to pull back a few cases from the local liquor stores, but I think the exposure in the city is well worth it."

"I'm glad you think so. I'm so excited. I never thought we'd have the opportunity to have our wine in New York." Despite her earlier reluctance, she was almost giddy with enthusiasm.

"Me neither." He grinned. "It's a chance we shouldn't pass up."

Natalia knew Sam's simple smile was as animated as he got, even on happy occasions. "Make sure you get the price we talked about," he said. "Tell Mariella if she can't pay what we want, it won't work for us."

"Okay. I'll call her."

But she didn't call. She waited another day. Another day, she hoped the pills would start to work and she would get some sleep. Then she could ship the wine to the city and not have any contact with Mariella or Marc. But nothing was helping. She had followed Mariella's instructions perfectly and there was no change. The rational thing to do was to find a place in Connecticut to help her. Nevertheless, she knew deep in her heart that she wouldn't. She would end up at Mariella's center eventually, of that she was sure.

Sleep deprived and exhausted, Natalia had no choice but to pick up the phone.

"Mariella?"

"Yes."

"Hi. It's Natalia."

"Hello, dear. Has it been ten days already?"

"You don't fool me, Mariella. You know it's been over two weeks."

"I'm assuming the supplements must have helped, or you would have called sooner."

"No, I'm sorry to say, they haven't helped. I even gave it a few extra days."

"Don't get discouraged, dear," Mariella reassured her. "There are other things we can try."

"I'll think about it, but I do have good news. I would like to have our wine at your center if you're still interested. I know it took me longer to decide than agreed, so I won't be upset if you went elsewhere."

"Of course, I'm interested. I'm a very patient woman, Natalia. I wanted your wine and I waited until I heard from you. I couldn't be happier. I think this arrangement will work out for both of us."

"I think so, too. This is a first for us, to go outside of our local area."

"When can you come down to go over the numbers and sign a contract? Have you thought of a price?"

Natalia explained everything to Mariella exactly the way Sam told her to.

"I think that's very reasonable. If you're coming down anyway, why don't you pack a bag and stay? We can go over some of the treatments that might help you sleep."

"I don't know. This is all so frustrating. I've always been a good sleeper."

"Eventually this will affect your health. Insomnia can cause many problems. If you don't want to come here I understand, but promise me you'll take care of yourself."

"I liked your facility very much." Natalia laughed. "At least I know I'll like the wine."

"There won't be any alcohol during therapy. Alcohol doesn't help you sleep. It actually makes it worse."

"Whatever," Natalia said. "When do you want me to come?"

"It will take my lawyers a couple days to draw something up. Today is Sunday. How is Tuesday? Does that give you enough time to take care of things up there?"

"Why? How long am I going to be there?"

"Pack for a few days. You never know."

"You never know what?"

"Good-bye dear. See you Tuesday."

♨♨

Natalia told Sam where she was going and why.

"Don't worry about anything here, Nat. Do what they tell you and get better." He embraced her. "I need you well rested for the spring cleanup."

"Thanks, Sam. I'll fax the contract to you when I get there."

"I'll be waiting for it. Now, go take care of yourself."

Natalia was packing when she felt Giovanna cheerfully blow into her room. "Why are you so happy I'm leaving? Are you planning a weird party with your other unworldly friends?"

Feeling Giovanna stop cold in front of her, she said, "Oh, I'm sorry," as Giovanna let her know it had been a very long time since she'd been to a party.

Natalia sat on the edge of the bed and looked around the seemingly empty room, not knowing exactly where her invisible friend was. "I wish you would tell me who you are and why you're here. Maybe I could help you."

At that moment, Natalia felt a whirlpool of cool air wrap around her tightly. Even though Giovanna's temperature was chilly, the warmth of her love came through.

"I know you do," said Natalia, closing her eyes. "And for some strange reason, I love you, too.

♨♨

When Natalia arrived, Mariella was in the lobby. "Hello, dear. Oh my, you look awful! You have terrible circles under your eyes."

"Thanks. It's nice to see you, too."

"I'm sorry, I'm just surprised. You didn't look this tired the last time I saw you."

"I hardly slept last night. I was nervous about coming down here today."

"There's no need to be nervous. It'll be very relaxing, I promise."

"I hope so."

"Shall we do the paperwork first?" asked Mariella. "Get that out of the way?"

"Sure. I want to fax the contract back up the vineyard and have Sam look at it." Natalia paused. "It's not that I don't trust you."

Mariella cut her off. "Natalia, I wouldn't think you were a good business woman if you didn't look after your own assets. I would do the same thing. Who's Sam?" she asked as they walked into the elevator together.

"Sam and my father are best friends. He came to work at the vineyard many years ago and stayed even after my parents retired to Florida. I've known him all my life and love him very much."

"Did you discuss our business arrangement with him?"

"Yes. He really encouraged me to do it. He thought having our wine in the city was a great idea."

"I hope I get to thank him someday," said Mariella.

She had multiple copies of the contract ready. Natalia read them over. Everything looked fine to her, but she still faxed the agreement to Sam.

"With that behind us," said Mariella, "let's talk about you. Tonight, we'll do a routine polysomnogram. This test will help us figure out what your sleep disorder is." Mariella briefly described how Natalia would be hooked up to electrodes and monitored all night. "The doctor will explain everything. You can ask him any questions that you have."

She got up and walked to the door. "Let me show you to your room. I'm sorry we don't have a suite available right now, but in the next day or two you should be able to move into a nicer room."

"I only need a room with a bed and hopefully a good night's sleep." Natalia had to give Mariella credit for keeping her word. There had been no mention—or sight—of Marc since she arrived. That changed when she picked up her suitcase, opened the door, and found him standing there.

"Hi, Natalia."

"Mariella, you promised."

"What did you want me to do, dear? If I told him not to visit for a few days, he would have known something was wrong."

"Natalia, are you sick?" he asked "You don't look so good."

"I'm starting not to feel so well." She glared at both of them.

Mariella's phone rang and she went in the other room.

Marc stood within inches of her. Would he touch her? She breathed a sigh of relief when he shoved his hands in his pockets and asked, "How have you been these last few weeks."

"Cranky."

"Just your usual self, then?"

"Natalia," said Mariella, coming out of the kitchen, "you're going to have to give me a few minutes before I take you to your room. I'll be right back. Marcos, come with me and leave her alone."

"Sure." He followed his aunt to the door. She walked into the hallway, and Marc shut the door behind her remaining in the room with Natalia.

"Marcos," Mariella called through the door. "I don't have time for this. I have to go."

"Then go," he yelled back.

"I don't think this is a good idea. She's tired and irritable."

"It'll be fine. Go do what you have to do."

"Be careful, dear," she said.

The smile Natalia heard in Mariella's voice made her suspect the woman had planned the whole thing.

♨♨

"What do you want, Marc?" Natalia asked.

"I want to talk to you about a couple of things."

"A couple of things? In which order? Your birthmark and how I knew about it or what I'm going to do about it?"

"We'll get to that, but first things first." He put his hand out. "Shake my hand."

"No. We've already met."

"What are you afraid of?"

"Nothing."

"Then shake it."

"I don't want to." She crossed her arms defiantly over her chest.

"You really are the most stubborn person I've ever met." Before she could stop him, Marc touched her forehead. She jumped from the shock.

"Stop it."

He touched the tip of her nose.

"Stop it, I said."

"No."

Natalia uncrossed her arms and reached her hands out toward him. As they stood holding hands, Marc appeared not to want to let go. When she started to squirm uncomfortably, he let his hands drop to his side.

"It's just me, right? You can touch other people and not get shocked?" he asked.

"Yes."

"Me, too."

"You're enjoying this, aren't you?"

"Yeah, I am. I don't know if anyone has mentioned it to you, but you're a little bit of a hot-head. At least you're calmer today."

"Maybe one or two people." She gave him a smirk. "I'm too tired to fight today."

"I guess we better get everything done today, then."

"Great."

"Do you still feel like you know me from somewhere?"

"Yes. Unfortunately."

"Does—"

"Look, I can save you a lot of time. Let's get it all out in the open. Yes, I feel drawn to you, and I don't know why. You already know I like your birthmark and tattoo. I have an overwhelming desire to look at them whenever I see you. I know I can't, though, because I'm afraid I'm going to want to kiss it again. I don't know why, and it bothers me. Yes, I think we have some weird connection I can't even begin to explain."

"Wow, I guess the key is to get you while you're sleep deprived. You told me things I wasn't even going to ask. You really want to see my birthmark?"

"Yes."

"Even right now?"

"Did you not understand what I just said?" she snapped.

"You really are cranky. I thought you were too tired to fight."

"Sorry." She sighed. "Yes, even right now." She walked over to the picture window. Marc stood beside her, and they watched the busy city below without saying anything.

♨♨

As much as Marc wanted to have this conversation, now that they were having it, he found it disconcerting. How was this woman able to stir all these strange emotions in him? Natalia was honest. She'd told him everything he asked—and more. Should he be as open about what was going on in his head? If he said the words aloud, it would acknowledge he had feelings for her, and that brought up guilt and fear.

He stared straight out the window and didn't look at her when he spoke. "The first night we met and were in my office, I didn't want you to leave. I didn't understand it then, and I still don't. I called you to come to lunch because I wanted to see you again."

"I know. I felt it, too. I would've been content to stay and talk with you all night." She glanced in his direction. "Did Mariella tell you I was coming today?"

"If I say 'yes,' will you be mad? It wasn't her fault. I wouldn't leave her alone and kept asking if she heard from you."

"No, I'm not mad. It's all so complicated."

"I'm not used to anyone liking my birthmark. Most people recommend a plastic surgeon while telling me how sorry they are I have to live with something like that."

"People really say that to you? I'm sorry. I hope you never take their advice. It really is a part of who you are."

"You're the only person who's told me that. I know it's ugly, but I want to keep it. And you appreciate that."

"It's not ugly," Natalia whispered. "It's quite beautiful."

Every time she told him it was beautiful, he wanted to wrap his arms around her and thank her. He knew he couldn't do that and tried to push the thought from his mind.

"Mariella will be back soon," she said. "I should go upstairs and get ready for my treatment. You need to go home or to work, whichever it may be."

"Work," he said. "I have to go to work soon. Are they hooking you up to the polysomnogram tonight?"

"Yes, I think so."

"I'll come back tomorrow and see how you did."

"No. Please don't. Whatever this thing is between us, we have to let it go. You have a wife and a good life here in the city. I'm happy at the vineyard. We both need to move on. I'm sure we'll see each other occasionally. I have to keep an eye on Mariella and my wine." She smiled at him. "Let's leave it at that. Agreed?"

"I'll agree only if you promise to come to the restaurant whenever you're in the city. Risotto Smeralda is on the house whenever you do."

"My mouth is watering already." She laughed. "Sure, I would like that."

"Good. If I have time tomorrow, I'll try to call you and see how the test went."

Marc had plenty of time. Tomorrow was his day off. He also had no intention of keeping up his end of the deal. Things were set in motion, and there was nothing either one could do about it.

CHAPTER 6

"The worst thing in the world is to try to sleep and not to." – *F. Scott Fitzgerald, 1896-1940, American author*

Natalia Santagario?"

"Yes."

"Good evening, I'm Dr. Alex Mikowski. Don't you look comfortable?" he asked, chuckling.

It was ten o'clock at night. Natalia was snuggled in a luxuriously soft bed with wonderfully fluffy pillows. "Hi. It's nice to meet you."

A jolly man of smaller stature with a white beard and glasses, Dr. Mikowski reminded her of svelte Santa Claus.

"Did Mariella go over this procedure with you?"

"Yes, she did a little. She said you would explain everything as we went along."

"Of course and please ask any questions. This test is a routine polysomnography. I'm going to put these electrodes on your chin, scalp, and the outside of your eyelids. They have to stay there the whole night. Are you okay with that?"

"Yes."

"You haven't had any medication, alcohol, or caffeine this evening, correct?"

"Yes."

"Good. We're going to observe your heart rate and breathing while you sleep. Even if you don't sleep well, these must stay on all night. There's a camera in the corner of the ceiling. While you're sleeping, we'll be recording you. Are you comfortable with that?"

She doubted anyone was comfortable with that. Who wants to be filmed while sleeping? It's such a vulnerable state to be in. She thought it was nice he asked but didn't think it mattered what she said. They were going to do it anyway. So she said what she was sure everyone in this position before her had. "Yes, that's fine."

"We're going to monitor your REM sleep or rapid eye movement. In REM sleep, the voluntary muscle system in your body turns off. It's almost a type of paralysis. The only voluntary muscles that move are your eyes. This is when you dream." Dr. Mikowski attached the electrodes to her face. "We'll also check your NREM sleep or your Non-Rapid Eye Movement sleep. Generally people go back and forth from REM to NREM sleep every ninety minutes or so. Typically there should be four to five cycles of sleep each night."

He asked if she had any questions. "Try not to think about us watching you. Just relax and go to sleep."

"Okay. I'll try."

She laid there in the dark, trying not to feel self-conscious. Taking a deep breath, she began to unwind. The bed was extremely comfortable, and she hoped to get some much needed sleep. Thinking about her day, her mind drifted to Marc. Even though she knew it was best not to see him, she was glad they talked. She went over their conversation in her head and was soon asleep.

At some point, like every night, her eyes popped open. She didn't know what to do. She assumed they knew she was awake. *They* were the professionals. The last thing she wanted to do was roll over and face the camera. So she laid there and tried to will herself to sleep. But sleep wouldn't come. There wasn't a clock in her room, but she knew she had been awake for hours.

There was a knock on her door.

"Come in," she said.

Dr. Mikowski burst into her room. He seemed in good spirits. "Good morning, Natalia."

"Hi, Doctor. Aren't you the cheerful one in the morning? What time is it?"

"It's seven a.m. You didn't get much sleep last night, huh?"

"It was the same as every other night."

"How do you feel?"

"I'm tired."

"I'm sorry about that, and we're going to do everything we can to get you back to a normal sleep pattern. Let me take those electrodes off, and you can get up. They'll be bringing you breakfast soon."

"Thank you."

He told her he would come see her as soon as he got the results from the test then left.

She got up and went into the bathroom. When she came out, Mariella was standing there. "Good Morning, Natalia. How did you sleep?"

"Not very well, I'm afraid."

"After breakfast we're going to start the maintenance wakefulness test."

"What's that?"

"It's a test that tells us how alert you are during the day and how well you are able to stay awake for long periods of time. There are usually four tests with two hours in between."

"It's all day?" Natalia didn't want to complain but staying awake while you were tired didn't appeal to her.

"Yes, dear. I'm sorry," Mariella said. "And it can be tedious at times. I'll be around most of the day. I'll try to see you when I can."

"Then, what?"

"Then we wait for the results. This test may take a little longer to get back, so we can look into some other options.

"Like what?"

"Have you ever been to a chiropractor?"

"Yes. About five years ago, I hurt my back, working in the vineyard."

"Good, I'll make you a couple of appointments over the next few days. Then how would you feel about a nice massage with aromatherapy?"

Natalia couldn't remember the last time she pampered herself. "Mmmm. I may never leave"

"While you're with the chiropractor, she may talk to you about acupuncture. If you'd like to try it, she would be the one who would do it. I can tell you from my own experience that it works."

"I don't mind looking into it."

"That's it, dear. We want you to relax. Here comes your breakfast. I'll come get you when it's time for your next test.

♨♨

"Hi. Natalia?"

"Yes."

"I'm Matt Davenport, the technician who's going to administer your next test."

"Hi."

"First, how does the temperature in the room feel? Is it too hot or cold?"

"No, it's very comfortable.

"Good. Now I'm going to shut the blinds and put a dim light behind you. You'll be sitting in this recliner, and I have to place sensors on your face and chin. They are connected to our computer. Okay so far?"

"It sounds very exciting." She sat in the recliner and tried to relax.

"Yeah, I know." He smiled. "Then we wait and see if you can stay awake. It'll be quiet and calm. You can't fail the test. If you feel the need to sleep, then please do so. Don't make yourself stay awake. Do what your body needs to do. Ready?"

"Let the party begin."

Matt put the sensors on her and went into another room where he spoke to her through an intercom. "Okay, Natalia. I need you to look straight ahead and try to stay awake."

Natalia sat there, feeling ridiculous. Were they all looking at her? This had to be the most absurd thing she had ever done. She was exhausted and thought she would fall asleep from pure boredom. Her mind kept wandering to Marc. In order to make herself stop thinking of him, she counted the diamonds on the wall. The next thing she knew, Matt was shaking her.

"Natalia, you can wake up now. You did well and stayed awake for almost fifteen minutes."

"How long did I sleep for?"

"We only let you sleep ninety seconds," he explained. "This way it won't affect the next test. You can get up now and occupy yourself for two hours, then come back here."

"Okay, thanks."

The next test she did about the same. The third test she fell asleep sooner, after about nine minutes. There was only one more test to go, and she was glad.

She decided to go outside and walk around. The building had what she assumed was a beautiful garden in the summer, but since it was February, there were only bare bushes and trees.

There was no place to sit. All the benches were covered for the winter. The fountains stood still, a little water frozen in the bottom of each one. The sun was trying to win its battle with the clouds, but it couldn't break through. It was cold and bleak. Natalia thought it might snow, but it felt good to be outside and get some fresh air.

It had been an extremely boring day. It was five o'clock and her last test wasn't until six. She thought about Marc. He hadn't come to see her, but she'd told him not to. He was only doing what she asked. Although, he did say he would call.

She looked at her cell, no messages. What would she do if he did call? It would be better not to talk to him. It was too damn confusing when he was around. She looked at her watch and realized she'd been outside longer than she thought. She went back inside and headed off for her last date with Matt.

"Natalia, that's it," he said after the test. "You're all done for today."

"I didn't fall asleep that time. Is that okay?"

"Yes. It's fine. Don't worry, there is no right or wrong."

"Thank you. Is Mariella around?"

"No. She went out, but she'll be back later."

"I guess I'm on my own then."

CHAPTER 7

"Anyone can be passionate, but it takes real lovers to be silly." – *Rose Franken, 1895-1988 Playwright and Novelist*

As Natalia walked back to her room, her stomach growled. The first thing she needed to do was get something to eat. She opened the door to her room and was startled when she saw Tony, Giuseppe, and Marc sitting there. There was a delicious smelling pizza on the table as well as a deck of cards and poker chips.

She couldn't help but laugh. "What are you doing here?"

"Wednesday and Thursday are our days off," said Giuseppe. "Marcos told us how boring the tests are and said we should visit you."

"That was very thoughtful of you."

"You said that silly card game was more fun if we were drinking but we can't find any wine. Mariella is out, and her apartment is locked," said Tony. "Marc doesn't have a key."

Natalia gave the three men a sly smile. "I know I wasn't supposed to, but I brought some wine with me. Promise not to tell Mariella?"

"Ah." Tony grinned. "Marc knew you'd have wine. It seems he knows you too well."

Marc shrugged. When she went to get the bottle of wine out of her bag, he followed her. "How did the tests go?"

"Okay. I didn't sleep well but it's what I expected. You're right, today was very monotonous. This is just what I need, a little company. How did you know I had wine with me?"

"I don't know. I get the feeling you're not someone who always follows the rules."

"If it's your night off, shouldn't you be home?"

"Simone, that's my wife, is working late."

"Oh, well thanks for this. Let's eat, I'm starving."

After they ate, they played Natalia's one card poker game until Tony spoke up. "Do you know how to play real poker?"

"I've played once or twice. I guess I could try." She listened intently as Tony explained the game and wrote down what beat what on a piece of paper.

"Let's try five card stud," he said, dealing the cards.

"Oh! Is this the one where I can pick new cards if I want?" she asked innocently.

"You don't pick them. I give them to you. Don't forget to ante up."

"Sorry." She threw a blue chip into the middle of the table.

"No, Natalia," Tony snapped as if losing his patience with her. "Not a blue one. Everyone threw in a red one. Please pay attention."

"I didn't think it mattered."

"Yes, it matters. They're all worth different amounts."

"Okay, I have it now." She looked over her cards at the men. "Let's play."

She carefully watched the men's mannerisms as they were dealt their cards. Giuseppe sat up a little straighter with a good hand but slouched a bit with a bad one. Marc tended to lean back and relax when dealt good cards. Tony was the easiest to read. He had no poker face at all. Natalia lost the first few hands and folded a couple of times.

She looked at Tony. "I'll take three cards, please."

Giuseppe folded, Marc had two pairs, and Tony had three of kind. He went to reach for the pot, ignoring Natalia.

"Excuse me, I have a full house," she said, showing them her cards. "I'm sure it was beginner's luck."

Her beginner's luck continued until she had a pile of chips in front of her. The paper Tony had written for her was on the floor.

"So, who taught you the game?" Marc asked. "You seemed so innocent in the beginning, you played us well."

"My brother and his friends taught me at least twenty years ago."

"How do you know we weren't taking it easy on you because you didn't know the game?" asked Tony.

"What do you have in mind?" asked Natalia.

"Strip poker."

She laughed. "How old are you? I don't want to get arrested for having a buck-naked, under-age kid in my room."

"Very funny. I'm twenty three."

"You're on."

"Here are the rules. Jewelry doesn't count."

"I don't have any jewelry on."

"Neither do belts or shoes. Socks do—if you want them to. So everyone can leave their socks on. Or use them to stall."

"I don't think this is the proper thing to be doing," said Giuseppe.

"Oh, have another glass of wine and relax," said Natalia. "We'll go easy on you."

Marc asked her to come to the side of the room. "What are you doing?"

"Are you going to get all proper on me, too?"

"No. Who doesn't love strip poker? But we both know what's underneath my shirt."

"I know, and I would love to see it, but I can't."

"Then why are doing this?"

"I'm expecting you not to lose."

A half-hour later Tony had lost his shirt, as well as his socks. Everyone else had managed to stop at no more than being barefoot. The next hand found Natalia and Giuseppe betting. When she put down a straight and saw his face drop, she assumed he didn't want to take his shirt off. "I'm sorry, Natalia," he said laying down a full house. "No one expects you to take off your sweater." His face turned slightly red as he spoke.

"Yes, we do," said Tony.

"You need a girlfriend," she said, raising an eyebrow to him. "It's fine Giuseppe. I play fair and square."

"Natalia, you don't have to prove anything," Marc chided. She crossed her arms grabbing each side of her sweater and started to pull. "Natalia, stop it!"

She yanked her sweater off and sat there with a burgundy Santagario Vineyard t-shirt on. "Gentlemen, it is winter. Didn't you mother teach you to layer your clothing?"

"Is there another shirt under that one?" Tony quipped.

Natalia turned to him. "You *really* need to get laid."

"That's enough, you two." Marc's grimace suggested he was biting his cheeks, trying not to laugh. "Natalia, considering you're a forty year old woman, why do I have to be the mature one here? Come on, I have time for one more hand, then I have to go."

Giuseppe dealt the cards, announcing deuces were wild. Again, it was between Natalia and him. This time he put down a straight.

"Giuseppe, you shouldn't have made deuces wild." She placed her cards on the table and showed three fives and one deuce. "You're a dear sweet man, and no one is going to make you do something you're not comfortable with."

"No, I shouldn't have agreed to play if I wasn't going to play by the rules." He started to unbutton his shirt.

"What's going on here?"

They all twisted their heads to the door and saw Mariella standing there. Giuseppe groaned a sigh of relief, and Natalia started giggling.

"I'm sorry Mariella, but I don't think Giuseppe has ever been happier to see you."

"Is that wine? Where did you get that from?"

"I brought it," the three men all said in somewhat unison.

"Where did you get wine with a Santagario label on it? We haven't signed the paper work."

Natalia was touched they were willing to take the blame for her. "Thanks guys, but it's mine, Mariella."

"I thought I told you alcohol makes sleeping worse."

"I haven't had a glass of wine in over two weeks, and I still can't sleep."

"The party's over. You three get out now!"

The three men did what they were told and got up to leave.

"Thank you for visiting me. I feel much better." Natalia hugged Tony. "No hard feelings?"

"Nah, it was fun."

"*Buena sera*, Natalia," said Giuseppe, kissing her on the cheek. "Good luck with Mariella."

"I can handle her." Out of the corner of her eye, she saw Marc walk toward her. "You better get going." She made sure she didn't touch him.

"I have a few minutes. Do you want me to explain to Mariella? She's tough. I grew up with her." He stepped closer and Natalia backed up.

"No. I have the advantage. I won't sign the contract if she gives me a hard time."

"I heard that," said Mariella.

"Mariella, I'm kidding." Natalia faced Marc but lowered her head, not wanting to look at him. "Good night, Marc. Thanks, again."

"Natalia, come with me." Mariella said as she walked out the door.

"Mariella, it's late and I'm tired."

"You yourself said you won't be getting any sleep."

Natalia followed her into the elevator. As the doors shut, she saw Marc standing there watching her leave.

"Natalia, I'm disappointed with you. You knew the rules."

"They surprised me, and we needed something to drink with our pizza. I wouldn't have opened it if I was alone."

"Whose idea was this little party?"

"I have no idea."

"Only Marcos knew you were here. He's not going to be able to keep away. Neither are you, dear, just so you know."

"We reached an agreement yesterday. We're going our separate ways." She neglected to mention that within twenty-four hours, Marc had broken their agreement, and she was glad.

"We'll see who's right and who's wrong. Here's your paperwork from Sam."

Natalia looked everything over, happy to change the subject. "Sam says everything's in order. Where do I sign?"

"Right here, dear."

Natalia signed the papers and handed the pen to Mariella.

"Here's to a long and prosperous business relationship?" Mariella said. "Should I open champagne?

"I thought alcohol made sleeping worse," Natalia teased. "No, thanks, I'm tired. Thank you again for giving the vineyard some extra exposure. I'm going back to try and get some sleep."

Mariella handed her a paper with her appointments for tomorrow. She had the chiropractor at ten and maybe acupuncture at eleven. Then she had time to exercise and sit in the steam room, then a massage after lunch.

"Well, that's a full day. I won't be bored tomorrow."

♨♨

Natalia's morning went well and after lunch, she went back to her room for a quick shower before her massage. She was surprised to see Marc sitting there watching TV.

"I could've sworn I locked the door."

"I know the owner."

"Why are you here?

"I'm off today, too. I'm bored."

"What do you usually do on Thursdays?"

"Follow women around. Today is your lucky day."

"I won't be too much fun to follow around today. Maybe you should bother someone else."

"No. I'm good."

"I have a massage at three."

"I'll be here when you get back."

"What for? It'll be after four when I get back. You'll need to be getting home."

"We're going to hang out for a while."

"No. We aren't."

"Look, it's almost three. You'd better get going. They don't like it when the clients are late. It messes up the schedule for the rest of the day. Go on." He sat there smugly. "Oh, and can you try and be in a better mood when you get back? Thanks."

She mumbled some obscenities and called him a not so nice name in Italian under her breath.

"Now, now, Natalia. That won't work with me. I understand everything you're saying. For the record, I'm not above calling you a few names as well, in English or Italian. I might even remember a little French from college—"

Infuriated, she slammed the door on him while he was talking. She tried to reap the benefits of her massage, but all she could think of was Marc and his damn birthmark. True to his word, he was there when she got back.

"Marc, please, I thought we had an agreement."

"We do, and that's why I'm here. I'm busy this weekend with work and some function with Simone. Then I work until Wednesday. I think you'll be gone by then."

"Yes, I'm going home tomorrow, after I get my results. I've decided to find a facility closer to home to help me."

"Oh," Marc said somberly. "So after tonight, we each go our own way."

"Yes."

"Then I think we should order Chinese food, rent a movie, and wish each other well."

She knew the worse thing she could do was agree to his proposal, but like every other time he was near, her will power had run off somewhere. "That's it? Dinner, movie, and we're done?"

"Cross my heart. I have to be home at ten."

"You sound like a teenage with a curfew."

"Yes or no?"

"Yes," she said and told him what she wanted to eat.

"Jesus, you eat a lot."

"Life is to be enjoyed. Food is a great thing."

Marc laughingly agreed with her. "What kind of movie? Please not a chick flick."

"Yuck. For me the scarier the better."

"A girl after my own heart."

"Surprise me—but I loved *The Grudge*."

♨♨

Natalia was through showering before he got back. She combed out her wet hair, put on a pair of sweats, a t-shirt, and applied a smidgen of make-up. She refused to get all dressed up and act like it was a date. The problem was where to eat. She was still in a small room, her suite not ready until tomorrow. There was a little table in her room but only one chair. She certainly wasn't going to sit on the bed with him and eat. The floor would do. She pushed the bed to one side to make room. She was getting paper cups out of the bathroom when Marc walked in.

"Excuse me. Have you heard of knocking?"

"Sorry, I'm too comfortable around you, I guess."

She quickly changed the subject. "What movie did you get?"

"*The Grudge* was gone. They did have *The Ring*."

"Oh, perfect. I love that one, too. Can you put it in? I'm bad at the DVD stuff."

She opened all the cartons of food and put them and some paper plates on the floor in front of the TV. Then she went to the closet and dug out the last bottle of wine, which she hid after last night. Marc opened the wine and poured them each a little while she fixed him a plate from the buffet spread out before them.

He put the movie in and sat down next to her. "You look nice tonight."

"These sweats are hand-me-downs, and this is my brother's old Navy t-shirt."

"It doesn't matter. I think you look good. It's nice to meet a woman confident enough not to cover herself up in a lot of make-up."

"Let's watch the movie," she said, inching away from him.

Since Marc had never seen *The Ring*, Natalia had fun trying to scare him. She was impressed. He didn't scare easily. Maybe he was a horror fan. When the movie was over, she started to clean up. "I'm sure Mariella won't appreciate the mess in here."

He poured them each a little more wine. "Wait. You forgot your fortune cookie." He handed her a cookie and her wine. She took it, being careful not to touch him.

"Do you know the old joke about adding 'in bed' to the sayings to make them risqué?" she asked.

"Of course, I'm related to Tony remember?"

"Who told Tony?"

"I may have mentioned it to him while I was in college." Marc grabbed a fortune cookie for himself.

"That's what I thought. What's your fortune say?"

He opened his cookie and read it aloud. "You use your creative talents to transform a business environment."

"In bed," they said together and laughed.

Natalia read hers, "You will meet hundreds of people."

"In bed," they announced together. "Sounds fun but exhausting." She giggled.

He picked up a different bag.

"You have more?"

"These are the *other* fortune cookies you can buy at any participating Chinese restaurant. I knew if anyone would enjoy a dirty fortune cookie it would be you."

"You do know me too well. I'm going to need more wine for this."

He poured wine in her little cup and held the bag open for her. "Ladies first."

She picked a cookie and started giggling before she even opened it. "Sex is like snowfall. You never know how many inches you'll get."

"In bed." They were almost crying from laughing so hard.

Marc opened his. "Sex drive begins with puberty and ends with marriage."

The minute she heard him utter the word, Natalia stood, picked up all the fortunes on the floor and threw them in the garbage. She was angry with herself. Marc shouldn't be here, and she shouldn't have allowed this evening to go on, much less, let her guard down and have fun with him.

"It's almost nine. You better get going." She fidgeted a bit, putting her hands in and out of her pockets. "I feel like I'm always thanking you. I do appreciate you visiting me since all my friends are over an hour away." She lowered her eyes to the floor.

He got up and went to her. "Natalia, I was happy to keep you company. I like spending time with you." He gently lifted her chin and ran his fingers down the side of her face. "I don't want to go. I want to stay with you, but I can't."

She felt a stream of shocks follow his fingers down her face like a teardrop. "I know," she said softly.

"I'm sorry."

"Don't be. It's just the way it is. I'm glad we had a chance to meet and have some fun."

She went to open the door. He put his arms around her. She didn't resist and hugged him back, feeling the shocks sporadically striking where their skin touched, holding on to each other longer than they should have until Natalia pulled away.

"I'll never understand the shocks," Marc said.

"Me either, but it is cool, don't you think?"

"Yes, it's very cool and I like it."

"You really need to go," she said, trying to be firm.

"Nat, I—"

"Please don't. I'm going home tomorrow.

"This is really good-bye then?" he asked solemnly.

"Yes, it is. Take care of yourself."

"You, too." He put his coat on and left.

CHAPTER 8

"Put your ear down close to your soul and listen hard." – *Anne Sexton 1928-1974 American poet and writer*

Natalia had told Marc she was going home, but she wasn't. She had weekend plans with Mariella. On Friday, they shopped and had dinner. It was a good day and the subject of Marc never came up.

That all changed on Saturday afternoon. After her appointments on Saturday morning, Natalia knocked on Mariella's door.

"Hello, dear, come in."

"Are you ready? The movie starts at two p.m."

"Yes. How have you been sleeping?"

"There hasn't been any change. I feel good though, very relaxed. I hoped the treatments would help, but they haven't."

"After the movie, will you come back so we can have a talk?"

"I'm not going to talk about Marc. We've gone our separate ways."

"I wanted to talk about your sleep issue, but I see he's the first thing on your mind."

"No, he's all *you* ever want to talk about."

Mariella only smiled. "Let's go. I don't want to be late."

After the movie, Natalia and Mariella were sitting in her living room. Natalia made some tea.

"You shouldn't have that tea this late. It won't help you sleep," Mariella said.

"I don't think it matters much and it tastes good."

"Marcos calls every day asking if I've heard from you."

"Mariella. Stop trying to connect my sleep problems with Marc. One has nothing to do with the other."

"Did he come to your room the other night with dinner and a movie?"

"Yes. Do you have some sort of tracking device on him? Doesn't he have any privacy?"

"He walked around the city then came here for a few minutes before going home."

"What does that have to do with my sleep problems?"

"Natalia, if you would be honest about your feelings, things might go a little better for you."

"I can't." Natalia regretted her decision to come back to Mariella's apartment.

"Well, I can, so you'll have to listen to me. I've been a big believer in reincarnation for over thirty years. I think it explains many things in our lives—our fears and phobias, our likes and dislikes. Do you know anything about it?"

"Yes. I've read about it. I don't know that I believe it, but I'm open-minded about most things."

"Good. I also think most of the people in our lives are souls we have known before. We know some better than others, and some we have a very strong connection to. I think you know where I'm going with this."

"Yes, I do. Have you had this talk with Marc, or am I the only one lucky enough to hear your ideas?"

"Only you, dear. Even you said you were open-minded to most things. Marcos is not. He's very touchy about his birthmark, and that's a big part of this. I believe birthmarks are reminders of things that happened to us in previous lives. Through the years, I've often wondered what Marcos had to go through to get those scars, but I could never tell him that. Then out of nowhere, you show up and seem to understand his birthmark."

"I don't understand it. I have no idea what those marks mean."

"But you could find out." Mariella looked Natalia straight in the eye. "You could go back into—"

"Oh, no, Mariella. I came here to get some sleep, not be an experiment."

"You wouldn't be an experiment. The two doctors on my staff have been doing past-life regressions for years. It's a new practice *here*, that's all."

Natalia looked out at the statue of Columbus. It was getting dark. The city was aglow with lights and so alive. Yet, she felt stuck in some sort of limbo she didn't understand.

"Natalia, why did you come to me for help? I could have referred you to plenty of places in Hartford or Stamford."

"I like you and I like it here. It's easier to get help from people you know and trust."

"You knew Marc would be here. You could have declined on the wine and therapy, but you didn't."

"No."

"You could have told Marc and his cohorts to leave your room Wednesday night and told him it wasn't appropriate for him to be there on Thursday night. But you didn't."

"No," Natalia said, feeling ashamed.

"Well, dear, it's just going to get worse. You're both drawn to each other. Ignoring it won't make it go away."

Natalia continued to look out the window with her back to Mariella.

"Will you please take these few books on the subject of regression back to your room? Look through them and think about what I said. That's all I'm asking you to do." Mariella said.

This being a rare occasion when she was at a loss for words, Natalia took the books and started to leave.

"I know it's a lot to think about, Natalia, but I know you'll make the right decision. You need answers as much as he does."

♨♨

Sunday morning Natalia's eyes popped open at six a.m. She had stayed up reading until two-thirty in the morning, only getting a few hours of sleep. She wasn't sure how much longer she could go with such little sleep.

The past life regression subject made her uneasy. But after reading the books, she had a better understanding of it. Still, she needed time to think—away from everything Tremonti. She dressed and headed outside for a brisk walk.

She found the streets of New York empty, quiet, and cold. All the wonderful sounds and smells were hidden away somewhere. New York City may never sleep, but it does rest on Sunday mornings between six and eight o'clock.

After exploring the streets for forty-five minutes, she walked up to the statue of Columbus. Pigeons were taking off and landing on him. Natalia smiled. She was sure Columbus would be thrilled with the admiration the city gave him, but not about being a pigeon perch.

She looked up at him half expecting him to say something. However, he was the strong, silent type and didn't offer her any advice. No, she was on her own, the only one who could make the decision that had to be made.

♨♨

Sunday night Natalia knocked on Mariella's door to return the books.

"Natalia, have you eaten? I have a nice antipasto."

"No. That'd be great."

"Did you get a chance to look over the books?"

"Yes. We can talk about it while we eat."

Half way through their meal, the doorbell rang. Mariella answered the door, and Natalia could hear Marc's voice in the other room. "Mariella, do you have my tux? Simone thinks it's here."

"Yes, dear. It's in the closet in the second bedroom."

"Thanks."

Mariella glanced at Natalia. She shook her head. Marc didn't know she was there and Natalia wanted to keep it that way.

"Where are you going tonight?" Mariella asked Marc.

"I don't know. I haven't seen or heard from Simone for weeks, then out of the blue, she needs me to attend some function tonight. I hate this tux." Marc sighed. "Have you heard from Natalia?"

"I'm sure she's fine, dear. Why not have Simone pick you up here?"

"Yeah, let me call her."

Mariella went back to Natalia. "Please think about what we talked about. Every day he asks about you."

"Why can't he be regressed?"

"He's afraid. He doesn't want to go back and remember his parent's accident."

"I understand that, but this is different. This is past life regression."

"He doesn't believe it. He thinks you're born, you live, and you die. He assumes you can't go further back than childhood, and that's when the accident occurred."

"Why did he say Simone was away for weeks? He told me she was at a dinner the other night?"

"He hasn't said anything about Simone to you?"

"No."

"They haven't lived together since July. She's a little *confused* right now and wanted some time to figure things out. When she's not traveling, which isn't often, she stays in the apartment above the restaurant. Unfortunately, sometimes they go weeks without talking."

"Oh." Natalia was surprised at Mariella's words. "Where is he?"

"In the second bedroom."

♨♨

Natalia knocked on the door.

"Hold on, Mariella," Marc answered. "Is Simone here already?"

"No. Not yet," Natalia said, standing in the doorway.

He turned around. "I thought you went home."

"I lied. I can't keep seeing you. It's too hard."

She walked toward him and looked into his eyes. "Can I see it?"

"Why? No—I don't think so. Not tonight."

"It's important. Please."

He hesitated but eventually turned his back to her. While he took off his shirt, Natalia stared at the floor. When she slowly looked up at his shoulder, she was again amazed at how his birthmark affected her. This was only the second time she had come face to face with it. She had seen it plenty of times in her mind. Lately it was all she thought about.

She walked up behind him and asked him to sit on the bed. As if something else was instructing her on what to do, she took off her sweater. She kept her bra on, for which she was grateful, as it seemed she had no control over her actions.

She sat behind him and traced his birthmark with the tip of her finger, feeling the expected shocks. Tenderly kissing his shoulder, she felt a surge of jolts hit her as her stomach brushed against his lower back. Slowly and deliberately, she continued to press herself against him. She thought she heard him say her name, but all she could do was her put arms around him and lean her head on his back. She welcomed the small parade of shocks flowing between them. It was warm and soothing and just what she needed.

♨♨

Marc had been taken by surprise when he heard her voice and turned to face her. He was happy to see her, but when she asked to see his birthmark, he didn't think it was a good idea for either one of them. He also knew he couldn't refuse her. Taking off his shirt, he was aware of her behind him. He sat on the bed, expecting the shock as she touched and kissed his shoulder. But when she embraced him and her body met his, it was a sensation he could have never imagined. He heard himself utter her name.

Instead of answering him, she rested her head on his back. Like a gentle massage, shocks ran up and down his spine. He held her arms around him tightly and put his head down. It was the most peaceful and serene feeling he'd ever had.

It wasn't sexual. Although if someone saw them and didn't understand what was happening, they would certainly think it was. In reality it was much deeper, and something he was sure neither one of them had ever experienced. It was the coming together of something. Something that had been separated for a time, but found its way back together. Within a minute or two, their breathing was in sync, and she seemed as content to sit there as he was.

Mariella opened the door and saw them sitting there, turned away and left them alone. Natalia tried to get up.

"No," Marc said. "Not yet." He held on to her arms even harder.

"Marc, if I don't get up now, I might not ever."

"I said not yet."

She didn't say anything and let her head relax against his back. After a few more minutes she said, "Marc, I need to go, please."

He slowly and unwillingly let go of her. She stood behind him and pulled her sweater over her head before he turned around. "Thank you for letting me spend this time with you. I know it was intense, but it's helped me make a necessary decision."

He continued to sit there with his head down, not responding to her. She knelt down in front of him and asked him if he was all right. He gazed into her eyes and saw they were full of tears. He took her hand, kissed the inside of her palm, let the shock come, and put her hand down. "Yes," he said.

She got up and walked out the door. He let her go and said nothing.

♨♨

Marc walked out of the bedroom without his tux on.

"Are you all right, Marcos?" asked Mariella.

"No, I'm not. Did Natalia go back to her room?"

"Yes, dear. I have good news, though. She agreed to undergo hypnosis to get the answers you both need."

"She did?"

"I thought you'd be happy."

"She shouldn't have to do it alone."

"I have two doctors here tomorrow. Sometimes you have to find your own answers and not let others do all the work for you."

"Or maybe we shouldn't find out at all."

"Marcos! You don't mean that. You've been obsessing about her since you met."

"I have to get dressed. Simone will be here soon." He turned away from his aunt, went in the other room, and slammed the door. Sitting there with Natalia helped him make a decision as well. He needed to get his head on straight. Straight toward Simone, where it belonged, not in the opposite direction toward Natalia, the direction in which he'd been happily heading in the last few weeks. That ended tonight.

CHAPTER 9

"Relationships are like glass. Sometimes it's better to leave them broken then try to hurt yourself putting it back together." – *Author Unknown*

Marc came down the stairs the next morning and saw Simone's luggage at the door.

"We got home late last night. You didn't have to get up. I have a car coming to take me to the airport," she said. "Thank you again for coming with me. You were your charming self, like always." She smiled.

"You're welcome." As Marc took her hands in his, he was blatantly reminded that at Simone's touch he felt no shocks. For the hundredth time he had to force Natalia out of his head. "Would you consider not going on this trip? I was hoping you and I could go away for a few days instead."

"Marc, I have to go. I've worked hard on this account, and I'm the only one who can present it."

"How about you work on our marriage?" he snapped.

She walked away from him toward the door. "I thought maybe we could go more than one day without fighting."

"You'd have to be here more than one day at a time for that to happen."

"I'll wait outside. The car should be here any minute."

"Simone, wait. I'm sorry. I don't want to fight with you. It's just...I've had a lot on my mind lately, and I'm confused right now. I need you. I need my wife back. Please."

"Marc, I'm sorry, too. I know you're confused. So am I. I appreciate how patient you've been with me, letting me have my time alone these last few months. I don't know how many other men would've been as supportive."

"My patience is running low. I don't want to live like this anymore. Do you?"

"No," she said.

"I want you to be honest with me. Tell me how you feel."

"Marc, do we have to do this right now?"

"Yes, I want to know."

She sighed. "I have a restlessness inside me. I feel like there's a whole world out there to see and experience. My job is exciting. It allows me to travel and come in contact with so much. We got engaged straight out of college and then married. We didn't travel or do anything but work. I feel like I already did the conventional marriage thing for all those years. Now things are different, and I have several opportunities."

"And I'm holding you back from all that?"

"Not you." However, when she looked at him, Marc saw tears rolling down her face. "Maybe being married is, though. Both my marriage and my job are huge commitments. They're important to me, and I love them both. But I'm not sure I can do two important things at the same time and do them well."

Can't or won't? Marc thought but kept it to himself. "I can take time off from the restaurant and travel with you. I'd be willing to do that."

"I know you would." She took his face in her hands and kissed him softly. "You are the kindest, sweetest man I know. It would work for a while, but you'd soon be unhappy. You're a homebody. You want a more traditional life and marriage. Then we'd have the argument about kids again and end up right back here."

Marc knew she was right. He never enjoyed a vacation lasting longer than a week, always anxious to get home to his bed and home cooked meals. His favorite thing to do in the winter was curl up by the fire and watch football or a good movie.

She was also right about the subject of having children. She had been clear from the beginning she didn't want children. He was twenty-three when they'd had the conversation. At the time, kids were the last thing on his mind, so he agreed. As Simone became more adamant about not having kids, his longing to have them became stronger, especially these last few months.

"It seems we want different things at this point in our lives," he said.

"Yes, it does."

"Should we talk to someone? A counselor?" He'd asked her this many times and always got the same answer.

She hesitated a moment. "We could, but I don't know when I can arrange an appointment. My schedule is full the next few weeks."

"You have to make a decision then."

"I need more time."

"No. I'm sorry. This arrangement only works well for you. When you need a husband, you show up here and crawl into my bed or dress me up in a tuxedo, and we pretend we're a happy couple. Then you're gone again for weeks. As your escort last night, I didn't even get the benefit of you in my bed. I was an ornament on your arm. When I did everything you wanted me to do, I wasn't needed anymore."

"Marc, that's not true. I'm sorry. It was very late. I was tired and had to get up early."

"Don't apologize. I wasn't in the mood anyway." He saw her glare at him and knew he'd gone too far. "Nothing had to happen if you were tired. It would have been nice to have you next to me. We could have talked and maybe gotten a little of our connection back," he said softly.

"Marc, I do love you."

"Then please stay here and don't go on this trip."

"I have to go. Please don't do this to me right now. It's not fair. " They both heard the car horn beep. She put her coat on and grabbed her suitcase.

"Simone, please. You have to make a decision. Will you at least come home after your trip?"

"I—can't. I love you and want you to be happy." She kissed him again, this time on his cheek. "I'll call you when I get back from D.C." They heard another beep, longer and louder. "Good-bye, Marc."

Marc stood alone in the foyer looking at the back of the door. He turned and walked into the kitchen and stared at the phone. What the hell was he supposed to do now? She can't do what? Make a decision? Does she want him to make it for her? It was apparent she wasn't coming home after her trip. Who the hell knew when he'd see her again? It could be weeks. Did she expect him to be here whenever she needed him? What about when he needed her?

"Good bye, Simone." He picked up the phone and punched in the number of his lawyer.

CHAPTER 10

"I have fallen in love many times...always with you." – *Author Unknown*

Marc arrived at nine-thirty a.m. and found Mariella in her office.

"I'm sorry, Marcos," she said. "Natalia's already gone in with Dr. Ellis. I did talk to Dr. Collier and she has time this morning if you'd like to...find the answers you need."

Marc had made his decision on his ride to the Center.

"I'll do it on one condition. I don't want to go back to the accident. I won't go back any farther than when I'm five or six. I must have met Natalia as a child, and that's why she has such an impact on me."

"All you have to do is explain this to Dr. Collier," Mariella said.

"One other thing. No hocus pocus regarding past lives. You know how I feel about that. I mean it, Mariella."

"Yes, Marcos, I know."

There was a knock on the door and Dr. Marcia Collier stuck her head in. "Good Morning, everyone." She was a pleasant looking woman in her fifties and was Marc's favorite doctor here. He was glad that Mariella had arranged for him to see her. "Hello Marc."

"Hi, Doc."

"Are you ready?"

"No, not really."

"You'll be fine. Most people don't realize how relaxing this is. You'll be in control the whole time, don't worry."

"Okay. Let's go before I change my mind."

They walked into her office, and he sat down. She went over the procedure and asked him if he understood what would be happening. She also asked him permission to record his session.

"So what would you like to accomplish today? Mariella told me you're here because of your birthmark."

"Yes. I met a woman for the first time in December. Yet, I felt like I knew her right away. Out of nowhere, she drew my birthmark without ever seeing it. We must have met before. She's twelve years older than me, so it must have been when I was a child."

"If you've met her before and want access to that information, it should be fairly easy to retrieve. What's her name?"

"Natalia."

"Let's begin," Dr. Collier said gently. "I would like you to close your eyes and take a deep breath. When you exhale, try to release any stress or tension you feel. When you inhale draw in energy from a source that is comfortable to you. Focus on your breathing, finding a place within that is peaceful, and allow yourself to go into a deep relaxation. You will only go as deep as you're comfortable with." She sat patiently while Marc relaxed—as much as he could.

"Marc, I want you to go back to when you were a child. Tell me when you get there."

Marc assumed he would have to concentrate on going back to his childhood. Instead, he found it came easily to him. In his mind, his saw his life rewinding like a movie and was able to stop it where he wanted.

"I'm five years old."

"Do you remember seeing Natalia during this period?"

"No."

"That's okay. We'll go through the years and you tell me when you see her."

Marc allowed his younger years to move forward slowly, looking hard for Natalia. He went through his teens and into his early twenties. There was no sign of Natalia. He was becoming anxious.

"Marc, just keep breathing. There's no reason to get upset. We'll find her. Just rest and let your stress go." When Marc had calmed down, she told him she'd be right back.

♨♨

Dr. Collier went looking for Mariella. When she found her, she explained that Marc was becoming extremely agitated. "He didn't meet her before last December."

"Of course, he didn't," Mariella said. "Take him back farther. He won't go if he doesn't want to."

"I know," Dr. Collier concurred. "But I thought he was clear, it wasn't what he wanted."

"I know, but he needs the answers to his questions. I'll take full responsibility if he's angry."

Dr. Collier went back to Marc's room and quietly sat down next to him.

"Marc, are you still feeling relaxed?"

"Yes."

"Do you still want to find Natalia?"

"Yes."

"In order to do that, we have to go back further in your memory. Are your comfortable with that? You can only go there if you want to."

"Yes."

"Are you positive?"

"Yes."

"We're going to have to go deeper into relaxation." Within a few minutes, she had gotten Marc where he needed to be. "Marc, I want you to visualize a long hallway. Down this hallway, there are many doors. Each door represents a past life. Can you find the one that shows us the first time you met Natalia?"

"Yes."

"Can you tell me about the door?"

"It's very old."

"Ancient?"

"Older. Prehistoric."

"Would you like to open this door?"

"Yes."

♨♨

"Natalia, are you comfortable?"

Natalia was in a reclining chair in a dimly lit room with soft music playing in the background. She had met Dr. Elizabeth Ellis for the first time this morning and liked her immediately. "Yes, thank you."

"Have you ever been hypnotized?"

"No."

"Most people don't know this, but you'll actually be awake. Just in a very deep state of relaxation. You'll be in full control of what you say and do. I have no mind control over you. Do you have any questions?"

"No. I'm ready."

"Okay, Natalia," Dr. Ellis said soothingly. "As you go deeper into your relaxation, I want you to think of a safe place where you enjoy going. While there, you feel like you want to sit down and relax. You're comfortable there and realize this place has special energy. This energy will permit you to connect to infinite knowledge. Only you can allow yourself to go there and to do that you must be in a very deep state of meditation. I'm going to count backwards beginning with five. I want you to sink deeper after I speak each number. By the time I get to the number one, you should be at the deepest point at which you're comfortable. Five. Four. Three. Two. One."

Dr. Ellis gave Natalia a few minutes then asked, "How you are feeling?"

"Good. I'm very relaxed."

"Now, I want you to envision a long hallway. There are many doors down this hallway. Each door represents a past life you've had. We won't open every door, just the ones you want to, the ones that will be helpful to you at this time."

"Okay."

"I want you to find the door that will show us the first time you met Marc. Do you see it?"

"Yes."

"Can you describe it to me?"

"It's...old."

"Hundreds of years old?"

"Much, much older."

"How old?"

"Prehistoric."

"When you open the door, what do you see?"

Natalia sat quietly for a few minutes before she spoke.

"My mate and I are wandering in the snow. I am with child. The rest of our tribe has died off from a sickness. We come across another tribe and watch them from the hills above. My mate will hunt for an offering, and maybe they'll let us stay with them. He finds me shelter underneath some rocks, covers me with animal skins and gently touches my face. I smile and nod. I know this is how it has to be. He's gone a long time. I don't know what I'll do if he doesn't come back. I'm happy and relieved when I see him with a large animal tied to a stick. I shouldn't have worried. He was the best hunter in our tribe. We look at each other and start down the slippery embankment.

"Some one sees us walking down the hill and tells the elders of the tribe. They are waiting when we arrive at the bottom. They are cautious at first, but impressed with the kill. They could use another hunter, and this is much needed food. They realize I will need the help of the women of the tribe very soon.

"We are allowed to stay, but we don't know for how long. We build a dwelling from animal skins we've carried with us and from wood we find. We keep to ourselves, except when there are jobs to be done. Since the child will come soon, my job is to soak bark, strip it into thin pieces, and make rope for the hunters.

"My mate makes sure I have enough food. He was a highly respected member of our tribe, and wears strings of large animal bones and teeth around his neck as a sign of leadership. One younger male keeps touching it. My mate offers one to him in return for extra meat, which he gives to me. I have chosen well."

♨♨

MARC...

"I see the male and female walk down the hill towards us. I am curious about them but keep my distance. The elders will decide if they can stay or not. To show he is a skilled hunter, the male hands the elders a large animal he has killed. The female is with child. One of the elders tells me to take the male and help clean the animal. The female goes to the dwelling with the other females."

♨♨

NATALIA...

"My mate comes to tell me he is going hunting with the other males of the tribe. He touches my stomach and smiles. The next day, I'm not feeling well. I go to one of the older women and tell her I think the child is coming."

"Natalia," Dr. Ellis interrupted briefly. "Do you want to relive the whole birth?"

"No! It was so cold and long and hard."

"Continue after the baby is born."

♨♨

MARC...

"I take the new male and the other males out for a hunt. I know he's a good hunter, but I'm the leader of the hunt in this tribe. We walk for a long time. The sky is dark. We find shelter and try to get some rest before early morning when the animals start to stir. We wake up to animal noises in the woods and come upon a pack of wild boars. The new hunter knows he must contribute to this kill if he and his mate are to be fully accepted into the tribe.

"Everyone is quiet, waiting, and watching the beasts' movements. The new hunter charges one of the animals, spear in hand. We scream for him to stop, but he doesn't. The male boars have their tusks up and are ready to attack. We try to surround one or two of the animals when the new hunter hurls his spear at one of the large boars. It grazes the beast but doesn't wound it enough for us to catch him. There is much confusion and spears are thrown in every direction.

"When it's all over, the new hunter and another male are dead—gored and trampled. I have a spear in my left shoulder, and I'm bleeding. Someone pulls the spear out. I scream. They pack snow around my wound and cover it. They lay me on an animal skin and pull me back to the tribe. I am unconscious for most of the journey. The two dead hunters and one dead animal are brought back as well.

"When we get back, the elders come to see us. They are happy about the kill but not that two more are dead. I don't tell them it's the new hunter's fault. I don't want them to cast the female out with her child. The other hunters look at me but won't go against what I say.

"The women look at my wound and give me dried fruit that's been stored for the winter. They tell me the child has been born. I go into the dwelling and see her wrapped in animal skins, feeding her child in front of the fire. She looks at me and is terrified. I give her the string of bones and teeth her mate wore and look at her sadly.

"She starts to cry. A woman comes in to cut some of her and the child's hair to put with her dead mate. We wrap our dead. Far away from our dwelling, a fire is going. We put each body on top of the fire. They will now go the way of our ancestors."

♨♨

NATALIA...

"I stay in the dwelling with the older women. I look at the hunter's wound each day. I know a little about healing. The wounded hunter is kind to me, and I know it's because of him I'm allowed to stay. One day he shows me his dwelling and looks at me. I take the string of bones and teeth and put them around his neck. He smiles and tells me he will take good care of me and the child.

"Slowly, the weather changes, and the days of the sun are longer. I am with child again. As we lay on our animal skins, he turns on his side. I look at his wound. It has healed, but it's left a mark."

"Natalia, you had another child?" asked Dr. Ellis.

"Yes, two more. We had six winters together and were as happy as life would let you be at the time. With the longer days, we moved around and foraged for fruit, herbs, and plants. The males hunted. We would settle somewhere for the darker, shorter days. One winter a sickness went through the tribe."

♨♨

MARC...

"Many in the tribe were sick and dying. We needed food. I took two males and left to go hunting. When we returned the children were dead, and she was dying. The women came to take care of the children's bodies, but I told them I would do it. I was heartbroken as I wrapped each of them, a piece of our hair in their hands.

"She was lying there coughing, burning hot as any fire. I stayed with her. She smiled at me but cried for our children. Soon she closed her eyes and her breath stopped. Tears ran down my face as I got her body ready. I carried each body out and laid them atop of the fire. That night I started coughing and by the time of the sun, I was burning hot. Those left tried to help me, but I told them to leave. I went into my pouch and put the children's hair in my hands and her hair on my chest. I lay down. That's how they found me."

"Marc," Dr. Collier asked. "Are you okay?"

"No...I don't think so," he said, wiping his eyes.

"Marc, that life is over. It's two thousand-ten and you and Natalia are fine. Take a deep breath and relax."

After a few deep breaths, Marc's anxiety subsided. Dr. Collier asked him if he was feeling better.

"Yes."

"Do you want to continue?"

"Yes."

"Is there another door you would like to open? Do you know Natalia again?"

"Yes. We have many lives together before I get the second mark."

"Do you see the door to the life when the second mark appears?"

"Yes. It's made of stone and very old. We don't have much time together."

♨♨

MARC...

"We are in ancient Britain. It's approximately two thousand BCE. I'm making the long journey to what you now call Stonehenge. We gather there for the longest day of the year to remember our dead and those who came before us. Then we walk up the river to a similar structure made of wood. Here we have a fertility ceremony. It's a two-day celebration and feast. Each year, hundreds of people come from all over. It's an important ceremony for all of us.

"It's early in the morning and we gather to watch the sun come up through the two main stones. It's a beautiful sight and we're happy. The festival can begin. I'd seen her on our journey here, but she had to stay with her clan. As we walk up the river, I look for her again. We take the long walk together.

"When we get there, we have to separate. We all have jobs to do. I tell her I will find her later. The feast begins. The fires are burning, and the drums are beating a festive rhythm. This is a fertility ceremony so we have sacrificed animals and brought gifts to the gods. We hope in the spring, the Gods will share their fertility with the people, the crops, and the animals.

"I see her in the crowd, and we dance around together. We make our way away from the feast and into the woods. Under the stars, we lie together. I roll on my side, and she curls up behind me. She sees the mark on my back. I tell her it came with me from birth. The elders think the God's have given me special gifts. She tells me if it's from the Gods it must be good, and she kisses it. She has her arms around me and pulls me towards her again. I am the happiest I have ever been."

♨♨

NATALIA...

"After the morning sunrise, we start on the path up the river to the wooden structure. We have to be there and be ready for sunset. He finds me, and I am happy to make the journey with him. When we get there, we have things to tend to and must leave each other. We gather at dusk. The structure is in alignment with the sunset on the longest day. He comes up behind me. We watch the sun go down together.

"He is kind to me, and I'm happy to lie with him. He tells me the mark on his shoulder is from the Gods. I kiss it because the Gods think he's special, and so do I. The next morning he leaves to go hunting for the next feast."

♨♨

MARC...

"I have to hunt for the evening festival. When the celebration begins, we search until we find each other. We eat and dance. Soon she pulls me into the woods. I have lain with other women but this so different. I think the Gods have sent her just for me."

♨♨

NATALIA...

"He's lying on his back and I'm curled into his side. I'm almost asleep when he screams. He bolts up and there is a snake on the ground underneath him. It bit him. I pick up a rock and hit the snake until it's dead. He's struggling to get his breath. I look and see the bite on his shoulder near the mark of the Gods. I grab his water pouch and try to get him to drink, but he can't. I run and get the members of his clan. They come, and I show them the snake.

"They take my mate and lay him down near the main fire of the festival. He looks at me and reaches for my hand. I pull him up on my lap, his back to me. I put my arms around his waist. The elders are asking the Gods to help them. I'm crying and yelling at the Gods as well. The difference is they are begging, but I'm angry.

"His breathing is getting worse. He grabs my arms around his waist and holds them tightly."

Dr. Ellis saw Natalia trembling in her seat. "Natalia are you all right? Do you want to stop?"

"I'm scared for him."

"I understand, why don't you go to a time when all this has passed?"

♨♨

MARC...

"There's a lot of confusion. I don't feel good. It's hard to breathe. Everyone is yelling and screaming. I want it all to stop. She's behind me with her arms around me, and I'm glad she's there. I hold her arms close to me. The elders ask her to let go of me so the Gods can see my mark, but she refuses. She tells them if the Gods put the mark there, they would know it. She doesn't let go of me. Again, I'm glad. She kisses my mark, and I feel her tears. I'm really grasping for breath now. I don't want to leave her."

"Do you?" asked Dr. Collier softly.

"Yes," he said in between labored breathes.

"Marc, I want you to leave that life behind. You're back here in your present life, and you can breathe normally. Please take some deep breaths."

When he was calmer, Dr. Collier asked him a few questions.

"How many lives have you had?"

"I don't know, hundreds."

"All of them with Natalia?

"No, we can't always be together."

"How many lives have you had with Natalia?"

"We've been together for most of our past lives. I don't like to come back without her, but sometimes we have to."

"Are you still feeling all right?"

"Yes."

"Do you want to open another door?"
"Yes."

CHAPTER 11

"Men never do evil so completely and cheerfully as when they do it from religious convictions."
– *Blaise Pascal, 1623-1662 French Mathematician and Philosopher*

"Natalia, would you like to open another door?" asked Dr. Ellis.

"Yes."

"Is it related to Marc's birthmark?"

"Yes."

"You can begin whenever you're ready."

"We are in Lisbon, Portugal. It is fifteen-oh-six. My name is Aelah Couto. My husband Josue and I have recently arrived in the city. He's a cobbler. We have a baby girl, Renata. We are *Conversos,* which means we are Jews, forced to convert to Christianity by King Manuel. Most people refer to us by the derogatory term *Marranos,* meaning pig or swine. The first time I meet Sergio Araujo is when he comes to get his shoes repaired. I like him right away."

"Do you know Sergio in this life?" asked Dr. Ellis.

"Yes, it's Marc."

♨♨

MARC...

"I heard there was a new cobbler in town. I walked in and there was a pretty, young woman holding a baby. I told her my wife, Lettie, and I had a baby boy, Paolo, about the same age. I told her husband what I needed and left. When I returned to pick up my shoes, I mentioned that Lettie hadn't been feeling well, and I didn't like leaving her alone while I was out on the fishing boats. Josue immediately offered Aelah's help, and she happily agreed. I don't know why, but I was glad for the chance to see Aelah a little each day.

"Lettie liked Aelah. I would come home and find them laughing together. We didn't have a lot of money, so all I could offer was fish. Aelah always smiled and said, 'thank you.' I didn't want to think about how each day, when Aelah left, I tried to touch her hand."

♨♨

NATALIA...

"Lettie was sweet, and we became friends. Paolo was a good baby. I was happy to help her. I told her she would be better soon, not to worry. She had to get better because I had eaten enough fish for this lifetime. She laughed. And she did seem to get better, so I didn't come as often. One day when I arrived to check on her, she was burning with fever and could barely stay awake. I wiped her face with cold, wet cloths and waited for Sergio to return. He was grateful I stayed and asked if I could come the next day. He looked worried. I said I would be back. He took both of my hands, held them tight, and told me how much it meant to him that I was taking care of Lettie. It was a thought I shouldn't have had, but I liked how it felt when he held my hands."

♨♨

MARC...

"She never arrived the next day. Was it because I held her hands a little too long? It wasn't proper, but I don't regret I did it. Right now I had to take care of Lettie and Paolo. I hated to leave Lettie alone, but I had no choice. I needed help and went to Lettie's sister, Nisalda. I wasn't fond of Nisalda, but I picked up Paolo and ran to her cottage."

♨♨

NATALIA…

"Josue told me not to leave. It wasn't safe. Local Conversos had been arrested for preparing a traditional Passover meal. After their release, the townspeople were angry. Later in the day, two Dominican Monks walked through the streets, yelling that the *Marranos* were heretics and should be killed. It was April nineteenth, fifteen-oh-six. A riot broke out in the street. Rocks came through our windows, and people started shouting at us. Josue thought it best to split up and meet in the woods outside of the city.

"'Josue! What are you doing? Renata comes with me.'

"'No, she will slow you down. I can tie her tightly to my chest and still move quickly. I want you to go run as fast as you can and get away.' He kissed me, told me he loved me, and dashed out the back.

"'Josue, come back. I want Renata.' I put my cloak on and went after him. I saw two men run towards him and grab him. 'Please don't hurt him.' I tried to help him but I was crying and tripping on my cloak.

"'My baby. Please, my baby.' They dragged him out onto the street. 'Josue!'

"The two men stopped and looked at me. 'Get her, she's with him.'

"'No! No she is not. She's a patron of mine. That is all.'

"Josue's eyes told me not to contradict him.

"'Please, he's a good man. You've made a mistake.'

"'Everyone knows the new cobbler is a *Marranos*,' said one of the men, pulling him into the street. As they were knocked into by a mob of people on the prowl, Josue broke free and ran to me.

"'Aelah, go, run. Hurry.'

"'Not without you.'

"'No, they know who I am. It won't be safe for you to be with me.'

"'Josue, please come with us,' I sobbed. 'Give me Renata, please!'

"'Yes.' Josue and I were struggling to get our baby untied from his chest when someone shouted, 'There he is!' In a moment, Josue was no longer standing next to me. Four men pulled him away from me. I screamed but there were too many people in the street blocking my way.

"'Wait, he has a baby,' someone shouted.

"'One less Marranos to worry about,' a woman yelled.

"I saw the pyres burning but wasn't prepared for what happened next. They beat Josue over the head with large rocks. When he could no longer fight back and was limp in their arms, they threw him on the burning flames. A noise wouldn't come from my mouth. I had to get to them before they burned to death. I pushed through the crowd screaming, 'They have my family by mistake. My baby. Please help me!' Finally, a man took hold of me and brought me to the side. He said he was sorry about my family, and the only thing left to do was go to church and confess to Jesus. My sins must be great for God to take my baby, but being a loving and merciful God, He would forgive me.

"'God bless you, child,' he said and walked away. I spat at him and watched him grab another man and beat him. How could he think anything I had done in my twenty-years was worse than what he was doing now?

"I made my way back to where I thought they took Josue and Renata. The mob had moved on from that part of the street and it was eerily quiet. I tried to call out their names, but instead I found myself throwing up. The death and devastation on the street was horrifying, and the smell of burning flesh was unbearable. I knew they were dead. I heard more people approaching and, with a stabbing pain in my heart, ran down an alley into a small crevice between two buildings. I waited there for the mob to move past and claim their next victims.

"Natalia," Dr. Ellis said. "I want you to come back to your present life. This is too stressful for you."

"No." Tears were streaming down Natalia's face. She crossed her arms around her stomach and rocked back and forth in her chair. "I want to remember."

"Then leave the spot where you're hiding and go to a time when you feel safe."

♨♨

MARC...

"Lettie was dying. I knew it. With Nisalda there, I ran to the city to get a physician. King Manuel's men were on the outskirts of the city and not letting anyone in. I pleaded with them, explaining my wife was dying, and I needed help. They told me I would be killed if I went into the city. The mob was out of control, and that would leave my wife to die alone.

"'Please,' one soldier told me. 'Go home and be with your wife. Most of the physicians were *Conversos* and are probably all dead.'

"I had no idea what he was talking about. Why would anyone want to kill the doctors? The only thing I could do was go home. I sat with Lettie and held her hand. I rested Paolo on her chest. She smiled and told me she loved Paolo and me. She squeezed my hand one last time and was gone. I rested my head on her stomach and sat there until I heard Paolo crying. I knew he was getting hungry and didn't know what to do. I held him in my arms, looking out the window, trying to comfort him. In the distance, I could smell the smoke and see the glow of the fires.

"The sun hadn't risen yet when there was knock on the door. I opened the door. Aelah was standing there. She looked like she had been through hell. There was smoke and dirt on her face. She was crying, and it looked like she had gotten sick all over herself.

"'Aelah, what has happened?'"

♨♨

NATALIA...

"I told him everything that was occurring in the city. Sergio was pacing back and forth with Paolo, who was screaming. I couldn't imagine where Lettie was. I knew she wasn't feeling well, but she was always able to nurse Paolo. When he told me she had passed, I couldn't believe it. I didn't think I could cry any more than I already had.

"'Sergio, I'm so sorry. I never meant to burden you at this sad time in your life. I can sneak back into the city. I know where the mobs have been and I can bring back a priest for you.'

"'Absolutely not, Aelah. It's not safe. We've all had enough death for one day.'

"Paolo started crying harder, and my breasts, already full, began to seep milk. A sorrow I couldn't imagine filled my heart as I thought of Renata. I grabbed Paolo from Sergio, pulled my blouse down and put him to my breast. He latched on as if he hadn't eaten in days. Hearing all the noise, a woman appeared from the back of the house. She looked at me and asked who I was and what I was doing."

♨♨

MARC...

"I explained to Nisalda that Aelah's entire family had perished in a riot in the city.

"'Sadly, Aelah lost her baby this evening but she has found it in her heart to nurse Paolo for us. I was afraid he would die of hunger.'

"'I know who you are,' said Nisalda. 'You're a *Marranos*.'

"'Nisalda! Stop it, right now. Lettie and Aelah were friends. Do not speak to her that way.'

"'I can take care of Paolo,' said Nisalda. 'He doesn't need milk from some Jew.'

"Pack your things right away. I will take you home as soon as the sun rises."

"'And have that *Marranos* stay here with you? It's not proper. It will become a source of gossip throughout the city.'

"'The city is all but destroyed and many people are dead. I doubt who is staying here with me is of any concern to those who have survived.'

"I looked over at Paolo and he was asleep, full and happy."

♨♨

NATALIA...

"Sergio was coming toward me when he screamed. Nisalda, in her anger, had thrown hot coals from the fire at Sergio's back. Paolo shrieked, and I thought he'd been hit. I stood and yelled at Nisalda. 'What are you doing? Have you gone mad?'

"'I won't have you staying here.'

"I saw Sergio turn toward her in a rage and put his hands around her throat. He demanded she leave right now and didn't care how she got home. I thought he was going to kill her, and I shouted at him that Lettie wouldn't want this. He let go of her. She gathered her things and left.

"When she was gone, I carefully removed Sergio's shirt to see how badly he was hurt. The coals had landed on his left shoulder and his skin was red and inflamed. Inside his burn were three other strange marks.

"I couldn't help myself and I gently touched each of them. I applied honey to the burn and covered it with a cloth. He thanked me for everything and asked if I would stay with Paolo while he tried to get a priest for Lettie."

♨♨

MARC...

"No one was allowed in the city. I spoke with one of King Manuel's officials and explained I needed a priest. He took me to a small church outside of the city and introduced me to Father Cabrel. The priest was very obliging. He and his carriage driver followed me back to my cottage. I showed him to the room where Lettie was. I spoke quietly to Aelah, advising her that due to the trouble in the city, she should come in the back room and pray with us. She nodded. I worried how Aelah would do with Roman Catholic prayers, but she recited them perfectly. When we were done, I helped Father Cabrel's driver lift Lettie's body into the church carriage. It was the hardest thing I ever had to do. Aelah asked me if I was all right. When I saw how happy Paolo was, I told her yes.

When we went back inside the cottage, I offered Father Cabrel a small glass of wine, and we talked about the riots.

"'There are problems in the city with the *Conversos*. Anyone helping the Jews is being attacked by the mob, as well. You aren't hiding any Jews are you? If you are and they find out, they'll come after you, too.'

"'No, this is my sister and her baby. Her husband is off at sea for a few months, and she has been here to help Lettie.'

"The priest looked suspicious and asked Aelah, "This is your child?"

"I have him at my breast, do I not?"

"Yes. May I see him, please?"

The priest took Paolo and undid his blankets. When he saw that Paolo wasn't circumcised he seemed pleased.

"'I'm sorry,' Father Cabrel explained. 'Many of the *Conversos* are still practicing their Jewish rituals in hiding. I had to be sure.'

"He handed Paolo back to Aelah, made the sign of the cross on his head, and blessed him."

♨♨

NATALIA...

"After Father Cabrel left we looked at each other, exhausted. Sergio told me to lie in the back room, but he woke me a few hours later because Paolo was crying. We slept most of the day. When we awoke, I made something for us to eat. I asked to see his burn.

"We sat by the fire so I could get a better look. His skin was still red and sore. I applied new honey and told him I thought it was healing well, but it may leave another mark on his shoulder. Paolo was playing on Sergio's lap when he started to cry."

♨♨

MARC...

"She was sitting by the fire, nursing Paolo. I was so happy he was alive that I kissed his small face. Then I kissed the exposed curve of Aelah's breast and the top of her head.

"'I don't know how to thank you for this.'

"'I'm the one who is grateful to you. If you hadn't let me stay here, I'd surely be dead. I love Paolo and am happy to help him.'

"She stood and said she would keep Paolo with her. Tomorrow was Lettie's funeral and she wanted me to get a good night's rest.

"The next day, I took Paolo with me, and when we arrived at the church no one was there but Nisalda. I was glad. I wasn't up to speaking with anyone. After the Mass, Nisalda came over to me and asked whether the *Marranos* was still at the cottage with me.

"'Stop calling her that horrible word. Her name is Aelah. You're fortunate I allowed you to attend Lettie's funeral after what you did to me. I no longer consider you part of our family and hope to never have to see you again.'

"I walked away and never looked back."

♨♨

NATALIA...

"When he kissed me last night, I couldn't breathe. I didn't understand what was wrong with me. Josue had been dead for barely a day. I tried to put that behind me and again busied myself fixing food. I knew Lettie's funeral would be hard for him. When he returned, he told me about Nisalda.

"'Lettie told me she thought Nisalda was in love with you.'

"'Yes, Lettie told me that as well. Nisalda has never been kind to me. Is that how you love someone?'

"'Love is strange. When the riots began, Josue wanted us to separate. He took Renata. Why would he do that? Take the baby, run, and leave me behind? Renata belonged with me. Although when the two men came after me, he did protect me. Then when he got away, he told me to run and leave him behind. He said he loved me but sometimes I don't know what to believe.'

"'I'm sure he was frightened and wanted you to be safe at any cost.' He touched the side of my face. 'How could anyone not love you?'

"My heart was pounding, and I didn't know what to say. I told him I should tend to his burn. When I saw how sore it looked, I felt terrible and for some reason I gently kissed his shoulder.

"'I'm sorry to have caused such trouble. You wouldn't be hurt if Nisalda wasn't angry with me. I think I should leave. You can find a wet nurse for Paolo. Nisalda is right. If I stay, it will cause you nothing but grief.'

"I rested my head against his back. It wasn't respectable but I couldn't help myself. He turned to face me and asked me not leave. He and Paolo both needed me. Then he kissed me."

♨♨

MARC...

"I couldn't let her leave. I had just buried my wife, but I had felt drawn to her from the first day I saw her. Some may say the devil had my soul and maybe he did, but I didn't care. I kissed her and she didn't pull away.

"'Aelah, I'm sorry about the kiss, but I won't apologize for my feelings for you. I know you just lost Josue and Renata and I, Lettie, but I've had a strong desire for you since we first met."

♨♨

NATALIA...

"Tears were rolling down my face when I thought of everyone who had passed, especially my Renata. We both had suffered such sadness and tragedy over the past couple of days, we needed a distraction from all the heartache that had come our way.

"'I'm sorry they're gone as well, but not that you kissed me or my feelings for you.'

"He wiped my tears away and for a night made me forget all the horror I had seen the last two days. In the morning, he rolled on his side and I put my arms around him. I kissed his shoulder and told him I would kiss it each day to show him how sorry I was to have caused him pain.

"'None of this is your fault. You have given me the chance to be happy again.'

"He made me promise I wouldn't leave the cottage. He was going to see what was happening in the city and if any fishing boats were going out to sea. He told me he loved me and I told him I would be there when he returned."

MARC...

"Having Aelah in my bed was wonderful. I loved Lettie, but the marriage bed seemed to embarrass her, although she never refused me. Lettie was tiny and somewhat fragile, where Aelah was voluptuous, passionate, and uninhibited. The way she used her mouth—"

"Marc! I'm glad your time with Aelah was pleasurable," said Dr. Collier.

"Yes, very," he said, cheerfully reminiscing.

"These are personal recollections and you should keep them to yourself as a lovely memory. Why don't tell me what happened next?"

NATALIA...

"Sergio left and Paolo was hungry. I didn't see or hear Nisalda come in, and she surprised me when I looked up.

"'What have we here? I'm surprised you even waited until my sister was dead before you found your way into his bed. I see you're a whore as well as a *Marranos*.'

"'That may be, Nisalda, but I would rather that then an old maid who has never been loved and never will. You should leave. He'll be back soon.'

"'No, he won't. I know where he went. You'll be the one leaving.'

"'I love him and he loves me.'

"'How can that be? He just buried his wife. Unless you have bewitched him with some old Jewish mysticism? I'm sure the Spanish Inquisitors will be very interested in hearing about this.'

"'You wouldn't.'

"'Of course, I would. When they are through with him, they'll come after you. They don't appreciate good Christian men getting involved with female *Marranos* and their magic. You wouldn't want to see your beloved Sergio hanging from the gallows after being tortured, would you? For a few hours of pleasure in his bed? But we can avoid that frightful situation if you do as I say.'

"She looked at me with such hatred in her eyes. I thought she was the most repulsive woman I had ever met. She ordered me to leave the city and never come back. She would tell Sergio she caught me stealing his money and that I was leaving and taking Paolo with me. If I didn't do what she asked, she would notify the Inquisitors immediately. I hoped in my heart he wouldn't believe her malicious lies, but I agreed to her terms.

"'Can I have some privacy to get dressed?'

"'A whore with modesty?'

"Nisalda laughed at me, took Paolo from my arms, and left me alone in the room. I dressed with a heavy heart but knew leaving was the best thing for Sergio. I didn't want to put him in any danger. As I was leaving, I tried to touch Paolo one last time but Nisalda pulled him away from me.

"'Be careful, Nisalda. What if your accusations are true, and I do have knowledge of magic? If I can make someone fall in love with me in one day, sending someone to their grave shouldn't be a hardship at all. I would watch my back if I were you.'

"I walked out the door and started the long trek back to the city."

♨♨

MARC...

"I had forgotten to tell Aelah to bolt the door and not answer to anyone, but it was too late. When I got back to the cottage, I heard Nisalda and Aelah arguing. When I saw Aelah leave, I let her get a little ahead and followed her into the city.

"I couldn't believe the devastation and destruction that had occurred in the last three days. There were fires burning and the dead were lying in the streets. I put my coat over my face to fend off the smell. I kept going until I found where Aelah used to live, assuming she would go back to see if anything was left of her home. She was sitting in a corner of a room holding a small blanket and crying. When she saw me, she ran and hugged me. I knew she was scared and told her I heard everything Nisalda said.

"I explained that she, Paolo, and I needed to leave Lisbon. It was the only way to be together and be safe. We journeyed back to my cottage and I asked her to wait in the woods for me. I went inside and pretended to be surprised to see Nisalda.

"'What are doing here? Where is Aelah?'

"She's gone. I discovered her stealing your money. I think she was going to take Paolo and leave. You were a fool to let her—"

"No, Nisalda. You are the fool. I told you to leave Paolo and me alone.

"I won't. He is my nephew and I won't have that whore raising him. I will call the Inquisitors and her fate will be in their hands.

My fury took over and I reached for her. She was frightened, her bravado from before all but gone. I held her against the wall. I had hoped it wouldn't come to this, but she gave me no choice. I thrust a pillow over her face and pressed hard. She struggled for a minute and then went limp. I let go. Nisalda fell to the floor. I picked up Paolo. He was asleep, and I was glad he didn't have to see his father do such a horrible thing. I ran outside and gave the baby to Aelah.

"Aelah could tell I was shaken and questioned me. I told her not to worry. I had taken care of everything. I asked her to please be careful and take Paolo back to her home in the city. I would meet her there.

"I went back inside and carried Nisalda a mile into the woods to a small pond. I found a spot on the embankment and stood her up. I slid her down into the water, purposely allowing her shoes to leave a trail to the water. She floated face down and became tangled in some rocks. I sat down on a tree stump and looked up to the heavens.

"'Lettie, I'm so sorry for all this. I did what I had to do for Paolo. I know you were fond of Aelah, and I hope you are pleased she is taking care of us now. I apologize for desiring her before you left me. I don't know why I had feelings for her. I was very fortunate to have you as my wife. Paolo and I are happy again. I hope that you can give us your blessing. Please forgive me.'

"With all the confusion in the city, I hoped it would be some time before someone came looking for Nisalda. I packed the things I thought necessary and the little money I had and went back to Aelah."

♨♨

NATALIA...

Sergio came back with all his belongings and said we were sailing south to Sines and on to the Azores. When I asked him about Nisalda, he put his head down and started to cry. He wasn't proud of what he had done, but he did it to protect Paolo and me. For that reason, he would live with it. I wrapped him in my arms and told him Lettie would forgive him.

"We went into a room that hadn't received too much damage. Sergio lit a fire and gathered blankets while I rummaged around for stale bread, old cheese, and a bottle of wine. While we ate and drank, Paolo decided he was hungry as well. He fell asleep at my breast and Sergio laid him down. I was returning my blouse to its proper place when Sergio took my hand and pulled me on top of him, kissing me. Once again, he took me to that blissful place I had never truly been before. He told me he loved me.

"I curled up against his back. I put my arms around him, kissed his shoulder, and told him I loved him, too.

"'Are you really going to kiss my shoulder every day?'

"'Yes.'

"'Good. I like it.'

"'I do, too.'

"'I thought when we arrived at the Azores, we could get married.'

"'I would like that.'

"'Would you be opposed to being married in the church?'

"'I have no loyalty to either religion. I was born in to one and forced into the other. Neither was my choice. I don't think the Hebrew or Christian God is fond of me, and I'm certainly not fond of either one of them. After what I've seen the last few days, neither one is worthy of any worship.'

"'I struggle sometimes, too. I don't understand why certain things happen but I always try to keep my faith. You haven't had it easy but please don't speak like this in front of anyone. You will be named a heretic and taken away from me. I couldn't bear that.'

"'I won't speak of it again. I want to make you happy, not some God who thrives on violence. If the church is important to you, that's what I'll do. I've lived as a Christian for the past ten years. I know what to do. I am sorry, but I can't promise my heart will be in it.'

"'Can you promise *me* your heart?'

"'Yes, of course.'

"'That's all I want.'

"With Paolo between us, the three of us nestled close together and fell asleep. When we arrived at Sines, we had enough money for passage to the Azores and a little left over. I held Paolo and looked out at the sea and to our new life."

CHAPTER 12

"Are we not like two volumes of one book?" – *Marceline Desbordes-Valmore, 1786 – 1859 French Poet*

Natalia," said Dr. Ellis. "How would you like to take a break? I'd rather not take you out of your deep state of relaxation, but I think it would be best if you let your sub-conscious rest a bit. I have to step out for a few minutes. When I return, we can continue if you'd like."

"I would like that."

Dr. Elizabeth Ellis quietly left Natalia alone and walked into the hallway. She purposely decided to pass by Dr. Collier's office on her way to see Mariella. Marc's session had started a little later than Natalia's, and she hoped she wouldn't have to wait too long to talk to Dr. Collier. Luckily, with a trip to the vending machine, by the time Elizabeth arrived at Marcia's door, she was coming out.

"Hi, Elizabeth."

"Marcia, I'm glad I caught you." I would like to talk to you and Mariella about Natalia's regression."

The two doctors knocked on Mariella's door. They found her listening to Marc and Natalia's session. The doctors had streamed the audio through the computer to Mariella, who burned it onto a disk.

"Mariella, I know there is patient confidentiality we have to be careful about, but can you at least tell me if Marc is remembering the same lives as Natalia?"

"Yes, Elizabeth. Their recollections are almost identical with each other's."

"Are Natalia's memories as intense as Marc's? He is reliving a lot of emotions, and I have to calm him and persuade him back on track."

"Natalia's been upset a few times during the session. Right, Marcia?" said Mariella.

"Yes. They are extremely attached to each other."

"I think each life they spent together has made their bond stronger," added Dr. Collier.

"It's truly fascinating how long they've been together. When do you think their first life occurred? Eight to ten thousand years ago?" asked Mariella.

"At least, maybe older than that," Marcia agreed. "They had fire and the beginnings of society, but no agriculture. They were still a nomadic people."

"Do I dare say this is my first *Twin Flame* case? I've read textbook cases but have never had the opportunity to see one first hand." Elizabeth looked at her watch. "I better get back and check on Natalia. Mariella, you're familiar with Marc's birthmark. How many more lives do you think are associated with it? Natalia can go back one more time, but no more. It's been emotional and stressful for her today."

"There's only three small round brown marks left that haven't been explained. I can't imagine there are three more lives, each leaving him with one small mark in the same place. Let's hope not anyway. I was hoping they would both get the answers they need today." Mariella walked with the doctors to the door. "Thank you both for working with them. I appreciate it. When you are finished, would you like to explain the *Twin Flame* theory to them or do you want me to?"

"I'd be happy to talk to Natalia about it. Their case is intriguing me," Elizabeth said.

"I'll talk to Marc as well," Marcia said. "I had a case where two people were very connected, but they weren't together nearly as long as Marc and Natalia. So I'm very interested as well."

"Thank you, again," said Mariella. "I may stick my head in and check on them. I'm curious to see their reaction when you tell them they are literally the other half of each other."

CHAPTER 13

"We don't waste people the way white society does. Every person has their gift." – *Joseph Medicine Crow, 1913 - Crow Tribal Historian*

"Natalia," said Dr. Ellis.

"Yes?"

"How many more lives are related to Marc's birthmark?"

"One more."

"Do you see that door and would you like to open it?"

"Yes. It was our last life together before this one."

"Have you been back without Marc before your present life?"

"No. We've been together our last few lives."

"Take your time and start whenever you're ready."

♨♨

NATALIA...

"It's eighteen fifty-five, and I'm living in Nebraska helping my husband's aunt and uncle on their farm. I'm not happy with my situation. I can't remember the last time I made a decision for myself. My father was a doctor. He loved medicine and science and taught me to love it as well. He told me it was important for me to read and think for myself. When he died, my mother couldn't handle her *untraditional* daughter and married me off to the first person she could find. That man was Nathan Morgan. I lost my father, his name, and pretty much who I was in one clean sweep. Now I'm Lilly Morgan.

"I go into Belle Terre one day to get supplies. A young boy is struggling to put the heavy bags of feed on my carriage. A man comes over and helps him. They seem to know each other and talk a bit. As the man turns to leave, he gives me a puzzled look but then smiles. I ask the boy who the man was.

"'That's Lucas Jolibious. He's a half-breed but everyone in town knows and likes him and his two brothers. Their father started the trading post outside of Belle Terre. He was French but married an Omaha woman.'

"I give him a nickel for his help.

"Now, I'm in Aunt Matilda's sitting room with a group of women, and they are teaching me to sew. This is the most monotonous thing I've ever done. I know I will die of boredom.

"The women are talking about how their organization helps the Indians on the Nemaha Half-Breed Reservation. I immediately think of Lucas and wonder if he lives on the Reservation.

"The women ask Matilida to go to the reservation with them the next day, but she declines. I offer to go in her place, but she quickly tells me it isn't a good idea, and that Nathan would agree. The women in the group try to persuade her, but I know arguing will do no good. However, I know how to be careful and quiet. If I am lucky and no one sees me leave, they will have an extra member tomorrow, after all."

♨♨

MARC...

"It's eighteen fifty-five, and my white name is Lucas Jolibious. Although, my Omaha tribal name is Hu'ton-ton. When I'm not trading or interpreting, I live on the Nemaha Half-Breed Reservation in Nebraska.

"I saw her one day in town, but the first time I meet her, she arrives with a group of women who call themselves The Society to Aid the Indians.

"There aren't many of us on the reservation that want their aid.

"The next time I see her, she jumps off the carriage and walks toward me with Mrs. Baxter, the woman in charge of the Society. Mrs. Baxter introduces her as Lilly Morgan.

"We shook hands, and I had the same strange reaction in my stomach I had when I saw her in town.

"She was pretty, but so were many other women, and they didn't make my stomach go upside down. Her hair was long and light brown, her eyes a deeper, darker brown. She had a nice smile."

♨♨

NATALIA...

"I saw him standing there. My heart was pounding. I had been hoping to see him, but I didn't think it likely. He was average height and looked more Indian than white. His hair was as black as a crow's feather, and his complexion was a mixture of both races. It was his eyes, though, that were piercing. They were a combination of brown and blue, a color I had never seen. When he looked at me, I felt as if was looking into my soul. He had an air of confidence about him and spoke English very well.

"'I'm Lucas. It's nice to meet you.'

"'Mrs. Baxter thought I could help with the children.' I said.

"'Let me show you around.'

"'Lucas, I don't know if it's proper for you to be taking a married lady around without a chaperone,' Mrs. Baxter chimed in.

"'Ma'am, how long have you known me? My father raised us to be gentlemen.' Lucas smiled. Mrs. Baxter blushed and agreed with him. So—he was charming as well.

"We walked around and instead of the usual awkwardness of two strangers making small talk, our conversation was easy and relaxed. I told him about my life in Boston, my father, and my arranged marriage. He explained his father was a French trapper and trader who met up with the Omaha people. He fell in love with their ways and with his mother—an Omaha woman—the first time he met her. He has two brothers and one sister. All of them were educated in St. Louis, sent there by their father.

"'When I'm not trading, I interpret for your government because of my knowledge of your language and customs.'

"'It seems you've had a much more exciting life than I've had.'

"'Not true," he said. "I've never been Back East to see any of the big cities.'

"'It's beautiful here. Back East is crowded and noisy. You're not missing much.'

"'That's what Belle Terre means in French, beautiful land.'

"'You speak French as well?'

"'A little. My father would speak to us in French when we were younger and my mother spoke to us in our native language.'

"'Where is your family now?' she asked.

"'My two brothers live here on the reservation. My sister married a white man and settled in Virginia. My parents live in Washington, DC. My father works for the Bureau of Indian Affairs.'

♨♨

MARC...

"I didn't understand why I was telling her the story of my life. I had just met her, but my words flowed freely from my mouth.

"'What do you know about the group of ladies you arrived with?' I asked.

"'Not too much. They told me they provide support and help, so your people can adjust to living in our society.'

"'What if we don't want to live in the white society? Most of us here like our Omaha ways and traditions and don't want to change. But they keep pushing your culture and religion on us.'

"'I'm sorry. I had no idea. No one should be forced to live a life they don't want to live. My life right now certainly wasn't my choice, so I understand how you feel.'

"I looked into her eyes and thought they were the kindest, truest eyes I had ever seen. At that moment, I knew she was different from anyone else I'd ever met. We continued to walk. My son, who was nine, and my daughter, who was seven, ran over to me. Before Lilly could ask, I pulled her aside and told her my wife died in childbirth. With trading and interpreting, I was gone from the reservation quite a bit and never wanted to marry again. She touched my arm gently and again told me she was sorry. Then she sat down on a tree stump so she was at the children's level.

"'Hi there. I'm Lilly. It's very nice to meet you.'

"'My name is Non-ke'-ne,' my son said.

"My name is Raw-zi," my daughter said.

"'You have beautiful names. You'll have to teach me how to say them properly.'

"'Don't you want to know our white names? Everyone like you always does.'

"'Which one do you like better?'

"'I like my Omaha name,' said Non-ke'-ne.

"'How about you, hon?' Lilly asked my daughter.

"'I like both of them.'

"'What's your other name?'

"'Anne.'

"'Well then, I'll surprise you. Next time I see you, you try to guess which name I'll call you that day. If you're right, I'll have a surprise for you.'

"'What about me? My other name is Andre.'

"Lilly laughed, 'Oh, how silly of me. Of course, I'll have a surprise for you, too.'

"I watched her talk with them. She was at ease, and I could tell the children liked her. A man calling her name pulled me from my thoughts."

♨♨

NATALIA...

"I was talking to Lucas's children when I heard him calling me. A shiver went down my spine as I looked over and saw Nathan. He was angry and told me to get on the cart. I argued that I came with the women; and I should go back with them.

Nathan didn't agree. I turned to say good-bye to the children but they were standing behind Lucas. I apologized and climbed up on the cart next to Nathan. Lucas followed me and offered his hand to Nathan.

"'I'm Lucas Jolibious. Nathan Morgan, right? Your uncle knows my father. Lilly was a big help today. I hope she'll be able to come back.'

"'I know what's best for her.' Nathan pulled the reins on the horse, and we headed for home.

"'Why are you always embarrassing me, Lilly?'

"'How is helping upstanding women in town embarrassing? I would think you'd be glad I was doing something worthwhile.'

"'Working on the farm and having babies is worthwhile. But you can't seem to do either, can you?'

"We had been married almost a year and I wasn't pregnant yet. He blamed me.

"A few days went by and it was Sunday, a day of rest. It was a beautiful summer day, and I went for a walk. I started thinking about Lucas and wondering how I could get back to the reservation. I had no idea where it was. I was lost in my thoughts when I heard a horse and cart coming up behind me. It slowed down and stopped next to me. There was an attractive woman sitting in the front. She was dressed in a black and red dress with sequins around the edge. She had a small, stylish hat with a feather on her head. There was a nice looking Negro man sitting next to her, and three women in the back.

"'Darlin,' what on earth are you doing out here all by yourself?' she asked me.

"'I was going for a walk, and I guess I went farther than I thought.'

"'I'm Amelia Labonte. This is Kaleb and that's Sadie, Clare, and Emma in the back.'

"'Ma'am.' Kaleb tipped his hat at me.

"'I'm Lilly Morgan. We have a farm that way somewhere. I'm not sure where I am.'

"'We're on our way to the reservation. Jump in the back and we'll bring you home after our business there.'

"'I know Lucas Jolibious,' I said proudly. The girls in the back giggled.

"'Do you?' Amelia smiled. "'That's who we're going to see. Get in.'

♨♨

MARC...

"Every time I saw her, she was jumping off a carriage that belonged to someone I would never expect her to be with. Today I had to laugh. I wondered if she realized who she was riding with. I didn't care. I was happy to see her.

"'Lucas, it seems we picked up a friend of yours.' Amelia said.

"'Lilly, I wasn't expecting to see you today. Does your family know where you are?'

"She smiled. 'No, but I'll worry about that later.'

"'Then come with me.'

"'Lucas, no, there's no need for her to come,' Amelia protested. 'We'll take her home afterwards.'

"'She can be trusted. She's coming.'

"I lifted her up on the back of my horse. She put her arms around my waist and rested her head on my back. A peculiar feeling came over me. I took off before Amelia could argue anymore. I asked Lilly how she came to meet up with Amelia. Then I told her who she was.

"'Amelia is a very well-known madam and owns a large brothel outside of Nebraska City.'

"'The girls in the cart work for her?'

"'Yes, but what I have to talk to you about is what's going to happen next.'

"'I think Amelia and Kaleb like each other. I could tell by the way they looked at one another.'

"'That would be dangerous for them.' I took a deep breath. 'Lilly, please listen to me. This is important. What you're going to see today, you can't speak of to anyone. It's a secret that must be kept no matter what. If that scares you, I'll leave you here and pick you up later. You can't tell what you don't know.'

"'I'm not scared. I've never felt more alive than I do today. I won't tell anyone, I promise.'

"'Good.'"

♨♨

NATALIA...

"I had never met a real Madam before. I suppose I should be appalled but I liked her. I had a small pang of jealousy that Lucas knew them, and I wondered how well. But it felt so good to have my arms around him, I soon forgot about the girls. I couldn't imagine what they could possibly be doing that was so risky, but I soon found out.

"We stopped in front of the same sort of dwelling made of earth, sod, and wood that I saw the other day. This one was at the farthest edge of the reservation. We heard Amelia's cart rumbling toward us, a cloud of dust behind her.

"She wasn't happy we had taken off before she was through talking. 'Lucas, I don't like this at all.'

"'I really want to help,' I pleaded. 'I won't tell anyone, I promise.'

"'You're young and naïve. You don't know what you're getting yourself into. Lucas shouldn't ask you to do this.'

"'Please,' I said.

"Amelia sighed and gave in. 'All right. If you get in trouble you can work for me. You're young and pretty. The men would love you.'

"'Amelia!' Lucas took my arm and pulled me toward him. 'Lilly won't get in trouble. If she does, I'll take care of it.' He and Amelia glared at each other, the defiance so thick, the air felt heavy.

"'That's enough you two,' Kaleb growled. 'We have more important things to worry about, don't you think? Lucas and Amelia shot him dirty looks, but both relented.

"The three of them walked over to the cart and helped the girls in the back down.

What happened next took me by surprise. Lucas and Kaleb climbed into the cart and pushed all the hay out on the ground. They got on their knees and pulled up the boards. A trap door fell open, revealing a false bottom. Lying there were five Negros all squeezed together—four adults and one child. Lucas and Kaleb helped them up and out. They moved slowly, obviously stiff and achy from being crowded in such a tight space. Their eyes seemed to have trouble adjusting to the light.

"They were parched and scared, but Amelia, Kaleb, and the three young women were at their side immediately, with food, water, and a reassuring smile. The little girl started sobbing. Not knowing what else to do, I scooped her up in my arms and gave her a hug, some water, and food.

One by one, we helped each of the slaves down to the river. They washed up a little and then hid in a small cave until dark. That was when Amelia told me she was taking me home while the rest of them got the supplies ready for the next leg of the trip to Canada.

I didn't want to leave but knew I had to. Before I left, I went over to the little girl. I didn't even know her name. I told her to be brave. This wonderful group of people would take good care of her and get her to a safe place. I gave her a hug and climbed up next to Amelia on the cart.

"'Will Nathan be angry with you again?' Lucas asked.

"'Yes. He's always mad about something. I'm used to it.'

"'Thank you for helping and for keeping our secret,' Lucas said.

"He gently touched my hand. I smiled and said good-bye.

"On the way home, Amelia explained that she moves the slaves from Missouri, a slave state, through the territories of Kansas and Nebraska. Her brothel outside of Nebraska City is also a stop on the way to their next contact in Canada.

"'Aren't you afraid of getting caught?'

"'There have been rumors, but no one has ever proved anything. Sometimes they send men to check my place of business, but men are easily distracted in certain company. We know how to distract them.' She winked. "'It gives us time to move someone if we have too.'

"'It's very brave of you to do this. You're a good person.'

"'I don't think too many people would agree with you.'

"'They only know one part of you, not all of you.'

"The smile disappeared from her face. 'And they won't either, will they?'

"'No. I promise.'

"'Here we are," She stopped the cart at my door. 'Remember what I said. If you get tired of being the good wife, you can have a job with me.'

"'Don't tempt me. Good luck with everything.'

"When I walked inside Nathan was waiting for me. As expected, he was extremely angry.

"'Lilly, this behavior of yours has to stop. Now you have a whore bringing you home and it's almost dark outside. You're bringing shame to this family.'

"'I went for a walk and got lost. Amelia was kind enough to bring me home. Instead of being mad, you should be grateful. Were you even worried about me? Anyway, I like her, and so would other people if they would get to know her. I'll talk to whomever I like. I don't care what you or other people think.'

"The shock from his slap didn't register until I tasted the blood in my mouth. He'd always had a temper, but he'd never hit me before. A natural reflex took over. I didn't even think about what I was doing. I slapped him hard across the face. Furious, he grabbed me and threw me against the wall. My back hit the corner of the table. I slid down the wall to the floor and curled in a ball, covering my head. He kicked me, yelling obscenities. His uncle Henry ran in and pulled him off me. He dragged Nathan out of the room and called for Matilda.

"She helped me up to the couch. I was sobbing—and bleeding. She left for a few minutes, returned with warm water and a cloth, and gently cleaned my face, wiping my tears away. It was the nicest she had ever been to me.

"Henry brought Nathan back. Nathan had tears in his eyes. He promised he would never hurt me again. As he moved toward me, I inched closer to Matilda.

"She hugged me. 'Lilly, if Nathan says he's sorry and won't hurt you again, he won't. He's a man of his word.'

"'I didn't do anything wrong. I got lost, and Amelia brought me home, nothing more.'

"'I know dear, but in his defense he just wants a proper wife. Is that too much to ask?'

"'Lilly, please believe me,' Nathan begged. 'I'm so sorry. 'I don't want you to be afraid of me'

"I looked around the room at the three of them staring at me. So, this is how it was going to be. I sighed and slowly nodded my head. Nathan held my hands and thanked me. We went upstairs to our room where I changed and carefully climbed into bed. He kissed me good night and told me how important I was to him. When he was asleep and snoring, I quietly got up and put a few things in a bag. Silently, I crept down the stairs to the barn.

"Gritting my teeth against the agony in my back, I saddled up a horse and led it outside. My body ached as if I'd been beaten with a hammer. In more pain than I'd have ever thought possible, I hoisted myself onto the horse and started down the long, dark road to the reservation."

♨♨

MARC...

"It was late by the time Amelia left and for some reason I was tired. My brother and his family had my children so I stayed at the lodge on the outskirts of the reservation. When I woke up and went outside, I saw her sleeping about a hundred feet away, wrapped in a horse blanket. Her horse was tied to a tree. As I got closer, I saw her face was swollen and bruised. I picked her up and brought her inside the lodge.

"'Lilly, wake up. What happened? Did you fall off your horse?' When I laid her down, she moaned. 'Does something else hurt?'

"'My back,' she said half asleep.

"I sat down and she curled up next to me. I put my arms around her. She went back to sleep. When she woke, she told me what had happened between her and Nathan. I was so enraged, I thought I could kill him.

"'Lilly, I'm so sorry. I won't let you go back there. Will you stay here...with me?'

"She looked at me with her sleepy eyes and put her arms around my neck. 'Yes.'

"'*Lilly*! Are you in there?'

"'It's Nathan. How did he find me so quickly?'

"'Stay here,' I told her.

"'No,' she said and followed me out.

"Nathan was standing there with a shotgun in his hand. I saw my two brothers and three other men of the tribe hidden in the woods behind him. I asked him to put the gun down. No one needed to get hurt.

"'Shut up,' he bellowed. 'I came to get my wife.' Then he looked at Lilly. 'I see you ran back to the half-breed. You're coming home with me.'

"'I'd rather be dead. Go ahead and shoot. I'll never go back with you.'

"'Lilly, please," I said. 'That's not helping.'

"Nathan was taken by surprise when my brothers and the other men jumped him and pushed him to the ground. They tied his hands behind his back, gagged him and pulled him onto his horse. They explained that Nathan had come to the reservation looking for me and, considering how angry he seemed, they'd decided to follow him.

"I introduced my brothers to Lilly using their white names, Charles and Pierre. I told them she would be staying with me on the reservation from now on. Lilly apologized for bringing trouble to the reservation.

"We decided the best the thing to do was take Nathan to the sheriff. Charles and Pierre took him with them. Lilly and I made a stop at the Morgan farm on the way to town. Henry came out when he saw us.

"'Lucas, is that you? Lilly, where have you been? We've been looking all over for you. Thank you for bringing her home.'

"'I'm sorry, Henry,' I said. 'But we're taking Nathan to the sheriff. I thought you should know.' We rode off and left Henry standing there.

"By the time we arrived, my brothers were already talking to the sheriff.

"'Hello, Lucas,' the sheriff said. 'I hear there was some commotion on the reservation this morning.'

"I was about to answer when Henry appeared on his horse. Now that everyone was there, I told the sheriff the whole story.

"'For many years we have lived fairly peacefully with the folks in town. We haven't had much trouble, but when we did, you brought the young men back to the reservation and told us to take care of it. And we did. We appreciate that, and we're returning the favor. Nathan belongs to you, and you need to keep him away from the reservation. If he comes back again, I don't know how much patience we'll have for him.'

"The sheriff turned to Nathan. 'Son, why did you go there this morning?'

"'I went to get my wife back. They're putting strange ideas in her head. She belongs at home with me, and I had every right to go get her.'

"'Ma'am, did Nathan do that to your face?'

"Yes. I don't want to go back. I want to stay on the reservation of my own free will.'

"'Nathan, did you hurt her?'

Nathan hung his head, humiliated, then he tried to defend himself. 'Yes, but you don't know what she did—'

"'Hush up, Henry muttered, "You'll only make things worse.

"'Henry,' said the sheriff. 'You and I have known Lucas and his family for a long time. We are both friends with his father. They have every right to ask Nathan to stay away from the reservation. I'm sure you wouldn't want someone coming to your farm and causing trouble.'

"Then he turned to Nathan. 'Son, I know you haven't lived here but six months or so, but we have an amiable relationship with the tribes around here. We'd like to keep it that way. So, stay away from the reservation.'

"I gave Henry back the horse Lilly had taken last night and went over to Nathan.

"'Her heart belongs to me now. I hope you will respect that. We don't want any trouble.'"

♨♨

NATALIA...

"We returned to the lodge so I could get my bag. Lucas's children were waiting for us. They were adorable and I couldn't help but smile when I saw them.

"'Lilly! We heard you were here. We're happy to see you. Do you remember what you told us yesterday?'

"'Of course, I do. Go tell your father what name you think I'm going to use and then I'll decide.'

"Lucas stood behind them and pointed at me. I assumed that meant their white names.

"'Let's see—today I think—I'll call you Andre and Anne.'

"They both giggled and came looking for their surprise. I found some hard candy in my bag and gave it to them. They were thrilled. There wasn't much hard candy on the reservation.

"'What happened to your face,' asked Anne.

"'I had an accident. I'll be fine, hon. Don't worry.'

"The four of us walked back to the main part of the reservation. I wasn't sure what to expect or where I would be staying. Lucas showed me his lodge. It was near his brother's. We went inside. He sat down looking very tired. I asked him if he was all right. I felt his head, and he was warm. He assured me he was fine and wanted to show me around.

"I was in awe at the size of the reservation. Lucas described everything to me as we walked through all the different areas. We came upon a two men that were dressed differently than the other men. I thought they were women until I got closer.

"'Who are they and why are they dressed like that?' I asked him.

♨♨

MARC...

"'Lilly, I think I need to explain a few things to you. I should have done it before you decided to stay. You may change your mind. Because of my education and trading with the white people, I understand your ways and how they differ from ours. First, where would you like to stay tonight?'

"'I would like to stay with you, but I know I can't. I'm married to someone else and your children are there.'

"I smiled. 'You have to decide what's best for you, but you can stay with me if you like. The children won't care and neither will anyone else. My people are comfortable and open about sex.

We believe it's a gift from the Great Spirit and should be enjoyed. When a couple is courting, chastity is valued but not expected. If a couple wants to be married, they usually elope, or spend a few days away together, come back, and live in the man's lodge. They may have a feast to celebrate.'

"'Sounds good so far.' She touched the side of my face. 'Lucas, your fever is worse. How do you feel?'

"'I'm fine. Let me explain about the men you saw. They are *Mixu-ga*. We consider them both male and female. When a boy is twelve, he must go off on a vision quest. He will fast and pray for four days. In his dreams, the Moon Goddess visits him. She asks him to choose a warrior's bow or a burden strap, used by the women. If he chooses the burden strap, he lives the life of the *Mixu-ga*. They are highly respected members of the tribe. We believe they have a connection and an understanding of the spirit world the rest of us do not have. They have healing powers and are the wisest members of the tribe. They are expected to live by a high moral code, but our moral code and the white moral code differ.

"'What I mean by that is they often take on the women's role and cook, sew, and make pottery and baskets. If they like, they can wear women's clothes, and they usually have a strong relationship with another man in the tribe. Since their physical being is male, they are stronger than females and have more stamina. When a woman is at the end of her pregnancy or nursing, the *Mixu-ga* will take on her jobs as well as his own, and do both well. They also go to battle and on hunting trips.

"'The white society only sees the homosexual aspect of the *Mixu-ga*, but we put spiritual nature above sexual nature. The white settlers call them *Berdache*. This is offensive to us. I've heard many different translations of the word, none of them nice or accurate.'

"All of a sudden, I felt dizzy and almost fell to the ground. 'Lilly, I think you're right. I don't feel very good. I need to lie down.'"

♨♨

NATALIA...

"By the time we got back to his lodge, Lucas was burning up with fever. I was afraid it was small pox—this is how it started—and I knew I had to get him away from the reservation right away. I told Lucas's brothers what I was doing. They wanted to come and help me.

"'I can take care of him. I had cowpox as a child. It's a milder case of small pox. But I need you to stay away from us. It's the only way to keep you and the whole reservation from getting sick.'

"I didn't hear Lucas's children come up behind me. They looked scared, so, they must have overheard our conversation. I did my best to reassure them. I told them my father was a healer where I lived, and I would take could care of their father. Charles and Pierre picked them up and carried them into their lodge.

"Moving lethargically, Lucas clambered onto his horse. I climbed up in front of him and told him to hold on. When we arrived at the lodge on the outskirts of the reservation, I helped him off the horse and inside. He was shivering. I wrapped a blanket around him, laid beside him, and put my arms around him, trying to keep him warm. It was a restless night for both of us.

"The next day was a beautiful day, and I thought some fresh air might do him good. Still sore from Nathan's reprimand, I struggled to help Lucas up and outside. I helped him to lie down on a blanket and ran to the river for some water. When I got back, he was semi-conscious and throwing up. I pulled him up on my lap and leaned him forward so he could vomit. Then I ripped a large piece of my dress off, dipped it the water and began to wash him.

"'Lilly,' he whispered.

"'I'm here. Can you take a little water?'

"He nodded.

"Ripping another piece of my dress, I soaked it in the water and put it to his lips. I told him to suck on it slowly. 'Go easy, but you need to keep drinking.'

"'It's good. I'm so hot.' He fell asleep. I had taken off his shirt to wipe him down with cool water when I saw it. On his left shoulder was the strangest birthmark I had ever seen. There was a large, light red mark with three smaller jagged marks inside of it. I sat there frozen, mesmerized by it. Finally, I gently touched it and for some reason, kissed it. When my lips met his skin, it felt like it was on fire. He started throwing up again. It snapped me out of whatever was wrong with me.

"'Lilly,' he whispered again.

"'I'm still here. I'm not going anywhere.'

"'What's wrong with me?'

"'I'm not sure, but I'm going to take care of you. I love you.'

"I was still behind him with my arms around his waist. I leaned my head against his back. I thought he was asleep, but he put his arms over mine and held tight. My body ached. I was so tired, I closed my eyes. I heard someone calling my name and jumped. Charles and Pierre, as well as the *Mixu-ga* were standing in the woods.

"'Don't come any closer,' I told them.

"'Is he worse?' asked Pierre. 'We saw him getting sick. We were watching from the woods. You really do love him, don't you?'

"'Yes.'

"The *Mixu-ga* came forward. 'I'll sit with him. You rest and eat.'

"'*No*! I should know if it's smallpox by tomorrow. If the red marks appear. I don't want anyone else sick.'

"'Lucas is respected in the tribe. It would be an honor to sit with him. I am the healer of the tribe. It is my duty.'

"'Lilly, please,' Charles pleaded.

"'He's burning up with fever,' I said. The *Mixu-ga* immediately lifted Lucas up in his arms and started toward the river.

"'Where are you taking him?' I yelled, running after him.

"'Lilly, he knows what he's doing,' Charles called from his spot in the woods.

"The *Mixu-ga* walked into the river and completely immersed Lucas underwater for a few seconds. He kept him in the water, dunking him under a few more times while speaking over him in their native language. When he carried him out,

Lucas was shivering. He took him back to the lodge and put a blanket over him.

"'Better cold than burning hot,' he said and sat down next to Lucas.

"I walked over to the woods where Charles and Pierre were waiting. I kept a safe distance from them while explaining the *Mixu-ga* couldn't return to the reservation. I went back and asked the *Mixu-ga* if he could help get me Lucas back inside. He picked him up, laid him down inside, and chanted over him again.

"'You can't go back,' I said. 'You have to stay here with us. If it's small pox, you'll give it to everyone at the reservation.'

"'I will cleanse myself in the sweat lodge.'

"'You and other people sweating next to each other is the worst thing you could do.'

"'I won't go against Wakon'da, the Great Spirit. It's part of our healing ritual.'

"I sat down on a tree log and let out a frustrated sigh. I remembered my father saying he didn't understand human beings and their religions. So often people are afraid of offending a God or Gods they can't see, even at the expense of the living, breathing people they care about.

"'Can you build a sweat lodge here? I need your help with Lucas. I'm very tired and my back hurts.'

"He touched my face. I hadn't looked in a mirror but I knew the bruises were there.

"'Your husband did this to you?'

"I nodded. He walked towards the woods and from a safe spot spoke with Charles and Pierre.

"'Yes. I will stay,' he said to me. 'Charles and Pierre will bring food and supplies and leave them on a rock. Go stay with Lucas. I will do what needs to be done out here.'

"I thanked him but also felt a sense of relief and hoped the reservation would stay free of the illness. I found Lucas asleep so I nestled up against his back and slept, too. When we woke a few hours later, he a small red rash on his stomach but was much cooler.

"'I feel a little better,' he said. "'It is small pox?'

"'Yes. When the rash appears the fever breaks a little, but it will go back up.'

"'Why are you doing this? Will you get sick?'

"'No, I had cow pox as a child, so I'm immune. It wouldn't matter though, I'm staying with you.'

"A look of panic came over his face. 'What about my children? Are they sick?'

"'No, don't worry. They're fine and staying with your brothers.'

"He seemed to relax. I brought him close, and he let himself melt into me. I held him tightly.

"'Lilly, I'm glad you're here. This may be the only time we have together. Small pox isn't a friend to the Omaha people or any of the tribes here. Thousands have died.'

"'Lucas, don't talk like that. I'm not going to let anything happen to you. Neither will the *Mixu-ga.* He's staying here with us now.'

"'His name is Wa-zhin'-ska,' he said, drowsily. 'Lilly, I'm getting tired again.'

"He rolled on his side revealing his birthmark. I stretched out behind him, traced it with my finger, and kissed it.

"'Why do you keep kissing my shoulder?' he asked. 'I felt you do it when my fever was high.'

"'Tell me about your birthmark.'

"'My mother was superstitious about it. My father said people were born with birthmarks all the time. It wasn't anything to worry about. I took my father's advice. I can't see it so I don't think about it.'

"'I like it. I don't know why.'

"'I like it when you kiss it.'

"I told him to get some rest. I went outside and saw a small tee pee off to the side. There was also another type of dwelling next to it. I looked around and saw Wa-zhin'-ska walking up from the river carrying quite a few large rocks in his arms. He put them in the odd shaped hut I assumed was his sweat lodge. He told me Charles and Pierre had left food for us. I went to the woods and gathered the fruit, vegetables and corn bread they had left.

"Wa-zhin'-ska was dragging large logs from the woods and putting them around the fire he had made, again showing his great strength. He had something cooking and asked me not to let the fire go out. He went into the sweat lodge. When he finished his healing ritual, he went in to Lucas and carried him outside by the fire.

"I tried to coax Lucas into eating something. Wa-zhin'-ska poured whatever he was cooking into a pottery cup and gave it to Lucas to drink.

"'What is it?' I asked.

"'It is a tea I boiled with purple coneflower and blazing star.'

"Lucas announced he wasn't feeling well and wanted to lie down. We helped him inside, and I curled up with him until he was asleep. When I went back outside, Wa-zhin'-ska was cooking fish and squash over the fire. He asked me to sit down and eat. I had never spent any time with someone of his sexual preference before. If I had, I wouldn't have known it. Men like him were not able to live freely in our world.

"'Lucas's fever is up, but not as high as before. He doesn't have many pockmarks on him. I'm taking that as a good sign. I remember my father telling me of people who were covered in red marks and never regained consciousness, their fever was so high.' He nodded but didn't answer me.

"'Is one of your parents white?' I asked him.

"'Yes, my father was white, not French, but American. He traded at the post in Bellevue and married my mother there. He was killed on a hunting trip in my twelfth summer. My mother died two winters ago.'

"'I'm sorry. When Lucas gets better, I'll be living on the reservation with him.'

"'I saw you two walking together.'

"'Lucas started to tell me about the Omaha way of life and how it differs from my world. But he didn't get the chance to finish.'

"'What is it you want to know? Is it me you wonder about?'

"'I'm sorry. I didn't mean to—'

"'I will tell you. You ask with a pure heart.'

"He told me about his life on the reservation, and he wasn't to question why he was different. It was the Moon Goddess's choice. He must follow her instruction. Then he got up and handed me a buckskin dress that he had made. It was decorated beautifully with beads. He wanted me to have it. He really was two different people, and I found him fascinating.

"He stirred the tea over the fire. "'When Lucas wakes up, give him more of this.'

"'Will you teach me how to make it?' I asked.

"'Yes, tomorrow.' He looked at me for a minute and said, 'This is your time of the moon?'

"I didn't know what he was talking about and told him so.

"'Are you bleeding?'

"'Yes.' I put my head down, a little embarrassed. 'How did you know?'

"He laughed a little. 'Why is it that white people don't like to talk about things that are part of nature? If you have pain, drink the tea, it will help.'

"'Why do you call it the time of the moon?'

"'It takes a month for the moon to go through its phases and ends with a full moon. It takes a woman a month to go through her cycle, ending with her bleeding. That's why women are of the moon.'

"'I never thought of it that way. What does your name mean?'

"'Wisdom.'

"'It fits you well.' I was tired and got up from my seat. 'I know I'm different from the rest of the tribe.'

He smiled. "'So am I.'

"'I don't know what's acceptable and what's not, but I want to thank you for all your help with Lucas and for the beautiful dress. It means a lot to me.' I hugged him and wished him good night. I checked Lucas and saw he had three large pustules near his birthmark. I kissed his shoulder, which had become a strange habit of mine, and fell asleep.

"Time passed and Lucas recovered. Wa-zhin'-ska stayed with us and never got sick. I wasn't surprised. There was something mysterious about him, almost magical. I didn't care what the reason, I was glad he stayed healthy."

♨♨

MARC...

"I was feeling much better, but Lilly told me I was contagious until my last scab fell off. What can I say about Lilly? I'd never felt so close to someone, and I hadn't even kissed her. When I was so sick and felt her kiss my shoulder, I knew she was with me and always would be.

"I was missing my children but didn't tell her. One day she said she had a surprise for me. I went outside and standing at the edge of the woods were Raw-zi' and Non-ke'-ne with Charles. I knew I couldn't get close to them, but at least they could see I was better. I couldn't hug them but I did hug Lilly. She pulled away from me and smiled.

"'I've been a very patient woman, don't you think?' She took me back into the lodge, pushed me down, slid on top of me, and kissed me hard. We loved each other with an urgency and passion I had never experienced before. She—"

"Marc. We've been through this already. Keep it to yourself as a nice memory," said Dr. Collier.

"Sorry." Marc sat quietly for a few minutes before he continued.

"While I was sick, our chief was killed on a hunting trip. Joseph LaFlesche was our new chief now, and he asked if my brothers and I would be his chief interpreters. We accepted and our first Indian agent, George Hepner, was assigned to us. We spent most of our time at the agent's house on the reservation. This is where Lilly signed the papers for her divorce from Nathan.

"It's February eighteen fifty-six. Lilly, myself, the Sheriff, a lawyer, Mr. Hepner, Nathan, and Henry were seated at a table. Nathan asked for the divorce on the charge of adultery.

"'I don't think she'll contest the accusation,' he said as he glared at her.

"I admired Lilly's strength and bravery as she sat there while the men looked at her disapprovingly. I stood behind her and put my arms on her shoulders.

"'I haven't seen her since June, and it's obvious she's at least seven months along with a baby.'

"'No. I don't deny it. I'll sign the papers. I want the whole thing over.' She held her head high as she spoke and signed the papers."

ꕥꕥ

NATALIA...

"It was March, a month after the divorce, when it happened. We were waiting for Amelia and Kaleb at the lodge. With the baby coming soon, I couldn't do much, so I went for a walk while Lucas got things ready for them. Most of the snow was gone. I was enjoying the sunshine on my face, when I felt a hand on my shoulder. I turned around and was face to face with Nathan.

"Hello, Lilly'"

"'What do you want?'

"'How is it that you can have *his* baby and not mine?' He had a crazy look in his eyes. I was scared, and wished I hadn't wandered so far away from Lucas.

"'I don't know.'

"'It doesn't matter, because I won't let you have that half-breed's baby.'

"Nathan lunged at me. I turned to run but slipped on the ice underneath the snow. He grabbed my legs and turned me over onto my back. He sat on my stomach with his legs straddled to my sides and held my hands over my head.

"'I hate you.' I spit in his face.

"He jammed his knee into my stomach almost knocking the breath out of me.

"'I'm sorry, I'm sorry.' I moaned. 'Don't hurt my baby.'

"I felt his knee in my stomach again. He got off me, and I tried to get up. He pushed me down and kicked me in the stomach. I was trying to protect my baby the best I could when he suddenly stopped.

"I looked up. Lucas was holding him by his hair, a knife at his throat.

"'I'm sorry I left you alone, Lilly. Are you all right? I want to make sure, but I can't let him go right now. I'm going to take him away from here. I don't want you to see what I'm going to do to him."

"'Lucas, no, if you kill him, they'll take you away from me. Please, I need you and so does our baby.'

"'No. I won't let him hurt you again.'

"Lucas, please.' I was sobbing. 'Take him to the sheriff.'

"Lucas appeared to think about it and finally threw Nathan next to a big tree. He smashed the back of his head against the tree until he was unconscious. Then he tied him to the tree and ran over to me.

He hugged me. "'Are you all right?'

"'I don't know. My stomach hurts. Go get your brothers. I'll stay here with him.'

"'I'm not leaving you here.'

"'I can't ride on a horse right now. I need to rest. Give me your gun. I'll shoot him in a minute if he tries to hurt our baby again.'

"Lucas reluctantly did what I asked and took off as fast as he could. After a few minutes, Nathan started to come to.

"'Lilly," he moaned as he struggled to free himself from the ropes that bound him. 'If you let me go, I promise to leave. I'll go Back East and never bother you again.'

"'Why should I believe you?'

"'He was going to kill me. He would have if you hadn't stopped him. I'm grateful for that. I owe you. You saved my life.'

"'You promise to never come back?'

"'Yes. There is nothing here for me.'

"I started to get up but the debilitating pain in my sides brought me to my knees. When it subsided, I walked over to him. Pointing the gun at him, I untied him. He stood, and I held the gun at this head.

"'Get out of here and never come back."

"I promise. Thank you, Lilly.' He started to walk away but turned back to me after he had gone about fifty feet and yelled, 'By the way, I know your secret. I saw you helping the slaves. I hope I don't slip and tell anyone. That would be bad for you, your half-breed, and your baby, don't you think?' He laughed and started walking away, assuming I was helpless to do anything. Determined to stop him, and ignoring the pain in my abdomen, I walked after him as fast as I could. When I caught up with him, he spun around. 'God will see you in hell, bitch.'

"'You'll be there before me.' I took the gun in both hands, swung, and hit him hard on the side of the head. He dropped into the snow. I fell to the ground, holding my stomach. I was still lying there when Lucas found me. I was shaking uncontrollably and crying. 'Is he dead? I think I killed him. I hit him with the gun.'

"'Don't worry, Lilly. As long as you're all right, I'll take care of it.'

"I heard him and his brothers talk in their native language. Charles and Pierre lifted Nathan up and carried him to the river. They laid him down with his head against some rocks. Lucas found a bottle of whiskey in Nathan's jacket. He took it, poured a little whiskey on him, and put the bottle in his hand.

"'Lucas,' I whimpered. 'The baby is coming. It's too soon.'

"He carefully put me on his horse and got on. 'Hold on to me,' he said.

I squeezed his arm as another contraction came over me. 'I'm sorry I let him go. He said he would leave us alone because I stopped you from killing him. He said he owed me, and I believed him.'

"'Lilly, I don't care about him. I care about you and the baby.'

"'Then Nathan said he knew about Amelia, and he was going to tell. I couldn't let him do that, so I hit him with the gun. Now the baby is coming and it's my fault. I'm so sorry.'

"'It's not your fault. We're almost back. I love you.'

"Back at the reservation, Lucas carried me into a lodge. Soon the women of the tribe were there to help me. They massaged my back and legs. Hours had passed and I was exhausted. Finally, I asked for Wa-zhin'-ska.

"'Please, I need him with me.'

"It wasn't long before he was by my side. He put his hands on my abdomen and began massaging it. Then he started to chant in his native language. I couldn't understand what he was saying, but it was calming. I didn't want him to stop."

♨♨

MARC...

"Twelve hours had passed and Lilly hadn't had the baby yet. I saw Wa-zhin'-ska go in with her. I was worried but knew I couldn't go in, just the women of the tribe. I was sitting, waiting for news, when I saw the sheriff walking toward me.

"'Hello, Lucas. You don't look so good. What's wrong?'

"'Lilly is in there with the women. The baby is coming and it's a little early. She's been in there since yesterday.'

"'I'm sorry to hear that.' He sat down next to me. 'Henry came to see me. Nathan never came home last night. We found him down by the river this morning near a lodge that belongs to someone on the reservation.'

"'Is he all right? What happened?'

"'He's dead. That's why I'm here.'

"'Oh.'

"'Lucas, I have to ask you a few questions. Who does the lodge belong to? It's down by the Big Nemaha River, near the fork in the road before the reservation begins.'

"'That's mine. I don't use it often. I was there this summer when I had small pox.'

"'Why would Nathan go there?'

"'When Lilly left, after he beat her, that's where I found her. I don't think she knew it was mine. It was the first lodge she saw, and she thought she was on the reservation. Nathan found us there. What made you look near the reservation?'

"'Henry said Nathan was very upset after he saw Lilly in her...condition. He thought he might confront her. You haven't seen him?'

"'No. I haven't seen him since Lilly signed the papers,' I said, surprised at how easy it was to lie when you are protecting someone you love.

"'You haven't left the reservation in the last twenty-four hours?'

"'No. I wouldn't leave Lilly like this. Especially after what happened when Raw-zi was born.'

"'Yes, I remember. I'm sorry to ask,' he said.

"'I understand.'

"'Wa-zhin'-ska came running out yelling, 'Lucas, it's a boy! He's small but he's crying.'

"'Sheriff, I'm sorry, but I need to see Lilly and the baby.'

"'Yes, of course. I'm glad everyone is fine.'"

♨♨

"Marc?" asked Dr. Collier.

"Yes."

"What happened regarding Nathan?"

"They said he was drunk, slipped on the ice, and hit his head."

"Was the baby okay?"

"Yes. We were very happy until eighteen seventy-seven when we died in our barn fire."

"You died together? That doesn't happen very often."

♨♨

MARC...

"Lilly was in there trying to get the horses out. I heard her screaming for me and ran in. I couldn't see very well, my eyes were burning from the smoke. I yelled for her but couldn't hear her answer. The horses were stomping and snorting.

"I was crawling on the ground when I saw her. She was lying there coughing and choking on the smoke. But she was alive and looking at me. She reached her hand out to me. I was almost to her when a large part of the ceiling fell on my shoulders, back and legs. I couldn't move and screamed from the pain. I was having trouble breathing when I saw her close her eyes. I shouted her name but her eyes stayed shut.

"The smoke had overtaken me as well. My lungs were on fire. I couldn't do anything but lie there. The heat was unbearable and soon I was gone. It was November twenty-first, eighteen seventy-seven.

♨♨

Marc was coughing as he relived the last part of his life.

"Marc, it's two thousand-ten, and you're in my office in New York City. You are not in the barn and there is no fire. I want you to take a few deep breaths. Fill your lungs in this body with cool, clean air. Relax and take your time."

Within a few minutes, Marc stopped coughing but Dr. Collier could see he was still upset.

"Marc, I think we've done enough for today. Unless there's another door you want to open."

Marc wiped his eyes for the second time today and said, "No. I have everything I need."

CHAPTER 14

"...and when one of them meets the other half; the actual half of himself, the pair are lost in an amazement of love and friendship and intimacy and one will not be out of the other's sight even for a moment..." – *Plato, 428 BC – 348 BC, Greek Philosopher*

Natalia eased out of her deepened state of relaxation as Dr. Ellis brought her back to her present life.

She slowly opened her eyes and tried to get her bearings. When Dr. Ellis asked her how she felt, she had to think a minute as to what the answer was.

"I have a lot of things going on in my head, that's for sure. But I feel good, well rested."

"Do you have any questions about anything you remembered?"

"No, I don't think so. It seems so unreal, but I know in my heart it all happened."

Dr. Ellis handed her a glass of water. Natalia, not realizing until then how thirsty she was, gulped it down. "That tasted good, thank you. At least I understand about Marc's birthmark now."

Understanding it made her feelings for Marc unbearable, but she couldn't trust herself to see or talk to him. The best thing to do was have Mariella explain to Marc, or better yet, have him listen to her session. She'd be home in Connecticut. Or she could travel to Europe. She had to be away from him, and the sooner the better.

"Natalia, I need to talk to you about Marc. He was here today. Dr. Collier regressed him as well."

Natalia sat there with her mouth wide open. "He's here? Right now?"

"Yes. He's through with his session. Dr. Collier is talking with him."

Panic clutched Natalia's stomach. Had Marc remembered everything they'd been through together? How they loved each other? She was afraid to ask, but something told her Dr. Ellis was about to enlighten her.

"Natalia, you don't have to tell me anything you don't want to, but you and Marc have a very strong history together. Did you have any feelings for him when you first met him in December?"

Did she dare say it aloud? "Yes." She sighed. "But he's married."

"I know," Dr. Ellis said sympathetically, and squeezed Natalia's hand. "Dr. Collier and I have enjoyed regressing both of you. We've never seen a couple that has been together as long and has such a strong bond as you two. We believe you two are what's known in our field of research as *twin flame soul mates.*" The doctor let go of Natalia's hand and sat back in her chair. "First, let me explain. There are three kinds of soul mates. The first type is a *companion soul mate.* These are souls you have a positive, albeit short relationship. You may meet them in another life.

"*Twin soul mates* are souls you have several lifetimes with and have a special connection to. They are usually family members and dear friends. They are often spouses.

"*Twin flame soul mates* have a much deeper, spiritual and intimate relationship with each other. When you first meet, you feel like you've known each other forever. The truth is you have known them forever due to countless lives spent together. Ancient cultures, and some therapists in our field today, believe twin flame souls were actually a single soul separated into male and female at its creation. The only way for those individuals to feel—"

"Whole is to find their other half?" Natalia asked.

"Yes," said Dr. Ellis, raising an eyebrow.

"I knew, the moment I opened the first life door, who and what Marc was to me."

There was a soft knock on the door. "Come in," Dr. Ellis said. Mariella walked in and sat next to Natalia.

"I know this is a lot to take in and process, dear. How are you doing?" Mariella asked.

Natalia sat there, trying to get a grip on the newfound knowledge swimming around in her head. "Since being regressed, I'm fully aware that Marc and I share an *essence* that's a fundamental part of our nature. We always have, and we always will. I don't know how I know, but I do, instinctively."

"Natalia, dear, you're going to have to talk to Marc. He was very emotional at the end of your last life."

"Emotional? About the fire? I didn't want to relive that over again. I'm sorry he's upset, but it's not a good idea for us to see each other."

"Well, dear, you don't have to worry about that right now. It's too late for you to go back to Connecticut. There's a refrigerator full of food in your suite. Go back and spend some time alone, thinking about what you'd like to do. If you have any questions, Dr. Ellis and I are here to help you."

Natalia stood and hugged Mariella. She shook Dr. Ellis's hand and thanked her for everything.

"Natalia, there is one other thing. If these memories are too much for you to carry around, Dr. Ellis may be able to have you forget them."

Natalia gave Dr. Ellis a questioning look. "Yes, I can try," the doctor said. "It's rarely done, but under the circumstances, I'm willing to do it. You'll still remember each other, but not the past lives you've shared or the tension in your present relationship. I'll keep two o'clock open for you, just in case."

"Thank you. That might be best," Natalia said and walked out the door.

♨♨

Marc was sitting in Mariella's apartment when she walked in. His expression was hard to read. She wasn't sure how angry he was with her, and she didn't care.

"Marcos."

"Mariella."

"I understand if you're upset with me, but I did it for your own good. Your obsession with Natalia and your birthmark was consuming your life. Aren't you glad you understand the reason behind your attraction for her?"

"Yes," he admitted. "Did she remember me the same as I remembered her?"

"Yes, you two have been together for a very long time. Did Dr. Collier explain to you about—"

"I already knew she was an essential element of my being. How could I not, after all we'd been through together? Those four lives are a small part of our existence together."

Mariella looked at her nephew. She'd never expected this. She had known he and Natalia were connected and needed the regression to help them move forward. However, the extent and depth of their relationship stunned her. She, like Dr. Ellis, had read about twin flame soul mates but never thought she would see a case first hand.

"Marcos, I need to tell you one thing. If you want to forget everything that happened today, Dr. Ellis may able to help you do that. Considering your situation, it might be best. It was hard for you to stay away from her before. It will be close to impossible now."

"If the situation you're referring to is Simone, our marriage is over. I called my lawyer this morning."

"What?" Mariella couldn't believe what she was hearing.

"I spent last night and this morning trying to get Simone to decide if our marriage was important or not. She couldn't and said she needed more time. It's been eight months of us living apart, and me not knowing where she is half the time. I felt I'd been more than patient, so I made the decision for her."

"I'm sorry. What did she say when you told her?"

"She doesn't know yet. She got on a plane to D.C."

"She doesn't *know*?"

"I asked her to come home after this trip, and she refused me. She'll find out whenever she gets back. I don't know when that'll be. She doesn't share that information with me anymore. Where's Natalia?"

"I don't think she wants to see you. Or should I say, she's afraid to see you."

"I'll talk to her. Please, is she in the same room she was in the other night?"

"No. I moved her to a suite the other day." Mariella handed him a plastic keycard to Natalia's new room.

CHAPTER 15

"There's love of course. And then there's life, its enemy." – *Jean Anouilh, 1910-1987 French Dramatist*

Natalia opened the refrigerator door, saw the food—and two bottles of wine. She would make do with the wine, but what she *really* wanted was a glass of whiskey. She rummaged around for a corkscrew, opened the bottle, and poured herself a big glass. Then she flopped on the couch, edgy and agitated.

She couldn't remember the last time she prayed. Actually, she wasn't sure if she ever really had. She went through the motions when she was young and sat in church with her parents but never cared about the prayers she was forced to memorize. Still, she found herself looking up at the sky, which in her case was a ceiling with recessed lighting.

"So, this is your brilliant idea? Twin flame soul mates, my ass! It's more trouble and aggravation than it's worth. What the hell am I supposed to do now? You know full well, he's going to come here. You also know I'm not strong enough to resist. Is this a game to you, screwing around with people's lives?" She felt her anger growing. "If you haven't noticed, our world has some serious problems that could use some attention. How about you focus on that and leave the rest of us alone? I'm so fucking pissed and confused right now. This is an impossible situation. And it's not fair!"

One of the bulbs in the recessed lighting popped and blew out. "I don't want to calm down!" Natalia shouted and slammed her wine glass down on the coffee table. Then she sat there frozen, realizing what had just happened.

"Giovanna, is that you? I didn't know you could leave the vineyard," she whispered.

No, it wasn't Giovanna. Natalia would have felt her immediately. Still, Natalia swore she heard someone tell her to calm down. Perfect. Now she had apparitions appearing where ever she went.

She picked her glass up, took a few sips, and tried to do what the voice in her head asked of her. Taking a deep breath, she muttered, "I'm sorry about the not-so-nice adjective. Sometimes when I get angry, I don't have the best control of my language."

She took another sip and continued. "Like I said, you and I both have a fairly good idea what's going to happen here. So here's the deal. After Marc's, um...visit...here tonight, I promise to forget all about him. I'll have Dr. Ellis do her magic on me, and I'll convince Marc to do the same. That way no one will know or remember whatever happens in this room. But I do have to see him and feel him just once in this lifetime. That's all I'm asking. Even after I've forgotten, I'll know deep in my soul that we had some time together, and I'll be content. That's the best I can do. Take it or leave it. After all, this is your grand design."

The gas fireplace lit up by itself, displaying a roaring fire. Natalia waited for the voice in her head, but there was only silence. "Well, what's that supposed to mean, yes or no?"

She stared at the fire and decided it could mean one of two things. One, the voice in her head agreed and wanted her to sit by the fire and have another glass of wine *or* the fires of hell awaited her. "You're insufferable, do you know that?"

She went back to the kitchen, grabbed the bottle of wine, refilled her glass, and then returned to the living room, curled up on the couch, and waited for the inevitable.

♨♨

Marc stood outside of Natalia's door. His heart had ached for her long before he called his lawyer this morning. With his back against the door, he slid down until he was sitting on the floor. He knew his marriage was over. It had been over for months, but both he and Simone were hanging on for some reason. Was it a fear of failure? Or of what other people would think? Who knew, but someone had to stop being the enabler. So he'd made the call. He had no qualms about going inside to see Natalia, even though he knew what would happen. He loved her more than anything and always would. She was his other half, for God's sake.

The minute he walked into her room, he would become the disloyal husband, even though he had been more than supportive of Simone in her quest to find herself. He would take full responsibility for his actions and the blame. He was the one doing the betraying, legally anyway. Simone wasn't concerned with whom he spent time. He knew that. She never asked whether he had met someone or what he did with his time while she was away.

He was happy to be the bad guy and let her be the innocent, unsuspecting wife. He would try to cause her the least amount of embarrassment if any of this was to come out, which he hoped it wouldn't. Even if it meant staying away from Natalia, after today, until the divorce was final. This wasn't about hurting Simone. It was about living his life with the person he was destined to be with, since the beginning of their time on earth.

He stood and swiped the key to Natalia's door.

CHAPTER 16

"What greater thing is there for two human souls, to feel that they are joined...to strengthen each other...to be at one with each other in silent unspeakable memories." – *George Eliot (pen name of Mary Anne Evans), 1819-1880 English Novelist*

When Marc walked in, the room was illuminated only by the flames flashing in the fireplace. Natalia sat on the couch, knees at her chest with her arms wrapped around them, holding a glass of wine.

"Hey, Nat," he said softly, sitting beside her. "Are you okay?"

She kept her head down. "I think so."

"This certainly wasn't what I expected." He took the wine glass from her hand and set it on the table.

"I guess we have the answers we were looking for."

He took her hands and was startled by the absence of burning energy. "No more shocks."

"I'll miss them."

"I've missed you." He leaned in and quickly brushed his lips against hers. She didn't pull away.

"I've missed you, too." She rose and he followed her lead, both of them instinctively knowing what they needed. She stood behind him as he unbuttoned his shirt and took it off. He walked toward the fireplace and sat down. He felt her hands slide down his back. She put her arms around his waist, kissed his birthmark, and rested her head on his shoulder. Like so many times before, he held her arms tight around him.

"I love you," she told him.

"I know, baby. I love you, too."

They were happily content—for a time.

Slowly, he undid his arms from hers and turned toward her, caressing the side of her face. His thumb swept across her lips. He kissed her softly, not wanting to push her if she wasn't ready, but she hungrily returned his kiss. He could taste the wine on her tongue. He kissed her harder.

Frustrated by the number of buttons on her blouse, he simply yanked it over her head and pulled her against him. His mouth found hers again, and this time he could feel all of her, each time she had loved him during their long and fervent past. He was thankful that of all the souls in the universe; she was his.

She shifted in his arms as he moved his fingers along her back trying to find the clasp to her bra. When he couldn't find it, he looked at her, dumbfounded, 'Nat, what the hell?"

"I thought you had at least done this once or twice," she teased him.

"I won't make you jealous and tell you how many times I've done this," he said with a sly smile.

"Be that as it may, it seems you need a little more practice." She guided his hands to the hook between her breasts. "Try again."

He sat there, admiring her lovely curves, moving his fingers across her silky skin. Slowly lowering his hand, he moved back. "No," he said huskily. "I want you to do it."

She paused before answering him. "I'm not twenty-eight any longer. I'm forty." Marc heard a hint of uncertainty in her voice. She sighed. "Let's just say...things may not be exactly the way they were when I was younger."

"I think you're beautiful," he told her.

She gave him a small grin and put her hand in his bringing him to his feet as she stood.

He felt himself harden as his eyes took her in. She slid her hands seductively down her stomach and undid the button on her low-rise jeans. She unzipped them slightly, enough to entice him. Then she glided her hands back up to her chest, leisurely unhooked her bra, and let it drop to the floor.

"You're perfect."

"No, I'm not."

"You're perfect for me," he said and let himself fall into her arms.

He crushed her against him, her warm, soft skin next to his. Wanting her in his mouth, Marc danced his lips and tongue around her full, round breasts. Natalia sighed with pleasure.

He smiled. "I see this is still your favorite place to be kissed."

"Wherever your mouth is on me is my favorite place to be kissed."

He felt her fingers move then fumble with his belt buckle. He stopped her.

"Nat, please, wait. I can't believe, I'm stopping you but I have to, for just a minute."

"Now what?" she groaned.

"Listen, baby, I have to say this."

"All right. I'll try to control my fortyish mid-life hormones." She smirked at him but didn't move her hand from his belt. Instead, she pulled him closer.

"We're crossing a line that we shouldn't. I did call a lawyer this morning, but it's only the first step to ending my marriage." He saw her flinch. "I know what I'm doing. It's a choice I'm making, but I don't want to drag you across with me unless you're sure."

"So chivalry isn't dead. Are you worried about my honor? I'm sure this is one of your many endearing qualities that kept me coming back to you for centuries."

She closed her eyes, so he again asked her if she was all right.

"I never thought I'd ever do anything like this," she confessed. "It's wrong, and I'm not proud of it, but I'm exactly where I want to be."

"I don't want this to hurt you in any way."

"It won't, and if it does, I'll deal with it. Your minute is up."

She yanked at his belt, and he pushed her into the bedroom. He shut the door and turned to see Natalia's back to him. The blaze from the double-sided fireplace radiated a warm ambiance into the bedroom. He took hold of the top of her jeans, already loosened, and pulled her toward him. With one hand, he swiped her long, dark locks to the side and slid his other hand down her sleek and sexy back.

He leaned his head into her neck and whispered, "Since the first time I laid eyes on you, in my mind I had us taking our time, unhurried and slow. Now that I have you—"

Natalia interrupted him by reaching behind and putting her hands atop of his. Together they slid her jeans down over her hips. She shimmied out of them. Marc groaned

"Have you—and your sweet, um...derriere in my arms," he continued. "I don't think I can wait. I'm a regular guy, and there's only so much I can take. I need you to make me whole."

She turned to face him and wrapped her arms around his neck. "You're no ordinary man. You're an important part of me, the part that makes me full and complete." Gently kissing him, she teased, "But you're also a man who needs to get out of his jeans if you want to move this along."

"I'm already working on it," he said with a wink.

He dumped his remaining clothes in a pile, lifted her with ease, and plopped the two of them on the king size bed so they were facing each other. True to his word, he was all over her. She freed herself from his embrace, urging him to sit up against the soft pillows.

"Comfortable?" she asked.

He nodded and she sashayed toward him on all fours. In one graceful movement, she had him straddled and was guiding him inside her. As her tightness and warmth engulfed him, he thought he would die.

"Oh, God! Nat, baby, you feel so damn good. Too damn good."

Throwing his head back, he moaned in mind-blowing pleasure. The passionate pace she set as she rode him nearly drove him over the edge. When he couldn't take it anymore without losing control, he grabbed her hips, slowing her thrusts. She clung to him, clutching the top of his shoulders. He grasped her face in his hands, gazing at her intently, but her eyes were closed.

"Baby, look at me," he demanded breathlessly. "I want to see your eyes."

They fluttered open. Her beautiful brown eyes were smoldering with desire, aglow with love.

He suddenly realized she was somewhere deep within him where no one else had ever been—a place only she could reach. She lowered her head to his, their foreheads almost touching.

He knew neither one of them could last much longer. When he felt her body start to spasm and her breath become heavier, he thrust his arms tight around her. Her lips purred his name and, with an urgency he'd never felt before, he slammed himself deep inside her. As they plunged off the cliff together, their bodies and souls became one. Together again, whole and complete. At last.

♨♨

Natalia braced herself on one arm, watching Marc's chest heave up and down. She couldn't help but let her fingers stroll down his wonderfully long and lean torso.

"Baby, that was..." he panted. "Well, I don't know what to say. I'm not sure there's a word to describe what happened between us."

"If my memory serves me," she said, kissing the middle of his stomach. "It's always been like this for us. We're lucky to be connected the way we are."

"Oh, I remember." He laughed. "Dr. Collier scolded me a few times for providing a little too much information regarding our past trysts."

"Good thing *I* don't kiss and tell," she said then winced as his phone went off. "Is it...?"

"No, don't worry. She rarely calls me." He leaned over, picking up his pants from the floor, searching for his phone. "It's Tony. I called in sick today from work," he said, placing his phone and wallet on the nightstand.

Natalia noticed his birthmark as he started to lie back down. She stopped him and traced it with her finger. Everything was there. The mark from the spear, the snakebite, the port wine stain from the burn and the small pox scars. She had a hard time fathoming how old the marks were and how long she and Marc had both existed.

"Did Mariella ask if you wanted to forget all this?" she asked.

"Yes, but I don't want to."

"Maybe you should think about it. I made a promise to..." It wasn't clear to her whom or what she made her agreement with. A deity she wasn't sure she believed in? "Myself that after our time together tonight, I would put all this behind me. I was hoping you'd agree to forget as well. It would save everyone, especially Simone, any humiliation and heartache. I don't want your family to be upset with you. I'll admit I'm being a little selfish. But being the other woman isn't sitting well with me. It's my own fault. I should get up and leave, but I won't. I can't."

"Baby, come here," he said, enveloping her in his arms. "You aren't the other woman. You and I are continual and always will be." He kissed the top of her head.

Tears stung her eyes as her heart swelled with love. "You always know how to make me feel better, don't you?"

"Maybe if I explain how it is between Simone and me, you'll understand."

"I don't know about that." She sat up and motioned to him. "Roll over."

She climbed on his back, one leg to each side and rubbed her hands together vigorously. When she'd built up enough heat, she began to knead his shoulders and neck.

"Mmmm. That feels good." Marc sighed. "I never said anything before because I thought it was a private matter, but last summer Simone got a huge promotion at work. Since then, things haven't been good between us. Her new job allowed her to travel and see the world. She told me how exciting it was and how much she loved her job. I was feeling a little left out but assumed the traveling would slow down once she met all her new clients.

"One day she came to me, apologizing for not giving me the time and attention she should. She said didn't know what to do about it. She was confused and thought having a little time on her own would help her figure things out. It hurt me. Still, I agreed to give her the time she needed. There's an apartment above the restaurant, so she moved in there. That was about eight months ago. In the beginning, we kept in touch pretty well. Little by little, she traveled more and more. She'd *forget to* tell me where she was going and when she'd be back. The last few months, I've rarely known where she was, with the exception of Christmas. She came home for a week so we could spend the holiday together, but it was awkward at best. Anyway, by then I'd met you, and you were all that was on my mind. She left before New Year's Eve. I worked at the restaurant that night—and thought about you. To this day I don't know what she did for the New Year or who she spent it with.

"After you sat with me last night, I was at the end of my rope. Simone had called me and asked me to attend a party with her, and I decided a decision regarding our marriage had to be made. She couldn't make one, so I did."

"I'm sorry. I'm sure it was hard for both of you."

"Don't be sorry. Simone and I had grown apart. I want children, she doesn't. Although, I knew that before we got married."

Natalia felt him move underneath her. She started to massage the middle of his back.

"This is where I want to be, with you," he said. "It's where I belong. She doesn't know I started the paperwork for the divorce, but she'll be relieved she wasn't the one to have to do it."

"What do you mean she doesn't know?"

"She immediately got on a plane and left."

"Marc!" Natalia pushed her thumbs, hard, into the base of his neck.

"Ouch! Nat, that hurt. I know I screwed up. I should have called her."

Natalia didn't want to argue with him. She wanted the little time they had together to be loving, even though she wasn't going to remember it. His speech hadn't convinced her to change her mind. She still intended to keep the appointment with Dr. Ellis and wanted Marc to come with her. Convincing him would have to wait until later. She still had one more question.

"Do you have a picture of Simone?"

"Nat," he whined. "Please, don't do this."

"Well, do you?"

"Yeah, but I don't think it's a good idea for you to—"

"That settles it. Let me see."

Still on his stomach, Marc clumsily reached over to the nightstand and grabbed his wallet. As he opened it several pictures fell out.

"Holy shit. I said one picture not the whole damn family album."

"Baby, must you, with the language all the time?"

"It's not all the time," she said, defending herself. "I've been trying to curb the cussing, but I've always been around my brother, his friends, and the men at the vineyard. It's the way I am. Take it or leave it."

"I'll take it. It's a part of who you are. That's what you told me. And you do have me in a vulnerable position. I don't need any more muscles tortured right now."

"Hey, you want to hear a great joke my brother tells every time he comes to visit?"

Her hands and arms tired, she stretched out on his back and whispered an obnoxiously dirty joke in his ear. He laughed, but knowing he was an old soul, Natalia thought he would have appreciated it more, coming from a man. Even at twenty-eight, Marc was a gentleman.

"Okay, because I love you, I promise not to swear for the rest of our short time together."

"I'll believe that when I hear it," he said, laughing.

She reached over him to take the picture from his hand. "Double holy shit! She's absolutely gorgeous."

"I told you it wasn't a good idea for you to see her."

"How the hell does someone get to look like that?"

"Simone may be beautiful, in the traditional blonde, blue eyed way, but she's never done to me what you just did to me, what I hope you'll do to me again. And she never will."

Natalia leaned over and put the picture back on the nightstand. "What does she—"

He twisted himself around, rolling her off his back, reversing their positions. Now behind her, he whispered in *her* ear, "No more about Simone."

His arms circled her waist, and he nibbled on her neck. Then his hands cupped her breasts and caressed them. Not moving his left hand from her breast, he trailed his right hand down between her legs, pausing then staying there. She let out a small groan, loving the way his hands and mouth moved over her. He always knew where and how to touch and kiss her, and she was helpless in his arms.

The next thing she knew she was on her belly, his fingers slowly drifting down her back. Giving her a tender love pat on her backside, he trailed his mouth along her spine. The sensation of his kisses traveling up her back left her breathless.

Turning to face him, she wrapped her arms around his neck and kissed him then eased him onto his back. As her tongue left his mouth, she let it glide over his lips, exploring his body from top to bottom. She nestled her head between his legs and felt his hands in her hair, tugging it gently.

"Baby, you're making me crazy," he gasped. "Have some mercy."

Natalia let him lift her toward him and onto her back. Impatient for the amazing things his body would do to hers, she pulled him inside her. Her legs tangled with his. He weaved his fingers around hers and pinned her hands on the sides of her head.

At first, he moved slowly, thrusting deep inside her, then quickened his pace. She arched her back as they were engulfed in love and togetherness once more.

♨♨

"I'm starving," Natalia announced as she got out of bed. "Mariella left food in the refrigerator. You're the chef. You heat up the food. I'll get the wine."

Marc lounged in bed with his arms behind his head. "I called in sick from work, remember? Anyway, I'd rather watch you walk around au natural. What are you looking for? "

"I'm cold. Where are my clothes? And if you don't want the food burnt instead of warm, I'd get up if I were you."

He laughed. "If you're cold, come back to bed." Pushing the blankets aside, he patted the spot on the bed beside him. "I'll get you something to put on—for a kiss."

The offer was hard to resist. He was deliciously good-looking, with his curly hair and brown eyes, broad shoulders, and strong arms. Not to mention what was still underneath the covers.

"Well, you are pretty cute. How can I refuse?" She climbed back in bed and curled into the heat of his body.

He lifted her face up to his and kissed her.

Her stomach made a loud growl.

"Sorry." She giggled. "When I'm hungry there's nothing I can do about it."

"Did you say something? I'm having trouble hearing you. Odd time of the year for thunder, don't you think?"

Still laughing, she pushed him out of bed.

"Wait here." He slipped his jeans on. When he returned, he took her hand and plucked her out of bed. "Put this on," he said, holding open his shirt for her. With her arms in the sleeves, he twirled her around to face him and buttoned the shirt from the bottom up, stopping to leave the top half open. "You look sexy in my shirt."

She stood on her tiptoes and kissed him. "Thanks, but right now I feel more hungry than sexy.

♨♨

Marc and Natalia rustled around the kitchen then hurried back to bed with plates of lasagna, salad, olive oil to dip their warm bread in, and a bottle of wine.

"Everything smells and tastes delicious," she said. "As much as I love Italian food, I could go for a thick, juicy steak, baked potatoes, mushrooms—you know, the works."

"The next time I cook for you, I'll make you the best steak you ever had. I have a secret marinade I use."

"You're promising to cook me a meal when you're going to forget you promised?"

"I'll remember. I'm not forgetting anything. If you want to keep the appointment with Dr. Ellis, go ahead. I don't want her or anyone else in my head."

He ripped off a small piece of bread. Dipping in the oil, he raised it to her lips. She opened her mouth, but took the bread in her hand and licked the garlic and oil from his fingers.

"Nice try," he said. "But don't try to distract me because you don't want to hear what I'm saying. After these past months of being confused about Simone, I'm finally thinking clearly, and I know what I want." Natalia started to interrupt him. "I'm not talking about this anymore," he told her firmly.

She sat staring straight ahead, gritting her teeth. He knew her mind was crammed with a vast amount of obscenities, all directed at him, but she was biting her tongue.

He couldn't help but smile. "Would you like more to eat?"

"Yes, some warm bread."

"I figured as much." When he came back with her food, she was pouring them more wine. He knew her heart and soul better than anyone, and after these last couple of hours, he knew every inch of her wonderful body. What he didn't know was about her life.

"Now it's your turn," he said, climbing in next to her. "All I know about you is that you own a vineyard, play a mean game of poker, have a ferocious appetite, and prefer top shelf whiskey. All qualities I admire, but I'm sure there's more to tell."

"No, not really. I went to college and came to work at the vineyard. I almost got married once. I would like to have a baby—"

"Me, too. See we're—"

She put her hand over his mouth. "But I know my age is working against me. Every time I turn around, I hear how old and decrepit my eggs are. Another reason you should meet with Dr. Ellis tomorrow and see what happens with Simone. My biological clock might be broken."

He removed her hand from his mouth. "There's nothing old and decrepit about you," he said, kissing her. "Simone may be able to give me a baby, but she won't. She's been very clear. At least you and I are on the same page. We could adopt."

"You're really starting to piss me off."

"I'll give you credit. You held your tongue longer than I thought you would," he teased. "When did you *almost* get married?"

"At the end of September. His name was Jacob. I'd rather not talk about it. It's embarrassing what a fool I was."

"I told you everything about Simone."

"I know, but she's in your life now. He's gone and you and I don't have much time left. I don't want to spend it talking about Jacob."

Fair enough." Marc took hold of her shoulders and turned her to face him. "I'm glad you didn't get married. Don't you see? My marriage is over and you never got married. The time is right. We're supposed to be together."

"Marc, please. You don't know that."

"Yes, I do."

She put her empty plate on the nightstand and yawned. "I know it's only eight o'clock but could we close our eyes for a few minutes? I'm exhausted. I haven't been sleeping any better."

"Sure, baby. I'm tired too. Having you on my mind lately has kept me tossing and turning."

She snuggled next to him, and he pulled the covers over them. There was a soft glow from the fireplace. Marc hit the switch so the lights dimmed, but didn't go off. He put his arms around her, holding her tightly, thinking how nice it was to lie there together.

"A nap it is," he said and closed his eyes.

♨♨

"Nat. Nat, wake up."

Natalia was comfortable and warm and didn't understand why she had to get up. They couldn't have been asleep more than an hour.

Marc was shaking her. "Nat, it's eleven in the morning. We slept fifteen hours."

"What? Holy sh—" She saw him standing there with a cup coffee. "—Cow. Holy cow. I'm sorry. I wanted a short nap. Jes...um...geez, I'm such a loser. I get to spend one night with you, and I sleep instead."

"Nat." He laughed, apparently at her struggle with word choices, "I told you to be yourself. It's fine. More importantly, we'll have plenty of nights together." He handed her a cup of coffee and climbed back into bed.

She sipped her coffee. "Wow, this is delicious. Thank you."

"So I brought you coffee in bed, no kiss for that?"

"Ugh, fifteen hour morning breath, just a minute." She got out of bed and went into the bathroom.

"That's what you're worried about? I had no trouble kissing your potty mouth."

"What potty mouth? I'm reformed."

She was brushing her teeth when he walked in. "How about a shower?" He asked, winking. She turned and smiled, but before she could answer him, he had her shirt unbuttoned and was kissing her.

♨♨

"Nat, I think you're trying to kill me," Marc said. "You give new meaning to the term *lather up*. I'll never look at a bar of soap the same."

A large bath towel wrapped the two of them together as they stood in the steamy and foggy bathroom. "I'm glad you enjoyed it as much as I did," she said with a twinkle in her eye. Laying her head on his chest, she tightened her grip around him.

"What's wrong, baby?"

"I'm sorry, but we need to talk about keeping this appointment with Dr. Ellis."

"Nat, this isn't your decision to make for me. I know how I feel about my marriage and Simone."

"So what's your plan? To blindside Simone with divorce papers when she returns? Is that fair?"

"I've already started the paperwork. I doubt she'll be blindsided."

"You don't know that. What if it's the wake-up call she needs to realize she doesn't want to lose you? She deserves a chance to have her say. I promise if you both decide it's not going to work, I'll be on your doorstep before you can say my name. But you can't make an honest decision with our past and present relationship in your head."

"You'll be in Connecticut with no memory of me."

"That's not true. We'll still know each other. Every other time, we've known how connected we are. We'll feel it again, I'm sure of it. We've been through too much together."

"And? I know you not telling me everything. What else is bothering you?"

"You do know me too well." She brushed her lips against his and put her arms around his neck. "It's hard to explain, but I feel we need to do things right this time. In the past, we did what we wanted, not caring about the consequences. People were badly hurt, killed."

"Are you thinking of offing Simone?" he quipped. "Because I wasn't."

"No." She gave him a smirk. "I'm not up to hurting anyone this time."

"You can't compare those times to now. We did what we had to in order to survive under difficult circumstances. There were babies at stake both times."

"I know but I still think we need to set things straight. Please come with me. We need to do this together. It's our karmic debt."

"Baby, I can't. I don't want to forget you. We just found each other."

"Marc, I love you with my whole heart and soul, and I wouldn't ask you if it wasn't important to me. I know it's hard. I don't want to forget you either, but it's the right thing to do."

He held her close, taking in her softness and warmth. Deep down, he knew he always had, and always would, do anything for her—but not this. He wouldn't lie to her. He'd agree to talk to Dr. Ellis, but he refused to erase his time with Natalia from his mind. Past or present.

"I love you too, baby. All right, I'll come with you."

♨♨

When Marc and Natalia walked into Dr. Ellis' office, Mariella was standing there. She immediately gave Natalia a warm embrace.

"Are you okay, dear? I know this is hard, after all you've been through."

"Mariella, I'm so sorry about last night. It was completely my fault."

"Natalia, stop it!" Marc snapped as he walked up behind her, taking a firm hold on her shoulders. "We've already talked about this."

"I'm not upset with anyone," Mariella said. "Some things are out of our control, and I believe this is one of those times. Whatever is destined to happen, will happen, and none of us can stop it."

They heard the door open and Dr. Ellis walked in. "Good afternoon, everyone. Are we ready to get started?"

Marc didn't answer, but Natalia quickly answered yes.

"Okay, here's the next step. You know firsthand that you never forget anything. It's all in your subconscious. As I told you yesterday, you're in control during hypnosis. I can't put ideas in your head, but I can suggest things. That's what I'll be doing today. My suggestion will be for you to put your past lives, as well as any other intimate memories you have of each other, in a certain part of your subconscious. Then I'll ask you not to go there to retrieve them. However, it's just a suggestion. There's no guarantee these memories won't come back. At first, it may start as bits and pieces and eventually everything may come back. The likelihood is greater for you two. You share an extremely deep bond, and your attachment to each other is much stronger than any suggestion I can give you."

"That's what I'm counting on, Doc," Marc said, hoping any instructions Dr. Ellis gave Natalia to forget wouldn't last long.

"Who would like to go first?"

"I'll go," Natalia said facing Marc. "I love you."

He squeezed her hands and nodded. No words would come from his mouth. She walked into another room with Dr. Ellis and shut the door.

When she walked out a little while later, she looked surprised to see Marc sitting there.

"Hi, Marc, what are you doing here?"

He thought he'd be able to handle her speaking to him as a casual friend instead of someone she had just given her body and soul to, but it felt like he'd gotten the wind knocked out of him. He forced the words out. "I was visiting Mariella before I have to go to work."

Mariella led Natalia to the door. "So, dear how did you sleep last night. That was your last session with Dr. Ellis. I hope your treatments here have helped."

"Actually, last night was the best sleep I've had in a while."

"I'm happy for you, dear," Mariella said as they walked out.

Marc sat on the couch with his head down, not wanting to watch her leave. When Dr. Ellis told him she was ready, he didn't get up right away. Instead, he wrote a note on a piece of paper, on the small chance Dr. Ellis changed his mind— although he doubted it—and put it in his wallet.

He walked into her office.

"Hi, Doc. I'm sorry for taking up your time, but I don't want to go through with this."

♨♨

Marc saw Mariella and Natalia in the lobby as he walked out of the elevator. He wasn't sure how to play his hand. Even though she'd been surprised to see him after her session with Dr. Ellis, he decided to be himself.

"Hi, Natalia."

"Marc, I just saw you upstairs. Are you following me?" she asked with a smile.

"Oh, look at the weather," said Mariella. "It's sleeting out. Why don't you two share a cab? Dear, are you catching the next train to Southeast?"

"Yes, I don't have a schedule, but they should be running every hour or so now."

"Marcos, are you going to work?"

"Yes."

It took some time standing in the sleet, but they finally flagged down a cab. Despite the umbrella Mariella had given them, they were soaked when they sat down in the back seat.

"Where to?" The cabbie asked.

"I'm going to Tremonti's restaurant on Fifty-Fourth Street then onto Grand Central for the lovely lady here." Marc faced Natalia. "So do you have plans for the weekend?" he asked, fighting hard not to touch her.

"No. I've been down here for a week. I'm going to relax and get some sleep. I hope the weather is nicer. If it's sleeting here, it's snowing up by me." The automatic message regarding seatbelts came on. Natalia snapped hers on.

"I would like to come to Connecticut and see your vineyard. If you're not up to it this weekend, I could come next weekend."

"Wait until spring when it's nicer weather before you and your wife visit. There used to be an inn on the property, and I still rent some rooms out. You can stay 'on the house.'"

Then everything went black.

CHAPTER 17

"True memories are not of mind and body, but those that remain forever written on the soul."
– *Elizabeth Barrett Browning, 1806-1861 English Poet*

Natalia opened her eyes to a throbbing headache. Had she'd been drinking? She didn't think so. Was her brother in town? She couldn't remember.

"Ouch," she moaned. "What the—?"

Mariella interrupted her before the onslaught of obscenities started. "Natalia, it's me, Mariella."

"Mariella?" She looked in the direction of Mariella's voice. "What the hell happened? I feel like I got hit by a frigging bus."

"It was a garbage truck, dear."

"Didn't I just leave your place? I feel like sh—um—I really don't feel good." *'Baby, must you, with the language all the time?'* She heard Marc's voice in her head.

"After you and Marcos left, you had a terrible accident. Your cab was behind a garbage truck when a bike messenger swerved in front of it. The truck driver slammed on his brakes. When the cab driver tried to stop, he slid on the icy roads and crashed into the back of the garbage truck."

"Oh my God! Is Marc okay?"

"Yes, he's in another room. Simone is with him."

"Can I see him?"

"I don't think it's a good idea for you to get up right now. You both were banged up pretty good. You had your seatbelt on. Marc didn't."

For a reason she didn't understand, a fear of Marc being hurt seized her in the gut. A strong reaction for someone she didn't know very well. "You said he was okay, though?"

"He is, don't worry. Let me tell the nurses you're awake."

A nurse arrived a few minutes later, took her vital signs, and asked her a few questions.

"On a scale of one to ten, how much pain are you in?"

"I don't know," answered Natalia. "Maybe a six or seven. I have a splitting headache, and my whole body is sore."

"You're very lucky you don't have a concussion. You can thank your seatbelt for that. Your friend didn't have his seatbelt on. You'll be fine but sore for the next few days."

"Marc didn't have his seatbelt on? He's all right, isn't he?"

She noticed the nurse and Mariella exchange a glance.

"Yes, he's fine. Let me help you to the bathroom."

When she'd finished using the facilities, the nurse helped her back to bed and hooked her IV up to the pain medication.

"The medicine will make you drowsy," she told Natalia. "But rest is the best thing for you right now."

"Mariella, please, what aren't you telling me about Marc?" As hard as Natalia tried, her efforts at battling the drowsiness from her IV drip failed her. "Mari..." She was asleep.

When she woke up, she'd lost track of time and had no idea what day it was. Her sleep had been restless, troubled, and filled with strange dreams about Marc.

A different nurse came in to see her. "I'm glad to see you're awake. Hungry?" When Natalia nodded, the nurse smiled. "Good. They'll be coming with your breakfast soon."

"It's morning? How long have I been here?"

"It's Wednesday morning, February thirteenth. You had your accident late yesterday afternoon. You woke up last evening for a few minutes then slept all night. Besides being hungry, which is a good sign, how do you feel?"

"I guess a little better than yesterday. Some parts are still foggy. I can't seem to get a clear picture of certain things."

"It's probably the pain medication."

"Can we stop it? I don't like all these weird things going on in my head."

"I'll have to ask the doctor. He'll be in to see you soon. Mariella Tremonti has been looking after you. Is there someone else you'd like to call? I can get your cell for you. It's in the locker."

"Yes, thank you."

"Look, here's your breakfast now."

A pleasant looking older woman came in and set the tray on her small table. She poured her some coffee and handed it to her.

'Nat, Nat. Wake up. We slept fifteen hours.'

"Thank you." Natalia took the cup, burrowed down in her bed, and wondered about all the things going on in her head. "Is Mariella in her nephew's room?"

"Yes, she arrived a little while ago."

"Can you ask her to come here, please? Thank you."

♨♨

Natalia glanced up when Mariella knocked on the door then walked in.

"Good morning, dear. It's good to see you up and eating. How do you feel?"

"Better than yesterday, but I'm confused. I'm having strange thoughts, and I don't understand them."

"Well, you *did* hit your head hard."

"I don't think I did. I had my seatbelt on. That's what the nurse said. Has Marc asked about me?"

"No, I'm sorry, he hasn't."

"I thought we were friends. It is because of Simone? I know I've never met her, but she couldn't possibly be upset if he wanted to see how the person he was in the accident with was doing."

"No, that wouldn't upset her."

"Why can't I see him?"

Mariella pulled a chair over next to the bed and took her hand. "Natalia, he doesn't remember anything or anyone, not Simone, or me. He received a hard blow to the head. The doctors think its temporary, but he isn't going to know who you are. Simone is having a hard time with it, and he's very frustrated. I think you should stay here and not add another face he's supposed to know. It'll upset him more."

Natalia leaned back in bed and tried to absorb what Mariella told her. She would do what the woman asked. For now. "Okay, I'll wait to see him. Thanks for telling me. I'm getting tired again.

I'd like to rest." Turning on her side, she waited for Mariella to leave.

When she was gone, Natalia called her parents in Florida and assured them she was fine. Her brother Robbie wasn't home, so she left him a message. She talked to Christine and Ellie and told them not to come visit her in the hospital. She wouldn't be good company right now and would see them when she got home. The last person she called was Sam.

"Hey kid, what happened down there? Mariella called and left a message. She must have gotten the vineyard number from the paperwork going back and forth. I was going to give you a few more hours, and then I was going to call you."

"Thanks, Sam. When they release me to go home, can you pick me up?"

"Of course, Nat. Whatever you need, you know that."

"I know. What would I do without you?"

"Just let me know where, and when to be there."

After dinner, Natalia decided to get up even though the nurses had specifically asked her not to. Screw them! And Mariella. She wanted to see Marc. After successfully making her way down the hall to Marc's room without the nurses noticing her, she looked through the small window in the door. There was a dim light on, but he had no visitors. He had his back to her. Was he asleep?

She tiptoed in and softly said, "Hello." If he *was* asleep, it shouldn't wake him.

He rolled over. At first, all she saw was his bruised, swollen face but soon got past that. He stared at her. As she looked into his eyes, everything came flooding back. Her heart raced. It felt as if a tsunami had crashed over her. She started to tremble. Her legs were shaking so badly, she didn't think they would hold her up. Stumbling backwards, she leaned against the wall so she wouldn't fall down.

"Are you okay?" he asked. "Do you want me to call the nurse?"

"No," she squeaked out. "I'm sorry. I should go."

"No. Wait, please come here."

She couldn't put one foot in front of the other, so she stood there.

"You took the trouble to come to my room, why won't you come in? Who are you?"

"My name is Natalia."

He continued to stare. "You know out of all the people who've come in here, you're the only one who seems familiar to me. Do I know you?"

"We were in the cab together when it had the accident."

"Oh. I'm sorry. Are you okay?"

She tried to pull herself together. The last thing she wanted was for him to see her like this.

"I think I'm a little better than you. They told me you weren't wearing your seatbelt."

"Yeah, I know."

"What the hell's wrong with you?

"You're actually going to yell at me right now?"

"It was stupid."

"If you were sitting there with me, why didn't you yell at me then?"

Then he started to laugh, and she saw him cringe from pain. Her heart ached, seeing him in such agony. She wanted to wrap him in her arms, but she didn't dare touch him.

"Finally," he said. "Someone who speaks her mind without worrying she's going to upset me. So, you know me. How about my wife?"

"I know your Aunt Mariella. I've never met you wife."

She wasn't up to spending any more time with him and wanted to leave before she burst into tears. "Well, good night. I just wanted to see how you were. Mariella says your memory loss is temporary. I'm sure you'll be yourself in a day or two."

"Will you come back and visit me again? I would like you to tell me how we know each other."

"I don't know. I'll try." She wasn't even out the door before the tears ran down her cheeks. The real sobbing didn't start until she was back in bed, alone in the dark.

The nurse came in to check on her and heard her whimpering. "Sweetie, why didn't you call us and tell us you were in this much pain? Is that what's the matter?"

"Yes." But it wasn't the physical pain that was making her cry. She welcomed the pill that would help her escape the real cause. She remembered everything. All their past lives, the night they spent together, everything. Marc didn't even know who she was.

When Mariella poked her head in Natalia's room the next day, Natalia couldn't hide how upset she was.

"What's wrong, dear?" Mariella asked.

"I went to see him last night."

Mariella sighed. "I told you not to."

"I couldn't help it."

"He didn't know you, did he?"

"No."

"Well, you knew that. Why are you taking it so hard?"

"I remember everything," Natalia whispered as her eyes began to fill.

"What do you mean *everything?*"

"I remember Marc, his birthmark, our regression, and everything that happened afterwards. I even remember walking into Dr. Ellis' office so I would forget. But here I am with a crystal clear memory."

Mariella let out another sigh. "I was afraid this might happen. Although, I'm not sure your memory coming back is all due to the accident. I think you two would have started to remember sooner rather than later."

"I'm sick to my stomach with guilt for sleeping with him. That's the only thing I'm glad he doesn't remember."

"Natalia, we've been through this, and you need to get a hold of yourself."

"It was wrong, and I knew it. I wasn't strong enough," she continued, as tears flowed down her face.

"You weren't the only one in the room. Acting like a martyr isn't going to change anything."

"Mariella!"

"I'm sorry, dear. Things are very complicated. I'm sure you know Marc started divorce proceedings. But after the accident, the hospital notified Simone because she's still his wife. She told me seeing Marc lying there injured made her rethink her priorities. I think she may actually want to work things out—after months of skirting the issue. Of course, she doesn't know Marc called a lawyer, and he doesn't remember."

Natalia needed to pull herself together. After all, this is what she wanted, for Marc and Simone to try working things out, barring any obstacles. Of course, she was supposed to be unaware of all of this, back to her life at the vineyard, thinking Marc just a friend. Something had gone terribly wrong with her plan.

She grabbed the tissue box, blew her nose, wiped her eyes, and took a deep breath.

"I apologize for all my slobbering," she said. "I know you're in a tough spot, Mariella. Simone is probably aware the conversation they had the other morning didn't go well, so maybe you could gently prepare her for what's coming. Other than that, it's none of my business. I'm going home tomorrow."

Mariella gently embraced her. "I'm sorry all this is happening, dear. I know how much you love him. Stay strong. Remember, whatever is supposed to happen, will. It always does."

After Mariella left, Natalia was determined not to let this situation turn her into a sniveling, helpless crybaby. She couldn't remember the last time she'd cried this much. She was on her own and had to take care of herself. Deciding she needed some closure—and she hoped it would ease her conscious—she opted to meet Simone and wish her and Marc well before leaving the hospital. Yes. She needed to face the situation head on.

She walked into the bathroom and looked in the mirror. Ugh! Her eyes were swollen and red, her hair greasy and lying flat against her head. After washing her face and pulling a brush through her dirty mane, she ventured back down the hall.

When she peered in Marc's room, she saw Simone and Mariella standing next to his bed. The pictures didn't do Simone justice. She was even lovelier in person. She was impeccably dressed, her hair and make-up perfect. Natalia stood there—a mess, in her baggy hospital gown and bathrobe—feeling as though she was about to do something foolish. She knocked on the door and walked in anyway.

"Excuse me," she said quietly.

Marc looked up. "Natalia?"

"Hi."

"You *know* who she is?" Simone demanded, apparently stunned, although, Natalia didn't think it sounded like an accusation—more like she was hopeful his memory was coming back.

"No," he said. "She came here last night to see how I was. She was in the cab with me when we had the accident. I thought she seemed familiar, but the doctor said it was probably because she was the last person I talked to before the crash. I don't remember her, just a vague familiarity. She knows my aunt."

Natalia walked toward Simone with her hand out. "Hi. I'm Natalia Santagario."

Simone smiled and shook her hand.

That's when it happened. It was subtle, but the sensation was there. At first, Natalia thought her regression may have made her more sensitive, but Simone realized something as well. Natalia felt her jump slightly, as if she had been startled when they touched, then Simone gave her a curious look, obviously not understanding what had passed between them.

Natalia wasn't sure if Simone was friend or foe, but they had definitely known each other in another life.

Simone quickly composed herself, adjusting her skirt and playing with her hair, and asked Natalia how she knew Marc.

"I own a vineyard in Connecticut, and Mariella buys wine from me for her Center. I was leaving a meeting with Mariella when Marc and I decided to share a cab."

"Do you remember the accident?"

"Actually we were talking about you two coming to spend the weekend at the vineyard this spring. It used to be an inn, and I always keep a few rooms ready. Then I woke up here."

"That's very kind of you. Maybe we'll be able to take you up on your offer someday."

Sorry, the offer is null and void. "I better get back to my room," Natalia said to Marc. "I just wanted to see how you were."

"Thanks," he said with a smile.

♨♨

After dinner, Natalia decided she needed a shower. As she stepped into the small stall, she realized how much this shower was going to suck, compared to her last one with Marc. She let the hot water beat down on her back. It felt good. Shampooing her hair was almost like heaven. Almost.

After blow-drying her hair, she tried to cover up her bruises with makeup. Putting on a clean gown, she told herself the only reason she was going to see him was to say good-bye. She was leaving tomorrow. After checking herself in the mirror one last time, she made another trek down the hall.

This time he was alone. She knocked and walked in. Marc turned over and a smile came to his face. "Hi," he said. "Don't you look much better?"

"Thanks. A shower can do wonders for your soul. How's your memory?"

"It's the same. Everyone's frustrated, and I'm getting discouraged. They all bring pictures and videos but nothing comes to me. I'm sure they mean well, but it's like I'm outside looking into a crystal ball at a life that I don't remember."

"I think your being too hard on yourself. It's only been a couple of days. Maybe you're over-thinking it. Take a break and give your brain a rest." She hesitated. "When's Simone coming back?"

"She's not."

"Aren't spouses allowed to spend the night?"

"Yes, but she isn't resting well here. I thought a little alone time might be good."

"I'll leave you then." Natalia turned to leave.

"No. Don't go. You don't keep questioning me about 'the time we did this' or 'remember when we did that?' Some peaceful company would be nice."

She went to the other side of the bed and sat in the chair. He was on his right side, his back to her. He didn't roll over to face her, so she waited.

Finally, he said, "This is going to seem like an odd request, and if you're uncomfortable, I understand. Could you open the back of my gown and look at my left shoulder?"

Natalia was speechless.

"I'm sorry," he said when she didn't respond. "I shouldn't have asked, but I don't know what they're talking about. The doctors think I have a very unusual birthmark. They've never seen anything like it. Evidently my wife was appalled when I got some sort of tattoo."

"No, it's okay. I'll do it. " Natalia sighed. She didn't have to open his gown to tell him what was there. But he didn't know that. So, with a wavering hand, she undid the tie of his gown and pulled it off his shoulder.

"Well?"

"I think it's beautiful," she said softly. "The tattoo is of two colorful flames entwined together." Despite her earlier proclamation to stop crying, the tears flowed freely down her face. It was useless to fight them and she knew it. "You have a port wine birthmark with a few different brown marks in the middle of it, that's all."

"It's not horrible looking?"

"No, not at all. It's part of who you are." Afraid she couldn't trust herself not to kiss his birthmark, she pulled his gown up over his shoulder and retied it.

"Thanks," he said. "Would you mind sitting here with me a few more minutes? This is the calmest and most relaxed I've felt since I got here. The nurse gave me pain medication, and I can feel it starting to work. I would like you to stay if you don't mind." He kept his back to her.

"Sure."

In a few minutes, he was breathing heavy and snoring lightly. She got up to leave, but before she did, she leaned over and kissed his shoulder through his gown.

"Good-bye," she whispered in his ear. "I love you." He started to stir as if he heard her words. She quietly crept away and left his room.

Sam would be here in the morning, and she and Marc would go their separate ways. She hoped he'd remember Simone, work things out, and be happy. As for her, all she could hope was her memories would fade, and at the very least, she'd be content with her life.

CHAPTER 18

"Friends will keep you sane, Love could fill your heart, a lover can warm your bed, but lonely is the soul without a mate." – *David Pratt*

When Natalia walked into her kitchen, she was greeted by a vase of fresh flowers on the table. "Oh, Sam, they're beautiful. Thank you."

"I wish I could take credit, but they're from Robbie. I did go to your favorite restaurant and buy a few dinners, though. They're in the freezer. I want you to rest and get back on your feet."

She was so touched, her eyes filled.

He put his arms around her. "Nat, what's wrong? This isn't like you."

"I'm sorry, Sam. It's been a difficult week. First, I was exhausted, and then we had the accident. I'll be back to my obnoxious self soon, don't worry."

He laughed. "Well, I must admit it hasn't been the same around here without your *lively* personality. I feel badly I didn't get the chance to meet and thank Mariella for calling me."

"We have a solid business arrangement with her. You'll meet her soon enough." She changed the subject. "Sam, please come back later and have dinner with me. I would love the company."

"Sure. Go relax and I'll be back soon."

Still sore from being jostled around in the cab, she curled up on her couch with a blanket. A cool breeze swirled around her head. She couldn't help but smile.

"Hi, there. I missed you, too."

Giovanna's presence churned around a little faster.

"Don't get excited. I'm fine." Natalia giggled. The chilly breeze flew by her face. She crossed her arms and cocked her eyebrow. "No, I don't want to talk about Marc. You still haven't told me how you know about him."

She felt a flurry of activity around the room. "All right. All right. He's fine. Don't worry. You need to drop it, though. I won't be seeing him anymore."

The two pillows on the end of the couch, and the magazines on the coffee table, flew to the floor. Natalia heard the door to the kitchen slam shut. Giovanna was gone.

"Drama queen," Natalia said and closed her eyes.

♨♨

Over the next couple of weeks, Natalia started feeling better—physically. She threw herself into her work. There was plenty to do to get the gift and wine shop ready to open in the spring.

Christine and Ellie came to visit once a week, and one night they ventured into town for dinner. Natalia tried to have a good time and enjoy their company, but her thoughts kept wandering to Marc.

"Nat! We're talking to you." Ellie frowned. "Have you heard a word I said?"

Startled, Natalia apologized. "I don't mean to be such bad company."

"Please tell us what happened in the city," said Christine. "You aren't yourself, and we miss you. Maybe we can help."

"There's nothing to tell. I went to get help for my sleep problems then I had that stupid accident. I think I have the winter blues, that's all. I'm always restless this time of the year."

"This isn't being restless," said Ellie. "You're sad all the time. You can tell us. We're your best friends."

"I know and I appreciate it. If there was something to tell you, I would. How about we get out of here and go see a movie? My treat."

♨♨

Marc was in a room full of people, but he felt lonely and disheartened. According to the pictures and videos he'd been made to look at, time and time again, these people where his family and friends.

His wish to remember his life was two-fold. First, it would make life easier if he knew the woman with whom he was living and sleeping. As of now, it was awkward at best. Even more so, since—soon after Marc came home—a man showed up at the door with a large manila envelope and asked to see his wife. The envelope was addressed to Simone, and its return address indicated it was from a local law firm. Simone was visibly upset, and Mariella ushered her into another room. When they came out, his wife was calmer and explained to him that it was a work-related matter.

Second, he assumed that after his memory returned, everyone would finally leave him alone. For the past month, it had been the same thing. More people, more pictures, more questions. But no answers came to him.

He stood abruptly and went upstairs. He didn't want to be rude. They seemed like nice people and their intentions were good, but he'd had enough. Alone in his bedroom, he sat down on the edge of the bed and thought about Natalia.

Over the past four weeks, she'd popped into his head at the weirdest times—not that he minded. He often thought of her and hoped she was well. There was something different about her. He wondered how well he had known her. She was the only one who was even vaguely familiar to him. But she wasn't in any of the pictures he'd seen. No one mentioned her except for the one time Tony and Giuseppe asked Mariella how she was. Marc never asked about her, thinking it was inappropriate to ask about Natalia when he didn't remember his own wife.

His wife—he let out a sigh. Simone was going away for a ten-day business trip. Regretfully, he was somewhat relieved she was leaving. After last weekend and this past week, maybe some time apart was what they needed.

His doctors thought a change of scenery might do him good. Marc agreed. He didn't think staying in the house, where a life he couldn't remember surrounded him, was a good idea. He'd ask Mariella if he could use the apartment above the restaurant. It would be easier for work, not that work was going any better than the rest of his life.

He could drop by at Mariella's center and maybe, if he was lucky, he'd see Natalia. In the hospital, he had heard her say she'd been in the city for a meeting with Mariella. He had a few questions regarding the accident, and she was the only one who could answer them. Yes, a few days in the city were just what he needed to feel better.

♨♨

The middle of March was unseasonably warm. Natalia welcomed the opportunity to work outside, cleaning up from the winter on the vineyard grounds. She loved the change from winter to spring. A fresh start, a new beginning—just what she needed.

Her friends, Rachel and Bob, owned a catering company and rented out the space where the inn once was. They had a few bookings for March, and she was looking forward to the excitement, as well the people these events would bring to the vineyard. A small part of her hope for the chance to meet someone new. Although the other, larger part knew it was impossible. Marc was always front and center in her mind and heart. Could you really ever forget your other half?

Shaken from her thoughts by the cell phone vibrating in her pocket, she flipped it open.

"Natalia?" asked a familiar voice.

"Mariella?"

"Yes, dear."

"How is...everything?"

"Marcos is fine dear, physically anyway. His memory hasn't returned, and it's been stressful for everyone."

"I'm sorry to hear that." She refused to feel any empathy for him. He wasn't hers to worry about. "Is the wine arriving like it's supposed to?"

"Yes, and we've had quite a few compliments as well." Mariella hesitated a moment. "Simone is going away for a week or so. I'm picking Marcos up. He wants to stay in the apartment above the restaurant."

"What do you mean pick him up?"

"Marcos and Simone live in New Jersey."

Natalia was surprised at how much she didn't know about his life. She always saw him in the city and assumed that's where he lived.

"I can't imagine what any of this has to do with me."

"He would like to see you. He has a few questions about the accident."

"I've told him everything there was to tell." Natalia felt something tug at the work gloves she had tucked in her jeans back pockets. The next thing she knew, the gloves were at her feet and a breeze was in her face. She asked Mariella to hold on.

"Stay out of this. I'm warning you," Natalia said to the emptiness of the outdoors. She reached down to pick up her gloves. They shot across the ground out of her reach. "I'm not going to see him and that's final." She took a few steps and leaned over for her gloves and, again, they moved out of her grasp. Exasperated, she shouted, "Keep the damn gloves. I'm done for today anyway."

Natalia walked back toward the house, resuming her conversation with Mariella.

"Natalia, who were you talking to?"

"No one important. I'm sorry Mariella, but there's nothing more I can do for Marc." Natalia turned off her phone and went inside.

The next day when a strange car pulled up outside of her house, she wasn't necessarily surprised.

"Mariella, I said no and I mean it. It's a busy time here. I couldn't possibly leave right now."

"Natalia, I'm sure everyone who works here is very capable or you wouldn't have hired them. Don't be such a control freak."

"*I'm* a control freak? You're here to practically kidnap me."

Mariella laughed. "You do know me too well, don't you, dear?" She walked toward the men working in the vineyard. "Excuse me, who's in charge here?"

"I am," said Sam.

"Hello, I'm Mariella Tremonti."

"It's good to finally meet you," he said, extending his hand. "I'm Sam Belfry. I wanted to thank you for calling me about

Nat's accident. When I picked her up from the hospital, she said it was better not to bother you. I am grateful, though."

"It's nice to meet you, Sam. Natalia speaks fondly of you. Thank you for persuading Natalia to have your wine at my Center. We've had a wonderful response to it."

"I'm glad. We work hard to make a good wine."

Mariella sighed. "I'm here because I need Natalia's help with something in the city. But she thinks she can't possibly leave today."

Sam laughed. Natalia glared at him.

"Mariella," he said. "May I call you Mariella?"

"Of course."

"Nat likes to think she's useful, but lately, she's just in the way. She isn't herself and has been in a foul mood since she came home from the hospital. I don't know what's wrong with her. She won't talk about it." He chuckled. "I love her, but please take her. It might do her good." He walked away, still chuckling.

Revenge will be mine, Sam. Just you wait.

"Get in the car, dear," Mariella said.

♨♨

"Natalia, your vineyard is beautiful. Maybe the next time I visit, Sam could give me a tour. He's quite attractive—in a rugged kind of way."

Natalia had ridden in silence since leaving the vineyard, but this was the last thing she had expected Mariella to say.

She laughed. "Actually, you and Sam would make a perfect couple, Mariella. He's just as stubborn as you."

"I'm glad you think so." Mariella smiled.

Natalia retreated back behind her façade of silence until they started across the George Washington Bridge, and Mariella spoke again. "I was wondering if we could talk about the date your last life ended, November twenty-first, eighteen seventy-seven."

"Please, Mariella. I didn't want to relive it with Dr. Ellis, and I don't want to go there with you."

"I know, dear. Just let me say one thing, and we won't speak of it again."

"Why do you bother to ask?"

"Marcos got his tattoo on the twenty-first of November last year. It was the Monday before Thanksgiving, and one hundred thirty years to the day of you and Marco...passed."

Natalia stared at her. "I remember him telling me that he had a burning sensation on his shoulder the day he got the tattoo."

"You started not sleeping well around Thanksgiving, right?"

"Yes."

"I wouldn't be surprised if it was the same date."

"Do you have a point to all this?"

"I think you both knew somewhere in your subconscious, your meeting was approaching." When Natalia rolled her eyes, Mariella added, "Just think about it."

"I don't want to think about it. What good did it do for us to meet? Nothing can come of it. I'm trying to get on with my life, but here I am, sitting in your car, going to see him. I don't know how I let myself get into these situations."

"You can't say no, dear. It's that simple."

Sitting in traffic on the upper level of the bridge, Natalia looked out her window at the Hudson River below her. Keeping her eyes on the cold, grey, white-capped water, she said, "You know the night we spent together? Well, we slept for fifteen hours. We were exhausted."

"Are we really going down this guilt-ridden path again?"

"I want you to know it wasn't all about sex. It was so much more than that. It was about *being together* on every level."

"I believe you. I'm sure you felt safe and loved and that you could be your true selves. What's better than that?"

Natalia didn't answer, because there *was* nothing better than that.

Soon after crossing the bridge, they pulled up in front of a beautiful colonial home in a perfectly manicured neighborhood. The house wasn't huge, but it was too big for a couple who probably weren't going to have children.

"Mariella, I don't belong here."

"You're here to help Marcos, that's all.

They got out of the car and rang the doorbell. Simone opened the door looking perfect. Natalia, who'd been snatched from working outside at the vineyard, wore dirty, old, ripped jeans and an even older sweatshirt. She had no makeup on and her hair was pulled back with a rubber band. She looked down at her hands. There was dirt in her fingernails. Great. Just great. She probably had food in her teeth as well.

She knew what was going to happen next, and it did. When the two women looked at each other, the feeling of déjà vu returned. She could tell that Simone felt it as well. Her shoulders dropped, and she let out a small sigh.

Simone gave her a puzzled look, but once again, quickly pulled herself together. "Natalia, right? I'm glad to see you recovered from the accident."

"Thank you."

"Come in." Simone gave Mariella a questioning glance. "I wasn't expecting both of you."

"I had my first visit to the vineyard this morning," Mariella said. "There's some paperwork Natalia has to sign, and I thought it would be easier if I picked her and Marcos up on the same trip, before taking them to the city."

Natalia stepped into the open foyer and admired the décor, especially the chandelier hanging from the ceiling. It was old, rustic, and lit by candles. Mariella and Simone went to the right, but a painting in the small room to the left caught Natalia's eye.

"Natalia, this way," called Simone "the cleaning lady just finished in there."

Natalia turned to say something, but Mariella gave her a warning glance and shook her head.

She heard footsteps coming down the stairs and before she knew it, she was face to face with Marc. Her heart was in her throat. She had to catch her breath.

"Hi, Natalia." Marc smiled. "Does my aunt always work this fast? I told her I wanted to talk to you about the accident, but I wasn't expecting to see you so soon."

"Oh, yes. Mariella is always on top of things."

"I'm sorry I didn't get to say good-bye before you left the hospital. I'm glad to see you're fine. You look good."

Liar, I look like I just got through wrestling with a pig.

"You look much better than the last time I saw you, too. How are you feeling?"

"Okay, I guess. I'm looking forward to a few days in the city."

"Well, let me find Mariella."

"I'll put my stuff in her car," Marc said walking away.

Natalia wandered upstairs and poked her head in the room where she heard Simone and Mariella talking.

"Sorry, Natalia, I have to finish packing for Europe," said Simone. "Come in."

Perfect, I get to spend time in their bedroom. This day was going down the proverbial toilet. Fast. Natalia assumed this was her hell for sleeping with him. Let the punishment continue. She deserved it.

"Simone, I think you're overreacting," said Mariella.

"No, I'm not. He's not even trying. He mopes around all day, and when people come to visit, after a little while he disappears."

"Maybe he needs some peace and quiet to get his head in order?" offered Natalia.

"Natalia, this isn't any of your concern. I'm sure you're trying to help, but you barely know him or anything about the situation."

Mariella shot her a look, and once again, Natalia bit her tongue.

"The other night at my company dinner he wouldn't mingle with anyone," Simone continued. "He sulked all night long. He used to be charming and personable at my work functions. All he could muster up was telling my boss and his wife a filthy joke he thought someone from the Navy told him."

"Can I use your bathroom?" Natalia asked.

"It's down the hall."

Natalia shut the bathroom door, put the lid down on the toilet, and sat. She had needed to get out of the bedroom and away from Simone. It scared Natalia that Marc remembered the joke she'd told him. She wanted him to get better and remember his life, but she didn't think she was up to having him remember her. Not right now, anyway.

When she returned to the bedroom, she waited outside in the hall but could hear Simone and Mariella talking.

"Why don't you two go away together? Have a few days on your own?" asked Mariella.

"We tried last week. It didn't go so well. He couldn't, well, you know."

Natalia walked back into the room. When Simone saw her, she continued. "Except for that one time, things in that department have been going well. He was hesitant at first, of course—to him I was a stranger. But let's just say in the end, I persuaded him."

Natalia wished Simone would zip the damn suitcase—and her mouth—and they could be on their way. "Mariella, it's getting late. I'd like to get back to Connecticut tonight."

"Of course, dear," said Mariella. "If Marcos is ready, we can go."

Marc was already outside by the car when they came out. Simone came over and kissed him hard while Natalia and Mariella stood there, watching uncomfortably.

Her patience already thin, and feeling she had nothing to lose, Natalia let her tongue loose. "Okay, you two, we need to get moving. Either get a room and *try again*, or let's go."

"You told them?" Marc asked and pulled away.

"I was explaining to Mariella the doctors think there's nothing wrong with you except too much stress." Simone glared at Natalia. "*She* must have been eavesdropping."

Mariella shoved Natalia into the backseat of the car.

"What?" Natalia asked innocently. "You're the one who made me come here. Maybe you should think twice next time."

Marc sat in the front with his aunt. He looked back at Natalia. "I didn't want Mariella to make you do something you didn't want to."

Natalia sighed. "It wasn't that. I was a little busy at the vineyard."

Mariella got in the driver's seat and started the car.

"I'm sorry Simone decided to go into our personal life," he said.

"Don't worry, Marcos," Mariella said. "We're not going to talk about it anymore."

"We had to listen to her drone on about it," said Natalia. "To be fair, we should hear both sides."

"Ignore her, Marcos."

Natalia assumed Marc would be furious with her. Instead, he had an amused look on his face. "Still speaking your mind, I see," he said.

Natalia didn't answer. They stared at each other until she thought her heart would break in two. Finally, she looked away and put her head against the window. Closing her eyes, she plotted Sam and Mariella's demise and thought about a night that happened four short weeks ago.

CHAPTER 19

"Guilt is the price we pay willingly for doing what we are going to do anyway." – *Isabelle Holland, 1920-2002, Author*

Natalia opened her eyes as they were pulling into the parking garage underneath Mariella's Center. "I thought we were dropping Marc off at the apartment. Why are we here?"

"Mariella and I are having dinner together tonight. I'll walk to the restaurant tomorrow."

"Natalia, I was hoping you'd stay for dinner. That way Marcos can talk to you about the accident."

"I don't think so. I need to take an early train back. Sam has to pick me up at the station."

"There's no need to make Sam drive to the train station tonight. I have plenty of room here. Relax," said Mariella.

Natalia opened the car door and got out. She was furious with Mariella for putting her on the spot like this. They got into the elevator. Natalia sulked in the corner and didn't say anything. When they walked into Mariella's apartment, Mariella had Marc put his things in the same bedroom Natalia and he had been in the night before their regression. She didn't want to remember how it felt to sit there with him that evening, but it was all she could think about.

"Marcos wants to shower before dinner," Mariella said to her. "That'll give you time to go downstairs to the boutique and get some decent clothes to wear. I'll call them and tell them to put it on my account."

"This wasn't part of the deal, Mariella. I said I would talk to him and that's it."

"So you can talk over dinner."

"Why are you doing this? Don't you want him and Simone to work things out? It seems like you're sabotaging his marriage and trying to push us together."

"Natalia, everything isn't about you. I'm not doing either of those things. The only thing I want is Marcos to get better and be happy. He asked to see you and that's what I did, nothing more. I've already told you, I truly believe whatever is supposed to happen, will happen. We're only along for the ride." Mariella handed her a room key. "Be back for dinner at six-thirty."

Natalia took the key and went to find her room. It wasn't the same room Marc and she spent the night in, but it looked exactly like it. She fell into the couch and looked up at the recessed lighting on the ceiling.

"So you're going to make my life a living hell. Is that the way it's going to work? This isn't my fault. I kept my end of the deal. I forgot about him. I can't help that we had an accident, and now I remember everything."

She sat there, thinking. "I was with him from four in the afternoon until two the next afternoon. That's twenty-two hours, *but* we slept for fifteen hours, and I don't think that should count. I was technically only with him for seven hours and that's all I'm paying for. That's when our...lapse of judgment occurred."

"Mariella picked me up at eleven this morning. I'll go to dinner, be nice, and stay until eleven tomorrow morning. I'll take whatever you throw at me until then and not complain. I'm taking into consideration my afternoon with Simone as part of that punishment. That's twenty-four hours of living hell and then I'm absolved. Enough is enough."

Content with the deal she made with *who* or *what*-ever, she left to go to the boutique in the lobby. Mariella had called ahead and they were expecting her. She picked out a nice pair of jeans, a silk blouse, and a pair of expensive shoes she knew she would never wear again. When she was checking out, she noticed a beautiful bracelet in the case.

"Can I see that please?" The woman laid it out on the counter. "Oh, it's lovely. It's my birthday dinner tonight, and Mariella told me to pick something nice out for myself. Could you put that on her tab as well?" Natalia could play Mariella's game, too.

After running into a small gift shop, she bought make up and a brush then went back to her room. She showered and dressed, but before leaving, she took the pillows and blankets off the bed and put them on the couch. Sleeping in the bedroom would be a torturous reminder of Marc. While making up her bed, she noticed two bottles of Santagario wine in a tastefully decorated basket on the hearth. She ripped it open, grabbed one bottle of wine and took it to dinner.

She waited outside Mariella's door and finally knocked. It was best to keep moving along. Marc answered the door, looking handsome in his jeans and sweater. "Hi, Natalia. Don't you look pretty tonight?"

Every fiber in her being told her to turn and walk away. She didn't. She vowed to keep up her end of the deal. She walked in. Mariella was putting dinner on the table.

"Dinner smells wonderful. Thanks for having me," she said. "I'm hungry."

"Of course, dear, I hope you like tuna with risotto and salad."

Natalia smiled. "I've been told I'll eat anything."

"That's a nice bracelet you have on. Did someone give it to you?" Marc asked.

"Yes. Mariella gave this to me for my birthday. Wasn't that thoughtful of her?"

"Oh, when was your birthday?"

"Last week," Natalia lied. Her birthday was months away.

"Happy belated birthday," said Marc.

When she looked at Mariella, she saw a sly smile on the woman's face.

Natalia was taking a sip of wine when Marc asked her, "Do you mind if I call you Nat?"

Of course, she minded. Nat was what he'd called her when they were together. "I prefer Natalia if you don't mind."

"Oh, okay. Natalia, the doctors think something is blocking my memory. They think if I can figure out the last few hours before the accident, it might help me break through. Had we been together for a while before we got in the cab or had we just seen each other?"

Natalia looked at Mariella. "We saw each other in the lobby."

"We didn't have lunch or spend any time together before that? Mariella told me we've eaten together a few times."

"No."

"Did I mention to you in the cab where or what I was doing earlier? You're the only person I know who saw me that day."

"Look Marc. I said we saw each other in the lobby and that's it. If I had something else to say, I'd say it. I'm sorry I can't help you. Where's the wine?" Natalia held out her glass, while Marc poured a little wine in. "No, fill it up. To the top."

"I don't doubt that if you had something to say, you'd say it," he said. "I was hoping you'd know something that would help. Simone was away. I wasn't at work, so I can't imagine what I was doing that morning."

Taking a shower with me is what you were doing. She choked on her wine as the image popped into her head.

"Are you okay?" He handed her a glass of water.

"Yes, thanks, I'm fine."

Natalia had had enough. She was wrenched with guilt for sleeping with him, as well as for having the answers he needed to help him remember but being unable to tell him. It would only hurt him and Simone in the end.

"I think you need to give it more time. You're too hard on yourself. It's only been a month," she said sympathetically. "Why don't you take these few days by yourself and do something you like?"

"I don't *know* what I like. Everyone focuses on me not remembering them. They don't realize I don't know anything about myself, either."

"You like horror movies, Chinese food and playing cards," Natalia said and immediately regretted it.

"How do you know that?"

"It came up in the few conversations we've had. I'm sorry that's all I know. " Turning to Mariella she said, "Thank you for dinner, but I'm tired. I think I'll go back to my room."

She got up and Marc walked her to the door, putting his hand gently on her back. *Always a gentleman*. Still, she flinched at his touch.

"I'm sorry you're leaving so soon. It's been nice talking to you."

"It's been nice seeing you, too, Marc." And she meant it, happy to have the opportunity to spend a little time with him. "Good night."

Back at her room, she turned the fireplace on and poured a glass of wine. She heard a knock on the door and panicked, but figured it was Mariella scolding her for leaving so suddenly.

"I'm sorry, Mariella. I can't help you with Marc anymore. It's too hard for me."

There was silence for a moment than another knock. "It's me, Marc. Can I come in? I have another question."

Her eyes shot up to the recessed lighting. "Are you freaking kidding me? I know I said I would take whatever you gave me and not complain, but this it too much. Everyone has their limits."

"Natalia."

"Sorry, Marc, not tonight. Can't we talk tomorrow?"

"Please, it's about my birthmark. Simone wants me to see someone about having it and the tattoo removed. In the hospital, you said you liked it. Do you know why I got it or what it means?"

"No. I don't."

"I told her what you told me. That it was part of who I was, and I was keeping it. If she loved me, she should love all of me."

"Good for you," she managed to squeak out.

"Can I come in for just a few minutes?"

Natalia didn't answer him.

"If you want, we can talk about how I'm impotent. You said you wanted to hear my side of the story. Remember?"

Between her tears, she couldn't help but laugh aloud a little.

"Was that a laugh I heard?" Marc asked.

She pulled herself together. "No," she said coldly, turned the deadbolt, and walked away.

♨♨

Natalia looked at the clock. It was nine-thirty in the morning—only an hour and a half to go. In a little while, she would go up to Mariella's apartment, say good-bye to the two of them and get herself to the train station. Then her penance would be complete. She was folding up the sheets and blanket from her makeshift bed when the knocking began.

"Natalia, its Mariella."

She opened the door. "Mariella, I apologize for leaving so suddenly last night, but I had to get out of there."

"That's fine, dear. There are more pressing issues at hand now. Your friend, Rachel, the caterer has been trying to call your cell."

"I know who she is, Mariella. I didn't get a chance to grab my phone charger yesterday during my abduction, so my phone's dead. Why, what's wrong?"

"It's has something to do about them not being able to cook for the event on Saturday night."

"What? How did she know where I was?"

"I guess Sam told her."

"Let me see the phone."

Mariella handed her the phone and gave her some privacy.

"Hello, Rach? What's wrong?...Yes, I know and I'm sorry...I'm sure she needs you...You've always been able to find someone to fill in other times. It's hard to believe that everyone's booked in March...It's a wedding rehearsal dinner, so I would guess we can't reschedule...Yes, I know I haven't been myself lately...Okay, fine. I'll take care of it. Tell Sandie I wish her well."

Natalia sat down on the coffee table and buried her face in her hands. In a low voice, she started mumbling to herself. "What am I going to do now? My whole life right now is one big clusterfu—"

She saw someone out of the corner of her eye. "Marc, how did you get in here?" She looked over at the door and it was wide open. Mariella never closed it when she left.

"Mariella said you needed a chef," he said. "As you know, I'm a chef. An almost unemployed chef, but I can still cook. Things aren't going so well at the restaurant, and they've cut my hours."

Natalia heard the words come out of his mouth but couldn't believe what he was offering. "Are you out of your mind? Thank you, but no. Do you see the time? It's ten-fifteen, and I only have forty-five more minutes until I'm done. And I really mean it this time."

"What?"

"I'll figure it out myself. Go back to your family and get better. Leave me and my—" she looked at the clock—"forty minutes alone."

"Are you done rambling yet? I'd like to help you. If I've done something to hurt you, I want to make it up to you."

"Why would you say that?"

"Last night when you thought I was Mariella, you said it was hard for you to be around me. So I figured I did something to upset you. But you were so nice at the hospital, I don't know what to think." He took a few steps closer to her. "Look, I wouldn't ask but I need to feel useful. Everyone thinks I've lost my entire mind, not just my memory."

She looked at him standing there. Besides being handsome, there was an innocence about him since he lost his memory. She wanted to reach out and touch him, but she wouldn't make that mistake again.

She willed herself to say no to him. *Just say it. It's a simple word and a strong word. Two letters, one syllable. N-O. Easy and straightforward.*

"Fine, you can cook for me on Saturday. Oh, and by the way, you do owe me. What you did to me was horrible."

"What did I do?"

Natalia smiled. "I'm not going to tell you. Then I can torture you until your memory comes back."

"Good." He laughed. "When do we leave?"

"You don't have to be there until early Saturday morning. I'm sure Rachel has everything ordered already."

"No, I want to see the kitchen and the menu. It's already Wednesday. Anyway, I won't know how to get there if I don't come with you. In the hospital you said you always had a few rooms ready." He lifted one shoulder in a half-shrug and smiled.

"You remember that with no problem, huh?" She was in such deep shit right now. She was usually a strong willed person.

How was he able to take her will power and throw it somewhere so far away that she couldn't even get a glimpse of it? "Where's Mariella?"

"In her apartment, I think."

"I want to leave soon. If you're not ready, I'm leaving without you. I have to talk to your aunt for a minute."

"Don't leave without me. I have to run across the street to the store. I'll be right back." Marc ran out of her room and closed the door behind him.

♨♨

Natalia burst into Mariella's apartment without knocking, demanding some answers.

"How'd you do it? Call Rachel and threaten her? And how did you know who she was and where to reach her?"

"It was easy, dear. You do know you're website has a link to Rachel's catering company. And I wouldn't have such a successful business if I didn't have a gift of persuasion when needed."

"You mean gift of manipulation, don't you? You're not even going to deny it?"

"No, dear, not at all. I initially called and told her who I was and how I knew you. I was going to ask her if Marc could help them. I explained how, right now, cooking was all he had that made him happy. Then she told me their daughter, Sandie was getting divorced. Did you know that?"

"Yes, I knew."

"Her daughter spent a bad weekend with her ex-husband, arguing about the kids. Rachel and her husband felt they needed to be with her this weekend but didn't want to say anything to you because you've been—"

"Not myself. Yeah I know."

"I think she was almost relieved I called. See dear, things always work out the way they're supposed to."

Natalia sighed and sat down. "What is it you want from me, Mariella?"

"I want Marcos to be happy, I've told you that. This isn't the first time he asked about you. Memory or not, he will always find his way to you. He can't help himself. Being with you is second nature to him. You can't say no, either, can you?"

"It's not fair. You don't know how hard it is for me."

"Yes, I do. I remember how close he and I were and he doesn't. Our relationship wasn't passionate or intimate like yours, but I've always taken care of him. I miss him as much as you do. I would like him back."

"The difference is you're allowed to have him back. I'm not."

"You're wonderful at seeing things from his side. Maybe you could try to see things from my side as well. We want the same thing."

"This is Simone's job, not mine."

"Be that as it may, she's not here and you are. He wasn't happy before the accident with Simone, and he's not happy now. I can tell Simone is getting restless again. Spending a month at home with a husband who doesn't remember her is taking its toll. When the divorce papers arrived, she was upset but we had a long talk. She understood why he did it. The morning she left after their conversation, she wasn't sure what to do about their marriage. But when he got hurt in the accident, she thought she'd made a mistake. Even so, she jumped at the chance to go away for these ten days. She loves him in her own way, but they are growing apart and this accident hasn't made things any better."

"I'm scared, that's all. I would like to spend time with him, but you're going to have to come as well. I don't think I can be alone with him."

"I would love to, dear. I can't come until tomorrow, though. I have to take care of a few things."

"Marc wants to come with me today. He says he needs to do chef things in the kitchen or something."

"Then let him come. It's better than having him sulking here all day. Can you control yourself for one night?"

"Yes. That's not what I'm afraid of. Believe me, I have enough guilt for two lifetimes. I won't be doing that again. I'm worried I'm going to tell him what he wants to know. It breaks my heart to see him so sad and not able to remember—when I can help him."

"You'll do fine, dear. It's one evening. Thank you for helping him like this."

"Well, you went to so much trouble manipulating the situation, it's the least I can do," Natalia said. "You do owe me, though."

"I'm not sure I do, dear," said Mariella. 'Take off the bracelet."

Natalia took it off, not caring about it. She was mad last night, that's all. She handed it to Mariella.

"Now, I owe you," Mariella said.

CHAPTER 20

"Whatever our souls are made of, his and mine are the same." – *Emily Bronte, 1812-1848 Author of Wuthering Heights*

Natalia and Marc were in Mariella's car driving up a dirt hill full of potholes and ruts. After a couple of miles, they came upon a small but elegant sign that read "Santagario Vineyards" with a picture of the family crest.

"You don't believe in a lot of advertising, do you?" he asked.

"Everyone who looks for us always finds us."

"You live in the middle of nowhere."

"Yeah, and I like it."

They passed a large building and she explained how it used to be a busy restaurant and inn, but had to shut down in two thousand-three. After Nine/Eleven, tourism was down and business wasn't so good.

"Keep going past the inn," she said. "The main house is up the road a bit."

They pulled up in front of a large white farmhouse with a wrap-around porch, complete with rocking chairs.

"Wow, Natalia, what a great house. It looks very New England. What are those buildings in the back? Is that where you make the wine?"

"Yes. You can drive up a little farther and see the grapes if you like."

He was obviously amazed at the acres and acres of grapes spread out before him.

"As much as I like wine, I don't think I know too much about how it's made. You'll have to teach me."

"I thought you were here to cook."

"It's always good to learn new things."

"You won't be here long enough. It's a lengthy, involved process."

"It's not that far away. I don't mind driving anywhere for something worthwhile," he said, shooting her a thoughtful look.

Uneasiness started to creep into the pit of Natalia's stomach. "Let's get back. Do you want a tour of the house before you go to your room in the inn?"

"I'll stay in the house, it looks big enough. How many bedrooms do you have?"

"Four," she said as her uneasiness grew.

"Four? You won't even know I'm there."

Yes, I will. "What will people think? You're married."

"I don't picture you caring what people think. Anyway, what people? The last house I saw was a mile down the road. Natalia, it's two thousand-ten, not the middle ages."

"Okay," she said hesitantly. "But while you're here, you're on your own. I'm used to living by myself and like my alone time. Got it?"

"Yes, Ma'am."

They drove to the farmhouse and parked out back. About a hundred yards away, set back in a clearing, was a cabin. "That cottage belongs to Sam. He's like a father to me. I couldn't run the place without him. You'll meet him tomorrow. Let me show you around inside."

"Where's the rest of your family?" he asked.

"I have a brother, Robbie. When he came home from the Navy, he and my parents had a falling out, and I took his side. My parents weren't happy with me, but they were more upset with him. When they retired to Florida, I found myself in charge. My brother lives in New Hampshire."

"You don't see them much?"

"No, and I miss them. My brother is due for a visit soon, though."

She led him in the back door through her modest kitchen, then into her enormous family room, complete with a floor-to-ceiling fieldstone fireplace. She watched his eyes scan the room, admiring it.

"What a beautiful fireplace," he said. "We have a small gas one in our house. I don't think we've had a fire since I came home from the hospital." He walked toward the hearth. "It seems Simone and I don't sit and relax together much."

"Let me finish showing you around." The last thing she wanted was to hear was what he did or didn't do with his wife. "These stairs will get you to your room," she said, pointing up the flight of stairs. He followed her into the foyer. "And so will these."

"Ah, two staircases leading down from the bedrooms. Very handy if someone who isn't supposed to be here needs to leave in a hurry," he said with suggestive glimmer in his eyes. "I'll have to remember that."

As they climbed the stairs, Natalia could feel him behind her and wished she hadn't agreed to this arrangement. This was going to be one big train wreck when all was said and done.

"Here's your room," she said stopping in front of a door.

"Is it your brother's?"

"No, I always keep his ready for him. If you need anything, let me know. Good night."

"Natalia, how can I let you know if I need something when I don't where your room is? And it's early. I'm not ready for bed yet."

"Oh, I guess you're right."

"Why don't you tell me what you need me to do for the event on Saturday?"

"How about you cook?" Natalia's tolerance for their togetherness was near its breaking point.

Marc opened the door to his room and sat his bag down. "Are you not going to be able to relax with me here? I guess I shouldn't have come."

"I told you this wasn't a good idea."

"No, you ranted on about having forty-five minutes left and some other craziness. I thought you were different from everyone else." He sat down on the top step and put his head in his hands. "I thought coming here and getting away would be good. I could cook and maybe figure a few things out. I guess I was wrong." He stood and raked a hand through his hair. "I'm not up to driving back to the city tonight. I'll leave in the morning and won't be any more trouble." Dejected, he walked into his room.

Natalia leaned against the wall listening to him. When he was through, she burst into laughter. "Gee, maybe you could hold a lost puppy in your arms while telling your tale of woe. You know, for effect."

"Didn't work, huh?"

"No."

"See, you are different. If I whine enough around my family, they let me get my way. You know me better than they do."

"That's mature."

"If they want to treat me like a child, the least I can do is act like one."

"I'm not sure that's going to help you get better."

"Friends?"

"Fine, I'll play nice."

"Not too nice I hope. That won't be any fun."

"Come on, I think Rachel left the file for the event in the kitchen."

She rummaged around the kitchen until she found Rachel's paperwork and handed it to Marc. Then she opened a bottle of wine and poured them each a little.

"No wonder my aunt wanted your wine in her guest rooms. It's really good, Natalia."

"Thanks. Did you look over the file? It's a wedding rehearsal dinner for fifty people."

"Where does all the food come from?"

"A local butcher in town. And it looks like she ordered everything already."

"It should be easy enough."

"I'm sorry it's not fancy. I'm sure you'd rather be making a gourmet dinner."

"Hey, I'm just happy to be doing something productive." He shrugged. "It'll be fun."

"Rachel has a list of high school and college kids that help here. We prefer the bartenders to be at least twenty-one. I'll have to look at her list and see who she uses."

Marc's phone went off. "Hi, Simone. Yes I can hear you."

He got up and walked into another room.

Natalia sat at the kitchen table and watched as her wine glass slowly tipped over and wine spilt out. She waited for the cool breeze.

"Why do you have to make a mess to make a point?" She got a towel and started to clean up the wine. "I don't care if you like him or not. He's only here for a short time to help while Rachel's away."

The file for the party blew off the table.

"Why can't you behave yourself?" Natalia felt a cool breeze right in her face. "No! Leave him alone, do you hear me?"

Natalia was on her hands and knees on the floor picking up the papers. She saw him grab the towel and wipe up the wine that was spilled all over the table. "Were you talking to someone?" he asked. "What happened in here?

"I knocked over my wine, and I didn't want it to spill on the file, so I pushed it away. It fell on the floor." She sighed. "How's Simone's trip going?"

"Good. She's in Paris."

Natalia picked everything up off the floor and tried to put it all in order. "Why didn't you go with her?"

"The trip didn't interest me at all." He poured her some more wine and sat down at the table. "Sometimes I feel like a carnival attraction. People can't believe they actually know someone with a bona fide case of amnesia. Of course, they're intrigued and have a hundred different questions. I'm tired of it all."

She put her hand on top of his and squeezed it. "I'm so sorry this happened to you." At his touch, she let herself remember for a brief moment how it felt to have his hands on her then quickly removed her hand from his. "Listen, we've had a long day. Let's call it a night. I'm going upstairs. Make yourself at home. There's a TV in the family room and a computer in the library. Good night."

"Good night. Natalia?"

"Yes."

"Thanks for everything."

"Sure."

♨♨

Marc looked around Natalia's library. She was well read, with an eclectic variety of books, fiction and non-fiction.

The framed photos she had scattered in different places didn't tell him much. He saw pictures of her skiing with friends who were all female. There were pictures of Natalia with a man who Marc assumed was her brother, since he was wearing a sailor's uniform. What he didn't see was a picture of her and a man who she might be in a relationship with. He checked out her family room.

Not discovering much about her, he went upstairs to his room. A cool breeze blew by him. He went to shut the windows but found them closed. He put it down to an old drafty house. Natalia left towels on the bed and he decided to take a shower. He went into the bathroom, turned on the shower, got in, and realized he left the towel in the other room. But when he got out, there was a towel there for him. He was sure he'd forgotten it. He must be more tired than he thought.

As he brushed his teeth, he thought about his day. When he woke up this morning, he never thought this was where his day would end—in Connecticut, in a house that belonged to a woman he barely knew but who seemed familiar to him, when no one else did. As strange as it might be, he was glad to be here.

For the first time since the accident, he was relaxed and at ease.

When Natalia had taken his hand and told him she was sorry, an odd sensation came over him. He didn't understand it but he was grateful for her support. She was the one person who seemed to see things differently from everyone else. He wondered if she was still awake and looked at his watch. It was later than he thought. He still had a few questions for her, but they would have to wait until tomorrow. As he climbed into bed, a cool draft brushed against his back. He pulled the blanket up around his neck and fell right to sleep.

The next morning he woke up early and went downstairs to make coffee. He searched the cabinets but couldn't find the coffee. He was about to give up when he heard a door creak open behind him. He thought it was Natalia, but when he turned around a long, thin, pantry door, hidden in the corner, was open. He looked inside. The coffee was sitting on a shelf. He grabbed the few things he bought at the store yesterday, and in a few minutes, the pot was brewing.

"Good Morning," Natalia said as she walked into the kitchen. "How did you sleep?"

"It was the best night sleep I've had since the accident. All the fresh air, I guess."

"I see you found the coffee. Most people have trouble finding it. I don't know why I keep it there."

"It took me awhile, but I finally found it."

"Mariella will be coming this afternoon."

"I know and I'm fine with her coming, but I'm here to help you and get away from everyone pressuring me. If she brings up the accident or my memory, I'm going to ask her to leave. I want you to understand that before she gets here."

"Don't worry. I'll have Sam keep her busy."

"When do I get to meet this elusive Sam?"

"He should be here any minute. He usually comes knocking when he thinks the coffee's ready."

Marc poured two cups and handed her one. As she took it from him, another odd sensation came over him. For a moment, he had the distinct impression of another morning he had handed her a cup of coffee. He let himself feel a small bit of optimism that his memory was returning. A knock at the door yanked him back from his thoughts.

"Come in, Sam," Natalia called.

"Good morning, Nat. How was your time in city?" Sam gave Marc a puzzled look, walked over to the counter, and poured himself coffee. "I hope you're in a better mood than when you left."

"Yes, Sam, I feel good. I planned your early demise from this world the whole car ride, and it made me feel much better. I want you to meet Mariella's nephew."

Sam turned and moved toward Marc with his hand extended.

"Good morning. I'm Marcos Tremonti, but please call me Marc." he said shaking Sam's hand.

"Good to meet you. I'm Sam Belfry. I met your aunt for the first time a couple of days ago, and she seems like a nice lady."

"Thanks."

Sam was a tall, well-built man in his early sixties. If Marc had met him elsewhere, he would have thought him a cowboy or rancher of some sort. He wore blue jeans, a flannel shirt and cowboy hat. When he took off his hat, he had a thick mane of white hair. His face was weathered, yet, despite his worn features, he'd aged very well and was handsome and fit. His strong handshake matched his well-toned physique.

"This is great coffee. Nat, you didn't make this. Marc?"

"Yes. I'm glad you like it."

"It's got a good flavor to it, not too overpowering, just right. What is it?"

"Sorry, Sam, it's a top secret ingredient I'm not allowed to divulge."

Sam laughed. "What if I figure it out?"

"If you can figure out the main ingredient, I'll give you the recipe."

"You're on."

"Sam, I'm glad you like Mariella because I need you to pick her up at the train station at one o'clock," Natalia said. "You might also have to bartend for me on Saturday night."

"And...?"

Now it was her turn to laugh. "Well, I thought maybe you could pick up the food Rachel ordered on your way back."

"What happened to Rachel and Bob?"

"They want to spend time with their daughter," she said. "Let me call Mariella. I'll be right back."

"So, Marc," Sam said, "I'm glad to see you're better after the accident. Nat told me everything. I'm sorry about your memory."

"Thanks. I'm hoping a few days away from everything that used to be my life will help me."

"Good luck but be careful what you wish for. There are a few things from my life I wish I had no memory of."

Marc thought he saw a quick look of regret on Sam's face.

"Okay," Natalia said to Sam as she entered the kitchen, "Mariella's all set. Pick something up for dinner tonight. Marc is cooking for us. He's a chef without a kitchen, and I don't want him to lose his touch. Ask Mariella what his specialty is."

"You can ask me. I'm standing right here. If I'd forgotten how to cook, I wouldn't be much help to you this weekend, would I?"

"Sorry," said Natalia.

"Natalia, I don't think Sam should pick up all the food today. Tomorrow's Friday and we can prepare some of the food, but some of it we need to do on Saturday."

"You're in charge. Tell Sam what you want him to do."

Marc took Sam aside and marked on Rachel's papers what he wanted picked up that day. Then he whispered to Sam about dinner that night. He didn't want Natalia to hear.

"Will do, Marc." Sam grinned. "Nat if you need anything else, call my cell. I have a few errands, so I'll see you both later."

"It was nice to meet you, Sam."

"Same here, Marc." Sam filled up his coffee cup one more time and walked out the door.

"Marc, I'll meet you back here at eleven," Natalia said. "I'll show you the kitchen and we can get the tables and linens ready."

"Where are you going?"

"Every morning I go for a brisk walk through the vineyard."

"Sounds good, I'll come."

"No! Alone time, remember?"

"What am I supposed to do till then? I was going to make you breakfast."

"I don't care what you do. It's not my problem."

Marc was taken aback by her abrupt mood change. "Are you not taking your medication like you're supposed to?"

"What?"

"One minute you're fine, the next you're snapping my head off. Maybe you should see someone about it. I can recommend a good head doctor if you need one," Marc grinned. He could tell he was making her even angrier, which amused him.

"Look, I didn't think the deal was I had to entertain you twenty-four/seven."

"If this is how you treat all your guests, no wonder the place shut down."

"If you wanted hospitality, you should have checked into the Hilton. It's in the next town up. Be back here at eleven." Natalia slammed the door on her way out.

CHAPTER 21

"The minute I heard my first love story I started looking for you, not knowing how blind that was. Lovers don't finally meet somewhere. They're in each other all along." – *Jalal ad-Din Rumi, 1207-1273 Persian Poet and Mystic*

Marc arrived at eleven on the dot.

"At least you're on time," Natalia said.

"I didn't dare be late. I figured you'd throw me in some old wine cellar you keep for people who piss you off. I expect it's pretty full down there."

"Nah, only half full." She gave him a small smile. "Sorry, I'm not always in the best mood in the morning."

"I'll remember that." They walked toward the inn and once they were inside, she gave him a tour. The main dining room was huge and all four walls consisted of full-length windows. There were large exposed beams on the ceiling, recessed lighting, and a fireplace in the corner. Marc thought the views were probably beautiful in the summer and fall. Even today, on a cloudy March day, it was very charming. Natalia took him into the kitchen.

"Wow," he said. "I wasn't expecting this." Against one wall there were two huge commercial gas stoves and ovens with a grill between them. On the other wall were two big stainless steel refrigerators and one big freezer. One long counter ran down the middle of the kitchen with large sinks and two dishwashers. Dark cherry cabinets filled the remaining space on the walls and underneath the counter. There was every pot and pan he could ever need hanging from the ceiling. He was very impressed and told her so.

"It was a popular restaurant in its day. Maybe it can be again someday. I'm glad you like it. So you can work your magic. No problem?"

"No problem."

"All right, enough with your brains. I need your brawn. We have to get all the tables, chairs and linens out of the closet over there."

They started bringing out all the chairs first before rolling out the tables and setting them up. He thought they worked well together. He also thought it might be a good time to ask her a few questions.

"So, we've only known each other since Christmas?" he asked her.

"Yes."

"Is this the first time I've been here at the vineyard?"

"Yes."

"So we only saw each other in the city? Please say something else besides yes."

"Uh-huh."

"Smart ass," he said and made her laugh.

"Were we friends?"

"Yes."

"Come on, Natalia. Mariella told me you've been to the restaurant. We've had lunch and you've met Tony and Giuseppe."

"Okay, if I tell you the whole torrid story, will you leave me alone?"

"Torrid? I can't wait to hear it."

"I went Christmas shopping with my friends, Christine and Ellie, and we came to your restaurant. It was crowded. We sat at the bar with drinks and appetizers. You were bartending because someone on the staff called in sick. When it came up that I owned a vineyard, you asked me to lunch to meet Mariella. That's how our business agreement began. I talked to her about my sleep problems that day.

"I came to the restaurant one morning to meet Mariella and take a tour of her center. She was late. We sat and played cards with Tony and Giuseppe. Altogether, I've been to your restaurant three times. We saw each other three or four times while I was getting treatment for my sleep issues, when you came to see your aunt.

"We got in a cab together once. That didn't end well. After that, I saw you three times in the hospital. That's it." She sat down in one of the chairs. "I know it's a shocking tale. Are you going to be able to handle it okay?"

"Yes, I can handle it okay," he said mockingly. "Because I don't believe you." He sat down next to her. "You know, I do plan on remembering eventually. Then we'll see if your story changes, won't we?"

She stood. "Please don't make it into something it wasn't because you need to fill in some blanks in your head."

He was going to say something, but she suddenly turned around and went to get the last table in the closet. It was too heavy for her, and she almost dropped it.

"Nat, let me get it. It's heavy. I don't want you to hurt yourself."

"Natalia," she snapped. "Didn't I tell you that at the dinner the other night? Is your short-term memory gone as well?"

"Is there some warning you give before your huge mood swings? Does your head spin and your eyes turn red, and I didn't notice? What's the matter now?"

"Nothing's the matter. I hate this part of the job."

"If you hate it that much, I'll do it. I told you I'd do whatever you needed."

"Good, I'll be back later." She left without saying anything more.

He went about his work, wishing he could figure her out. Something inside told him she was leaving a few things out of her account of their relationship. He seemed to upset her easily. That told him two things—either they didn't get along before or there were some feelings between them that went beyond friendship. He smiled and wondered if that was a possibility. It wasn't a thought he should be having. Simone would be home in ten days. Besides, he was sure Mariella wouldn't have suggested he come here if anyone suspected they were having an affair.

He would remember sooner or later. He hoped sooner.

♨♨

Natalia stormed into her house. What the hell was wrong with her? Did she think she could spend this much time with Marc and not have it affect her? She needed Mariella to get here so she didn't have to be alone with him.

Her stomach growled. She made two sandwiches, grabbed some chips, two bottles of water, and went back to where he was.

"Hi. I'm sorry about before." She handed him a sandwich and water. "I was getting hungry and thought maybe you were, too."

"Thanks. Yeah, I'm hungry." He took a drink of water. "I've been thinking. You know how you bite my head off every few hours, storm out mad, then apologize? Why don't you stop biting my head off? It's much more efficient."

"Or, I could stop apologizing. That would save time, too."

"I like my idea better."

"I'll think about it." She looked around the room. He'd done a lot of work while she was gone. "The place looks great. You did a good job."

"I moved the tables closer to the windows. I saw lights out on the terrace and thought it'd be nice if the guests could see the outside lit up."

"You're right. It's pretty out there at night."

"Glad you approve."

"I have one more thing I need your help with."

"Sure. Lunch was good, thanks."

She led him out back to a small shed. "When I was recovering from the accident, I collected large dead branches from the woods, painted them white and strung lights on them. Sam helped me put them in the pots but that's as far as we got. Can you help me carry them into the dining room?"

As he lugged the ten large pots to the dining room, she directed him where to put each one. She plugged them in. "Let's see how they look," she said, softening the recessed lighting with a dimmer switch.

"How do I turn on the outside lights?"

"There's a switch outside by the door."

When he came back inside, both of them looked at the hard work they had done during the day and were satisfied with the outcome.

"The room has a lot of ambiance, especially with a fire going," Marc said.

"I agree. I couldn't have done it without you. Thanks again. Let's go back to the house. I don't know what's taking Sam and Mariella so long."

"They're back. They were here, and we put all the food away. I thought you saw them. It was when you were back at the house."

"I must have just missed them. I came around the back way. Let's go."

♨♨

Sam poured Mariella a glass of wine and sat on the hearth in front of the fire. She sat down next to him. "You make a nice fire, Sam."

He thanked her and thought about how well their day had gone. He hadn't known what to expect when he picked her up at the train station. She was a successful business woman who lived in the city. He was a man who lived and thrived in the country, but they fell into an easy conversation.

He'd been lonely and full of regret for many years. It surprised him that at this time in his life, he would meet someone. He'd had women through the years but hadn't met anyone he wanted to have a serious relationship with, until now. There was something different about Mariella, and he liked her.

"I had fun spending the day with you," he said. "I'm glad you're here for a few days."

"I enjoyed your company, as well," she said.

He heard the door and glanced up as Natalia and Marc walked in.

"There you two are. Marc, let me show you what I bought for dinner. Mariella was a big help." Sam gave her a sly smile, and saw her cheeks turn a slight pink.

"Mariella, are you blushing?" asked Natalia.

"No dear, not at all."

Sam and Marc went into the kitchen. "Perfect, Sam. I'll get everything ready then I'd like to take a quick shower. I need you and Mariella to keep Natalia out of here. I don't want her to see what's for dinner."

"We'll try," Sam said. "But Nat can be very stubborn."

"I understand."

"You sure are going to a lot of trouble to surprise someone you *supposedly* didn't know very well and don't remember."

"If you have something to say, Sam, then say it. If you can help me remember her, I wish you would. No one else will. Not even Mariella."

"I don't know anything. She never spoke of you until the accident. I will tell you she's been miserable and keeps to herself since coming home from the hospital. That's not like her.

"I thought she was upset after Jacob, but I've never seen her this...sad. This morning she seemed happy again. I only know what I see, but if I were a betting man, I say you two knew each other better than anyone is letting on."

"Thanks for being honest, Sam. I think so too, but I can't explain why."

"I'm sure you'll figure it out. Let me try and get rid of Nat so you can cook." Sam walked in on Natalia and Mariella talking.

"Nat, why don't you take a shower while Marc's cooking? Then we can eat earlier."

"Good idea, I won't be long," she said and went upstairs.

As soon as she was gone, Sam grabbed Mariella by the hand. "Marc needs us to help him surprise Nat," he said and pulled her into the kitchen. "What do you want us to do?"

"I thought it would be nice to eat by the fire in the other room. Can you two set a table up out there?"

"Sure, dear," said Mariella.

Sam and Mariella went to work, carrying out a table and chairs and sitting them in front of the fire. He told Mariella where she would find the plates and silverware, and left to get a couple bottles of wine.

♨♨

Marc left Mariella making a salad and Sam in charge of keeping Natalia out of the kitchen. When he came back from his shower, he found the three of them in the family room.

"I'm hungry," said Natalia. "What's cooking in there?"

"You're always hungry, Nat," said Sam.

"Don't worry, Natalia," Marc said. "It won't be much longer. Pour me a glass of wine, and I'll be back in a few minutes.

As soon as he entered the kitchen, Marc felt a chill. He rubbed his hands up and down his arms to shake off the feeling, but it wouldn't go away. He hoped he wasn't coming down with something.

He opened the cabinet where earlier in the day he had put some of the ingredients Sam bought for him, but they weren't there. Irritated, he glanced around. Everything he needed, including utensils and a bowl, was on the counter. He supposed Sam could have put them there. No. Sam didn't know his recipes.

Hell, Marc didn't even understand why he remembered how to cook, but couldn't recall his own family. The doctor's only answer was the human brain still held many secrets the medical community had yet to uncover.

Since everything was ready for him, he shrugged, decided not to worry about it, and got to work. It had to be Mariella. She was the only one here who would have a clue about the way he cooked.

He put the last dish in the oven and went to set the timer on his watch, not trusting he would hear the oven timer from the other room. But there was no watch on his wrist. He remembered taking it off for the shower. He started to go back upstairs when out of the corner of his eye he noticed his watch on the kitchen table. He felt another chill and slowly slumped onto a chair.

What the hell what was going on?

♨♨

"Are you all right?" Natalia asked Marc as he joined them by the fire. His face was pale, his expression bewildered.

"Yeah, I'm fine. I had a little trouble in the kitchen, remembering a thing or two, that's all. I could use a glass of wine, though."

Natalia handed him a glass, and he no sooner sat down, when his watch went off.

"Good news, everyone. It's time to eat." He stood. "Sam, can you help me for a minute?"

"Sure." Sam followed him into the kitchen.

"Natalia, come sit down," Mariella said. "Marcos has worked very hard to make a special dinner for you."

Natalia smiled and thought about how nice he'd been to her all day. Even when her frustration at being alone with him turned to anger, he teased her instead of getting upset. Now he wanted to make her a special dinner and he didn't even remember her. She tried hard not to become sidetracked by his kindness. He wasn't hers, and she had to keep her head on straight.

"I'm sure whatever he makes will be delicious." She licked her lips in anticipation. "I'm starving."

"Good." Marc set a plate down in front of her. "Dinner is served."

She gaped, speechless, when she saw the food in front of her. Marc had served her a mouth-watering filet mignon, sliced and cooked to perfection, with a delicious wine sauce drizzled over the top. Accompanying the steak was a double baked potato and sautéed mushrooms. The plate was beautifully garnished, and in the center of the steak, was a lovely purple flower.

She gulped and willed herself not to cry. He was standing next to her, waiting for her to say something.

"You remembered?" she barely whispered as she looked up at him.

"No, I'm sorry." He sat next to her. "I found a note in my wallet." He took it out and showed her. It said, '*Important. Remember to cook Nat steak dinner with marinade, baked pot, m'rooms.*' "I thought you could tell me what it was about."

She felt his eyes on her as he sat there hoping for an explanation, but all she could muster up was a show of gratitude.

"Thank you so much. It's my favorite and its looks great. Come on everyone get your plate. We don't want this wonderful dinner to get cold." She began to cut her steak, not looking at him. Eventually, she saw him get up and go back in the kitchen.

Mariella leaned over and whispered in her ear, "Are you all right, dear?"

"Yes. I'll be fine."

She tried her best to get through dinner, but it wasn't easy. When had he written the note? Was it when she was getting dressed that morning? Or when she went in with Dr. Ellis?

He promised her he would remember to cook her dinner and even with his memory gone, he'd kept his promise. Having him here was going to be harder than she thought. She already loved him with her whole being, but after spending yesterday and today with him, she loved him more—if that was possible.

"Marc, everything was delicious. Thank you very much," she said when they were done.

"Sam and Mariella helped. They should get some credit, too."

"Not at all," said Sam. "It was the best steak I've ever had.

"Marcos, I've had this many times," Mariella told him. "But I think you may have outdone yourself this time."

"I'm glad you all liked it. It was the least I could do."

"Mariella and I will clean up," Sam said. "You two had a busier day than we did. Right, Mariella?"

"Yes, of course." After a few trips, everything was in the kitchen and Sam and Mariella never came back into the family room.

"So, you used to let me call you Nat. That's what I called you in the note."

"No, you did what you wanted."

"Why did I write the note?"

"I don't know. So you would *remember*?"

"Ah, there's that biting sarcasm I haven't heard in a few hours. Why was I supposed to cook you dinner?"

"You lost a poker bet." It was the first thing that popped in her head.

"To who?"

"Me."

"You beat me at poker?" Marc began to laugh.

"Yes, I did. Laugh now, but you didn't think it was so funny when you were sitting there with half your clothes off."

He was laughing even harder now. "You bet me at strip poker?"

You think this is funny, let me tell you what really happened. After we were through screwing around on your poor wife, you got up and brought me some really good food in bed. All I did was bitch and moan that I was tired of Italian food and wanted a steak dinner. And you're always so fucking nice—did I mention that you don't like my obscene language—you promised to cook me a steak dinner. Isn't that hysterical?

"Don't be so cocky," she said. "You can't remember a goddamn thing. You suck at poker."

"I don't know why you're getting so upset. I paid my debt and made you a great meal. What's the big deal?"

"Tell Sam and Mariella I'll see them in the morning." She stomped toward the stairs.

"I will remember someday." Marc said with a wink. "When I do, we'll have to play again and see who's sitting there with half their clothes off."

Natalia left him downstairs, still chuckling to himself. She went into her room and immediately felt a cool breeze.

"What do you want?" She heard the bathroom door shut. "No, absolutely not. I'm warning you."

The gentle wind blew by her, out her bedroom door and into the hallway. "I'm not in the mood for you tonight. Leave Marc alone and while you're at it, leave me alone, too." She slammed her bedroom door and got ready for bed.

CHAPTER 22

"Love is composed of a single soul inhabiting two bodies." – *Aristotle, 384 BC – 322 BC*

When Natalia walked into the kitchen the next morning, she found Marc, Mariella, and Sam having coffee and talking.

"Is it Amaretto?" Sam guessed. "I think there's a little Amaretto and cinnamon in the coffee."

"Oh Sam, you're so close. I do use cinnamon, but no, it's not Amaretto."

"Hazelnut?"

"No." Marc laughed. "I'm not sure you're going to guess, Sam."

"Don't be so sure, Marc. I have a secret weapon."

Natalia could tell they were both enjoying the wager they had going. "Good morning, everyone. What smells so good?"

"Look, dear," said Mariella. "They went into town early and got bagels. Marc is making breakfast."

Marc opened the oven door and took out a cookie sheet full of half cut bagels. After he put a bagel on a plate for each of them, he took a bowl of whipped cream out of the refrigerator. He put a scoop of cream on each bagel then drizzled it with vanilla.

"Is that real whipped cream?" asked Natalia.

Marc handed her a plate. "Of course."

"It looks great. What did you do to the bagels?"

"It's easy. Sam and I cut them in half, scooped out the middle, and chopped it up. Then we heated up eggs, milk, butter, cinnamon and vanilla on the stove. We stirred the pieces of the bagel into the mixture, poured it back into the bagels shells, and baked it. It's like a pudding. Add the whipped cream and you're good to go."

"Wow. That was wonderful." Natalia had finished her bagel and was licking her fingers by the time Marc was through explaining how he made them. "Is there more?"

"Yes, there's plenty. I'm glad you like them."

"Are you going to do this every morning?"

"Sure, if Sam helps me. He makes quite a good sous-chef."

Sam shrugged. "Oh no, I'll stick to making wine, Marc. You make the food."

Mariella got up. "Thank you both for breakfast, it was very good. I'm glad you're cooking again, Marcos." She kissed him on the cheek. "I have a few phone calls to make. Let me know when you need me to do something."

Sam followed her out the door.

"What time do you want to meet at the inn?" Natalia asked.

"Whenever you get done. We have all day."

She conned him out of a little more whipped cream on her bagel.

"You have quite the appetite, haven't you? You know this is full of fat and calories?"

"That's what makes it so good. I'll walk another fifteen minutes this morning. Not everyone gets to have a live-in chef for a week. I'm going to enjoy it."

"Good attitude. I tried to make these for Simone one day, and she barely ate half of one."

"She doesn't know what's she's missing."

"Let's just say she's a conscientious eater."

Natalia enjoyed her breakfast, but had a twinge of guilt over her behavior last night. Marc did make her a great dinner and breakfast. She should try to make it up to him. "Would you like to come with me on my walk through the vineyard this morning?" she asked him.

"I thought you liked your alone time."

"I do, but our tours will be starting in a couple months. I could use the practice."

"Sure. I would like a private tour."

She gave him a smirk. "Sorry, I already asked Mariella to come. I think there's old boots in the shed that might fit you. It's muddy up there. I'll meet you in fifteen minutes."

When she got to the foyer, he was there, waiting for her. "Looks like you're stuck with me. Mariella is still on the phone and can't come."

Natalia shook her head. "You two are unbelievable. And people think I'm controlling."

They walked to the bottom of a fairly steep hill and looked up. "Up there?" Marc asked.

"Up there," she said, smiling.

She liked to the get the hardest part of her walk out of the way first, and the views from the top were gorgeous. It wasn't difficult in the beginning, but the farther they traveled, the more muddy and slippery it became. There were some small patches of ice under the fallen leaves.

She thought Marc did well for a man not used to hiking in the woods. He slipped a few times, but recovered well, and soon had no problem maneuvering the tricky paths through the aisles of grapes. When they got to the top, they stopped and looked out over the grapes, to her house below.

"All this property belongs to you?"

"Yes, as far as you can see. It takes quite a few grapes to make a bottle of wine. We've already started to clean up from winter. That's what we were doing when Mariella came the other day. In April, we'll start pruning the vines back. The grapes won't be ready to harvest until the fall."

"It seems like a lot of work. You must have a lot of help."

"Sam takes care of that. He has a good group of men that know what they're doing."

Marc took a deep breath. "The air is so different here than in the city. You can almost smell spring coming. No wonder you like it so much."

"Every season brings new scents. I love the smell of the warm soil in the summer. In the fall when the air is cooler, you can smell the dried leaves and even the grapes. It's wonderful."

"Thanks for letting me come with you this morning. I'd like to come again."

It was a chilly morning and Natalia thought he looked adorable with his red cheeks and nose. "Sure. I do this every morning, even in the rain, unless it's pouring. I like having the company."

"Good. It's a date," he said.

She wished he would stop saying things like that, but it wasn't his fault. After last night, she vowed not to let her aching heart turn to anger and make her defensive with him. She wasn't sure how successful she'd be, but she'd try her best.

"If I'm going to work off all those bagels and whipped cream, we need to step up this walk. If you can't keep up, go back to the house," she teased.

"I can keep up. Let's go."

♨♨

Marc was already in the kitchen at the inn when Natalia walked in. Sam and Mariella arrived a few minutes behind her. Marc had the menu in front of him and assigned everyone a job.

"Sam, remember all the bread we left on the counter last night? Can you cut it up and put it in the food processor to make bread crumbs?"

"I don't know why not. It doesn't sound too hard."

Mariella followed Sam and began to help him.

"Wow. She has it bad." Natalia nudged Marc's arm and smiled. "You used to be the apple of her eye. It looks like you have some competition."

"I've noticed. I think your Sam has it just as bad, don't you?"

"I think they're cute together. Sam's been alone a long time."

"I don't know for sure, but I think Mariella has, too. I'm happy for them. But now that she's helping Sam, I need you to help me with the appetizers." He showed her the list of appetizers and told her what to do.

"I don't know. I don't want to screw anything up. I'm not that good in the kitchen. When I help Rachel I usually chop or grate and clean up."

"They're having chicken and beef kabobs. Do you want to cut up the meat?"

"Perfect. I can't screw that up—I don't think."

He put bacon on the griddle to cook and began to cut up bread for the pinwheel appetizers.

Mariella came up beside him. "Sam's doing fine over there. Let me help you." She mixed up the cheese, garlic, parsley, and herbs and spread it on the bread he had cut up.

"Did you used to help at the restaurant? You're good at this."

She gave him an affectionate smile, "Maybe once or twice."

He was glad Mariella had come, so he was able to spend some time with her. His cousin Tony mentioned to him Mariella had raised him and they had been close.

"I'm done," announced Natalia. "Where's the marinade? Do you want me to put the meat on the little sticks now or tomorrow?"

"The marinade is in the refrigerator," Marc told her. "And you can put the meat on the *skewers* now."

She playfully stuck her tongue out at him and grinned. "I'm sorry I don't know the correct chef terminology. Is anyone else getting hungry?"

"How can you be hungry?" Mariella appeared not to understand Natalia's enthusiasm for food. "Those bagels were filling."

"I took a long walk this morning. Anyway, that was breakfast, and it's past lunch time now."

"Actually, I could eat something, too," Marc chimed in.

"Let me finish and I'll make a sandwich for whoever wants one," Mariella offered.

Sam was done. He handed Marc a large bowl full of breadcrumbs. Mariella was through with her job, too. She and Sam left to go make sandwiches. Marc breaded the salmon steaks, and decided he would bake them now, and then heat them on the grill before he served them tomorrow night. He placed the breaded salmon in a baking dish, picked it up, and headed for the oven. Now, how to open the door?

"Natalia, can you open the oven door for me?" he asked, assuming she was still in the kitchen. "My hands are full."

He heard the door open and started to thank her, but when he turned around, she wasn't there. The oven door was open, but he was alone in the kitchen.

"Marc, I'll be right back. I have to go back to the house for a minute," Natalia yelled from the dining room.

"Did you open the oven door for me?"

"No, was I supposed to?"

"No, I have it." He put the salmon in the oven and set the timer.

Natalia had put all the meat on the skewers. Marc needed a container to put them in, so he could seal them overnight. As he looked around the kitchen, talking to himself about what he needed, he heard a crash.

Way in the back of the room, one of the top cabinet doors was open. Two big plastic containers with lids had fallen onto the counter. He stood there contemplating the strange things that had happened to him over the last two days, when the oven timer went off.

He took the salmon out of the oven and leaned against the counter.

"I'm not sure what's going on," he said. "Or who or what you are. But thanks for helping me out."

He felt a cool breeze blow past him. This time, he knew it wasn't a draft.

♨♨

After cooking all day, the four of them decided to go into town for dinner. Natalia noticed Sam had changed since Mariella arrived as he entertained them all evening.

She was enjoying their night out, even though she was very aware of Marc when he choose to sit next to her. Using the excuse of giving the waitress room to put the pizza on the table, he moved his chair closer to hers then stayed there. He filled her mug with beer when it got low and put another piece of pizza on her plate when she finished the first one.

He grinned. "I don't want you to be hungry."

"Very funny," she said.

To make matters worse, whenever he talked to her, he touched her arm. She turned to Mariella, begging for help with her eyes.

"Natalia, can you show me where the ladies room is?"

"Of course," she said, getting up so fast her chair nearly fell over.

They walked into the bathroom together. "What's wrong, dear? Aren't you having a good time?"

"Yes, I'm having a good time. *That's* the problem."

"What do you want me to do?"

"I want you to tell them we have to get up early tomorrow and we should be going."

"I'm having fun, and I like spending time with Sam. I haven't had this much attention from a man in a long time. I'm going to enjoy it. You know I don't believe in coincidences. People come into your life when they're supposed to. I'm surprised it happened at this point in my life, but we like each other. Don't you want Sam to be happy?"

"Yes, I do. I'm not trying to deprive you of Sam's attention. Can't he shower you with his charm back at the house? I can't spend any more time with Marc today. It's too much. Please."

Natalia grabbed Mariella's hand before she could answer and dragged her back to their seats. The waitress had taken their plates away, but everyone sat nursing their beer.

"Would you like more beer, Nat?" asked Sam.

Natalia put her hand over the top of the mug and looked at Mariella. "No, thanks. I'm getting tired." When Mariella didn't say anything, Natalia softly kicked her under the table.

"Ouch. Natalia that was my leg," complained Mariella.

"Sorry," she said, shooting daggers at the woman with her eyes.

Finally, the waitress bought the check. "My treat," said Natalia as she handed over her credit card.

"What's your hurry?" asked Marc.

"It's time to go. We have a busy day tomorrow."

CHAPTER 23

"For I have found the one whom my soul loves." – *Song of Solomon*

It was Saturday evening and only two hours until the party. The four of them had spent the day getting the dining room ready and finishing the last few appetizers. Natalia did what Marc told her and didn't say much. She preferred to watch him.

He threw himself into his work. It was obvious how much he loved to cook. He never seemed pressured and was always polite. He really was too damn nice all the time. It wasn't normal.

"Mariella, did you bring black pants and a white shirt?" she asked.

"Yes, dear, I did."

"Where's Sam?"

"He's changing."

"All the kids who are coming to help should be here by five-thirty. I'll be back by then. I'm going to get ready."

When she returned, the room looked beautiful. Sam plugged the trees in and had a roaring fire going.

"Nat, the place looks great, don't you think?" he asked.

"Yes. I wish I was having the party instead of working at it."

Marc came rushing over to her. "I need to take a quick shower and change. Can you do me a favor? You know the four platters with grapes, cheese, and crackers on them? Can you put them together for me? I ran out of time. All the cheese is cut up in the refrigerator."

"Sure."

"Thanks." He placed his hands on her shoulders and kissed her on the cheek. "You look great by the way."

She saw Sam watching her but ignored him. She found the large platters, put a bunch of grapes in the center of each one, and spread the cheese and crackers around.

A bunch of teenagers burst through the door, talking and laughing. "Hi, Natalia."

"Hi, everyone. Thanks for helping us tonight." She quickly went over with them what the party was and what they needed to serve. When she saw Mariella and Marc, she introduced everyone.

Soon after, the engaged couple and their parents arrived, complimenting Natalia on how wonderful the room looked. She was surprised at how quickly the room filled up. Before she knew it, the party was in full swing. Everyone scrambled to their places. Sam was bartending, Mariella was pouring wine, and Marc had the kabobs on the grill.

Natalia was stirring a large pot of risotto on the stove when she overheard one of the teenage girls gushing over Marc. The girl's name was Katherine, but everyone called her Kat. She asked Marc what she could do for him—more seductively than she should have at seventeen years old.

"Watch out. I think you have an admirer," Natalia said, winking at Marc.

"Katherine, come here." Marc took the kabobs off the grill and put them on three trays. "It's time to take these around to the guests. Have a couple of the guys help you."

"Can't Natalia do it? I'll stay here and help you."

"No," he said. Natalia felt his arm around her waist, pulling her close to his side. "I need Natalia here with me."

Disappointment washed over Kat's face. "Fine," she said and sulked off to serve the kabobs.

When she was gone, Natalia thought Marc would take his arm away, but he didn't.

"Let go of me," she said firmly.

He dropped his arm and walked to the grill. "The main course will be ready in about an hour."

♨♨

Natalia slumped on her couch in the family room, barely able to keep her eyes open. By the time the last guest had left and they'd cleaned up, it was after midnight. She couldn't imagine what was taking the others so long to get back.

"Hey, Nat," said Sam as the three of them walked in. "You look tired."

"I am."

"I thought I'd treat everyone to Sunday Brunch tomorrow morning." Sam announced. "What do you say?"

"Sounds good to me," said Marc.

"That's very sweet of you, Sam," Mariella added.

"Nat, how about you?"

"Whatever, Sam" Her head was pounding. She couldn't care less about breakfast. "Thank you, everyone. I really appreciate all your help. You did a great job. Marc, everyone raved about how good the food was. The bride-to-be and her parents were very happy at the end of the night." She struggled to her feet. "I'm exhausted. I'll see everyone in the morning."

♨♨

The coffee was ready when Natalia walked into her kitchen the next morning. Marc did make delicious coffee. She wondered if there was a class for that at "chef school."

Sam knocked and came in. "Good Morning. You should start getting ready for brunch. I want to leave here by eleven."

"Thanks, Sam, but I'm not going. Please don't give me a hard time."

"Whatever this thing is between you and Marc, you need to work it out—one way or another."

"There is no *thing*. He's married. Why would there be a thing?

"Nat, I was there last night, remember? Is Mariella up yet?"

"I don't know. Go knock on her door."

The next interrogation came from Mariella and Sam together.

"Why aren't you going, dear?" asked Mariella. "We've worked hard for the last two days. It'll be nice to have someone cook for us this morning."

"I want the three of you to go and have a good time. I won't be good company today. I'll see you when you get back." Natalia went up to her room. She knew Marc would try to talk her into to going as well, so she dressed in a hurry and left.

She ran up the hill at the back of the vineyard. In the woods behind the last row of grapes was an old building. From the outside, it looked like a shack that was falling apart. She kept it that way.

Inside, however, it was quite charming. A few years ago, she had a contractor come and redo the interior. It was one small room, whose décor included a small sink and microwave in the corner, one mug and a few tea bags. She had a small bookshelf with her favorite books, which she loved to read over and over again.

This was her refuge. She came here when she needed to think and be alone. No one knew she had this place, not even Sam. She curled up in the recliner she'd bought second hand, pulled a blanket over her, and closed her eyes.

♨♨

Marc, Sam, and Mariella returned from brunch around two o'clock. Marc enjoyed himself but missed Natalia. He went upstairs to see if she was in her room.

"Natalia, are you in there?"

He knocked on the door, but there was no answer. He felt a cool breeze blow behind him and wondered what unexplained thing was going to happen next. When he looked down the stairs and saw the front door wide open, he was relieved. It really was a draft this time.

He ran down the stairs and out the door to the front porch. He didn't see Natalia or anyone else. While he stood on the porch, the door slammed shut behind him. As peculiar as this was, he couldn't really say he was scared.

"Okay," he said. "I'm out here. Now what?"

It felt like someone pushed him. He almost fell off the steps of the porch, but he caught himself and sat down. He didn't know what he believed about the paranormal realm. Was he a skeptic when it came to the supernatural?

His head doctor was going to love this! Marc thought his biggest problem was getting his memory back. Could he be losing his mind as well? There was one way to find out.

He stood up. "This isn't going to work. If you want me to go straight, touch the back of my head. If you want me to go left or right, touch my shoulder. There's no need to push, all right? Is this about Natalia?"

He felt a tap on his head, so he walked straight back and up the hill through the grapevines. When reached a spot where he had to make a decision to go left or right, he felt a pat on his right shoulder. He walked down through more vines to the last row of grapes. Now, there was just woods.

"Now what?" He felt a tap on his head. "There's no place to go."

Feeling a nudge forward, he walked into the woods. It was thick with hemlock trees and difficult to walk through. About a half mile in, he saw an old shack and felt another pat on his head. He walked up to the door and knocked. When no one came to the door, he turned to walk away. A cold blast of air hit him in the face and stopped him in his tracks.

"What? No one's here." He'd barely finished his sentence when a harder, colder gust of air assaulted him. "Why am I not surprised you and Natalia have the same *temperament*?" He knocked again.

"Look, there's no one here. I knocked twice."

Something smacked him upside the head.

"Ouch. All right, all right."

He turned the doorknob. The door opened and he went inside. Curled up in chair was Natalia. He thought she was asleep until he saw that she had headphones on.

"Natalia." He shouted, so she could hear him, and watched her head pop up.

She stared at him, flabbergasted.

"What are you doing here?"

"I've been looking for you since before we got back from brunch."

"How did you find me here?"

"I'm not sure."

"That's not an answer."

He shrugged. She was right, but he didn't care. "Wow, it's really fixed up in here. You wouldn't think that from the outside. Did Sam help you?"

"No."

"Is this your hiding place?"

"I'm not hiding."

"How often do you come here?"

"I come when I need time to myself?"

"Like today?"

"Yes."

"Am I bothering you? Do you want me to leave?"

"I thought Mariella said you have a doctor's appointment this week."

"Yes, we're going back tonight. Mariella wants to be back here on Tuesday. You have another event on Friday night."

"I know the schedule. I think a couple days apart would be good for everyone, don't you?"

"Is it because I kissed you on the cheek last night? It was just a peck. Don't be upset."

She sighed. "You found me. What do you want?"

"Who's Jacob?"

A strange expression flashed across her face. He'd gotten that look from just about everyone at one time or another. It was usually when he asked about something he should already know. Everyone thought he was remembering, but he wasn't.

"Have you already told me about him? I'm sorry, I don't remember. Sam mentioned you were in a bad way after Jacob, that's all."

"Sam has a big mouth."

"You know everything about me, and I know very little about you. It doesn't seem fair, does it?"

"I'll tell you about Jacob if you tell me how you found this place."

"Deal, but let's go back to the house before it gets dark."

CHAPTER 24

"Our soul mate is the one who makes life come to life." – *Richard Bach, 1936 - Author*

I don't know where Mariella and Sam are," Marc said. "But it looks like the fire is almost out."

"Just throw a log on and poke it. The hot coals will catch it on fire."

Marc did and in a few minutes, there was a warm glow coming from the fireplace. Natalia sat down on the floor in front of the hearth.

"I could use a drink. I haven't talked about this since it happened."

"Let me get you some wine."

"I'd really like a whiskey."

His eyes widened. "You're full of surprises"

"Not really."

"I should know you drink whiskey?"

"It's come up once or twice."

"So, from what I can gather so far, our relationship consisted of strip poker and whiskey. Is that about right?"

Natalia giggled. "I guess so."

"No wonder I like you so much." He stood, asked where she kept it, and came back with two glasses of whiskey on the rocks.

"Thanks." She took a sip. "The man who had been our accountant for many years retired, and the firm assigned Jacob to our account. We met for lunch one day to go over the books, and I liked him immediately. He was smart, funny, and nice-looking. One day he called and asked me to dinner and I accepted. We hit it off and within a month, he had moved in. Not full-time but he was here Thursday until Monday. I liked the arrangement. Tuesday and Wednesday were days to ourselves. I didn't ask him what he did on those days, and he didn't ask me.

"We were together for about a year when he took me to Newport, Rhode Island, for the weekend. He surprised me with dinner at an expensive restaurant and asked me to marry him. He got down on one knee, told me he loved me and wanted to spend the rest of his life with me. I said yes and everyone in the restaurant started clapping for us. We spent the rest of the weekend in a beautiful suite at a four star hotel. It was very romantic. We had a wonderful time."

Marc got up and paced around the room.

"What's wrong," she asked.

"Nothing, I just need to stretch. When you say you spent the weekend in your suite, you don't mean it. You must have done some sightseeing."

"No, I've been to Newport plenty of times. I mean we barely left the room."

"I need more whiskey." He stormed into the kitchen, rattled at the thought of her in a hotel room for two days with some man, having a wonderful time. Because of what Sam told him, he assumed it didn't end well, and Jacob hurt her. The thought of her being hurt bothered him more than anything else.

The bottle of whiskey he left on the counter moved slowly toward him. He felt a gentle breeze. No longer unsettled by his new friend he said, "Thanks."

As he filled his glass, he turned to look over his shoulder. "What? Did you say something?"

"Yes...I feel better. Except now I'm hearing voices in my head...Okay, I'll calm down and let her finish the story." He started to walk back to Natalia then stopped. "Yes, I'm going to tell her about you. It was part of the deal...Oh, she does know about you. I thought so...She told you to leave me alone, huh?...Don't worry. I'll make sure she isn't mad at you."

He walked back to the family room. "Go on," he said to Natalia.

"When we got back home, Jacob wanted to get married right away. I didn't understand the rush, but I agreed. I don't know why. I guess because I was getting older and thought it was my last chance to get married, and I really did love him.

"He didn't spend the night here before the wedding. The next day when I was ready, Sam came to pick me up but when we got in the car, it wouldn't start. Sam tried everything. I called Rachel, she lives the closest, and she came as quick as she could. She wasn't happy I was getting married at the Justice of the Peace, but she drove us anyway. I told her we were having another ceremony with family and friends in the coming weeks."

"I tried to call Jacob, but his phone went right to his voice mail. By the time I got there, we missed our appointment and had to reschedule for another day. Jacob was furious with me and started yelling, screaming, and accusing me of all kinds of things. I had never seen him so angry. No one had. He was always easy-going and good-natured. Everyone liked him."

She wrapped her arms around her knees. "I was glad Sam was there. He told Jacob in no uncertain terms not to come back to the house to see me. Sam would be staying with me, not in his cottage. Two days later, Jacob called and asked to see me. I told Sam to let him come. I wanted to hear what he had to say.

"When he arrived, he was almost despondent. He hadn't shaved, and his clothes were a mess. I think he'd been drinking. He tried to hug me, but Sam stopped him. Jacob stood at a distance and told me no matter what happened to him, he wanted me to know he really did love me and always would."

"That's when the police arrived. They asked me if Jacob D'Alton lived here. I said no, but he was here at the time. When Jacob saw them, he looked defeated but relieved at the same time."

"Long story, short, Jacob had a gambling problem. Most Tuesdays and Wednesdays, he spent at the casinos here in Connecticut. He had a large gambling debt to some not-so-nice people. He'd become desperate and fixed the books of two of his clients. He'd also taken five thousand dollars from me. He wanted to get married in a hurry, so he could get to my assets, pay off his debt, and continue gambling."

"Nat." Marc hugged her. "I'm so sorry you had to go through all that."

She drew away from him. "It was months ago. I'm fine now. Please, call me Natalia."

He ignored her. "Nat, I wish there was something I could do for you. I'm glad Sam was here."

"I am, too. I don't know what I would have done without him. That said, if I were you, I wouldn't push my luck. I don't like to be called Nat. I thought I'd been very clear on that, and I've been told I have a bit of a temper."

He stared at her. She was the only person he knew who could turn feelings of sympathy into anger and frustration with just a sentence or two and in less than a minute.

"Why don't you say what you mean? You always do. You don't want *me* calling you Nat. Sam calls you Nat all the time. Everyone else wants me to remember, but you go out of your way to keep me from remembering you. You're so goddamn aggravating," he yelled.

"Screw you. I'll do whatever the hell I want. You're here to cook, not tell me what to do."

"Screw you, too. Maybe I'm through cooking for you."

He stomped upstairs as she stormed into the kitchen. He waited at the top of the stairs and in a few minutes, she came out of the kitchen carrying the bottle of whiskey.

She glared up at him. "How did you find me in the woods today?"

"That's it? We were just having an argument."

"So? I said what I wanted and so did you. It's over. I know I have a temper. I'm well aware of all of my flaws. But the good thing about saying what's on your mind is I feel better afterwards, and I'm able to move on."

"You're out of your mind."

"So you want to keep arguing? You need to learn to drop things when they're over. It's just like your birthmark all—."

"What about my birthmark? What do you know about it?" he demanded as he rushed back down the stairs.

"I know what you told me in the hospital and after dinner at Mariella's. That's it."

"How many times have you seen it?"

"And you think *I'm* aggravating? I saw it in the hospital."

"Was that the only time?"

"I may have seen it once or twice before that. You were always on some pity party over it. It was irritating, and I told you so."

"You told me it was a part of who I was."

"I know. I still believe that."

"Simone hates it. Since I don't remember why I got the tattoo, she wants me to at least get that removed."

"Yes, I like your birthmark and tattoo but I can understand why Simone might not. You should have told her you were getting a tattoo or at least that you would like to get one. I'm sure it was a shock to her. Even though I understand Simone's point of view, please don't have it removed. I think it's too important to you." She tapped her glass to his. "Cheers. Now I think you have something to tell me."

"Why is it important to me? Why won't you help me remember? What are you afraid of?"

"I'm not afraid of anything. I don't think you should make any decision until your memory returns. You don't want to regret it when you do remember. Give yourself a little more time."

"I don't know why, but I feel like I'm supposed to have the birthmark and tattoo. I want to keep it." He drained his drink, grabbed the bottle and poured himself one last glass. "I suppose that's all you're going to tell me."

"Yes. That's it."

"Have I mentioned how goddamn aggravating you are?"

"Yes. Twice now."

"You don't really care, do you?"

"No. Please tell me how you found me. I really need to know."

"Oh, so when *you* really need to know something, I'm supposed to tell you, but not the other way around, right?"

"Right. Finally, you understand how it works. You've been a little slow."

She gave him a small smile. It only upset him more, and he turned his back to her. He felt her closeness then a quick kiss on his cheek.

"Please."

He turned to face her and their eyes locked. He wanted to kiss her back, but not on the cheek—on her full, inviting lips.

Then he wanted to run his hands through her long hair and down her curvaceous body. He took a gulp of his drink and sighed. "You don't fight fair. I'm only telling you because I want to, not because you want me to. Understand?"

"Yes."

He hesitated, choosing his words carefully. He didn't want to get his mystical friend in trouble.

"I've met your friendly apparition. She, for some reason I think it's a girl, introduced herself to me the first night I was here." He told her the entire story, from forgetting the towel in the shower to their crazy walk in the woods today. "She didn't speak to me until a little while ago when I went in the kitchen. It was weird. I heard her in my head."

Natalia's mouth dropped open. Literally.

Marc gently lifted her chin up and closed her mouth. "Are you okay?"

"You can feel...and hear her?"

"Yes. So can you. That's what she told me."

"No one else can. I've tried to tell Sam and my brother Robbie about her. I think they want to believe me, but I understand why they don't. They've never been able feel her. Neither can my friends. She didn't like it when Jacob moved in. She would open drawers so when he turned around he would walk into them. He was always dropping things and tripping over things that weren't there. He put it down to being clumsy but I knew it was her. When I tried to explain it to him, he laughed and said we should advertise the vineyard as being haunted. It would be good for business."

"Who is she?" Marc asked.

"I don't know. She won't tell me. I've asked many times. She arrived soon after my parents retired to Florida. Were you ever afraid of her?" asked Natalia.

"No, I never got a bad feeling from her. In fact, she always helped me. I wouldn't have found you today if it wasn't for her. She wanted me to find you and wasn't going to leave me alone until I did."

"I knew she liked you, and I told her to leave you alone."

"I like her and don't want her to leave me alone. I don't want you getting mad at her either. She was afraid you'd be upset with her, and I promised I wouldn't let that happen."

Natalia laughed. "I see she has you right where she wants, already. She isn't afraid of me or anything else. What good would it do me to get mad? I can't win an argument with her. She knocks things over, makes a mess, and wreaks havoc when she gets upset. You'll see someday, I'm sure."

Mariella and Sam burst through the door. "I better get you two to the train station," Sam said. "It's getting late."

"Sam, please help me with my bags," Mariella said and they disappeared upstairs.

Marc walked over to Natalia. "I guess I have to go. Mariella has a meeting tomorrow, and I have a doctor's appointment. I'll see you on Tuesday night."

"Have a safe trip back. It's nice to have someone else feel my Giovanna. That's what I call her. I'm glad that someone is you."

"Me, too." Before he could stop himself, he put his arms around her and gave her a hug. When she didn't pull away, he kissed the top of her head. "Good-bye, Nat." He put his hand over her mouth before she could say anything. "Let me call you Nat this one time. It feels right."

As he spoke, Marc felt the familiar chill wrap around the two of them. He looked at Natalia, still keeping his hand over her mouth. "She's here."

Natalia nodded. They heard Sam and Mariella come down the stairs.

"No one else can feel her?" Marc asked.

Natalia shook her head.

He took his hand away and stepped back. "Mariella, Sam, do you feel a draft in here?

"Marcos." Mariella frowned. "It's as warm as toast in here with the fire going. I can't believe you feel a chill." She felt his forehead. "Come on, dear."

He smiled at Natalia. She shrugged. He liked the fact he and Natalia shared a secret—a supernatural one at that.

She hugged Mariella and told Sam she'd see him in the morning for coffee.

"Marc, speaking of coffee," said Sam. "Can you make the coffee tonight before we go? I'm not sure I can go back to Nat's version of a cup of Joe."

"Sure." Marc walked in to the kitchen with a feeling of sadness tugging at him. He didn't want to leave and go back to the city. He'd only been at the vineyard a couple days but felt at home and happy. At least he'd be back on Tuesday, if only for a couple of days. Simone was back on Sunday. He realized he hadn't spoken to his wife since the night he arrived here. She hadn't even crossed his mind. Simone had an international cell phone and told him with the time difference it would be easier if she did the calling. But she hadn't called. The confusion and uncertainty of his relationship with Simone inched back into his brain.

He set the coffee timer for the morning and walked back in the other room trying not to think about how much he was going to miss Natalia.

CHAPTER 25

"A soul mate is someone who has locks that fit our keys, and keys to fit our locks. When we feel safe enough to open the locks, our truest selves step out and we can be completely and honestly who we are." – *Richard Bach, 1936 – Author*

As hard as Natalia tried not to let herself become accustomed to having Marc around, her heart was in her throat when he and Mariella walked through the door Tuesday night. She'd kept busy the last two days, but she'd missed him terribly. In another five days, he would leave again. This time for good. It would be hard to let him go, especially now that she knew he could feel Giovanna. It was one more thing that connected them when they couldn't be together. Well, she'd deal with that on Sunday. Right now, she was just glad he was back.

"Did you eat something?" she asked. "I can make sandwiches."

"We're fine, dear."

"Sam, guess what? Robbie is coming for a visit. He'll be here late on Saturday afternoon," Natalia exclaimed happily.

"That'll be nice. We haven't seen him since Christmas."

"I can't wait for you two to meet him," she told Mariella and Marc.

"We'd like that very much, right Marcos?"

"What? Oh. Yeah. Sure." Marc made his way over to Natalia. "Hi."

"Hi. How was your doctor's appointment?"

"Good. I guess."

"What's wrong? You seem far away somewhere."

"Nothing. I'm just glad to be back. After being here a few days, the city seemed loud and crowded. I love the city, but it's so peaceful here. I think it helps me get my thoughts in order."

"We have a lot of work to do, starting tomorrow. So enjoy the peace now."

"I will."

He took his things up to his room. When he didn't come back down, Natalia went up and knocked on his door.

"Marc? Are you okay?"

He opened the door. "I'm fine, just a little tired."

"We're all sitting downstairs by the fire. Why are you up here?"

"I'm not up to it tonight. I need a little alone time. I'd think you would understand that better than anyone."

"I do. Okay. I'll see you in the morning."

"I'll be ready for our walk."

"Good. I've gotten used to the company. I missed you the last two mornings."

"I missed you, too, Natalia. Good night," he said and shut the door.

When Natalia returned to the family room, Mariella was by herself.

"Where's Sam?"

"He went to bed. He has to get up early tomorrow."

"You know what I don't understand? Why does Marc remember how to cook, and some secret coffee recipe, and nothing else?"

"Natalia, I have something to tell you about Marc."

"What is it?"

"Don't be upset, but Marcos never forgot about you that afternoon with Dr. Ellis. Because he told you he would, he did go in and talk with her. He explained how he felt, and she told him if he was going to resist, her suggestion to forget wouldn't work anyway. He left and came to the lobby where he saw you."

"Why didn't you tell me sooner?"

"I didn't know until a week or so after the accident and you were already home. Dr. Ellis probably wouldn't have told me except when she heard about Marcos's memory loss she thought it important that I know."

"So he pretended not to know me?"

"I don't know. I heard him say hello to you. There's nothing out of the ordinary about that. I don't know about your conversation in the cab."

"He asked me what I was doing over the weekend. Then he said he would like to visit the vineyard. That was it."

"He didn't have to act any differently. He just couldn't bring up the last twenty-four hours he'd spent with you. Don't be angry with him, dear."

"I'm not. I shouldn't have pressured him into doing something he didn't want to do. You think it has something to do with his memory not coming back?"

"I don't think there's anything wrong with him. He's doing it to himself. Who knows what the reason is? I do know he's happy here with you. He was miserable in the city and getting him to keep his doctor's appointment was like taking a child for a shot. He told me he'd be content if he never remembered anything as long as he could live, work, and start a new life here with you."

"You told him that was impossible."

"Of course, I did. He knows he can't, but that doesn't mean he doesn't wish he could."

"Well, his time here is almost over. He'll have to go home and live his own life. I'm glad you told me. Good night, Mariella."

"Good night, dear."

♨♨

The next morning when Natalia came downstairs, Marc was waiting for her with a cup of coffee. "Do you want to eat before or after our walk?"

"What do you think?" she laughed.

"That's what I thought. I have scrambled eggs and toast ready in the kitchen."

"You're spoiling me. Not that I'm complaining."

When they got back from their walk, they went over everything for the event on Friday night. It was a wine tasting and silent auction to benefit the Parent-Teacher Organization.

The President of the PTO said they would set up the silent auction on Thursday. All Natalia was responsible for was the wine tasting and a large amount of appetizers. She had a few of the same high school kids coming to help again. One local wine shop was also coming with wine.

Friday night arrived and Natalia went upstairs to get ready. She was the hostess and MC for the evening and had to dress accordingly—which was her least favorite thing to do. She didn't mind hosting the affair. It was dressing up she wasn't fond of, especially the torture device known as high heels.

She put on her make-up and dried her hair. In her closet hung the black off the shoulder dress she intended to wear. That's when she spotted her black high heels on the floor looking up at her, as if mocking her. Natalia swore at them under her breath, picked them up and walked out the bedroom door. She felt Giovanna whiz by and groaned as she heard something fall to the floor. She turned and saw her one and only bottle of perfume on the floor.

"No. I'm not wearing that, it makes me sneeze." The bottle moved across the floor toward her. "No, I said."

The phone was ringing and she rushed downstairs to answer it. "Nat, where are you? It's six o'clock and everyone's ready," Sam told her.

"I'll be right there."

She opened the closet to get her coat and was knocked over by the smell of perfume. The bottle was on the floor and had been sprayed all over the small closet. She couldn't wear her coat. It reeked of perfume. She started sneezing immediately.

"If you think this is helping me, it's not." She sneezed again. "I'll take care of you later."

She sneezed her way back upstairs to get a shawl, Giovanna following her.

"Yes, I know you win. I can't do anything to you. I can't see or explain you, *and* you have Marc wrapped around your invisible little finger. I'm screwed and at your mercy. Happy?"

♨♨

Marc was in the kitchen waiting for Natalia. "Sam, did you call her? What's taking her so long?"

"She's on her way."

Marc heard the sneeze before he saw her. "God bless you."

"Thanks," she said as she took off her shawl.

Sam whistled at her. "Wow, Nat. You ought to show off your feminine wiles more often."

"These shoes are going to kill me. Mariella, I don't know how you do it every day."

Marc stepped behind her and put his hands on her shoulders. Her body stiffened.

"You look beautiful," he said. "You smell good, too. That's my favorite perfume. How'd you know?"

"I didn't. It's the only bottle I have. Robbie gave it to me for Christmas. Giovanna knew and practically sprayed the whole bottle on me. We had a fight. I'm still mad at her."

He laughed. "I would love to see you two go at it. I'm sure it's very entertaining. I told you she liked me."

"Then take her home when you go. She can live with you and Simone."

Two pans hanging from the ceiling fell down off their hooks. They both jumped.

"I guess she wants to stay here. I'll have to make sure I come visit you two."

"I should go. People are arriving, and I have to welcome everyone. Is the food ready?"

"Yes."

She relaxed when he removed his hands from her shoulders. Then he moved closer to her back. He took her long hair and put it to one side of her neck. She could feel the heat of his body against her and his breath whispering in her ear, "Good luck tonight, Nat. You'll do great."

She walked away.

Marc watched as Natalia greeted the crowd of people filtering in. When everyone was settled, she took the microphone and asked for their attention. She made a nice speech regarding the Parent/Teacher Organization, their importance in the educational system and the future of their children. She asked everyone to look carefully at all the wonderful items on bid and be as generous as they could. Then she invited everyone to enjoy themselves, the food, wine, and music. She was busy all evening and never came into the kitchen.

A small part of Marc was glad she didn't come back. How was he going to tell her that in the past two days he started to remember some of his life—but not her? It happened right after he left the doctor's office on Tuesday. The memories were like postcards from the past, flashing in his mind. The first thing that came to him was when he was a child with Mariella. Then bits and pieces of Simone. He willed himself to remember Natalia, but his brain wouldn't cooperate. He assumed he would be happy when he started remembering—and he was to a certain point—except he wished Natalia was part of his memories. He hadn't told anyone yet, not Mariella or Simone. He wanted Natalia to be the first to know.

♨♨

The evening wound down. Natalia reached for the microphone, read the items on the silent auction, and announced the winners.

After everyone was gone, she went into the kitchen with a big smile on her face.

"Thank you, everyone, for a great job," she said. "The PTO made a lot of money and everyone had a good time."

She hugged everyone, including Marc. "Once again, I kept hearing how wonderful the food was. I really appreciate everything you've done for me. The parties wouldn't have been so successful if it wasn't for you."

"I was happy to help. It was fun. There's no place I'd rather have been these last few days than here."

"It's getting late. Let me shut off everything in the other room." She started to turn off the music when she heard Sam yell at her, "Wait, Nat, this is one of my favorite songs." A Frank Sinatra CD was playing.

"Mariella, will you dance with me?"

"Oh, Sam, don't be ridiculous. There's no one here."

"Come on, humor an old man."

"It was always one of my favorites as well." Mariella walked with him onto the dance floor.

"They make a sweet couple, don't you think?" Natalia asked Marc. "I never thought those two would get together. Sam really likes her. I've never seen him like this."

"I hope it wasn't because of me Mariella never married and had a family of her own."

"Don't feel that way. She told me she loved raising you. At the time, her career was very important to her, that's why she never married."

"Do you know about my parents?"

"Yes. Mariella told me. I'm so sorry."

"It seems I didn't have too many memories of them to begin with," he said sadly. "Now I don't have any."

"You will. I'm sure of it." She gently touched his arm. "You're too hard on yourself."

"You always make me feel better." He gazed intently into her eyes. "Would you like to dance?"

"I can't dance."

"Yes, she can, Marc," called Sam as he and Mariella twirled around. "Don't let her fool you. She dances quite well,"

"Sam, what the hell's wrong with you?" yelled Natalia. "For twenty-five years you've kept to yourself and never talked about you or anyone else. Now you can't keep your mouth shut."

"Sorry, kid. I have a new lease on life."

"Great."

"Come on, Natalia. It'll be fun.

Against her better judgment, she let him take her hand. As they started to dance, Natalia immediately tensed up.

"You can relax, Natalia. It's just a dance."

"I know." She shook her shoulders and arms then laid her head on his chest. It had been a bittersweet ten days having him around, but she wouldn't have traded it for the world. She'd treasure these last few hours with him.

She thought she deserved to be able to take all of him, if only for a few minutes. The way he smelled—a combination of his aftershave and the food he had cooked—the way it felt to have him hold her. She pulled him closer and was in heaven when his arms tightened around her.

The song was over and Frank began to croon another when Mariella said, "Natalia, I need to talk to you."

Not now, Mariella.

"Natalia, it's important."

She continued to ignore the woman.

Mariella sighed. "Marcos."

Marc led Natalia to the other side of the room. She grinned.

"Marcos, I'm losing my patience, with both of you."

"What's so urgent it can't wait until the song's over?" he asked.

"Trust me, it's important," Mariella snapped.

Natalia patted Marc's shoulder affectionately. "I better go see what she wants."

He caressed the side of her face. "Hurry back so we can finish our dance."

Reluctantly, Natalia unwound her arms from Marc and walked over to Mariella.

"Natalia, you wanted me here to stop you from doing something you will regret, remember?"

"This is the time you pick to finally do something I ask you to do?"

"Simone comes home tomorrow."

"No, not until Sunday."

"She left me a message. I'm sure Marcos has one as well but I don't think he has his phone with him. I don't want you to get hurt, dear."

Mariella's words punctured Natalia's heart like and icepick. Logically, she knew her time with Marc would soon be over, but it still hurt like hell.

"I'm sorry, Mariella. You're right. I was weak and let my guard down. I shouldn't have. It won't happen again." She hugged her. "I am grateful I was able to have this last bit of time with him. Thank you for *arranging* it so that he could be here." She smiled through her tears. "It's time to let him go and get on with my life."

She took a moment to pull herself together. "I think were done here. It's late and I have a busy day tomorrow getting ready for Robbie to come. You all think I eat a lot? Wait till he gets here."

She tried to laugh. This time when she went back into the dining room, she did turn off the music and unplug the trees. Grabbing her shawl, she wrapped it around her and walked toward the door.

"Natalia, wait," said Marc.

"Marc, it's late. We're all going back to the house."

She hurried out door with Mariella, leaving Marc and Sam standing there.

♨♨

The four of them were having coffee in Natalia's kitchen. It was a morning ritual she enjoyed and looked forward to, she thought solemnly, as it was coming to an end.

"Hickory. Its hickory nuts in the coffee," said Sam.

"Sam, you're running out of time. Why don't you just man up and admit you can't figure it out," Marc teased.

"I can't do that," Sam said with a laugh.

"What happened to your secret weapon? If it's Mariella, I don't think she can help you with this."

"That's true, Sam. I'm sorry, but I don't know Marcos' secret."

"Don't worry, I'll figure it out. Mariella, I have to go into town, do you want to come?"

"Sure."

After they left, Marc sat at the kitchen table with Natalia.

"So, Simone comes home today?" she asked him.

"Yes. How did you know?"

"Mariella told me last night."

"Oh, so that's what happened last night. I would have told you but I didn't get the message until I was back in my room."

"Nothing happened last night. Anyway, I'm sure you're glad she's coming home."

"I need to talk to you about something. Are you ready for our walk?"

They walked to the hill and stood looking up at it. Natalia wondered if he was thinking the same thing she was.

"I guess this is our last walk together for a while," he said somberly.

"It's our last walk period. You're going home, and I know you'll be better soon. Wait and see. Before you know it, you'll have your life back and be happy."

"That's what I want to talk to you about." They started up the hill. "I had a nice time last night dancing with you."

Dancing with him and how it made her feel was the last thing she wanted to talk about. If Mariella hadn't stopped her, she was sure they would have gone down that adulterous road again. In her head, she was glad they hadn't. But her heart and soul disagreed. She couldn't take much more of this. It was best his time here was over. What Marc said next, surprised her.

"I can't do anything about us until I figure out about Simone and me."

"There is no us."

"I'm not going to spend the little time we have left arguing with you. I did feel you pull me close to you last night. You didn't want to let go. You enjoyed it as much as I did."

"You're a good dancer, that's all."

"And you're the most stubborn person I've ever met. I knew there was something between us when you walked into the hospital room to see me."

She didn't know what to say, so they walked in silence until they reached the top of the hill. Together, for the last time, she thought, as they looked out over the vineyard.

"I'm really going to miss it here," he said. "But that's not what I want to tell you. I wanted you to be the first to know. I haven't told anyone, not even Mariella. I started to remember some things after I left the doctor's the other day." Natalia started to say something but he stopped her. "Let me finish. I have a few memories of my childhood and Mariella. I also have some of Simone." He took her hands. "I've willed myself to remember you, but I can't. Please, Natalia, tell me something about us. I know it'll help."

"I'm happy for you, I really am," she said as her heart was ripped from her chest. "You'll remember everything you're supposed to when the time is right. Whether you remember me or not isn't important. You need to remember your family and take care of them."

"Why won't you help me?"

"Marc, please. There's nothing I can do."

"I have to pick Simone up at the airport. I'm sorry I won't be here later when your brother gets here, but I'll come back to meet him. How long is he here for?"

"He'll be here for a week."

"Good."

"Meeting my brother should be last thing on your mind. Please, go pick up Simone and get on with your life."

"I have to tell Mariella. She doesn't know yet."

"She'll be thrilled. She's missed you so much."

He put his arms around her and embraced her tightly. She didn't have the strength to push him away. It took all her might to keep from sobbing and telling him everything he wanted to know. He kissed the top of her head and took her face in his hands.

"I'm sorry. I have to go, but I'll be back. I promise." He released her and walked down the hill alone. Natalia turned and headed in the opposite direction, thankful her brother was coming. This was one night she didn't want to be alone.

♨♨

Mariella was packing when Marcos knocked on her door. "What's wrong?"

"I have some news." He walked in and shut the door behind him. "I'm beginning to get a few things back. I remember some of my childhood and you." He opened his arms. Mariella fell against him and started to cry. He hadn't hugged her in weeks and it felt so good.

"I'm so happy. I've missed you more than you can imagine."

"I know and I'm sorry if I was distant and short-tempered with you. It's been nice spending time with you these last ten days and getting to know you again. I think it really helped me."

"I understand, dear. I knew you weren't yourself."

"I have a few memories of Simone as well. I'm going to the airport to pick her up."

"Oh. Anything else?

"Natalia? No, as hard as I've tried to remember her, I can't. Mariella, please tell me the truth. Since she walked into my hospital room, I knew she was different. Special. You already know I don't want to go back to the city. I'd rather stay here, but I can't."

"No, Marcos, you can't. Running from your old life isn't the answer. You have to face it head on. Now that you're remembering some things, it should be easier, especially if you have any decisions to make. I truly believe everything happens for a reason. You'll remember Natalia when the time is right."

"You sound like Natalia. Have you two been rehearsing your answers?"

"You told Natalia?"

"Yes, for some reason I wanted to tell her first."

"Really, not Simone?"

"No. I don't know why."

"Yes, you do, dear. How did she take it?"

"You know how stubborn she is. She said she was happy for me, and I think she is glad that I'm getting my memory back. But I think it bothers her that I don't remember her. She refused to help me, so I don't know what to do."

"You're going to pick up Simone and take care of that." Mariella kissed on the cheek. "It's good to have you back. I love you, Marcos."

"I love you too, Mariella. I don't have all my memory back, but it does feel good to be almost a whole person again."

CHAPTER 26

"If you love someone, set them free. If they come back they're yours; if they don't they never were." – *Gibran Kahlil Gibran, 1883-1931 Lebanese-American poet, writer, artist.*

Marc got to the airport and located Simone's arrival gate. He had a few minutes before her plane landed so he leaned back in his chair, closed his eyes, and thought about his life these past weeks. He supposed, in order to be fair to Simone, he had to be honest with himself.

He'd struggled with his feelings for Simone. Since the accident, he never felt at ease around her. Not only was she a stranger to him, she gave him the impression she wasn't comfortable around him either. When he came home from the hospital, the house didn't have much of a women's touch, which he thought odd. The plants were almost dead and the cupboards were bare. He found a huge pile of what he assumed were his dirty clothes in the closet. The bathroom didn't look much better than what you might find in a house full of college boys.

One day he heard Simone complaining she didn't know where the checkbook or the bills were. When he asked her about it, she said he'd been paying the bills because she'd been traveling so much. He found it hard to believe he would hide the bills away from her, but he didn't even know what day he was born on, much less how he handled money.

Then there was the intimate part of their marriage, if you could call two strangers constantly anxious around each other, yet living together, a marriage. One night he decided to make her a nice dinner but she picked at her food. She told him she watched what she ate so she would always look good for him. She took his hand and led him upstairs. He had wondered when this aspect of his marriage would come up and what he would do when it did. He told her they should give it more time.

"Marc, you're my husband, and it's what I want. Don't you find me attractive anymore?"

He noticed she never mentioned she loved him but when she started to undress, he didn't think about that. He found her very attractive. She was an extremely beautiful woman. When she started to kiss him and caress certain parts of his body, it wasn't long before biology, lust, and a longing to experience something that was part of his life took over, and he had no trouble partaking in what she had to offer.

That's when the trouble started. Simone thought being intimate together would make him remember her. She couldn't have been more wrong. Immediately afterwards, her eyes full of desperate hope, she asked him if he remembered her. He always had to say no. It wasn't something he could lie about. He knew he was hurting her. It was taking its toll on him, too, and he soon began to avoid her advances.

One day she announced she was taking him to an island in the Caribbean. She said it was their favorite place to vacation, and she was sure when they got there his memory would return. It was all she talked about. He feared he wouldn't be able to live up to her expectations and dreaded going.

The first night there, she planned a romantic dinner in their room. She lit candles, poured champagne and wore a wildly sexy piece of lingerie. She climbed into bed with him and asked him if this brought back any memories. Again, he had to say no. She started to cry. He felt horrible. He took her in his arms and told her how sorry he was. She kissed him and he kissed her back, but he felt nothing, except constant guilt-ridden depression. He pushed her away.

Somewhere in the back of his mind, resentment and anger crept in. He realized he had taken the whole burden of his memory loss on his shoulders, and she let him. She may as well have handed it to him. He was constantly apologizing and taking the blame for not remembering. It was exhausting to be made to feel everything was your fault. All she did was pressure him to remember her with no consideration how lost he was not knowing anything about himself.

Simone kissed him again. He felt nothing. At that moment, there was nothing desirable about her. She was devastated when he didn't get aroused. Like every other time she was upset, he apologized. No words of encouragement of understanding came from her. He felt like shit, got up, and spent the night on the couch in the other room. They left for home the next day.

Things hadn't been going well between the two of them when a man showed up with the package from the lawyer. Simone told him it was work related, but it couldn't have been good news. She became restless and troubled.

Two days later, he was at a work function with her when he found the note in his wallet about cooking dinner for Natalia. He smiled when he saw her name. He often thought about her. When Simone told him she was going to Paris for two weeks, he asked Mariella to call Natalia.

He heard Simone's flight announced over the loud speaker. He was here, as he should be. She was his wife and his first priority. Now that he had some vague memories of her, would he feel what he was supposed to when he saw her? He would know in a few minutes.

He searched for her in the crowd and finally spotted her, walking and talking with a man. He had his arm around her. They stopped, and she looked at her companion tenderly. He kissed her passionately. They started to separate and head in different directions when the man turned, grabbed Simone, and kissed her again. Simone didn't stop him.

She hadn't seen Marc. Thank God. He turned and walked back down the long corridor. Taking out his cell phone, her listened to her message once more. She apologized for calling so late and on such short notice. She assured him her company would have a car for her so he needn't come to the airport. She did ask him to call her as soon as he could. The bottom line was she wasn't expecting him to be at the airport.

He couldn't remember the last time he was this fucking angry. But then again, he couldn't remember a lot of things. What confused him was the reason for his anger. Was he mad at Simone or himself? These last ten days with Natalia, he'd been the happiest he'd been since the accident. She was stubborn and spoke her mind, but he didn't care. He liked that she and Sam went about their lives and seemed happy to have him around. They included him. There was no pressure to remember this or that. In stark contrast to Simone, Natalia told him he was being too hard on himself, and everything would come to him in time.

He had, for the last ten days, behaved the best he could around Natalia. Most nights he tossed and turned thinking about her across the hall from him. Each night, he wanted to knock on her door to see if she would let him in, but he didn't.

He and Natalia had gotten closer since he came back on Tuesday. On Wednesday and Thursday after working all day, they made popcorn and watched horror movies. After the movie, they would talk for hours, then go upstairs and say good night.

Last night was the hardest. He thought if anything was going to happen it would have been last night. Natalia had finally let her defenses down. They'd enjoyed dancing and holding each other. He hadn't wanted to put Natalia in an awkward position—he was married—so when her mood suddenly changed after talking with Mariella, he let her go. That didn't change the fact he felt a connection to her that was getting stronger and harder to fight each day.

He took out his cell phone, called his home number and left a message for Simone.

"Hi Simone. I didn't get your message until this morning. I wish you had let me know you were coming home a day early. There's an event tonight at the vineyard, and I can't leave them hanging without a chef. I'll see you tomorrow."

It wasn't a message most husbands would leave after their wives were gone for ten days. Right now, he didn't care. Let her figure it out. He swallowed hard and said, "I hope you had a good trip." Then he hung up the phone.

Leaving Mariella's car in the airport parking lot, he hailed a cab and told the driver to find the nearest liquor store. Marc bought a bottle of whiskey and climbed back in the cab. After he opened the whiskey and took a gulp, he explained to the cabbie where he wanted to go.

CHAPTER 27

"Each unveils the best part of the other. No matter what else goes wrong around us, with that one person we're safe in our own paradise. Our soul mate is someone who shares our deepest longings, our sense of direction." – *Richard Bach, 1936 - Author*

Natalia heard the knock on the door and dashed to open it. When she saw her brother, she jumped into his arms and squeezed him tight.

"Robbie, I'm so happy to see you!"

"Hey sis, it's great to see you, too." He hugged her then put her down.

"Hi, doll," quipped the good-looking man with him.

"Ben!" She jumped into his arms as well. "I'm so glad you came. I needed to see both of you so much!" Tears streamed down her face.

"What's wrong, Sis? We don't usually make you cry when we visit."

"I don't want to talk about it. I'll tell you later. Right now, I need you to get the cards and poker chips. I'll get the whiskey and order pizza."

"Oh, shit," Robbie said and glanced at Ben.

A couple hours later, the pizza boxes were empty, the whiskey bottle low, and Natalia had most of the chips in front of her. "Are you two letting me win?" She was starting to slur her words.

"Never, doll. We taught you how to play. Remember? You're beating us fair and square," Ben said with a wink.

She had already told Robbie about Marc, minus the part of spending the night together, via email these last few months.

Tonight she told him how he left to pick up Simone at the airport.

"Come on, sweetie," said Robbie. "I know you're hurt, but you knew he was married. Let's go for a walk outside. It'll help clear your head."

"No, it's too late for a walk. It's my deal, I think."

Ben took the cards from her hands. "We've had a long day traveling and we're tired. We can finish tomorrow.

Someone was banging on the door. "Do you always have people at your door this late?" Robbie asked.

She shrugged. Robbie answered the door. "Hi, is Natalia here?" She walked over and saw Marc, looking handsome, but drunk.

"Oh, God," she groaned. "I need more whiskey."

"No! It's all gone, doll," snapped Ben.

"I have plenty." Marc pulled a bottle out of a brown paper bag.

"At least you're good for something." She grabbed the bottle from him. "What are you doing here, and who's blowing the damn horn?"

Marc yelled something to the man outside on the horn then turned back to her. "Hey, Nat, I promised you I would be back, didn't I?"

"Don't call me that. Who's out there?"

"The cabbie needs a few hundred dollars, and I don't have it. Did you know it costs three hundred dollars, plus tip, to take a cab from Kennedy to here? I tried to tell him how unreasonable it was but he won't listen to me. I think if we ignore him, he'll go away." He staggered to the table. "Hey, you're playing poker, deal me in."

Robbie opened the kitchen cabinet, took out a jar and dumped all the cash out on the counter.

"Hey," yelled Natalia. "Get out of my swear jar. I'm not paying for this."

"Ben, how much cash do you have?"

Someone else was banging on the door. Robbie glowered at her. "Nat, how do you let things get this out of control?"

When Robbie opened the door, an angry looking cabbie stood on the porch. "Hey, that guy over there owes me a lot of money, and I'm not going anywhere till somebody pays."

Robbie took all her cash plus some of his own and Ben's, paid the driver, and sent him on his way.

"Come on, let's play," said Marc. "Nat, I think I can beat your cute little ass any day."

"Really? Think again *scassaca...scassaca...*"

"*Scassacazzo,*" said Robbie. "Natalia, stop it."

"Oh yeah? You didn't think I was a pain in the ass when you needed me to...you know...cook for you, did you?" Marc waved at Robbie and Ben. "Hi, is one of you Nat's brother? I guess I've forgotten my manners, among other things. I'm Marc," he said and held out his hand.

"Yes, I'm Robbie and this is Ben. Okay you two, we're done for tonight. Both of you have had enough to drink."

"No, I haven't had that much." Marc grabbed the bottle. "I don't know what makes you think that. Maybe I should catch up, though." He tried to pour whiskey into his glass, but spilled it instead.

"Robbie, I still want to play."

"Natalia, please don't be the whiney sister tonight."

"I'm not tired."

"We are," said Ben. "Marc, you take the couch over there." Ben took the whiskey bottle from him. "That's enough, Marc. Get some rest. You'll thank me in the morning."

Marc settled into the couch and turned his back to everyone.

"Okay sis, let's go upstairs."

"Wait"

"What do you need, doll?" asked Ben.

"Marc needs a blanket. I think there's one in the closet."

Ben got a blanket out of the closet and handed it to her. Tears filled her eyes. She couldn't believe Marc came back. Why didn't he pick up Simone, get on with his life, and leave her alone? She covered him up and couldn't stop her heart from sighing. Who was she kidding? She was glad he was here.

"Look how cute and sweet he is. I'm going to curl up with him for a few minutes. Not long...just a little while. Will you guys get me when I tell you to?" She started to sway as she rambled on.

"Natalia! He's married, give it a rest," Robbie said firmly.

"You think I don't know that!" She pulled the pillow out from under Marc's head and began hitting him with it.

He jumped up and covered his head with his arms. "Nat, what the hell? Stop it."

She hit him one more time, "Stop calling me that."

"Natalia, that's enough." Ben snatched the pillow from her and threw it back to Marc. "Go to sleep, Marc." He dragged Natalia over to her brother. "Here, she's all yours."

"Thanks," said Robbie. "Isn't it your turn to deal with her?"

She tried to wiggle out of Ben's military hold but couldn't. "Oh no, I had to do it last time."

"You know I can hear you," she said, still struggling against Ben's tight grip. He finally let go of her and she went right back over to Marc.

"No you don't. Leave him alone." Robbie grabbed her arm.

"I don't want to leave him alone, and I don't want to go upstairs." She crossed her arms defiantly. "I want to stay here with him."

"Your impossible when you get like this, you know that?" Robbie handed her back to Ben. "Keep her away from him. I'll be right back."

He returned with blankets and pillows from upstairs and threw them on the family room floor. Natalia could always count on her brother to be on her side. He handed her shorts and a tank top and directed her to the bathroom. When she came out, Robbie laughed. "Nat, you have everything on inside out."

She shrugged at him. "You're lucky I even got them on. I'm not feeling too well."

He led her over to their makeshift bed for the night. She flopped down next to Ben. Robbie turned off the lights and stretched out on the other side of her.

"You're a good brother." She kissed him. "And you're a good friend." She kissed Ben as well.

"Doll, you can't keep this up," said Ben. "You have to make a decision."

"Ben's right, Nat. Either, tell Marc how you feel about him and about your past together or send him on his way."

"I've been trying to send him away, but he keeps coming back. I can't tell him."

"You can and should. He has a right to know everything. He's living in limbo with not much memory of anything. How can he make a good decision based on that?" Robbie said.

"No."

"Try to get some sleep. We'll figure it out in the morning. You know I'd do anything for you, right sis?"

She rolled over to her brother and said, "Anything?"

"Of course."

"Then can you make the goddamn room stop spinning?"

"She doesn't handle her whiskey as well as she used to," Ben said.

"She getting old, and she's in loovvve," teased Robbie.

"I heard that," she said. It was the last thing she remembered.

CHAPTER 28

"We must realize that we seldom meet a person by accident. Almost everyone we meet in this lifetime is an old acquaintance we met in a distant past." – *Jaime T. Licauco, 1940- Parapsychologist and Author*

Natalia thought she heard someone knocking. She assumed she was dreaming and rolled over.

Then she heard the door creak open and someone say her name.

"Natalia? Are you here?"

Natalia pulled her head out from underneath the covers and looked up. "Simone?"

"Natalia."

"Do you have to shout?"

"I'm not shouting."

"Yeah, you are. What are you doing here?"

"Mariella sent a car for me. Why are you sleeping on the floor? Oh God," she put her hand to her mouth. "Is Marc in there with you?"

"No, I'm here with these guys." Natalia pulled the blankets off and revealed the two men lying there with her.

"Oh, my God. Who are they?"

"I don't know who they are. They're cute though, aren't they?"

Natalia was amused as Simone's cheeks turned bright at the sight of the men lying there. "Where's Marc?"

"Look over there on the couch. Please keep it down."

"Hey, doll, how are you feeling?" Ben asked groggily as he rolled over.

"Like crap."

"Well, you look worse than that."

"Natalia, have some self-respect," said Simone. "Marc, honey, please wake up."

"To what do we owe the pleasure of this lovely lady here this morning?" Ben asked as he propped himself up on his elbow.

Now Robbie was awake. "Good morning, ma'am."

Simone ignored them. Natalia rolled her eyes. She was having a hard time wrapping her head around Simone being there. Why on earth would Mariella send a car for her? Natalia didn't think her life could get any worse than it was at this moment. But right now, she had other things to worry about. She had to pee.

She pulled the blanket around her and walked into the bathroom. Ugh, she was a sight. Her hair was all over the place and there was so much mascara under her eyes she looked like a raccoon.

She tried to wash up a little, but didn't want to miss what was going on in the other room. She went and sat at a small table in the corner of the family room. Robbie and Ben were in the kitchen making coffee. Again, she was grateful they were there.

It sounded like Simone had finally gotten Marc up. He didn't look too good. Simone had gotten him some water.

"What do you want, Simone," he asked indifferently.

"What do I *want?* That's the welcome I get from my husband after being away for almost two weeks? You could at least pretend you're glad to see me."

"You're right. I'm sorry. How about this? Who the hell was he, Simone?"

"Who was who?" she breathed. "Can we please go outside?"

"No. You weren't ashamed of your public display of affection. So you shouldn't mind talking about it in public."

Simone obviously knew everyone was staring at her and she looked mortified. Natalia felt a twinge of sympathy for her. Everyone was capable of callous and unkind words if pushed hard enough, but she was still surprised at Marc's behavior.

"His name is Philip and he and I worked together for a few months." Simone stared at the floor while she spoke. "It's been hard having you not remember me, and I needed someone to talk with. When Philip noticed I wasn't myself at work, he asked what was wrong. He took the time to listen and asked if there was something he could do for me. It was nice to have someone pay a little attention to me. He and I like the same things. He understands how important my career is to me."

"We've had the same argument for months, haven't we?"

"Mariella told me you started to remember. Do you only remember the bad times?"

"Of course not. I only remember up until September or so. I don't remember any of the holidays up to the accident. I do remember you getting your promotion and how proud I was of you. I remember you being gone for weeks at a time then deciding to move out. I remember coming home every night by myself and never going out. I was the patient, supportive husband. I waited for you for what I assume was months. But your patience for me to get my memory back, wore thin by week three. The first chance you got, you ran off to Paris with some other guy."

"I didn't run off to Paris with him. I didn't even know he was coming. He didn't arrive until two days ago."

"Bullshit."

"Marc!" snarled Natalia. "That's enough. Obviously, you don't know the whole story. Until you do, leave her alone."

Both Simone and Marc's head whipped around. They stared at her, and it was obvious, neither of them had expected any defense from her.

That's when it happened.

When her eyes locked with Simone's, Natalia had the familiar sensation that she knew her. She could deal with that. What she couldn't deal with was Marc carrying on about being the good husband.

If he only knew, which he didn't, but he had no right to point his finger at Simone. Natalia didn't know what Simone's public display of affection was about, but how bad could it have been? Were they holding hands, maybe they kissed? Big freaking deal, compared to what she and Marc had done—and the fury, passion, and love they had done it with—anything Simone did was a mild offense.

"I didn't mean to butt in, but dredging up the past isn't going to help whatever your present situation is."

"I don't remember what our present situation is." Marc turned to Simone. "I'd like some answers."

"My job has caused many of our problems. I travel a lot and I enjoy it."

"Did I ever go with you?"

"Marc, please. Do we have to do this in front of everyone?"

"Yes! This is the first time since the accident we've had an honest talk."

"No, you never came along. You're a homebody and prefer a traditional life. We've already had this conversation."

"That may be so, but I don't remember."

"If you had come with me, you would've been alone most of the day and wouldn't have been happy. Then after a week, maybe ten days at the most, you'd have started wanting to go home. Then we'd have the same argument all over again about...having kids. I don't want kids and was very clear about that before we got married."

"I know, I remember that. I don't remember arguing about it."

"It's been bad, especially these last few months."

Out of nowhere, Robbie and Ben appeared from the kitchen with five cups of coffee on a tray.

"Coffee's ready." Robbie cleared his throat. "I have something I'd like to say."

Natalia groaned and held her aching head. She had suffered through plenty of Robbie's 'save the world' speeches.

"Excuse me," said Simone. "But who are you two?"

"I'm Natalia's brother, Robbie, and this is my best friend, Ben."

Natalia giggled. "Sorry, I couldn't resist."

"So," Robbie began. "Needless to say, most of us are strangers and yet we find ourselves in a very intimate situation. Since we've been privy to some of your conversation this morning, maybe we can help.

"You see, for most of my life, I haven't lived as myself. I was always trying to be what other people thought I should be.

It's not pleasant, never being able to be yourself, or at least only when you are around people you trust."

"Robbie," Natalia said slowly. "Are you sure you want—"

"Yes, Nat, I'm fine. Ben is my friend, but he's also my lover and has been for fifteen years."

Simone gulped. "You're gay?"

"Yes. I know we aren't what you'd expect, two big strapping men who drink whiskey and play poker. Anyway, when I told my parents, it didn't go well. They told me they loved me but couldn't accept my lifestyle. So after Ben and I left the Navy, we learned to fly small planes. The man who taught us was looking to sell his business, so we bought it. It's a small operation in New Hampshire but we enjoy it."

Ben handed everyone a cup of coffee as Robbie continued his speech.

"I'm sure you're wondering why I'm telling you this, especially since you don't know me. Well, it seems, from my point of view anyway, you two are going in different directions and are upset the other one doesn't want to follow." Robbie took a sip of his coffee. "Ben, great coffee, thanks. Simone, you don't want to have kids, so what?"

"The world is over populated anyway," said Ben.

"You were up front with Marc so he can't be upset with you," Robbie continued. "Don't let anyone make you feel guilty for not wanting children. Your career is important to you and that's great. We need strong, smart women who can lead the way in so many fields that have long been male dominated. Don't be ashamed of who you are.

"Marc, you're more traditional. I would love a boatload of kids, but I don't think it's in the cards for us." Robbie turned his attention to Natalia. "I'll leave that to, Nat, but maybe you can get a move on. I would like to be an uncle before I die, and you're not getting any younger."

She stuck her tongue out at him.

"Having a family and spending time with them is important to you, Marc. That's wonderful. So many people rush through life these days and forget to take the time to enjoy family and friends. There's no right or wrong. Everyone is different.

"You two have had a major crisis to deal with," he said to Marc and Simone. "If you really love each other, you should be able to get through it. Remember, there was something there in the beginning that made you fall in love. But you can't expect the other person to completely give up his or her identity to appease the other one. That won't work. It's okay to compromise but not to lose who you are. If you don't think you can respect each other's differences, maybe you should consider letting each other go. Then you can find someone who shares the same goals and dreams as you. And I'm not just saying that because Natalia is over the moon in love with Marc."

In Natalia's pounding head, it seemed like it happened in slow motion. She heard Robbie's words but it took a minute to register that he had just thrown her under one huge city bus. Simone sprayed her coffee all over the coffee table. Natalia jerked the blanket over her head and let her forehead drop to the table.

Robbie patted her back. "Sorry, Nat, it had to be said."

"*Ruffiano.*"

"Grow up," he ordered. "That's it, folks. Thanks for listening. Ben and I will make breakfast. I'm sure Natalia is hungry."

"Wait," Simone cried. "I don't really know what to make of all the things you've said, but I would like to thank you for understanding my side, especially about not having children. Most people make me feel selfish and shallow."

"You're welcome."

"Marc, where's Mariella?" Simone asked. "I would like to talk to her."

"I don't know. I'll go look in her room," said Marc.

They all waited in an uncomfortable silence for Marc to return. "She's not in her room. Sam would know where she is."

"Natalia," Robbie barked. "Get out from under there and take Simone to Sam's cottage to find out where Mariella is. We'd like to meet her, we've heard a lot about her."

"No," she muttered, from hiding place inside the blanket.

"Natalia, now," Robbie ordered.

"Why can't Marc take her? She's his aunt."

"Ben and I would like to talk to Marc, and I think Simone may have something she'd like to talk to you about."

"*Lo vado a legare le palle in un nodo.*"

"Ouch." Marc winced. "Why such destruction of the male anatomy?"

"Because she's *allupato,*" Robbie explained.

Marc gave a half laugh that quickly turned into a groan. "My head is throbbing."

"Fine." *Will this hell never end?* Natalia grabbed the whiskey, poured the last little bit in her coffee, turned to Simone and said, "Come on, then."

♨♨

Simone studied the curious woman walking next to her. She was certain she'd never met anyone exactly like Natalia before—or had she? Every time she found herself in a room with Natalia, she had an overwhelming feeling they knew each other. But that was impossible. She would have remembered meeting someone with her colorful personality.

"So, you're in love with Marc?" she asked.

Natalia sighed. "It's complicated and hard to explain, but I have feelings for him I shouldn't have."

Simone was surprised at her honesty. She thought she would at least try to deny it.

"While he's been here these last ten days, have you slept with him?"

"No, Simone. Believe me, it's not like that."

"Oddly, I do believe you. I think you're many things, but a liar isn't one of them. You speak your mind too quickly to take the time to make up a lie. Why don't you tell me what it *is* like then?"

Simone listened as Natalia explained how she and Marc met at the restaurant, meeting Mariella at Marc's request, the business arrangement with Mariella, and Natalia's sleep troubles.

"I didn't know how close Marc and Mariella were until I was at her center getting treatment. He came to visit a lot. Little by little, a friendship grew among the three of us. I had just gone through a bad break-up and was feeling vulnerable. Marc was easy to talk with. I knew he was married. It was never my intention to act on my feelings. That's why after the accident, I left the hospital without saying good-bye.

"When Rachel couldn't cook for the events, Mariella and Marc both pushed me to let him come and help. I tried to refuse, but when they both gang up on you, it's hard to say no."

"Natalia, you don't seem like a woman who's pushed around easily. Why did you really let Marc come?"

"I wanted to see how he was. I'd had no contact with him since the accident. Mariella and Marc both thought a little time away from the life he was supposed to remember would do him good, give him the opportunity to cook and relax. And it worked. By the time they left for a couple days and then came back, Marc had started remembering you and Mariella."

Simone stopped walking and turned to face Natalia. "Why did you stick up for me earlier? You don't even know me."

"Why not? I think when people say what's on their mind, it's assumed to always be negative. That's not true. When I see someone not being treated fairly, I don't like it. Marc wasn't being fair. Your conversation should have been in private. You should have insisted, but you didn't. You need to learn to stick up for yourself and not let people walk all over you. I won't always be there to rescue—"

Natalia stopped speaking abruptly and turned away from Simone. Simone could tell Natalia was as shaken as she was, by her own words. Simone often wondered if Natalia had the same sensation of knowing her, and now she was pretty sure she did.

"What did you say? How do you know that about me? Did Marc tell you?"

"No, Marc didn't even remember you until the other day. I've always been able to get a good read on people."

The two women stood there in silence until Simone spoke. "Thank you for being so honest with me, Natalia. I feel I should be honest with you."

"Okay."

"In an odd, twisted kind of way, I'm not that upset with you. I understand because I have some unresolved feelings for someone I shouldn't as well. I realize you can't always stop these things from happening."

"I was wondering why you've been so gracious to me. I can't honestly say I would be as patient with someone like me if the situation were reversed," Natalia admitted.

"I don't know about that. You may let your temper get the best of you but you always seem to be fair."

"And how do you know about me or my temper? We've only met three times."

Simone had no idea how she knew. "Mariella told me. Anyway," she said, wanting to change the subject, "I do have one more question. Why did your brother announce your feelings for Marc like that?"

"My brother's a pain in the ass." Natalia sighed. "Robbie didn't think it was a good idea for Marc to come here for almost two weeks. I downplayed my feelings for Marc to my brother but he saw through my denial. Lately, Robbie's big on honesty. He didn't think I could get over Marc and move on until I acknowledged my feelings to myself. He's very in your face sometimes."

"It was brave of him to be so open with us this morning. It will make us all think about our lives more carefully," Simone said as they started walking again.

"He hasn't had it easy, being gay. He never could understand why people define him by who he sleeps with. That's such a small part of who is he. He and Ben are wonderful human beings, but all certain people care about is their sex life. That's when he decided he was going to be truthful to himself and everyone else. Robbie doesn't think anyone can make a decision until they have *all* the information they can get on the subject. And make no mistake, if he thinks he has a fact or some words of wisdom that may help you make a decision, he'll tell you at a moment's notice. That's why he made his speech this morning."

The two women half smiled at each other. "We're here," said Natalia.

She knocked on the cottage door. "Sam, are you in there? Wake up. Did you leave Mariella in the city last night? She's not in her room. Sam!"

The door opened, "Don't worry, Natalia. I'm right here." Mariella opened the door with a sheet wrapped around her.

"Mariella," Simone gasped. "What are you doing?"

"Isn't it obvious, dear? Why are you so surprised? Love isn't only for the young."

Sam peeked his head out the door to see what was going on. "Mariella, who's this lovely lady?"

"This is Marcos' wife, Simone."

"It's a pleasure to meet you," said Sam.

"You, too." Simone sat down on a bench near Sam's front door.

"Nat, you look like hell," said Sam.

"Thanks. I think you had a better night than I did."

"I guess Robbie and Ben made it here last night."

"Yes, they're here."

"Rough night?" he asked.

"Last night is a little murky. Could you both come up to the house please? Robbie and Ben want to meet Mariella."

"Sure, dear," said Mariella. "Just give us a minute or two. I'm looking forward to meeting your brother."

"My head is spinning. I've only been here two hours and it seems everything is upside down," Simone said as Natalia sat down next to her.

"Welcome to my life," Natalia said. "Can I ask a favor, Simone?"

"Sure, why not?"

"Can I have five minutes with Marc before you leave? I want to thank him for all his help and wish him well. It'll be the last time I'll see him for quite a while."

"Yes. I would like to talk to him in private first, though. Is there somewhere we can go?"

"Take a walk out back in the vineyard. It'll be nice out there this morning."

CHAPTER 29

"Ti amo dal profondo del mio cuore con tutta la mia anima." (I love thee with the depth and breadth and height my soul can reach.) – *Italian Love Quote*

Marc started the conversation. "First, let me apologize for last night. I can usually handle my liquor better than that. I was confused and upset."

"No problem, Marc," Robbie assured him. "We understand better than you think because Nat told us everything, including things you don't remember. If I were you and living like that, I'd hit the bottle occasionally, too,"

"Why won't she tell me about us?"

"I'd better not say. If I told you, she really would tie my balls in a knot. No thanks."

Marc laughed. "You know Natalia was the only person who was familiar to me after the accident. I like it here and feel like it's where I belong. I don't want to leave, but I know my first responsibility is Simone."

"My main concern is Natalia. I don't want her hurt again. Yes, you have some decisions to make. I don't want you contacting her until you have everything resolved."

Marc studied the two men. If he'd been paying attention last night, he would have known Robbie was Natalia's brother. He was solidly built with a darker complexion, hair, and eyes than Ben. Ben was leaner than Robbie with sandy brown hair. He had striking blue eyes that seemed to twinkle whenever he spoke. Both men were nice looking, larger than life, and charismatic.

"If she gets hurt again," Robbie continued, "I'm going to have to kill you."

Marc was taken aback at first. But when Robbie punched him in the arm, Marc realized he was joking.

"Nah, I'm kidding. I hate violence. Ben, though, he's the Navy SEAL. He'll be the one doing the killing."

"Relax, Marc. I only ever do that as a last resort." Ben handed him a glass of water and an aspirin. "Here, it looks like you could use this."

Marc gulped down the water. It tasted good. His mouth was like cotton. "Thanks, Ben. Point taken, Robbie. Don't worry. I would never hurt her. I may not remember her right now, but I know she's very important to me."

"We know, Marc," Robbie said.

The door open and Natalia walked in.

"Did you find Mariella?" asked Marc.

"Yes. She was with Sam. I'll let her explain. Simone wants to talk to you outside."

"Natalia, wait."

"Simone is waiting for you." She walked away.

Marc found Simone in the vineyard.

"Let's go for a walk," she said.

They trudged up the hill in silence. They didn't make it to the top. Simone didn't have the proper shoes for hiking in the mud, and Marc was glad. He didn't want to go to the spot where he and Natalia stopped each morning.

"It's beautiful here," she said.

"Yes, it is. Did you enjoy Paris?"

"Yes."

"What did you want to talk to me about?"

"Do you have feelings for Natalia?"

He chose his words carefully. "I still don't remember her. I will admit I've enjoyed being here. I like her and Sam, and they've made me feel at home. What about you? How strong are your feelings for Philip?"

"He's been a good friend to me these last few weeks, since your accident. It was nice to have someone to talk with. I don't know, maybe I've been infatuated with his attention and not necessarily with him." She walked down a row of grapes. Marc followed. "You served me with divorce papers."

"I did?" He was stunned and wasn't sure how to respond. Should he apologize? "Oh—I'm sorry. I didn't know," he said, fumbling his words.

"Don't be sorry. We'd been living apart for about eight months. I couldn't figure out what I wanted to do about our marriage. We had a heated discussion, and you needed a resolution one way or the other."

"I don't remember that."

"When I heard you'd gotten into an accident and were hurt, it scared me. I decided it was time to change my priorities."

"But then I didn't remember you and—"

"And it was very hard to work on an already fragile marriage while dealing with another crisis."

"I understand. So, what do we do next?"

"I don't know. Do you want to come home and try again? It won't be easy. We have a few things to deal with."

"Yes, we do. Do you want me to come home?"

"Now that you're getting your memory back, I'd hate to give up without trying one more time. I don't know what will happen. We have different opinions on important issues."

Since Marc had no memory of Natalia, he'd do what everyone expected him to do—go home with Simone, whether he wanted to or not. He wasn't too confident they'd work things out, but he'd do the right thing. Even if doing what was right and doing want he wanted were two different things.

"I'm willing to try."

"I do love you, Marc."

Marc wondered what he should say to that. He cared about Simone but was it love? He didn't think so, not the way a man should love a woman. But again, he said what was expected of him. "I love you, too."

Even with their professions of love, real or not, they walked back to the house, not touching each other.

♨♨

Natalia took the eggs Robbie made for her and went to her room to eat. Sitting on the edge of her bed, she felt Giovanna blow by her.

"Yes, I know. I'll miss him, too, but there's nothing I can do."

Giovanna stirred up some more cold air right over her plate.

"Go ahead. I don't care if my food gets cold. I'm not even hungry this morning. This is hard enough on me. Please don't make it harder."

Within a minute, Giovanna was gone.

Natalia picked at her food. She figured she better see if Marc was in his room. She did want to thank him for everything. When she walked out her bedroom, Sam stopped her.

"Nat, can I talk to you for a minute?"

"Sure, what's wrong?"

"Nothing." He led her back into her room and shut the door. "So, this is it? Marc's going to leave, and you're going to let him?"

"Sam, what are you talking about? He's married. You knew this was a temporary situation."

"Don't be mad, but Mariella told me *everything.*"

"Great. I'm glad everyone's leaving. It's too crowded here for me. I liked it better on my own. At least I had my privacy. I don't appreciate being the subject of your pillow talk."

"You're right, and I'm sorry, but I need to tell you something. You know how your dad and I met. At a bar in Stamford one night?"

"Yes."

"But you don't know the whole story. I was getting drunk over a woman I was in love with. She was engaged to a wealthy Stamford business man from a powerful family. She and I were friends but our friendship went a little farther than it should have. One day she asked me why I hadn't asked her not to marry her fiancé. I told her I was afraid of what the scandal would do to my family. This man could literally ruin my family and me. I told her I loved her but she would be better off with him. He would be able to give her so much more than I ever could.

"She looked at me with such hurt in her eyes, I thought I would die. She got out of bed, and I never saw her again. The day she got married, I got drunk, like the coward I was."

"Sam, I'm so sorry. I never knew." Natalia leaned over and hugged her dear friend.

"I don't like to talk about it. I've regretted it up until now. I can't believe Mariella walked into my life one day and completely turned it around." He undid himself from her embrace and held her by the shoulders. "I don't want you to have any regrets like I did."

"I won't be the cause of his marriage breaking up."

"Mariella told me Marc hasn't been happy since the summer, way before he met you. She doesn't think Simone's happy either. If all the other things she told me are true, you'll always be the cause of everything he does. Not intentionally, of course, but there's nothing you can do about it."

"It's all true." This time she put her head on his chest as he wrapped his arms around her.

"Wow. If I hadn't heard it from your own mouth, I wouldn't believe it. Do you remember everything from the past?"

"Yes."

"I'm sorry, Nat. Please just think about what I said. If anything is worth fighting for, I think this is it. I've spent a lot of time with Marc and I know he loves you. I see the way he looks at you and acts around you. He doesn't understand it, but he realizes you two are connected somehow. At least give him a little hope that if things don't work out with Simone, he has a chance to be happy."

Sam squeezed her hard one last time and left her alone with her thoughts.

Natalia stood and walked out the door and down the hall to Marc's room. *All right, Sam. I'll tell him one thing but that's it.*

♨♨

"Marc can I come in for a minute?"

He opened the door with his face wet, his shirt off, and a towel around his neck.

"Hi," she said, trying to ignore how good he looked without a shirt. That in turn made her remember how it felt to have his skin next to hers, and she immediately made herself think of Simone. That always worked at making her feel guilty and horrible. "How are you feeling?"

"Better, now that I ate something. Ben gave me some aspirin. How about you?"

"Much better. I just need a shower. I came to thank you again for everything. I know in the beginning I wasn't thrilled you were coming, but I couldn't have done it without you."

"I told you before, Natalia. I was happy to be here. Come in, I'd like to talk to you."

She stepped in and Marc shut the door behind her.

He looked her directly in the eye. "Is what your brother said this morning true?"

"It's very complicated. I'm not sure you'd believe me if I told you."

"That doesn't answer my question. I was awake last night when you wanted to lay down with me. I heard everything you, Robbie, and Ben said."

"I was drunk. I didn't mean any of it."

♨♨

Marc's heart sank. He didn't know why he continued to hope she would admit to having feelings for him. Maybe he finally had to acknowledge the sooner he got over her and on with his life, the better he'd be.

"I guess it's a good thing Simone is back and I can go home with her. And to think I thought how nice it would be to stay here with you. Good thing you set me straight. I don't want to be somewhere I'm not wanted." He turned then paused. "Good-bye, *Natalia*. I think you should leave now." This time he walked away and didn't look back.

"Please, wait," she whispered. "You're birthmark."

He stopped but didn't turn to face her. "What about it? It's one more thing you won't help me with, when I know you can."

He knew she was behind him even before she touched him. The heat from her body radiated over his entire back.

"This has truly been a very unusual morning, wouldn't you say? Are you up for one more strange thing?" she asked.

"Whatever, Natalia. I've had enough of you and everything else. Do whatever the hell you want. You always do."

"Can you sit down for a minute?

"Why?"

"I need to tell you something."

It irritated him, but he did what she asked and sat on the edge of the bed. He couldn't say no to her. She sat behind him, slowly wrapped her arms around him, softly kissed his birthmark, and rested her head on his back.

"Nat, please don't do this if you don't mean it."

"Listen to me. I hope you and Simone work it out if that's what meant to be. But whatever you do, don't let her take this from you or tell you how horrible it is. It's a few different marks blended together to make one beautiful birthmark. I know you had to fight hard to endure all those scars and they're part of your body, heart, and soul. Please don't forget that. Promise me."

"Yes," he said, his voice breaking. He grabbed her arms and held them close to him.

The bathroom door slammed shut. "Giovanna is mad you're leaving. Don't be surprised if you're missing something from your bag when you get home. I'll leave you two alone to say good-bye."

Marc felt her kiss his shoulder again and heard her soft voice in his ear. "*Ti amo dal profondo del mio cuore con tutta la mia anmia.* And you thought I could only *swear* in Italian."

"Nat, please don't go. You can't say that to someone then leave. Why do you keep kissing my shoulder? Don't leave me with more questions than answers." He felt her try to pull away and tightened his hold.

"Please, let go of me. I can't do this again."

"Do what again?"

"You need to let me go. Everyone is waiting for you downstairs."

"I don't want to go. I want to stay here with you," he said holding her even tighter. "I love you, too."

She let out a small whimper. "I'm sorry. I shouldn't have come. It's making things worse. You have to go home now and deep down you know it. You have to try, and I mean really try, to work things out with Simone. It's the only way."

He slowly released her. She got up off the bed and was gone. One window slammed shut, then the other one. Even with the windows closed, the papers on his dresser and other small items lying around the room began to blow violently around. Marc rose and stood in the middle of the raging storm.

"You can be mad if you want," he said. "*Or* you can help me find a way to get back here as soon as I can. It's up to you."

♨♨

Natalia went downstairs and bumped into Mariella. Just the person she was looking for. When she was sure no one else was around, she gave her a piece of her mind.

"Why did you call her last night and then send a car for her, no less? Can't you ever stay out of anyone's business? There was no reason for her to come here. Marc would have gone home today and that would have been that. Instead, everyone's dirty laundry was dragged out in front of everyone else. It was humiliating."

"Sam and I talked it over and we—"

"That's another thing. I'm pissed that you told Sam about our regression. Isn't there some doctor patient confidentiality or something?"

Mariella tried to take Natalia's hands, but she ripped them away, crossed her arms over her chest, and turned away.

"I know you're not really that angry," Mariella said. "Your bark has always been worse than your bite. You and I will always see things from a different perspective. I called Simone to see how things were going now that Marcos is remembering. When she said he never came to the airport, I couldn't imagine what happened, but I knew something must have. I also knew he would come right back here to you, and he did. We heard the cabbie blowing his horn and saw Marcos go inside the house.

"I knew the longer he put off talking to Simone, the worse off he'd be. I thought it would be better to have it happen here. He's so much happier and relaxed here, more in control. If he went home where all his memories were supposed to be, I thought he'd get anxious again. I'm sorry if things were a little difficult this morning, but I'm sure everything that needed to be said was said. It may not have come out in the open otherwise."

"I don't know why you think you can manipulate everything to your liking," Natalia snapped.

"I don't. Well, not everything, just certain things. I want Marcos to be happy. I always will. Occasionally, I may have to get the ball rolling. If I didn't, everything that is supposed to happen still would, but it would take much longer. I don't always have the patience for that, so I move things along a little bit. That's all I do, get things moving, the rest is up to you and him."

"You may think your intentions are worthwhile, but you're still trying to control everyone's life."

"If that's the way you see it, dear, then so be it. I'm not sorry I did it and I'd do it again." Mariella put her arms around Natalia. "I'll be back in a few days. I know all will be forgiven by the time I get back."

"No!" Natalia pushed her away. "Not this time." To prevent her fingers from tightening around the woman's neck, she clenched her fists at her side. "You claim to be such an expert on past lives, telling me how rare and extraordinary the bond Marc and I share is. Well, I don't believe you. If you were really an expert, you'd realize that every time he comes here and leaves again, I lose a piece of myself. I can't and won't do it again." She closed her eyes briefly and whispered, "I don't have that much left." Hearing Mariella move toward her, she snapped her eyes open and backed away. "I said 'no.' The only thing you can do for me now is to keep him away from here. I don't want to see him again."

Mariella gasped. "You don't mean that, dear."

"Yes, I do."

Sam and Simone walked in. "I have everyone's bag in the car."

At this point, Natalia just wanted everyone the hell out of her house. She had plenty of misery to keep company. "Good-bye, Simone."

"Good-bye.

Natalia had no intention of hugging her, but she did extend her hand to Simone. Simone shook it and nodded. When Natalia heard Marc come down the stairs, she excused herself and went up the other stairs to her room. A few minutes later, Robbie and Ben knocked on her door and asked if they could come in. She opened the door.

"They're gone, sis. Are you okay?"

"Yes. Your room is ready, like always. I'm going to take a shower and a well-deserved nap. I love you guys."

"We love you, too, doll," said Ben.

The two men took turns taking her in their arms.

"Don't worry, Nat. Everything will work out," Robbie told her. "I'm sure of it."

"I'm glad you're both here." She turned away so they didn't see her tears.

CHAPTER 30

"He felt now that he was not simply close to her, but that he did not know where he ended and she began." – *Leo Tolstoy, 1828-1910 Russian Author*

The next morning when Natalia went downstairs, the coffee was brewing. She figured it was either Robbie or Sam who had made it. She poured herself a cup, thinking it had a familiar smell to it and when she tasted it she knew it was Marc's coffee. She ran outside looking for a car. When she didn't see one, she assumed he took the train. She flew back inside and barreled into Sam standing there.

"I'm sorry, Nat. He's not here. I made the coffee."

"Oh. I don't know what I was thinking. It was silly of me."

"No, it's not silly." He pulled her into his arms. "You know, over the last two weeks I've become quite fond of Marc. Mariella considers him a son, and I think if he'd spent more time here, I would have come to think of him the same way. I'm going to miss having him around." They let go of each other, and Natalia collapsed at the kitchen table.

"I had a chance to see him yesterday before he left," continued Sam. "He told me he never told another soul the secret to his coffee, but he wanted me to know. I told him I was having fun with him, and he didn't have to tell me, but he insisted. I was touched he wanted me to know. Do you want me to show you?"

"Why don't you tell me? That was something you two shared. I won't make the coffee anymore. That can be your job now."

"It's easy. After grinding the coffee beans, he grates cinnamon and adds that to the grinds. The secret ingredient is something called Cardamon. It's a tropical fruit seed from the other side of the world. He crushes that up and adds a little vanilla at the end. It might take me some time to get it right. Will it bother you if I make his coffee in the morning? I think it might be nice."

"No." She gave him a half smile. It was all she could muster. "I think so, too. I enjoyed our mornings here in my kitchen."

Sam poured himself a cup and freshened hers. They clunked their mugs together.

"Don't worry, Nat. Everything will be fine. I just know it.

After her conversation with Sam, Natalia went upstairs to Marc's room. She slowly turned the knob and walked in. She hadn't spent any time with him in here, except for their brief conversation yesterday, but she could feel him all around her. The bed was a rumpled mess. There were pillows on the floor. She didn't remember it being like this yesterday morning. He hadn't slept in the bed since Friday night. Saturday night he spent on her couch and last night he was in his own bed—with Simone.

Natalia crawled in between the cold sheets. She pulled the blankets up over her head and buried her face in the pillow. His aftershave lingered on the pillowcase. She inhaled deeply, breathing in the last bit of him she could. Then she rolled on her back and stared at the ceiling. Even though she and Marc weren't together in the traditional sense, they were still connected to each other in a deep and profound way, and always would be. Now that he was gone, she wasn't sure she could recover. Still, she had to try.

She got out of bed, ripped all the sheets and blankets off the bed, and headed for the bathroom. His wet towels were strewn all over the floor, there was toothpaste and shaving remnants in the sink. Natalia was stunned. She'd had no idea he was such a slob. His kitchen was always so neat and organized.

It took her over an hour to scour the sink, tub, and toilet. She scrubbed the bathroom floor, vacuumed and dusted the bedroom, and put new sheets on the bed. His towels and sheets, she washed in the hottest water she could—twice. With bleach. Then she opened the windows, wide, and let the fresh air cleanse his scent from the room.

When she was done, she stood in the spotless, disinfected room and scanned it every inch of it. Satisfied she had eradicated every trace of Marc, she shut the door and walked away.

♨♨

Natalia tried to get back to her normal routine at the vineyard, but it was hard. When she took her walk in the morning, she thought of Marc. When Sam and she had coffee in the kitchen, it reminded her of Marc. She considered walking somewhere else and drinking tea in the morning, but her heart wouldn't let her. She needed to remember Marc, not forget him.

Spring was a busy time and she still had a lot of work to do to get the wine shop ready for their May first opening. That was fine with her. The distraction working provided was vital to her survival.

Mariella lived with Sam for most of the week. She traveled into the city every Tuesday and came back Wednesday night. It gave her the opportunity to be semi-retired but still have her hand in the business she loved.

Robbie and Ben stayed on as well. Natalia and Robbie had talked the last few months about him returning to the vineyard. She wasn't sure how her parents would take it, but she didn't care. They'd left *her* in charge, damn it. She wanted Robbie and Ben there, and that's all that mattered.

On the last weekend of April, Mariella, Sam, Robbie, and Ben had planned a weekend in the city. That was also the weekend a Nor'easter decided to ravage the East Coast. Still, the four of them decided to keep their plans, despite the weather.

"Natalia, please come with us," begged Mariella. "There's plenty of room. You can stay in the apartment above the restaurant."

"Mariella, are you trying to work your manipulating magic again?" Natalia demanded. Me staying in the apartment above where Marc is working. What a great idea. She arched her brow in annoyance. *I don't think so.* "You go and have fun. I want to be alone anyway."

"Natalia, this isn't healthy. You need to get out," Robbie told her. "We're not going to let you turn into some recluse because your heart is broken. All you do is eat, work, read, and sleep. You're a beautiful woman with a lot to offer someone, and you're acting like an old maid. Marc has been gone for five weeks."

"I know how long he's been gone," she growled through clenched teeth. "When the weather is better, I'll get dressed up and go to Boston with Christine and Ellie. They've already asked me. But I need to stay away from New York for a while."

"Okay, doll." Ben shot Robbie a sideways look. "Maybe, she needs a little more time."

"Are you sure you'll be okay here, sis? I think the storm will be worse here than in the city."

"Yes, I'll be fine. I have everything I need." She mustered a rare smile. "Can you help me with something before you leave? I had a delivery come today and it's too heavy for me."

"Sure. We'll get it."

Robbie took Ben into the garage. They came back with a big box, opened it up, and pulled out a huge brown suede beanbag.

"After spending the night on the floor with you two, I thought I needed something comfortable to curl up in by the fire. Nice, huh?"

Mariella grinned and plopped herself right in it. "This is very cozy. Sam, come over here."

Natalia laughed. "All right, everyone. The beanbag's mine. Mariella, get out."

"Okay, dear, but I think you're going to have to help me up." Mariella put her hand out and Natalia pulled her to her feet.

"Thanks, everyone. Now get out of here."

She shoved them out the door before they started insisting she come with them again. She fixed herself something to eat and settled down with her date for the night—the beanbag and a horror movie.

Saturday morning she went for a brisk walk through the vineyard. When it started to rain, she headed home, showered, and drove into town. That night, she made herself an early dinner, lit a fire, and curled up in her beanbag—this time with a new book. *Robbie's right. I'm a boring old woman before my time.* She pushed the thought from her mind and opened her book.

Her eyes heavy, she put her book down.. The rain pounded on her roof, while the wind howled at her window. Natalia leaned her head back and closed her eyes, relieved she wasn't out in the storm.

♨♨

Marc watched Natalia sleep. She looked so beautiful, the glow of the flames illuminating her face, he could hardly breathe. And peaceful. Part of him, a small part, didn't want to disturb her. He considered curling himself into her and sleeping. But a much bigger, needier, part of him demanded to have her, awake and responsive. He gently caressed the side of her face.

She stirred and her eyelids fluttered open. "Hi."

Her soft whisper told him everything he needed to know.

"Hey, baby." He scooped her into his arms and ravaged her mouth with his tongue.

Natalia nestled against him then jerked away. "Did you rem—"

"Yes. I remember everything. How much we've loved each other. How you've been a part of me forever." He crushed her to him and took her mouth again.

She broke the kiss. "What about—"

He gave a strangled laugh. "Nat, please stop interrupting me. Don't worry. Simone left this morning with Philip. Any more questions?"

She relaxed in his arms. "No. I've been waiting for you."

"I'm glad. I'm sorry it took so long for me to get here."

"I didn't want you to come until you were sure about everything."

"I was sure before I left here that day. But you were adamant I leave, so I did."

"How about in the next lifetime you don't marry the first drop-dead gorgeous girl that catches your eye?"

"You almost got married."

"Yeah, but I didn't." She rested her head on his shoulder. "Tell me what happened."

"Please, baby, not right now. I need you to love me—the way only you can. I've missed you so much."

"I missed you, too."

He slipped the straps of her tank top down her arms and nibbled her shoulders then dragged her shirt down, setting free, first her left and then her right, ample breasts. He put his hands on her hips and lifted her to him, knowing how much she loved having her breasts fondled.

Her fingers speared through his hair as she murmured his name. He pushed her down on her back, savoring her taste, as his mouth and tongue trailed down her torso to the waistband of her shorts. He yanked them off and tossed them on the floor.

Sitting up, he began to take off his shirt.

"No, Let me."

She undid one button at a time, slowly, excruciatingly dragging it out until, at last, his shirt joined her shorts on the floor.

She wrapped her arms around his neck, snuggled into him, and crushed her lips to his. God, he loved how perfectly they fit together—in any position. How she melted into him until they molded into one

His hands moved down her back stopping at her lovely derriere. He pulled her closer to him. She eased back, grabbed his shoulders, and turned him so his back was facing her. He felt her lips on his shoulder then her hands snaked around to the button of his jeans. She unfastened him, slid her hands inside, and wrapped her fingers around him, bestowing on him a pleasure so intense he almost forgot to breathe. When she pushed his pants down, he had to concentrate to remember how to step out of them. She took his hand, led him back to the fire, and pushed him down into a sitting position on the beanbag. Moving smoothly on top of him, she guided him inside her, encircling his waist with her legs.

They swayed back and forth in perfect harmony.

He stared deeply into her eyes, saw her tears. "I love you so much," she whispered and made the small sound he loved to hear her make. She arched her back. Her body trembled.

Urgently, he tightened his embrace. As their thrusts became deeper, harder, and more desperate, his body surrendered to her love while his mind shattered in ecstasy.

♨♨

Marc laid on his back, his left arm stretched out. Natalia curled on her side, with her back to him, resting her head on his triceps. He stroked her hair as it spilled across his chest, loving the way it tickled his skin. "Hey baby, you know I love you more than anything, right?"

"Yes." She lifted his hand to her mouth and kissed the center of his palm. "I'm so glad your back."

"This is where I've always belonged, here with you."

"Can you tell me what happened now?"

"There's not much to tell. It was hard for me to concentrate on anything. I kept hearing you whisper in my ear that you loved me. But I made an effort like I promised.

"I tried to be more attentive to Simone—that was one of her complaints—and in return she didn't travel or stay late at work. The more time we spent together, the more we discovered we didn't have much in common anymore. Trying to find something do that we both enjoyed was challenging.

"I was getting more of my memory back each day, and I remembered a little restaurant in Soho that we liked. So we went. We ate dinner and actually had a nice conversation. Then we got the check and went home."

"Did you two, you know…get close?"

"That depends on what you mean by 'close.' Did we have sex? Yes, that one night, but that's all what it was—sex, nothing more. It was the nicest evening we'd had in almost a year. I think it was something we thought we should do, so we did it. It certainly didn't bring us any closer. Afterward, we laid there, not saying anything or even touching each other. Simone kept checking her phone, and when the call she was waiting for finally came, she got up and left.

"I didn't care because all I could think of was the napkin with the drawing of my birthmark in my wallet." She gave him a questioning look. He shrugged. "When you wouldn't help me remember, I asked G for help."

"G?"

"Yes, Giovanna is way too long a name. You don't mind do, you, G? She's here, you know," he told Natalia.

A puff of cool air blew over them.

"I know. I can feel her."

"Anyway, when I got home, instead of missing a few things like you thought, I found a napkin. I knew what the drawing was and saw your signature, but I had no idea what it meant."

"I had a feeling that's where the napkin went." Natalia chuckled. "Giovanna's been making such a commotion since you've been gone. I think she missed you almost as much as I did. When the napkin disappeared from the drawer I keep it in, I figured she was the culprit."

"Well, you were right. I took it out of my wallet and went downstairs. Simone was on the phone. She had a smile on her face."

"Philip?" Natalia asked.

"I don't know. I assumed so. I really didn't care. I went in another room, shut the door, and concentrated on the napkin. I'd been trying to look it at each day, hoping I'd remember you. I heard a knock on the door. Simone poked her head in and said she was going to bed. I told her good night and that I'd be up later.

"That was pretty much the beginning of the end. After that, we were polite to each other, but we went off in different directions. She started staying late at work again, so I didn't take time off from the restaurant.

One night I was in the shower and everything about you and me started to drift slowly back. I went to bed but just tossed and turned. I was keeping Simone awake so I went into another room. I had so many weird things going in on my head. Some were dreams. Some were memories. But by morning, I remembered everything you and I had been through.

"I wanted to come back then but I knew that if she was spending time with Philip, and I had no contact with you, it would be better for us in the end. I was becoming impatient, though, so last night I asked her if we could have a truthful conversation..."

♨♨

Marc poured Simone a glass of wine and they sat down in the living room.

"Thank you," she said as she took the glass.

"I've been home for over a month now," he told her. "And I'm not sure we're any better off than we were before the accident."

"I was hopeful in the beginning we might be able to get our connection back," she said. "But that hasn't happened."

"I have all my memory back now. I remember everything, including Natalia."

"I'm sure that's had quite an impact on you." She shrugged. "I'm not blind, Marc. It was obvious you had feelings for her, memory or not."

"Yes. I'm sorry."

She took a sip of her wine. "Since were being honest, I've been talking to Philip. We'd like to spend time together and see how it goes. I'm assuming you'd like to get back to the vineyard."

"Yes. I feel at home there."

"Marc, you're a graduate of a world famous culinary institute, but you want to settle for being not much more than a caterer?"

"It's simple, Simone. It makes me happy. The restaurant doesn't do it for me anymore."

"What will you do for money? I'm sure those jobs don't pay much."

"I'm hoping Natalia will let me earn my keep. I'll work in the vineyard, do whatever she needs."

"What did she say when you told her?"

"I haven't talked to her. I came home to work on our marriage."

Simone seemed surprised. "She doesn't know you want to come back?"

"No. Not yet."

"I don't understand what you two have in common, with the age difference and all."

"You'd be surprised."

"I think we should take Robbie's advice to follow our hearts and be who we are. I still care about you Marc. I want you to be happy."

"I'll always care for you, too, Simone. I hope Philip can make you happy."

"I think he can."

♨♨

Marc rolled on his side and pulled Natalia against him and traced the curve of her waist and hips with his fingers.

"Then she and I hugged and kissed each other good bye," he continued. "When I got up this morning, she was gone. I went to the restaurant and spent time with everyone there, telling them where I was going and why. Then I packed my things and here I am."

Natalia rolled over to face him. "With me."

"Just like I knew I'd be. Maybe you could not be so stubborn next time and listen to me, instead of taking the long way around for us to be together."

"Can we argue over who's right and wrong another time?" She pulled him on top of her. "I can think of something much more fun to do right now."

In the distance, they heard Natalia's front and back doors lock. A cool breeze swirled by and surrounded them then gently blew away. They glanced at each other and smiled.

♨♨

The next morning Mariella and Sam, back from the city, walked in and stumbled on Marc and Natalia asleep on the beanbag.

Sam immediately turned around.

"Mariella, you're going to have to take care of them. Nat's the closest thing I have to a daughter, and that's more information than I need on a Sunday morning," he said, heading for the kitchen.

Mariella looked down at Marc and Natalia completely intertwined and deep in slumber. The blanket wasn't doing its job of covering them up.

She leaned over them, kissed them affectionately, wrapped them in the blanket, and let them be.

CHAPTER 31

"You don't have a soul. You are a soul. You have a body." – C.S. Lewis, 1898-1963 British Author

Giovanna swirled cheerfully around the room as Marc and Natalia slept. Finally, they were together—as they should be, always. Fixing their mess had exhausted her, but she couldn't stay mad at them. She loved them too much.

Their soul group had journeyed through many lives together and usually everyone stuck to the plan they made before returning. At least Mariella, Sam, Robbie, and Ben had stayed on the right path. Giovanna wasn't sure why Marc, the level headed one in the group, had gotten off track.

This lifetime was an essential one for Simone. But she'd headed in the wrong direction. She was always the kind, but restless, one with a short attention span. Giovanna wasn't sure she'd have time to help Simone. That would have to be Natalia's job.

Natalia. What could she say about her? She was the strong one of the group that everyone depended on when things got rough. She was difficult sometimes, but she would fight with everything she had for you, if need be.

All in all, things were looking up. Giovanna needed one more thing from Marc and Natalia, but she wasn't worried. If she had to move them along to get what she needed, she would. It wouldn't be the first time.

CHAPTER 32

"The loneliest woman in the world is a woman without a close woman friend." -- *George Santayana, 1863-1952 Spanish Philosopher and novelist*

"What's up?" Natalia asked when Robbie pulled her aside early in June.

"This may come as a shock to you, but over the last few weeks Simone, Philip, Ben, and I have become friends."

"Oh." Natalia wasn't sure what else to say.

"Simone hired a lawyer and would like to talk to Marc about the divorce. She's a little apprehensive, though. She hasn't spoken to him since they said their good-byes." He squirmed a little.

"And?" she demanded.

"I was thinking that since you and Marc are family, and they're our friends, maybe they could come here one weekend. It would mean a lot to Ben and me if we could all get along and spend time together once in a while."

"Oh." Again, it was all Natalia could muster up.

She contemplated spending time with Simone. Marc never spoke ill of her, not that Natalia expected him to. There was no reason to. He didn't leave her because she was a horrible person. Then there was the nagging feeling she knew Simone. If she had already spent part of a lifetime with her, who's to say she wasn't supposed to do it again?

"Please sis, will you and Marc just think about it?"

"I think you should talk to Marc. If he's okay with it, so am I. I must admit I'm a little curious about Philip." She gave him a sly smile. "I would like to meet her new mystery man."

"Thanks, Nat. I appreciate it."

"No problem, but please talk to Marc."

"I will."

♨♨

Robbie found Marc, Mariella and Sam outside and pleaded his case to them.

"Oh," said Marc.

Robbie grinned. "You sound just like Nat."

"I, for one, think it's a wonderful idea," said Mariella. "Simone has been part of the family for quite some time, and I'm fond of her."

"What did Nat say?" asked Marc.

"She was fine with it."

"She was?"

"You haven't noticed my sister's odd?" Robbie asked him. "Most things that would bother other women—for instance, having your beautiful ex-wife around for the weekend—doesn't faze her. But something simple makes her fly off the handle."

Marc laughed. "Yes, I've noticed. I guess we do need to talk about the divorce. I don't want anything. She can have the house. We had separate accounts. I took my money from our one joint account and left hers alone. So the divorce should be easy."

"Then, you don't mind if they come for the weekend?"

"I'm sure it will prove to be interesting, but no, I don't mind."

Robbie found Ben back at the house and said, "Okay, my job is done. Marc and Nat agreed. Now it's up to you to convince Simone and Philip."

After forty-five minutes of begging, pleading and bribing them with private flying lessons, Ben got them to agree.

"Thanks," Ben and Robbie told them on the phone. "We'll see you in two weeks."

♨♨

Natalia was busy with appetizers. It was Friday night and there wasn't much time before Simone and Philip arrived.

Mariella was helping with the food, Sam was making a fire outside. Marc, Robbie, and Ben were bringing more tables and chairs out to the terrace.

Natalia sought out Marc and asked him what he planned to say to Philip.

"I'm not sure, but I think you're right. We should get it out of the way. It'll be awkward enough without dragging it out all evening."

"Just be honest with him."

"I know." He kissed her. "I'll take care of it."

When Philip and Simone arrived, Robbie brought them out to the terrace where everyone was waiting. Natalia thought they were all being nauseatingly polite with their happy handshakes and artificial kisses, but she followed everyone's lead.

Trying to be a gracious hostess, she asked everyone what they would like to drink. Out of the corner of her eye, she saw Marc talking to Philip.

"How about a beer?" Marc asked as he opened a cooler.

Philip nodded. "Sure."

Marc handed him one and led him away from everyone. Natalia couldn't resist. She followed them, but kept her distance—just close enough to hear what they said.

"Look." Marc ran his hand through his hair. "I think we should talk before the weekend gets started. When I saw you two at the airport, I was more than a little pissed and confused. I admit, I didn't handle it well, getting drunk and leaving, but that's in the past. I had enough of my memory back by that night to know our marriage had been pretty much over even before the accident. I'm where I want to be, where I've wanted to be since the first night I met Nat. That's why I came back here after I saw you two. I think we should put the whole thing behind us and try to get along this weekend."

"Simone is very important to me," Philip said.

"Good. I'm glad for both of you. Let's go back. There's plenty of food waiting for us."

Marc started to walk away.

"Marc, wait."

He turned around.

"Thanks." Philip extended his hand.

Marc took it. "Sure."

When they got back to the terrace, everyone had a drink except Natalia and Marc asked if she would like a glass of wine.

"I'll get it in a minute. You did great with Philip. I hope you don't mind. I may have overheard just a little."

"No, I don't mind." He brushed his fingers along her cheekbone. "I'll get your drink."

When he handed her the glass of wine, she thanked him. What he didn't know was that she was late for her period and hopeful. The rest of the night, she walked around pretending to take sips, but when no one was looking, she poured it out on the ground bit by tiny bit. Then someone would refill her glass, she'd have to go through the whole damn charade again.

Considering the circumstances, dinner went well. There were a few uncomfortable moments, but they got through them. They focused their attention on Simone and Philip. Philip confessed his first love was jazz, not advertising. He played the saxophone in a small jazz band with four other men. They didn't play many venues as they were all professionals with corporate jobs, but they enjoyed playing together.

"Every October we hold a large outdoor wine tasting event," Natalia told him. "In the past we've always hired a DJ, but I would love to have a live band. I already know the date. Would you consider playing for us?"

"I don't know. I'd have to ask the other guys."

She smiled warmly. "Well, I hope you'll at least think about it."

They were sitting outside by the fire having coffee when Sam and Mariella announced they were calling it a night. Simone and Philip agreed, so Natalia offered to show them to their room.

When they got upstairs, she showed them where everything was and told them to make themselves at home. For the first time since they arrived, she and Simone actually looked at each other. They hadn't spoken directly to each other, both of them preferring to speak in a larger conversation with other people.

"Good night," said Natalia.

"Good night," said Simone. "Thank you for your hospitality. You have a beautiful home."

"Thanks. If you need anything, let me know."

They both nodded and Natalia left. She didn't want to be rude, but she was anxious to get Marc alone to tell him she might be pregnant. She could take the test in the morning.

"A baby?" He grabbed her and spun her around until they fell on the bed together, laughing. "I love you, Nat. Should I set the alarm, what time do you take the test?"

"I love you, too, but leave the alarm alone. I'll take the test when I wake up—whenever that is."

Nevertheless, early the next morning he shook her awake, pulled her out of bed, pushed her into the bathroom, and handed her a box containing a stick to pee on.

Groggy, she stood in the bathroom, fumbling, as she tried to open the box. Suddenly, it flew out of her hands.

"It's too early for you this morning, Giovanna," she growled. "I don't even think the sun is up yet. Are you and Marc in cahoots?" She grabbed for the box. "Yes, I'm very excited. You know I've wanted a baby for a long time. It just takes me a minute to wake up."

"Nat, what are you doing in there?" Marc yelled through the door.

She yanked the door open. Giovanna blew a gust at Marc. He blinked and stumbled then grabbed a hold of the doorknob. "So that's what's going on in there," he said, laughing. "We might have an addition to our family. You'll behave and not be jealous, right?" he asked Giovanna.

An tender embrace of soft, cool air coolness wrapped around Natalia. She could tell from Marc's expression, he felt it, too. It was Giovanna's way of expressing her happiness.

"Can I have some privacy, please?" Natalia shut the door.

When she came out of the bathroom, she couldn't hide the grin. Marc, obviously interpreting it correctly, pulled her into a hug. Then he led her back to bed and eased her on top of him.

"God, Nat. I'm so happy."

"Me, too."

She didn't want to talk. Not when they could be celebrating their good news.

Later as she laid on her back, Marc traced circles around her belly button with his finger.

"A baby, I can't believe it. Do you feel okay?"

"Yes. I don't even feel pregnant."

"You will. But you'll be fine. You were every other time."

She cuddled into his side, reflecting on the fact it wasn't the first time they had a baby together. But to her, it felt like the other times were only stories, somewhere in the back of her memory—stories that didn't always have a happy ending. She thought about her children who had passed before their time. Then she remembered all the children she got to watch grow up. She squeezed Marc's hand.

He cupped her cheek. "Don't think about the other times, Nat," he said as if he were reading her mind. "We're all going to stay healthy and happy. Things are different now. You'll even have the luxury of a hospital this time."

"I know." She toyed with his hair. "I'm a little concerned about my age, though. I hope everything's okay."

"It will be. But if it's not, we'll get through it together. You know that," he murmured, holding her close.

"What's going to happen when we go downstairs?"

"I don't know," he said. "You think we shouldn't tell them yet? Although, I'm so excited I don't want to wait. And Mariella will be thrilled."

"So will Robbie and Ben. It's our other guests I'm worried about."

"You're right," he said. "I don't want to make Simone uncomfortable. The baby issue was a sensitive subject for us."

"I don't want to upset her, either. But if we wait until they're gone to tell everyone, they'll think we didn't want them to know." She sighed. "You decide. You know her better than anyone. I'll do whatever you think is best."

"I think it'll be hard for her to hear about the baby this morning, but in the long run—and that's how you have to think of Simone—she'll be glad she was included from the beginning."

"Good." She grinned. I'm volunteering you to make the announcement."

"Chicken?"

"That's right. Let's go."

When they walked in the kitchen hand and hand, everyone was having coffee.

"There you two are," Robbie said. "It's about time you got up."

Marc grinned. The happiness poured off him in waves. "Good Morning, everyone. We're glad you're all together." He slipped an arm around Natalia's shoulders. "We have an announcement to make. This may come as a surprise, but Nat and I are going to have a baby. We hope you're all as happy as we are."

When everyone started talking at once, Marc held up his hand. "It's early. We just found out this morning, and yes, we're very excited. Since everyone who is important to us is here, we thought it was a good time to share our good news." Mariella flew into Marc's arms crying. Then she pulled Natalia into a hug. "As far as I'm concerned, this is my first grandchild."

Robbie grabbed Natalia and squeezed her tight. "Oh, sis I'm so happy for you. I know you've wanted this for a long time." He kissed her forehead. "Have you told mom and dad yet?"

"No, not yet. I'll call them later. You know mom. She's old fashioned and won't appreciate me telling her this early in my pregnancy. You know how superstitious she is."

Natalia could tell he was happy for her. Still, there was a sad look in his eye. She hoped a baby might heal their family and they could all be close again. Robbie moved to Marc and held him in a big bear hug.

Ben came over to her. "Congratulations, doll. You know I love you like you're my own sister, right?"

"I know *Uncle Ben.*"

"Thanks, Nat. That means a lot to me." He kissed her then shook Marc's hand.

Then it was Sam's turn. "Well kid, it's been you and me for so long." He embraced her fondly. "Now you have Marc and a baby on the way, and I have Mariella." He shook his head, sighed then smiled. "So much change, but it's all good."

"Yes, Sam, it is all wonderful. Thank you."

Philip stayed back until the end, but finally came forward, shook Marc's hand, and kissed Natalia on the cheek. "Congratulations," he said.

Simone got up and walked out the back door. Philip started after her, but Natalia stopped him. "Give her a few minutes then I'll go talk to her."

♨♨

Simone stormed out the kitchen door and down a long row of grapes. She found a couple of old crates at the end of the row and plopped herself down on the hard surface. Irritated for letting Robbie and Sam talk her into coming, she decided to get the hell out of this place soon as possible. She and Philip had no business here.

She groaned when Natalia sat down next to her. She should have known the woman would come after her.

"Peace offering." Natalia handed her a pastry.

Although she was touched by Natalia's kindness, she wasn't about to eat the horribly fattening thing. When she made no move to take it, Natalia took a bite herself.

"I'm sorry, Simone. Marc and I didn't know what to do. We tried to consider your feelings, but I guess we screwed up. We didn't want to hurt you, but we also didn't want you and Philip to feel excluded because we didn't tell you at the same time we told everyone else."

Simone couldn't look at her, so she stared straight ahead.

"Look, I'm trying to do what Robbie asked of me. He'd like his family and friends to be able to get along." Natalia sighed. "Why don't you tell me how you're feeling? You need to get it off your chest, or you won't enjoy the rest of the weekend.

"That's the point," Simone finally said. "I don't want to enjoy the rest of the weekend. This is all too weird for me. My almost ex, his pregnant girlfriend, me, and my new boyfriend, all pretending to get along. People will think we're sick and twisted. It's not going to work out. It's too much."

"Why? Who decides what's normal? Don't worry what other people think. You always have the option of doing what you feel in your heart is right, whether the majority agree or not."

"You'll never understand. You seem fine with us being here. I don't get it."

"Oh, sure." Natalia rolled her eyes. "I have young, gorgeous, blue-eyed blondes with long legs, tiny waists—and boobs that haven't had gravity hit them yet—around here all the time."

"Come on, Natalia. You look great."

"Maybe, until *you* walk in the room."

"Marc doesn't even look at me anymore."

"He's a man with red blood and a working heartbeat. He looks at you"

"And that doesn't bother you?"

"I guess I could stress over changing human nature, but what good would it do me? Men look at women, and women look at men. Women are just more discrete about it."

"You don't have to worry," Simone told her "He's never looked at me the way he does you."

"What's really the problem?" Natalia took a deep breath. "Are you not over him like you thought you were?"

"No, I am. Marc and I are two different people now. Philip and I are good together."

"Then what is it?"

"This is hard for me. I haven't had a lot of girlfriends to talk to."

"I find that hard to believe. You're young and beautiful. You have a great job in the city, and you travel the world. You must have plenty of friends."

"Well, I don't." Simone studied her a moment. "It really doesn't bother you that I'm here this weekend?"

"No, not really. The way I look at it is, Marc was in love with you at one time. Mariella is very fond of you, and Robbie and Ben think you're great. So I figure you can't be *that* dreadful."

"You don't mince your words, do you?" Simone turned her head away and stared at the ground. She almost wished she had met her under different circumstances. Natalia might be the type of woman who could be her friend. God knew she needed a friend. She had Robbie and Ben, but she longed for a woman to share confidences with. Natalia didn't seem threatened by her beauty, like so many of the women she dealt with. "I feel like I failed at the whole marriage thing," she confessed. "I did everything wrong."

"You didn't fail. It was a lot to deal with. You and Marc decided together it wasn't working. When you both want the other one to be happy, and the way to do that is to let go, that's the nicest thing you can do for each other."

"I'm happy you two are having a baby. I know it's what Marc has wanted for a long time."

"I want it, too. I'm not getting any younger, you know."

Simone frowned. "I don't think I can come here and act like we're one big happy family."

"It would mean a lot to Robbie and Ben."

"I don't know."

"Think of it this way. You think I'm a bitch now? Wait until I'm fat, bloated, and hormonal. I'll probably be loaded with stretch marks, too. You don't want to miss that?"

Simone had to chuckle, but it felt strained. "You're a very strange woman."

"So I've been told. So, can we try and get along even if only when you're visiting my brother?"

"I suppose so. I do feel better. Thanks for listening, Natalia."

"Sure. Friends?"

A small part of Simone wanted to say yes, but women who had pretended to be her friend in the past had hurt her. "I don't think I'd go that far."

"Acquaintances?"

"No. We're more than that."

"How about two women thrown together, because of a relationship with members of the other's family, who are trying to get along?"

"Perfect."

♨♨

A little later Natalia asked Philip if he would like to see the wine making process. He nodded, and his eyes lit up.

While Sam and Marc showed him around, Mariella went to town. That left her, Robbie, Ben, and Simone sitting around bored. Just like she'd planned.

She got out a deck of card. "Let's teach Simone to play poker." .

Simone shook her head. "No, thanks. Really, I'll pass."

"Come on, Simone. It'll be fun," Ben said. "What else is there to do on a rainy Saturday?"

She gave in at his urging, so Robbie and Ben set up the game, putting a shot glass in front of everyone but Natalia.

Simone looked horrified. "What's that for?"

"You'll see." Natalia grinned. "I'll help you. I can't drink anyway." She set a bottle of whiskey on the table.

"I don't like whiskey," Simone said with a shudder.

"Have you ever tried it?"

She shook her head.

"Well, here you go then." Robbie handed her a shot glass.

Simone took a small sip, made a face. "Ugh, that's awful"

"Simone, what if I get you some champagne instead?" asked Natalia.

"Yes, I would like that."

Natalia came back with the champagne, popped the cork, and tried to explain the game to Simone. "Whenever you lose, you have to take a shot."

"You don't take shots of champagne, Natalia. You sip it."

"This isn't a formal affair, Simone. Drink the damn shot."

Natalia watched her take a few sips then gulp down the rest. "Good girl." Simone, apparently deciding she had the game figured out, began to ignore Natalia's advice. Before Natalia could stop her, she put the wrong card down. After a few bad hands, Simone's sips had become gulps, and she was giggling.

"Okay, this is the last hand," Robbie announced. "I think Simone has had enough poker and champagne."

Simone put her hand down. Ben immediately took all her chips. That's when Marc, Philip and Sam walk in.

"Hi, sweetie." Simone wiggled her fingers at Philip. Then she leaned into Natalia's ear. "I want to say something to him in Italian. Even when you swear in Italian, it sounds beautiful."

"Oh, no." Sam grabbed Philip and took him aside.

Natalia considered Simone's request. Hmmm. Should she do the polite thing or the fun thing? Oh, the hell with being politically correct. "Okay, repeat after me. *Mi amore, Philip, mi scopata facile.*"

Robbie blanched "Natalia!"

"What?" she asked innocently.

Marc laughed. "Baby, what are you doing? You should go easy on her."

Simone blinked like an owl. "What does it mean, Natalia?" She swayed in her chair. "I know amore is love." Robbie groaned. "She said 'Philip, my love I'm a woman of easy virtue."

Simone giggled. "Is that really what you said?"

"No. He cleaned it up. I didn't say—"

"I know what you said, now stop it," Robbie ordered.

"You want us all to be friends. I'm trying to do that by having some fun."

"Oh Natalia, you think we're friends?" Simone hugged her and knocked over her glass. "Robbie, leave her alone." Her words slurred. "Natalia, tell me what it means."

"Simone, I think you should lie down for a while." Philip scooped her up from the chair. "You're not used to having champagne in the afternoon."

"I'll tell you later," Natalia said. "You go with Philip."

When Simone came downstairs for dinner, she didn't look so good.

"Not feeling too well, huh?" Natalia asked.

"This is all your fault," Simone whined, holding her head.

"What did I do?" Natalia struggled to restrain her temper. "Maybe you should learn to eat something substantial instead of picking at your food or eating nuts and berries. You're an adult. You should know not to drink on an empty stomach."

"I'm not used to taking shots and playing poker at noontime," Simone snapped. "I don't live your decadent lifestyle."

"Decadent? Robbie, you, and Ben were drinking. I was not. And I'm the decadent one?"

"It was your idea."

"Maybe if you had listened to me, you wouldn't have lost so badly."

"You know what, Natalia? I was wrong this morning. We aren't friends or women thrown together to do whatever you said. You're back down to an acquaintance, a depraved one at that."

"That's enough you two," Robbie growled as he walked in.

"Stay out of it, Robbie," snarled Natalia. "This is between her and me."

"It's all right, Robbie," Simone said. "I can speak for myself. I would appreciate some water and an aspirin. Thanks."

"You two make my head spin." Robbie shook his head and left.

Finally Natalia said, "Come on, Simone, Marc made a great dinner. And Robbie needs to mind his own business."

"He's your brother."

"He's your friend."

Simone groaned. "Why do you always have to have the last word? It's childish and annoying."

"If you would stop talking, I wouldn't have to answer you, now would I?"

♨♨

The next morning everyone gathered outside to say good-bye. Natalia said goodbye to Philip first. "It was nice to meet you, Philip. I hope you had a good time." She hugged him. "Please think about playing at our wine tasting event. A lot of people attend. It might be good publicity for your band."

"Thanks, Natalia. I'll let you know."

When she stepped back, Simone was hugging and kissing Marc. Then he and Philip shook hands and even managed small smiles.

Natalia approached Simone.

"Good-bye. Thank you for coming."

"Thank you for having us."

The two women embraced clumsily.

Natalia whispered in Simone's ear, "What I really said yesterday was that you were an easy lay."

She studied Simone's expression. It was obvious she didn't want to smile, but couldn't help herself.

"Robbie would like us to get together again in a couple of months," she told her.

"Yes." Simone winced. "I guess we'll see you then."

"Have a safe trip back to New Jersey."

With a sigh, Natalia turned away. She wasn't exactly looking forward to the next visit.

CHAPTER 33

"The virtues we acquire, which develop slowly within us, are the invisible links that bind each one of our existences to the others – existences which the spirit alone remembers, for Matter has no memory for spiritual things." – *Honore Balzac, 1799-1850 French Novelist and playwright*

When Natalia picked up the phone, she was surprised to hear Simone's voice on the other end.

"Natalia?"

"Is everything okay?" Natalia asked. She couldn't imagine why Simone would be calling *her*.

"You tell me. Robbie said you went to the doctor, and they consider you a high-risk pregnancy. He's worried about you." Her voice hitched. "Is everyone all right? You and the baby?"

Touched by Simone's concern, Natalia smiled. "Yes, Simone. We're fine. They consider everyone in their forties to be high risk. I have to see the doctor a little more often than a woman in their twenties or thirties, that's all." She twisted a lock of hair around her finger. "Thank you for calling. It was very considerate of you. I'll be sure to tell Marc you called."

"Ben gave us a date in August to come back to the vineyard. Is that okay with you?"

"Yes, of course."

"When do you see the doctor again?"

"In two weeks."

"Maybe we could talk again after that."

"Sure."

"Goodbye, Natalia."

"Bye, Simone. Thanks, again, for calling. It means a lot to me."

♨♨

Two weeks later, Natalia stared at the phone. She'd told Simone she would call after her doctor's appointment, but everything went well. Maybe Simone only wanted her to call if something was wrong. She walked away then turned around and picked up the phone. Of course, she didn't have Marc's ex-wife's number on speed dial.

"Marc," she called into other room. "What's Simone's cell number?"

"Why?"

"I have to call her."

"You do?" He stuck his head in the kitchen where Natalia was.

"Yes. I do."

"Is this a prank call?" He laughed. "Are you mad at her?"

"Very funny. She wanted me to call her after my doctor's appointment, and I told her I would."

"I know baby, I'm kidding you." He gave her the number and went back to whatever he was doing.

Natalia told Simone about her doctor's appointment, assuming it would be a short conversation. To her surprise, they stayed on the phone for a half hour.

"Guess what, Natalia? My company is paying for me to take Italian. We have an office in Milan, and they want me to know a little of the language. Now, I'll know when you're having fun at my expense."

"No, you won't. They won't teach you all the good stuff. You'll have to come to me for that."

Simone giggled. "Okay, I will."

Natalia hung the phone up, thinking it was strange how the one thing she'd worried would cause problems between her and Simone—her pregnancy—had actually brought them closer together.

♨♨

"Natalia, are you in there? Robbie said you were up here." Simone knocked on the bedroom door then cautiously opened it and looked in. No one was visible, but she heard a horrible noise coming from the bathroom.

Opening the bathroom door, she saw Natalia, sitting on the floor getting violently ill in the toilet.

"Natalia! Oh my God, are you all right?"

Natalia nodded her head. Then she slowly sank back against the bathroom wall. "Well, this really sucks."

Simone grabbed a washcloth and ran it under the cold water. "You don't look so good."

Natalia's eyes were glassy. There was sweat on her brow, and she was pale as a ghost. Simone sat down and gently wiped her face. A feeling of déjà vu came over her. She jolted and studied Natalia intensely. Then she got up and ran the cloth under the cold water again.

"I thought it was called morning sickness," she said. "Its five in the afternoon, why are you sick?"

"Just lucky, I guess. I'm exhausted all the time, too."

Simone handed her the cool cloth. "Put this on your face. It might help you feel better."

"Thanks," Natalia said. "I know you feel it, too. We might as well stop ignoring it and admit it."

Simone didn't want to admit any such thing. "I don't know what you're talking about."

"Yes, you do. Ever since I met you in Marc's hospital room, whenever we see each other we feel like we've known each other before. Today was different, though. It felt like we had been through something similar to this at another time." She raised her head and met Simone's eyes. "Don't you agree?"

Simone took her time answering. "I don't like it. It gives me the creeps. What does it mean?"

"All the time you've spent with Mariella, she never told you her belief in reincarnation?"

"Of course, she did. I paid no attention to it. It's all nonsense." A suspicion struck her. "Don't tell me you believe it?"

"Let's just say I have an open mind on the subject. Anyway, it's nothing to be afraid of, and we may as well get used to it. I don't think it's going away." She struggled to her feet. "What are you doing here today?"

"Robbie and Ben are taking us out to dinner tonight. I thought it would be a good time to learn a little about your wines since we're helping at the wine tasting next weekend. It's a small tasting in your gift shop, right?"

"Yes. The big one is in October."

"Are you feeling better? Do you want to come downstairs? I'll make you a cup of tea."

"Thanks, Simone. That would be nice. Just let me clean up. I feel icky."

♨♨

Natalia was brushing her teeth when the cold blast of air blew by. She smiled. "Your coolness feels good today…What? Why are you sorry? Plenty of people get sick when they're pregnant. I'm sure it won't last long."

Natalia ran a brush through her hair and changed her clothes. Giovanna was still blowing around the room. "I don't know if I was sick the other times...Wait. How do *you* know about the other times?...No, wait. I want some answers, do you hear me?"

Natalia marched across the room after Giovanna, only to have the bedroom door shut in her face.

When she came downstairs, Marc, Mariella, Sam, and Philip were outside, having a beer. Simone handed Natalia her tea cup just as Robbie and Ben walked in.

"Are you ready to go?" Robbie asked Simone.

"Hey, doll, are you sure you don't want to come?" asked Ben.

Natalia snorted. "I would love to come, but I can't. Tell Marc to go. I don't expect him to sit here with me." She sipped her tea. It tasted wonderful. "Thanks for fixing this, Simone."

Natalia followed them outside. Marc was coming in and met her at the door.

"Thanks for your help upstairs, I appreciate it. I'll see you next week." Natalia hugged Simone and went back inside.

Marc had his back to her, busily doing…something.

"I wish you would have gone with them," she said. "I know I'm not much fun these days."

"Nah, I'd rather stay here with you. And we have the house to ourselves." He handed her a wine glass of ginger ale, decorated with orange slices and a small umbrella. "I bought gourmet saltine crackers for you, popcorn for me, and the scariest movie I could find."

Natalia threw her arms around his neck and kissed him. "I love you."

♨♨

Natalia handed Simone a burgundy Santagario Vineyard T-shirt.

Simone cringed. "I'm not wearing that!"

"Yeah, you are."

"You should really invest in fashionable attire, Natalia. A nice button down fitted shirt for the women would be much more elegant than a T-shirt."

"It's casual here, Simone. Please, just wear jeans and the t-shirt."

The advertising side of Simone came out full force. "Natalia, if you want people to take you seriously and recognize that you make a fine wine, you need to project that to them."

"If you want to accessorize your t-shirt and be fancy, go right ahead. But, please, put the damn thing on."

Natalia regretted her words later, when Simone walked into the gift shop looking absolutely stunning. She wore the Santagario shirt with a pair of fitted white jeans and a gold belt. Natalia thought her jeans fit a bit *too* tight, but no one asked her opinion. Simone had her hair pinned up to showcase her tasteful diamond earrings. Her make-up was flawless, and her lipstick matched the burgundy color of the t-shirt to perfection.

"I don't know how you do it, Simone. You look beautiful. I guess that's the upside to bringing so many suitcases for one weekend. You always have everything you need."

"I'm glad you like it. Are we ready to start?"

They walked over to a small bar where Philip was waiting for her. He had everything set up. Natalia gave him friendly pat on the back. "It looks great, Philip."

"Thanks," he said, kissing Simone. "You look stunning. Do you want to do the Chardonnay or the Seyval Blanc?"

"The Seyval."

"Good luck, you two." Natalia left them and walked back to the house, feeling a little melancholy. She came up behind Marc, wrapped her arms around him, and squeezed tightly.

"Hey, Nat, are you okay?"

"I guess. Simone looks beautiful today."

"She always looks beautiful. What's different about today?"

"She's exceptionally beautiful today."

He turned to face her. "After all this time, now you're jealous?"

"No. Not jealous, just a little insecure."

They sat on the couch together. She was frustrated with the debilitating tiredness that plagued her.

"Do you have any regrets?" she asked, feeling like a walking disaster. Lately, she didn't do anything but throw-up and sleep. It had been an effort to get into the shower this morning. She was sure if *she* had the choice, she would choose Simone over herself, hands down.

"Well, since you're asking." He let out a sigh. "Sometimes I think I got in over my head. The situation with Simone being here as often as she is—well, it's more than I bargained for." He dropped his head into his hands, and wouldn't look at her. "I'm sorry, Nat, I really am, but sometimes I wonder what I was thinking. What man in his right mind would leave a hot, twenty-eight year old blond bombshell for a forty-year old foul-mouthed tomboy?" He turned away from her, his shoulders shaking slightly.

Natalia thought he was crying. "You could at least look at me," she said, struggling to hold back her own tears.

He turned back to face her. His eyes were indeed wet—from laughing.

"Oh, baby, you really aren't yourself, are you?" he asked. "That's it? A pathetic 'you could at least look at me'? You can't even muster up a good swear word in English or Italian. Not even a small flare-up of that temper of yours. I know it's a cliché but—'Who are you and what have you done with my Nat?'"

She jerked away from him. "You're the only one who thinks you're funny."

"This isn't like you. You've always been happy and confident with who you are. That's one of the reasons I love you."

"I just wanted to be sure."

"After all we've been through I can't believe you have to ask. You know this is not only where I want to be, but where I belong. I couldn't be anywhere else and neither could you."

She knew he was right and didn't like whatever all these hormones were doing to her, but she was too tired to do anything about it. "Do you miss cooking?"

"I miss cooking for you. I'm looking forward to you getting your appetite back."

"I'm serious."

"Right now, no, I don't miss it. I like learning the wine business. You know Sam is thinking of semi-retiring. He and Mariella want to travel. When that happens, Robbie will need a lot help from Ben and me.

Natalia put her head on his lap. "I'm really tired."

"Go to sleep, baby. I'm not going anywhere. I love you."

"I love you too," She said as she drifted off.

CHAPTER 34

"They say it is to know the union with love that the soul takes union with the body." -- *Tiruvalluvar, 1st Century BC Tamil-India Poet*

A week before Thanksgiving Natalia and Mariella were in the kitchen making an early dinner. Robbie had taken Marc, Sam, and Ben to an agricultural company to buy new grapes vines.

"With everyone so busy for Thanksgiving and Christmas, I thought it might be nice if we all spent New Year's Eve together here," Mariella said. "How do you feel about that, dear?"

"Sounds like a good idea to me." Natalia reached for a tomato on the counter, but it rolled away from her. "Stop it right now, Giovanna," she mumbled under her breath. "I don't need you stirring up trouble."

"Did you say something?"

"No." Natalia got control of the tomato, only to find her knife missing. She let out a frustrated, "Ohhh," and turned her back on Mariella. "Why do you want me to do that?" she whispered through gritted teeth. "No, absolutely not."

"Natalia, who are you talking to?" Mariella demanded.

The back door opened and slammed shut.

"Natalia, please explain to me what's going on."

"See what you've done now?" she yelled.

"Natalia!"

"All right. Let's go in the other room. You may need to sit down for this."

She told Mariella the entire story of Giovanna. From her arrival at the vineyard to how the ghost helped Marc find Natalia's sanctuary in the woods.

"The most important thing is in the end, it was Giovanna who helped Marc remember me by slipping the napkin with my drawing into his bag before he left. I was so happy that he could feel her. No one else has been able to do that before."

Mariella sat listening intently. Natalia was surprised when she didn't necessarily seem shocked by Giovanna's presence.

"I hope you're not afraid," Natalia said. "She can by ornery sometimes but she likes you. That's why she wanted me to tell you about her."

"Why would I be afraid? I'm sure Marcos would have remembered you on his own, but I like the way she moved things along. An apparition after my own heart." Mariella smiled. "How could I not like her?"

"Did you feel her tonight?"

"No, dear, I didn't. I'm sorry about that. I would like to meet her."

"Even though we have our disagreements, I know she loves me and I love her. I wonder why only Marc and I can feel her."

Natalia saw Mariella's lips turn up in a smile, but had no answer for her.

♨♨

Natalia knelt on the floor near the Christmas tree wrapping gifts when Marc came in.

"There you are," he said, holding a small gift out to her. "Do you know what day it is?"

"I know there are only a few days left until Christmas, and I have a lot to do." She gave him a sly smile. "Although I do have a nagging feeling something important happened on this day about a year ago, but I can't quite put my finger on it."

He winked and knelt beside her. "Think hard."

Being six months pregnant prevented her doing any sexy slinking. Instead, she attempted to reach for him, lost her balance, and toppled over, arms and legs flailing like a rag doll stuffed with a fifty pound sack of potatoes. Giggling at the image, she brought her lips to his and kissed him softly.

"Happy Anniversary! December nineteenth, how could I forget?"

"Happy Anniversary, baby. I got you a little something," he said, handing her the small box.

When she opened it, tears filled her eyes. "Oh, Marc, it's beautiful."

He had taken the drawing of his birthmark and made it into a Christmas ornament. Enclosed in a glass sphere, the edges of the napkin were cut into the shape of a snowflake. The drawing, her signature, and the date were highlighted with glistening, gold paint. White glitter on the outside of the ornament shimmered like snow.

"I love it!" She rose and hung it on a branch in the front of the tree. "This has been the best year of my life. It had its difficult moments, but look how it's ending. We're together and having a baby."

"I know, baby. I couldn't be happier," he said, gently pulling her back down next to him. "I love you."

"So, I guess it's time for *your* gift."

She undid her robe and let it fall off her shoulders. His eyes devoured her recently curvaceous figure. It thrilled her.

"Nat, you were...voluptuous before but now you're...let's just say pregnancy agrees with you."

As he began to kiss her newly acquired feminine goods, she shed her robe completely, pushed him down on his back, and kissed him hard.

"Frisky, too, huh?" he said with a grin.

"Hormones. I'd enjoy it if I were you. I could have a mood swing at any moment."

"I'm not complaining."

She slowly undressed him. Her bulging belly made the logistics of lovemaking a little harder, so she turned her back to him. She could feel how much he wanted her. Widening her legs, she pushed her rear against him. He groaned, accepting the invitation. She pulled his arm around her and guided his hand between her legs.

"I got it, baby," he murmured breathlessly. "I know what to do."

"Mm, yes, you do." For her, the pleasurable combination of having him move inside her—as well as what his tender touch was doing to her—was too much to contain. As multiple shivers tap danced along her spine, she grabbed his hand, screaming out his name. Marc grasped her hand, squeezing it hard. "Nat, baby, you're the best anniversary gift—ever."

They lay together under the Christmas tree with Natalia's bathrobe covering them, Marc's hand resting on her belly.

"Have you felt Giovanna in the last few days?" she asked.

"I was going to ask you the same thing. I thought maybe she disappeared once in a while, and this was normal. It's been over a week since I've felt her around."

"I've never gone more than a day without feeling her. I'm worried. I don't know why she was here, and I don't know where she went." She felt the baby inside her move.

"Did you feel that?" he said. "Our little one is busy tonight."

"Yes, she is."

"You think it's a girl?"

"In the beginning I thought it was a boy," she said. "But the last few weeks, I really begun to think it's a girl."

"Well, either one is fine with me." He sighed. "Did you and G get in a fight?"

"No. The last time I felt her, she was very happy. Ever since I told Mariella about her, she's been on her best behavior."

"Don't worry, Nat. I'm sure she's fine. She'll be blowing around here and knocking things over any day."

"I hope so."

"Me, too. I miss her."

♨♨

It was about an hour before midnight. Everyone gathered in Natalia's family room.

"Natalia, you really are glowing this evening," Simone told her. "I guess it's true what they say about pregnancy."

"Thanks, Simone."

Simone leaned closer and whispered, "I think Philip is going to propose tonight. Isn't that exciting and romantic?" She sounded ecstatic. "Speaking of marriage, when are two getting married?"

"We aren't," they said together.

"Can't you two do anything you're supposed to?"

"We want the baby there with us. We also want the baby to be old enough to drop off with you and Philip while we go on our honeymoon?" Marc said with a chuckle.

"You can drop the baby off with us anytime. I'll pass it along to Mariella when it needs to be changed." Simone was laughing as she walked away.

Mariella came over to Marc and Natalia. "What's wrong with you two? Why so sad on such a happy occasion?"

"We're missing Giovanna," he said. "She hasn't been around the last couple of weeks. I don't know what could have happened to her."

Mariella led them to the other side of the room. "Don't worry, dear. I don't think she's gone very far at all," she said as she put Natalia's hands on her protruding stomach.

"What do you mean?"

"All those books I gave you. Did you read them?"

"Yes."

"What's one of the most important aspects of rebirth?" asked Mariella.

"That we choose our own parents, for lessons we either need to learn from them or teach them." Natalia froze. "Mariella, what are you trying to say?"

"Giovanna has been with you a long time and fought very hard for you two to be together. Now when you're almost seven months pregnant she disappears. I think she needed you two to be her parents. I wouldn't be surprised if she has been yours and Marcos' child before. You even said you could feel the love between you and her. For some reason it's important that you three have this life together."

"Why did she disappear now and not when I first discovered I was pregnant?"

"Dear, weren't you paying attention to what you read? In rebirth, the soul becomes attached in a spiritual way to the body at the moment of conception, but it can enter the physical body anytime between then and birth. Giovanna must have thought now was a good time to become reacquainted with being in a physical body again."

"Are you sure?" asked Natalia.

"Of course, I'm not sure. No one is sure of anything, really. I'm sure you and Marcos will always be together. Other than that, everyone believes what they think is right. We'll all find out one day, won't we?"

"Is that why she wanted me to tell you about her? She knew you would understand. Then you could tell us where she was and we wouldn't worry."

"Again, I don't know, dear. But I would like to think so."

Natalia turned to Marc. "Do you think it's possible?"

"I have no idea. After everything that's happened to us this past year, nothing could surprise me. I hope so. I miss her and she'd make a lively addition to our family."

Natalia put her and Marc's hands back on her stomach. "Giovanna, is that you?" Natalia asked and jumped when she felt a hard kick.

Marc chuckled. "I think that's our Giovanna, strong-willed, just like her mom."

Natalia threw her arms around him and kissed him.

"Hey, you two, the countdown is going to start," Robbie yelled. You can kiss at midnight." They hurried to join the rest of the family. "Five. Four. Three. Two. One. Happy New Year!"

"Anno Nova Felicia!" yelled Simone in very good Italian.

If they only knew what two thousand-eleven had in store for them!

THE END

ABOUT THE AUTHOR

Debbie Christiana remembers sitting in her room at eleven or twelve years of age pecking away at an old Smith-Corona typewriter, a gift from her parents. Even back then, the stories that appeared on paper were full of ghosts, skeletons and unexplained events.

An avid reader, she enjoys many different genres, but her true love is anything paranormal.

When not reading or writing, Christiana enjoys yoga, boating, and gardening. She lives in Connecticut with her husband and three children.

ALSO FROM BLACK OPAL BOOKS

CRAIGS' LEGACY
by Terry Campbell

DUTY CALLS
by Sherry Gloag

LAST WISHES
JORDAN DAVIS MYSTERIES – BOOK 1
by Alyssa Lyons

CLUBBED TO DEATH
JORDAN DAVIS MYSTERIES – BOOK 2
by Alyssa Lyons

BLOOD FEST: CHASING DESTINY
by Pepper O'Neal

MY KILLER, MY LOVE
by Mona Karel

RETURN OF THE LEGACY
PORTALS OF DESTINY – BOOK 1
by KH LeMoyne